PETER S. MICHIE'S MAP OF THE ENVIRONS OF RICHMOND AND PETERSBURG, VIRGINIA, MARCH 1865

Geography and Map Division, Library of Congress, Washington, D. C.

FAITH
of our
FATHERS

ONE NATION UNDER GOD

Volume Four

OTHER BOOKS AND AUDIO BOOKS
BY N. C. ALLEN:

Faith of Our Fathers Vol. 1: A House Divided

Faith of Our Fathers Vol. 2: To Make Men Free

Faith of Our Fathers Vol. 3: Through the Perilous Fight

FAITH

of our

FATHERS

ONE NATION UNDER GOD

Volume four

a novel by

N.C. ALLEN

Covenant Communications, Inc.

Cover design © 2004 by Covenant Communications, Inc.
Cover photograph (Union soldiers on horses) © Al Thelin. Cover photograph (View from south side of canal basin, Richmond, VA, april, 1865) by Andrew J. Russell, © Civil War Photograph Collection, Library of Congress. Used by permission. Flag illustration by Joe Flores.

Published by Covenant Communications, Inc.
American Fork, Utah

Printed in Canada
First Printing: October 2004

12 11 10 09 08 07 06 05   10 9 8 7 6 5 4 3 2 1

ISBN 1-59156-635-5

For my girls, Nina and Anna

And for Gunder, our newest addition—
I love you all.

LIST OF CHARACTERS

The Boston, Massachusetts, Birmingham Family
James Birmingham, the father, a wealthy iron magnate
Elizabeth Stein Birmingham, the mother, abolitionist descendant of Rhode Island Quakers
Luke, deceased
Anne Birmingham Gundersen, married to Ivar Gundersen
Camille Birmingham Taylor, married to Jacob Taylor
Robert
Jimmy

The Charleston, South Carolina, Birmingham Family
Jeffrey Birmingham, the father (James's twin brother), married to plantation heiress
Sarah Matthews Birmingham, the mother, plantation owner
Ben, married to Mary
Charlotte Birmingham Ellis, widowed
Richard, deceased
Emily Birmingham Stanhope, married to Austin Stanhope
Clara
Elijah, grandson, biological child of Richard and Mary (a slave)

The Birmingham Slaves, Now Freed
Ruth, the "matriarch"
Joshua, raised as Ben's companion
Mary, Ruth's granddaughter and Joshua's biological half sister, Elijah's mother, married to Ben Birmingham
Rose, Mary's younger sister, companion to Clara

The O'Shea Family, New York City
Gavin O'Shea, the father, deceased
Brenna O'Shea, the mother
Daniel, married to Marie Brissot
Colin, deceased

The Brissot Family, formerly of New Orleans, Louisiana
Jean-Pierre Brissot, the father, deceased
Genevieve (Jenny) Stein Brissot, the mother, sister to Elizabeth Stein Birmingham
Marie Brissot O'Shea, married to Daniel O'Shea

The Gundersen Family, Cleveland, Ohio
Per Gundersen, the father, deceased
Amanda Gundersen, the mother
Ivar, married to Anne Birmingham
Inger, their grandchild, Ivar's daughter

The Dobranski Family, Salt Lake City, Utah Territory
Eli Dobranski, the father; baptized Ben Birmingham years earlier on a mission to the Southern states
Ellen Dobranski, the mother
Earl, their oldest son
The Dobranskis also have seven other sons who do not play a role in this volume

Other Fictional Characters
Isabelle Webb, Pinkerton operative and friend to Northern Birminghams
Abigail Van Dyke, former fiancée to Luke Birmingham
Jacob Taylor, newspaper editor and husband to Camille Birmingham
Gwenyth Stanhope, Willow Lane estate manager

Nonfictional Characters to Whom Reference Is Made

President Abraham Lincoln

Jefferson Davis, president of the Confederacy

Alexander Stephens, Confederate vice president

Robert E. Lee, Confederate general

Ulysses S. Grant, Union general

Nathan Bedford Forrest, Confederate general

William Tecumseh Sherman, Union general

John Brown Gordon, Confederate general

Joshua Chamberlain, U.S. colonel

Winfield Scott Hancock, U.S. general

Andrew Johnson, U.S. vice president

William Seward, U.S. secretary of state

Edwin Stanton, U.S. secretary of war

Gideon Wells, U.S. secretary of the navy

Allan Pinkerton, private investigator

John Wilkes Booth, Lincoln's assassin

Lewis Paine, Booth conspirator

David Herold, Booth conspirator

George Atzerodt, Booth conspirator

John Surratt, Booth conspirator

Mary Surratt, John Surratt's mother and owner of boarding-house where the conspirators met

Major Henry Rathbone and his fiancée, Clara Harris, with President Lincoln the night of the assassination

TO THE READER

I would like to offer a note of thanks to those who have read this series and taken the time to let me know they've enjoyed it. It has been a labor of both love and frustration for me; as a rule, I enjoy research, but there were times when I felt depressed and discouraged by the things I read. I have learned much, however, and I hope I've been able to impart some of that to the reader through these books.

As was my goal from the beginning, I have focused my characters around those in history who knew better, who were years ahead of their time in terms of their attitudes and thinking, and who learned in spite of tremendous obstacles. My cast of main characters has been, for the most part, the minority—the compassionate abolitionists and the educated slaves. I thank the reader for indulging me in this.

I pledge allegiance to the flag
Of the United States of America.
And to the republic for which it stands,
One nation, under God, indivisible,
With liberty and justice for all.

CHAPTER 1

I see very plainly Abraham Lincoln's dark brown face, with the deep-cut lines, the eyes, always to me with a deep, latent sadness in the expression.
—Walt Whitman

* * *

1 January 1865
Boston, Massachusetts

Camille Birmingham Taylor floated in a haze, a place where she felt no pain and held a beautiful baby in her arms. She nuzzled the small, sweet head with her nose and whispered to the child, "I wasn't even aware you were with me, little one." The child opened her deep blue eyes and looked at Camille, the tiny brows creasing a bit as the infant tried to focus her gaze.

Camille felt a searing stab in her abdomen, and before her terrified eyes the world around her grew dark and the baby in her arms disappeared. "No!" she cried, choking on the word as the pain intensified and she reached in vain for her infant daughter. Her arms reached into nothingness, and she saw her hands straining and clutching at air.

Strong arms gripped her from the side and held her close, his very scent familiar to her. "Shhh, Camille, be still," he whispered in her ear. She calmed a bit when she heard his voice, her concern shifting from the vanishing child to her husband. He sounded horrible—something was wrong with him. He shifted and buried his face against the side of her neck, urging her to relax into the pillow beneath her head.

She felt his tears trickle against her skin, and her own eyes began to burn. "Jacob, don't cry, my love," she murmured, her throat feeling raw and sore. "Please, she'll be well. We'll find her, Jacob, we will."

He groaned softly and tightened his gentle grip around her. Someone placed a cool cloth on her forehead, and the sensation was divine. She was so warm! And her body felt as though it were being torn asunder. She pulled her knees up and tried to alleviate the pain radiating from her midsection, but no amount of twisting gave her any relief.

Another familiar voice sounded at her ear, and tears burned afresh. Her mother! Elizabeth would make everything all better; she would make the pain go away and would help her find the baby. Elizabeth could do anything. Camille turned her face toward her mother and tried to open her eyes, which felt puffy and swollen.

"Mama," she cried, and Elizabeth knelt close to the side of the bed, laying the back of her hand against Camille's cheek. "My baby girl is gone! I was holding her and then she disappeared. I didn't even know she was here. I would have taken better care of her—I wouldn't have let someone take her."

"Camille, it will be fine. She'll come back, you know." Her mother's words were comforting, but her face was as white as the sheet covering Camille's twisting form.

"You see, Jacob?" Camille turned her head again toward her husband. "It will be fine, just as I said. Won't it be fine?"

Jacob shuddered once beside her, and Camille heard Elizabeth sharply clear her throat. He immediately raised his head and looked at Camille through eyes that swam with tears.

He smiled a bit and nodded. "Everything will be fine now," he said. "As long as you're here, everything will be fine."

Camille looked at him, her fuzzy head beginning to clear and reason returning. The pain in her womb was so terrible, she was afraid she would die with it. "Oh, Jacob," she finally whispered. She raised a shaky hand to his side and gripped his. "I'm so sorry. I didn't know I was with child—I didn't know . . ."

"Shhh," he whispered, shaking his head. "Neither of us knew, sweetheart. There was nothing we could have done."

"Is she gone, then?"

He nodded, his expression pained. "Sweet Camille, I'm so very sorry."

"How big was she?"

Jacob glanced up at Elizabeth, panic crossing his face. "Darling," he said, still looking at her mother, "I don't think . . ."

Elizabeth sat gently on the side of the bed and Camille turned to face her. "She was this big, Cammy," Elizabeth said and cupped her two hands together.

"Where is she?" Camille looked at her mother's empty hands and felt her heart constrict.

"Your father and Ben buried her, my sweet."

"I didn't even see her. My own baby, and I never saw her."

"Ah, but you did. You were dreaming, and you saw her perfect and whole."

"Did they wrap her in a blanket?"

"Yes, love. They wrapped her in a soft blanket." Elizabeth's strong exterior finally slipped a bit; a tear escaped her eye and trailed down her cheek.

* * *

Jacob downed the fiery liquid in his glass and closed his eyes as it burned its way into the pit of his stomach. His father-in-law watched him from his position near the hearth.

"Better?" James asked.

Jacob nodded absently and set the empty tumbler on the polished wooden sideboard with a thump. He raked a hand through his hair—a gesture he'd been unconsciously repeating throughout the night and into the morning. "Thank you for being here," he said to James, hating the way his voice sounded. He cleared his throat and tried to steady it. "I couldn't have cared for her alone."

"None among us could ever do it alone," James said and left the hearth for a seat on a chair next to it. He expelled a tired breath as he sat, but managed a smile for Jacob. "A woman often needs her mother and the company of other women at times such as these. Leaves the rest of us to wander about and scratch our heads."

"Do you suppose they'll let me back into the room yet?"

"That's highly doubtful. You were fortunate to stay in there for as long as you did. Men just do not attend to these sorts of affairs, you know. The family physician is usually the only male allowed to enter." James softened his remark with a smile that appeared suspiciously wobbly. "She will be well, Jacob. The bleeding has stopped, and she no longer burns with fever. We have much for which to be grateful, and furthermore, you'd do well to get some rest."

"I want to be with her when she awakens."

"I believe I heard Elizabeth say that she and Mary will be taking turns keeping watch over her. I'm sure one of them will fetch you if you wish."

Jacob glanced at his father-in-law in frustration, wondering when he had lost control over his own household. James must have sensed his mood, because he added, "You will sleep better in the guest room, where every little sound won't have you sitting up in a panic. Truly, man. Go and get yourself some decent sleep. You're going to be of no help to Camille if you don't have your energy and wits about you."

Jacob felt the corner of his mouth kick upward in an involuntary smile. Life with Camille had proven to him time and again that she was a woman whose husband had indeed best have his wits about him, if only to maintain her pace. With a final, reluctant nod, he clapped James on the shoulder in thanks and quit the study, making his way up the stairs to the bedrooms. As he passed Camille, he looked in on her and was gratified to see that she slept, and that while her complexion was still pale, she wasn't nearly as sickly as she had looked hours before.

He nodded once to his mother-in-law, who sat in a comfortable chair next to the bed and kept her hands occupied with some of Camille's unfinished needlework. She gave him a weary smile, and he eventually turned from the scene and made his way into the guest room across the hallway.

His coat, vest, and tie had long since been discarded, and the state of his rumpled white shirt and disheveled breeches were testimony to his worry through the night. He didn't bother to disrobe, but quietly closed the door to the room and then fell to his knees beside the bed, giving thanks for his living wife.

* * *

3 January 1865
Boston, Massachusetts

Robert gently lifted the brass knocker on Jacob and Camille's front door, letting it fall back into place. In a moment, he heard footsteps on the other side and was soon admitted by a young woman in a maid's uniform who ushered him into the small parlor. It wasn't long before his mother appeared at the threshold.

"Well," she exclaimed. "To what do we owe this honor?"

"Can a man not see after the welfare of his sister?" Robert smiled and placed a kiss on his mother's cheek as she entered the room.

"Well, he certainly can. I just didn't expect it."

"How does she fare?"

Elizabeth's brow momentarily creased. "Well, considering. Her heart will take longer than her body to heal, I believe."

"Hardly surprising."

"True enough," Elizabeth sighed. "It's no easy thing for a woman to lose a child, no matter the age."

Robert had a fleeting image of his brother Luke, and he smiled at his mother, feeling a twinge of pain. "Camille will most likely bear other children, though, will she not?"

Elizabeth nodded. "Most likely. Would you like to see her now?"

"Yes."

Robert was not prepared to see his sister, usually robust and in the pink of health, looking so pale and forlorn. Her face looked unusually white against the darkness of her chestnut-colored hair. She appeared to have lost weight as well, making her green eyes appear huge in her petite face. He summoned a smile for her sake and took the chair next to her bedside. Clasping her lifted hand, he squeezed it gently.

"Don't look so worried, Robert," she murmured, the corner of her mouth lifting a bit. "This is but a passing thing."

"I would never worry about you. You can do anything, Cammy."

"My, with such effusive praise, you'll have me blushing."

"Sarcastic as ever. I believe that is a good sign, Sister."

Her eyes misted a bit. "Thank you for coming to see me, Robert. The company keeps me from thinking overmuch."

"I would have come sooner if I'd realized you wanted visitors." He tried not to allow his dismay at her distress show on his features. It was unsettling to see her unwell.

"Tell me something from the outside world, Robert," Camille said, shifting in the bed and wincing a bit. "Jacob refuses to share anything he thinks might cause me worry. He doesn't understand I'd rather have the distraction of a newspaper."

"I don't know, Cammy. I'd hate to find myself staring at the wrong end of his fist."

At that she laughed, but the sound was thready and weak. "He loves you, Robert, and you well know it. Come now. Tell me what you know."

"Hmm." Robert settled back into his chair, his one arm still resting gently at her side. "Well, Sherman is still camping out in Savannah. I suppose you'd heard we sent a ship of supplies down that way to aid not only our soldiers but the citizens of Savannah as well?"

She shook her head in the negative.

"It's a far cry from what Sherman gave Atlanta. I can't say that I blame him, really—his goal is an end to the war. By bringing it to the people's front doorsteps, it's a much faster guarantee."

Camille nodded, frowning. "I do understand that. I suppose I wish it didn't have to be so."

"He was right all along, you know. When South Carolina seceded, Sherman told a friend that it was bound to be an awful end, that this country would be drenched in blood."

"Ugh. He was right." Camille nodded slowly, and Robert wondered if she was remembering their shared experience at the first battle of Bull Run. "So he now lives temporarily in Savannah, you say? I admit, it makes me glad for cousin Emily. What a relief that her home won't be burned to the ground."

Robert nodded. "I've written to her and Austin—I'm still awaiting a reply. I'm curious to know firsthand how they are faring. I wonder if they haven't seen some hostility from their neighbors because of their Union sympathies."

"How much longer do you suppose Sherman will stay there?"

"It's anybody's guess, really," Robert said. "I don't imagine too much longer—I believe he'll start working his way north fairly soon. Pair up with Grant."

"Straight to Virginia?"

"Mmm, now regarding that I'm not certain. I've heard people say he'll work his way through South Carolina first. Thoroughly."

Camille's jaw slackened. "Oh, my. They'll tear the place to shreds."

He nodded. "Yes, they will. That's where it all started, you know."

"Oh . . . my." Camille's fingers knotted in the sheets. "I feel sorry for them, the people. Do you?"

Robert wished he could say he did. He wished he could tell his sister that his heart beat in trepidation for those whose rash, angry actions had culminated in four ugly years of bloodshed. He glanced down at his left arm, missing below the elbow. He had paid a price for the Southern rebellion, and at times he still felt very angry over it. Angrier still when he thought of the ultimate price the conflict had cost his family—Luke would never again be there to embrace them or someday have children of his own with Abigail, as he had dreamed.

He sighed, feeling very, very weary. "I suppose I do, Cammy. Truly, I don't wish innocent people to suffer. When I think back on the smugness with which the Southern states went about wreaking havoc on this country, though, I am angry."

Camille reached and took his hand into hers. "I understand," she said. "I do, Robert. I understand."

He cleared his throat. "Cammy, are you feeling any better? I'm so very sorry about your . . . loss."

Her eyes filmed over for a moment, and he regretted bringing up the subject of her baby. She squeezed his fingers weakly and gave him the ghost of a smile. "Thank you," she whispered and wiped a finger under her nose. "I feel awful about it, horrible that I didn't even know I was carrying her."

"Do you hurt much, still?"

She nodded slightly. "I do," she murmured through the tears that had thickened and now rolled down her cheeks. "I've been assured the pain will soon stop altogether, though." She paused. "I'm not so certain about the pain in my heart, however. I suspect that will remain."

* * *

Robert was deep in his thoughts as he reached the front door of Camille's house, preparing to leave after bidding his mother farewell upstairs. That was why, most likely, he wasn't aware of Abigail Van Dyke's presence in the parlor until he heard her voice.

"Robert, you're going to leave without saying a word to me?"

He turned in surprise, the thumping of his heart taking on its usual erratic beat at the sight of her.

"Abby," he said as he started toward her, meeting her halfway and flushing at the kiss she placed on his cheek.

She took his hand in hers and led him back into the parlor, brooking no argument when he said he'd just been on his way out. "Not without talking to me for a moment," she said and sat on a small divan, patting the seat next to her. "How have you been?" she asked, studying his face. He felt as though he were in a physician's examination room. "I've been thinking of you."

His tongue was stuck to the roof of his mouth, and he had to clear his throat to loosen it and find his voice. "Have you, now?" he said. "That's very kind. I've been well, thank you."

Her eyes narrowed. "You'll forgive me for saying that response sounded a bit forced."

"I . . . I . . ." He cleared his throat again. He couldn't look at the woman without feeling guilty for the fact that he was still in love with her. His dead brother's fiancée! It made him the worst sort of cad.

"What is it, Robert?" Abigail took his hand in hers and squeezed it gently. Her expression changed from skepticism to concern.

"It's nothing, Abby, truly. I *have* been doing well. I have moments of relapse, I suppose, but overall I've been happy."

"Robert, do I remind you of Luke? Is that why you practically run in the opposite direction each time you see me? If it's painful to speak with me, I do understand." She withdrew her fingers. "I should have been more compassionate . . . I never thought . . ."

"No, Abby, not at all." He reached for her hand, chagrined that he had caused her embarrassment. He clasped her fingers. "You must never think I do not want to be near you. I cherish our friendship very much. My memories of Luke are good memories, but no, you do not remind me unduly of him." He almost wished she did. Then perhaps he could squelch some of his own feelings for her.

She looked at him carefully, as if weighing his words. "I confess, I look for opportunities to be near your family, but not only because of Luke. You all remind me of him, but more than that, I have always *liked* all of you. You are a warm and humorous group of people, and I very much enjoy your company. I find tremendous strength in your mother. She mourns Luke's death, but not excessively. She's shown me how to be strong and continue living."

Robert nodded. "She's an amazing woman, and I'm glad you enjoy her company."

"I enjoy the company of all of you, Robert. That's why I would not want to cause you discomfort. I can clearly see that you choose to avoid me at times."

Robert sighed. Abigail was a bright woman. If he didn't explain himself, she would eventually work it out on her own. "You're a beautiful, beautiful woman, Abby. I've thought so for years. You were also engaged to my brother. I feel . . . I feel guilt when I look at you and still find you beautiful."

He looked down at their joined hands for a moment before finally mentally calling himself a coward for avoiding her gaze, which he felt keenly on his face. He glanced up and saw comprehension dawn on her features. Rather than withdraw her hand or turn away with a blush, however, she smiled. It was a pained smile, full of sympathy and something else he couldn't quite read.

"I understand," she finally said when he was wondering if she'd chosen not to comment at all. She opened her mouth, apparently searching for something she didn't know how to say. A faint flush eventually appeared across her cheeks, and she turned her head away a fraction but still maintained her hold on his fingers. She nodded a bit to herself and turned her face back to him, her eyes bright with unshed tears.

"I understand, Robert," she murmured, "and I do not object to the fact that you find me beautiful. I've heard everything you've both said and not said, and I hope you've heard the same from me." She gave his fingers another squeeze and released them, standing. He stood with her, confused.

"And now," she said with a slight sniffle, "I'm going to run from you for a while."

With that, she turned and left the parlor.

CHAPTER 2

The whole army of the United States could not restore the institution of slavery in the South. They can't get back their slaves, any more than they can get back their dead grandfathers. It is dead.
—*William T. Sherman*

* * *

5 January 1865
New York, New York

Marie O'Shea slowly walked along the length of beds in the large hospital room, wishing her sojourn down the hallway had been more productive, if not at least distracting. Her husband lay injured in a bed because of an accident that had befallen him while fighting a fire. The two days that had passed since she found him lying upon a board with a bandage about his head had given her time to think, to absorb her new reality.

She was beginning to find a problem, however, with being afforded so much time to think. She was becoming angry. The longer he lay still, unconscious of the world around him, the more she felt that if he ever did awaken, she might not have two kind words to offer him. He was home from the war, safe. They were married and happy—they had a life together that was more than she'd ever believed possible. Cared he so little for the whole of it that he thought nothing of risking life and limb? She knew of his penchant for seeking adventure, for trying to show his family and himself that he was a man of integrity; perhaps the thing that angered her most was that those close to him already knew these things.

Marie stood at the foot of his bed, her arms folded gently across her middle, and looked down at the man who was her husband. His face was nearly as pale as the bandage wrapped around his head, and he was very still. She knew a moment's panic that stole her breath until she saw the gentle rise and fall of his chest resume its customary pattern. Shaken, she sat in the now familiar ladder-backed wooden chair situated near his head and placed her hand on his shoulder. She revised her thinking a bit and admitted to herself that if—no, *when*—he awoke, she'd welcome the opportunity to give him a piece of her mind. She was angry, true, but beneath the anger lingered a deep fear that she might lose him forever.

* * *

Daniel struggled to open his eyes, confused that they were so heavy. Nothing felt familiar; he lay upon a hard bed, a strange smell assaulting his nostrils. He felt a weight upon his arm and turned his head, still struggling to lift his eyelids. As he turned his head, his face brushed against the familiar softness of Marie's hair, and an instinctive smile began forming on his lips until an intense pain halted its progress.

His face hurt—no, more than that, his entire head ached as though it had been split in two. He shifted his body toward Marie, groaning in pain when he realized that the pain wasn't singular to his head. Everything hurt. He finally succeeded in opening his eyes only to find it dark and Marie's lifting head but a shadow.

"Daniel?"

Her voice was so close—he should have been able to see her better.

"It's so dark," he croaked, his throat parched and dry.

"It's very late," she answered, and he heard her reaching for something near her side. The unmistakable sound of pouring water filled his ears, and when she pressed the cup to his lips, he gratefully sipped from it. That small effort left him exhausted, and he rolled back onto his pillow.

"Marie," he whispered, again wincing against the pain. "What is this? Where are we?"

"Oh, Daniel, you wretched man, you've had me worried sick. Not to mention the mothers." Daniel felt Marie's fingers close about his own and then registered the cool press of her hand against his cheek. "We're in the hospital. You're recovering from an accident."

"What . . . what accident?" He searched his memory in vain. He felt his heart increase in rhythm as he tried to remember something . . . anything. "I left the house," he murmured.

He sensed rather than saw Marie's answering nod. "You went into the city after receiving the summons. When you hadn't returned by morning, the mothers and I came looking for you." She moved her hand from his face and placed it atop his hand, sandwiching it between her two. "Finally, someone at the firehouse told me what had happened."

"What *had* happened?"

"Do you not remember any of it?"

He began shaking his head, but the movement caused shards of pain to slice through his skull. "No," he winced. "None of it."

"You were inside a burning building when the ceiling collapsed."

His discomfort intensified as he searched his mind for any small shred of recollection and found none. "Marie, I cannot recall any of it."

Marie's sigh was soft. "Perhaps it's just as well, my love. It can't very well be a pleasant memory."

He turned his face toward her again, his grip on her hand tightening fractionally. Even his fingers felt pain. "I hurt, Marie." It galled him to admit it, and he felt as low and humble as he ever had.

"Where, love?"

"Everywhere." He paused, squinting his eyes. "What is the hour?"

"Nearly two in the morning."

"Will you light a candle? You're but a shadow, and I would like to see your face."

She was slow to respond, and when she did, it was with a sense of confusion. "But, Daniel, there *is* a candle lit—just here to the side. Can you not see it?" The rustle of fabric signaled her movement, and in a moment, he felt a small measure of heat upon his face.

"The shadows are perhaps a bit lighter now, but I still cannot see you." Daniel shifted his weight to his side with a grunt and heaved himself up on his elbow. He passed his free hand slowly before his face.

"Sweet mercy," he heard Marie whisper on a thread of sound.

"I cannot see," he murmured, his heart beginning to hammer in his chest in earnest. "Marie, I cannot see!"

He heard a small clank as Marie placed the candle down and felt her arms steal around his neck. The mattress depressed at his side as she sat upon it and he lay back onto the pillow, still in her arms. "I am blind," he said, the sound muffled against her dress. His eyes felt the hot sting of tears then, and he knew it was futile to try to calm the rapid beating of his heart. The panic grew so intense that he wondered if it might kill him.

"Shhh," Marie whispered and gently placed the back of her fingers against his singed skin. "Perhaps it is only temporary,

Daniel. You'll yet see—as it is you *could*, in fact, see the light from the candle, yes?"

"A bit. I can see only dark shadows . . ."

"Well, then, in a matter of time I'm sure it will return as normal. In the meantime, I'll care for you."

He groaned a bit and closed his eyes. What a burden he'd become to his sweet wife. He'd intended to take her away from the awful memories of the recent past in New Orleans and give her a life of contentment and peace on his small farm in New York. Now it seemed all he'd given her was an invalid for which to care.

"You're not a nursemaid, Marie. This is unfair to you."

"I'm your wife, Daniel, and you are my dearest friend. I wouldn't allow anyone else to care for you."

As his frustration rose, he felt his old anger and self-deprecation rising along with it. "What is the extent of my injuries?" he asked Marie in strained tones, his voice still raw.

"You have a broken leg and possibly some cracked ribs. The back of your head, however, took the worst of it."

He absorbed the information for a moment before speaking again. "Marie, I am so very sorry."

* * *

7 January 1865
Savannah, Georgia
Willow Lane Plantation

Joshua Birmingham studied his surroundings. The irony of his situation wasn't lost on him; he was a former slave who now found refuge on a bed in a slave cabin. In truth it wasn't a typical slave cabin. It was clean, simply but adequately furnished, and cozier than any slave quarter he'd ever seen in South Carolina.

Before his escape to Boston, he'd spent time in this very cabin as a "slave" to Austin Stanhope, his benefactor and purchaser of his freedom. Joshua had never dreamed he would someday find himself at Willow Lane a second time, but once again, it had proved his salvation.

Gwenyth had found him, just as he'd hoped she would when he collapsed on the kitchen-house floor after escaping certain death at the hands of Confederate soldiers. Joshua was a Union soldier now, and the fighting he had seen had left him not only shaken, but physically wounded as well.

Gwenyth helped Austin and Emily manage Willow Lane Plantation, and under her watchful eye, he was slowly on the mend and grateful for her tender ministrations that were helping to heal not only his body but also his soul. He looked forward to her visits, which usually occurred several times a day, and looked forward to each coming conversation with her more than he had the last.

He hadn't seen Emily; in fact, Gwenyth had yet to tell his old friend and her husband that Joshua was on their property. Emily and Austin had their hands full with Sherman and his Union troops, and Joshua and Gwenyth had decided together that Emily had enough to worry about already.

Joshua wanted to see Emily, but not with the fervor or desperation he might have once imagined. He had been in love with the girl, it was true, but he found that in his mind the memories of her at Bentley were fond and gentle but had faded into the background of his thoughts. The love had transformed itself into something sweet and nostalgic, something he no longer yearned for.

It was fortunate for his heart that he had changed. To see her here with her husband again might well have done him in, were it otherwise. She was happy with Austin; he knew this, and more to the point, he didn't begrudge her that happiness. He had once assumed that the thought of her loving another man would kill him. How surprising then, and to his favor, that it wasn't true.

The door opened a crack after a soft knock sounded upon it, and he looked with anticipation to see Gwenyth enter the room. As always, the sight of her was as a breath of fresh air. She looked crisp and clean, every movement speaking of efficiency and capability. Her simple day dress of green calico was pressed and spotless, her hair held in a neat braided bun at the nape of her neck. She was a woman with pleasing features and bright eyes whose beauty rose in his estimation each day.

"I was beginning to wonder if you'd forgotten about me," Joshua said to her with a smile and wished he'd had the energy to don a clean shirt.

"Ha! That devilish smile of yours won't let me forget," she said as she closed the door behind her and went about the business of setting some fresh food on a small table near the hearth. "Sherman is making good on his promises all over the city. He's distributed the goods from up north and seems sincere in his promises to leave things here intact."

The aromas from the table made his stomach growl. "Am I to assume I get more to eat today than broth?" He sounded like a hopeful child, and she laughed.

"It's been for your own good, Joshua Birmingham, and you know it. But yes, today I've added a bit of meat and some vegetables to the mixture." She briskly prepared a small meal on a tray and carried it to the bedside, where he propped himself up further against the pillows. He gratefully took the food from her and, his mouth watering, tore a piece of thick bread and dipped it into the stew. The taste was like heaven.

"You spoil me, Miss Gwenyth," he said after swallowing and then glanced at her. "What do people say when you come traipsing over here every day with bandages and food?"

"I tell them you're one of the staff, an older woman, who is ill and needs special care." She winked at him. "If you don't mind people thinking you're an old woman, I expect we'll keep up this routine just fine."

"I'll be an old woman forever if it means you'll keep bringing me such good food." He took a swallow of the mild tea she had placed on the tray and wiped his mouth with a crisp, white linen napkin. "Miss Gwen, I am forever in your debt, and I admit this sincerely. I would be a dead man by now if not for your help, and I would have you know of my gratitude."

"And you know who I am grateful for?"

He shook his head.

"Whichever Birmingham it was who decided to let you learn to read and write. You have a wonderful mind, Joshua, and you express yourself beautifully. I'm glad to see your brain was given an opportunity to grow and stretch."

He turned his attention back to his food, suddenly feeling self-conscious. So many times in his life he had found himself having to explain his cultured speech to slave and white man alike. As a child, in fact, he had been better off speaking as the rest of the slaves on the plantation did. Less mistrust was fostered that way, and it had never been his desire to alienate himself from his people. But when he had been alone with Mary, Ruth, and Rose—well, Ruth had insisted he show her by example the things he had learned from Ben's schoolroom lessons.

"What about your own learning, Miss Gwenyth?" he asked, turning her comments back toward her. "You sound like a woman who was raised with a fair amount of education. And when I was here before, I knew full well who ran this plantation."

She smiled. "I have Mr. Stanhope and his parents to thank for that. We've each been blessed in our own way, haven't we, Joshua?"

"Indeed we have."

* * *

Gwenyth left Joshua a short time later, thoughtfully making her way back to the cookhouse. These stolen moments with him were quickly becoming the thing to which she looked the most forward during the course of her day. She was busy, trying to maintain the business of Willow Lane while at the same time feeding and housing hundreds of Union soldiers, and she was grateful that she was busy. It made the time pass quickly and gave her less time to think about the uncertainty of life these days.

In her quiet moments, however, she thought of the man she was hiding in the slave quarters until he was well enough to either rejoin his own regiment—wherever they might be by now—or sign on with Sherman. That was an interesting conundrum, however; Sherman had no use for black men as soldiers. How these Union boys would receive Joshua was anybody's guess.

Gwenyth gritted her teeth a bit and swallowed her frustration. Change was on the wind, but the wind often took its own sweet time. Of one thing she was certain: she'd hide Joshua in that cabin forever before she turned him over to men who would abuse him, or worse, turn him over to Confederates.

CHAPTER 3

Swift to its close ebbs out life's little day.
Earth's joys grow dim; its glories pass away.
Change and decay in all around I see;
O thou who changest not, abide with me!
—Henry F. Lyte, "Abide With Me!"

* * *

7 January 1865
Cleveland, Ohio

". . . ashes to ashes, dust to dust . . ."

Anne Birmingham Gundersen squinted against the cold winter wind that had become such a part of her life since her marriage. It was a colder and more brutal climate than she ever could have imagined, and to be standing out in it seemed tantamount to insanity. She pulled her black cloak closer about her shoulders, tucking the hood close to her ears and mentally blocking the droning voice of the pastor. She wished he would stop talking. The more the man talked, the more miserable she became at the thought of her father-in-law being lowered into the hard ground.

As if to echo her thoughts, her six-year-old stepdaughter tugged on her gloved hand. "Mama Anne," the child murmured a little too loudly.

"Shhh, sweet girl, we must be quiet for a bit longer," Anne whispered into Inger's blonde curls, which peeped out from under the fur cap tied securely beneath her chin.

"I want you to get him out of that box," Inger said flatly.

"Inger, hush," Anne whispered, pulling the girl closer to her side.

"I want my bestefar out of that box!" Inger looked at her with huge blue eyes that were beginning to fill with terrified tears.

Anne mentally cursed herself for not having explained things to Inger more effectively beforehand. She thought she had; apparently the little girl was still confused, and when Anne looked at the scene through Inger's eyes, what she saw was horrifying and morbid.

Without further thought, Anne stood and scooped Inger into her arms, carrying her briskly back toward the church that had been the place of Per Gundersen's funeral moments before. When Ivar began to follow her, she shook her head and whispered for him to stay with his mother, who looked uncustomarily near collapse.

By the time Anne reached the church and made her way inside, settling onto the last pew with the child nestled in her lap, Inger was sobbing in earnest.

"Inger, sweetie, he's not really in that box. Do you not remember what I told you?"

"But I *saw* him in there. He doesn't want to be in there. What will happen when he wakes up?"

"He isn't going to wake up, Inger. He's in heaven now, with Jesus." Anne rocked her back and forth, trying to explain what she really didn't understand herself. She had seen much of death in the past few years on the battlefield, and of one thing she was certain—it was awfully permanent.

"I want Jesus to get him out of that box."

"Jesus will get him out of that box, sweet girl, someday. And he won't awaken until Jesus is there to help him."

The gulping sobs tore at Anne's heart, and she felt her own eyes sting in kind. "Do you promise me, Mama Anne? Do you promise?"

"I promise. I promise, Inger, Bestefar is not going to wake up alone in that box. Do you believe me?" Anne pulled back from the child and looked into her eyes, ironically so like her own. "You know I wouldn't lie to you."

Finally, Inger nodded, her tears still streaming. "I will miss him, Mama. I will miss him so very much."

"Ah, Inger." Anne held her close again and closed her eyes, her own tears falling onto Inger's hat. "I will miss him as well."

* * *

Ivar kept a close eye on his daughter, who had firmly entrenched herself on Anne's lap throughout the funeral dinner and refused to move. Anne had become more of a mother to the child then Inger's blood mother ever had been. It was ironic, and probably good for Inger, that she actually resembled Anne. The two were nearly identical with thick, blonde hair and deep blue eyes. Inger's outburst at the graveside ceremony had caught them all by surprise, and he could only be grateful for Anne's quick thinking in calming the child's fears.

His throat constricted as he accepted the condolences of another family friend, and Ivar knew he would miss his father more than he could have imagined. Although Per's health had declined in recent months, his death had been unexpected. Ivar felt robbed of the time he would have still enjoyed in his father's company.

He looked over the fare being served in honor of his father's memory: fresh trout and boiled potatoes, lightly salted and buttered. On any other day it would have made his mouth water; now, unfortunately, he found he didn't have the stomach for much of anything. Amanda had outdone herself, though. His

mother had determined that the guests would eat well, and in
truth, the preparations for the event had kept her busy and close
to her friends, who were by her side to offer help and support. It
would be lonely when the whole affair was said and done, the
friends gone home to their own families.

Excusing himself from yet more neighbors and friends, Ivar
made his way to Anne's side and laid a hand on her shoulder. "If
you're tired, take Inger home. I'll stay here with Mama."

Anne shook her head. "I'm fine, and Inger is doing well
too," she said, giving the young girl a small squeeze. "We'll stay
until the last of the guests leave."

"Your eyes look weary, Anne."

"As do yours."

He shook his head a bit, the corner of his mouth tilting up
into a reluctant smile. She had always matched his will and his
efforts, even on the battlefield. Unless Inger became unmanage-
able, Anne would stay with him until the bitter end. He ordinarily would not have thought twice of it, but Anne had seemed
ill of late. She tired more easily than usual and had been battling
nausea for weeks. He wondered if she were expecting a child,
but supposed they probably wouldn't know for some time yet;
her courses had been irregular since her enlistment.

Her black gown made her features look gaunt and drawn,
and the fabric hung on her frame. Ivar clenched his teeth for a
moment in worry as he studied her and knew she was losing
weight. He had already asked her if she'd like something to eat,
but she had shaken her head, her expression paling even more
than it already was.

He leaned close to her ear and whispered in response to her
comment, "But you have not been well. I would not have you
overtired."

She reached up for his hand and gently clasped his fingers. "I
am fine, Ivar," she murmured. "How quickly you forget the
things we've endured together."

Images flashed through his head, memories of the first time he'd ever laid eyes on Anne Birmingham. She had been posing as a young man, but he had never believed her facade for a moment. His mind's eye saw her grimacing in pain as he dug a bullet from her leg, and he remembered her proud and fierce as she bartered for his life while he lingered inches from death in a prison camp.

He wondered what she thought of him now when she looked at him. He was still a much thinner version of the man she'd met all that time ago because of his time spent in Andersonville. His blond hair had thickened considerably in recent months, as opposed to the thinning that had occurred when he'd faced starvation in the prison camp. His stomach still gave him problems as well—he could tolerate only the mildest of foods, and sometimes not even those. It nearly drove his poor mother, who loved to feed people, crazy with worry.

He frequently reflected on the time he'd been a prisoner and grew angry at the premature toll it had taken on his body. His eyes still required the use of his spectacles, now more than ever it seemed, and Anne swore that was probably a result of Andersonville as well. Whether it was or wasn't, he knew he was aging. Farm life was good though, and he was regaining his strength by working at the things he loved most.

Ivar now lowered his stance to rest on his haunches and placed his arm about Anne's shoulders, pulling her close. Her hair was longer than he'd ever known it to be, and it smelled fresh as he closed his eyes and rested his face against her neck.

It was a miracle they had both survived.

* * *

Anne placed the warm cup of milk before her mother-in-law and studied her carefully as she took a seat opposite her at the well-worn, well-loved kitchen table. Amanda murmured her thanks and sipped the milk slowly, nodding her appreciation. "Just what I needed," she said.

"You'll sleep tonight, then?" Anne asked her.

Amanda nodded. "Ja, sure I will."

Anne snorted lightly and took a sip of her own milk. "As you've slept the past two nights?"

"I've slept."

"You haven't, Mama. You need some rest."

Amanda glanced at Anne and finally let out a bit of a sigh. "It's not so easy, you know."

Anne nodded. "Mama, I'm so sorry."

Amanda's eyes filmed over. "No more of that," she said, shaking a finger in Anne's direction. "No more sympathy for me. I do better without it."

"I know you do. I just want you to know how much I loved him too."

The silence between them was comfortable, and Anne stole a few glances at the woman she'd come to love. Amanda was strong, much like Anne's own mother, and sharing her mother-in-law's companionship made her feel a little less homesick for her family, far away in Boston.

Anne worried about her, however. She worried that Amanda might lose her sense of purpose, that she might feel adrift now that the husband with whom she'd spent the better part of her life was gone. There was no simple way to broach such a subject though, except through subtlety. Or perhaps distraction. Anne was not afraid to manipulate a good grandmother's emotions.

"Inger needs you now more than ever. And before long, she won't be the only little one around here calling you 'Bestemor,'" Anne said, innocently taking another sip of her milk.

Amanda's eyes fastened on Anne's face, comprehension dawning on her features. "Oh, Anne." Again, the woman's eyes misted. "Are you certain?"

Anne nodded, feeling a sting behind her own eyes. "I'm ill, I'm exhausted, and I cry for absolutely no reason. I keep waiting for it to pass, but it doesn't. I just feel . . . different. I can't eat a thing, and I haven't an appetite at all." Anne flushed a bit, embarrassed by the fact that she was embarrassed. "My body is changing . . ."

"Oh, Anne."

Anne wiped at a tear and tried to smile. Her efforts only produced more tears, however, and a laugh from Amanda, who rose and moved around the table to encircle Anne with her arms. "Oh," Anne muttered, frustrated. "I meant to comfort *you* tonight."

"Nonsense," Amanda said and planted a kiss on Anne's cheek.

"Will you help me? I'm very much afraid." Anne was shocked to realize the truth from her own lips.

"Of course I will help you. It's what a mama does."

* * *

9 January 1865
Ogden, Utah

The sparsely populated street held few homes—indeed the whole of the town could be missed entirely if one rode by quickly enough on a horse. The fledgling settlement had bigger, more exciting dreams on its horizon, but for now it was an isolated community that lay under a blanket of snow. For some of its inhabitants, however, the isolation had been a balm, a healing property that soothed and nourished until those who lived in it were again able to face life with a sense of renewed energy and purpose.

Sarah Birmingham watched her grandsons play together in her warm home while the snow swirled about outside. Her appearance was neat and tidy as always, and her small frame was clothed well in a day dress of sprigged muslin that showed her tiny waist to perfection. Her light brown hair was combed back into a braided bun, and her brown eyes missed nothing as she examined her surroundings.

The parlor was but an extension of Sarah herself; Jeffrey had taken great pains to see that many of their furnishings survived the trip west and were now fixtures in this new home. The chairs, the rugs on the floors, even the smaller adornments for mantelpieces and side tables were present and lent themselves to the beauty of the house.

She turned her attention to her grandsons. They got along well, Charlotte's son and Richard's son. It was good that there were two of them—the only other children in the vicinity lived an inconvenient distance away. Sarah was often struck by the family resemblance between the two, especially given that Elijah's mother had been a slave. The boys were most definitely Birminghams—nobody could dispute that fact.

She supposed that now, however, Elijah would be Ben's son more than Richard's. With an inward wince, Sarah acknowledged that if Richard had possessed any character in his short life, he wouldn't have fathered the child at all. Her son had raped a defenseless slave, and now he was dead after a lackluster military career with the Confederate Army. It grated against everything in her that was civilized to admit that one of her own flesh and blood could have been so utterly wanting in integrity and self-control.

But Richard was gone, so much of her old life was gone, and now Sarah herself was mother-in-law to a woman who had once been her own property. News of Ben and Mary's wedding had only just reached them, along with the news that, when the weather improved and was conducive to travel, the newlyweds would be coming west to see them and Mary's son.

Sarah had to admit a certain fondness for her grandson. Elijah had worked his charming way under her skin, and she often felt a smile tug at the corners of her mouth at the sound of his little voice. He was beautiful too. His clear features, olive complexion, and green-blue eyes were arresting.

He was beautiful like his mother.

Heaven help her, but Sarah had seen Mary's physical beauty when the girl had been but a child. The hard life of a slave had not diminished it in the least with the passage of time, but rather intensified the purity of her features and form. Of course Richard had been attracted to her. He would have to have been blind not to have noticed her.

Mary had always possessed an inner poise and grace that Sarah had occasionally found lacking in her own daughters, and it had grated on her all those years at Bentley. She pondered for a moment on her newfound, raw emotions for Ruth, Mary's grandmother and her own companion from childhood, and felt a stab of shame that the old feelings of proprietary ownership where Mary was concerned still lingered.

Sarah had, in recent weeks, bared her soul, her all, to Ruth. Her fears, her shame, her regrets, all that she had to offer that might afford her some absolution for her sins to Ruth. She knew a friendship with the black woman that she would never have with another living soul. So how was it possible that when she thought of her son Ben married to Ruth's granddaughter, Mary, she felt . . . disappointment?

Sarah had no say in the matter, at any rate. Ben had been lost to her for years—how many years was it? It had been nearly ten years since she had last seen her firstborn son. She and Jeffrey had driven him away, disgusted by his principles and his audacity. Now, her desire to see her boy again set her heart to thumping in her chest.

She caught a toy that Elijah had hurled into the air and tossed it back to him, smiling at his laughter. Perhaps, she mused, it wasn't just Mary herself who set Sarah's teeth on edge. Perhaps any woman at all wouldn't have been good enough in her mind for Ben. Or possibly it was just that she wanted some time with her son, all to herself, without the intrusion or presence of another woman.

Deep in her heart, however, Sarah knew that the only reason at all she was even going to be granted a visit with Ben was because they were coming for Elijah. She couldn't delude herself into believing that he actually wanted to see his mother again after all this time, especially given the nature of their parting. She had not been a good mother to Ben. Ruth had been Ben's mother, and that knowledge stung deeply.

What a wretched thing, that she had become so obsessed with her land and her holdings that she had turned the rearing of her children over to another woman! What kind of society did such a thing to a mother and her babies? What sort of God allowed it?

What sort of woman were you to embrace it?

A conscience was a vile, vile thing, Sarah decided as she watched William hurl the toy into the air this time. A conscience never left one at peace. It was so much easier to blame God, *anyone,* for her faults. Time, also, was her enemy. With each passing day, she grew more nostalgic for her children and their children. She had heard other women speak of fond memories when their offspring had been young, and she hated it. She hated that she could only bring to mind those things Ruth or other servants had told her through the years.

Now she felt more like an empty shell than a woman. Sarah was so uncertain of herself and prone to tears, which was something she'd never battled. She had no happy memories, very little to speak of in terms of warmth with her children, and she had no plantation. All that she had worked for was gone, and she was left to wonder why the world still held her in its grasp. She felt good for nothing, for no one. Her talents lay in managing large estates and a huge inventory of resources and staff. There was nowhere for her brand of womanhood to be useful, and she felt it more keenly each day.

Jeffrey entered the room and paused, watching the boys and offering a soft-spoken admonition that they take care, lest something in the room be broken by their antics. Sarah looked at her husband, who glanced in her direction with a quick smile and a wink, and felt something inside relax just a bit. Jeffrey was a constant, and he was still by her side after all that had transpired. She knew now that he had been making monetary investments of his own through the years; he was easily financially independent of her, where once he had been obligated to her for his every meal. He could have left—would have been justified in leaving as much as her mental state had been impaired—but still he stayed.

"How are you feeling today?" he asked her, sinking into a seat beside hers.

"Well, thank you. How did you fare at the meeting?"

Jeffrey nodded. "All seems in order. I do believe the lumber is a wise investment. And with the railroad completion in a few years, the opportunities will only increase."

Sarah smiled. All the years of her married life, Jeffrey had kept himself busy, becoming acquainted with people, working diplomatic circles, and keeping himself well informed. His continued movement and his involvement in their current surroundings was a comfort to her. She found that she very much liked the realization that no matter where they were planted, Jeffrey Birmingham would bloom.

CHAPTER 4

And in those times there shall many stand up against the king of the south: also the robbers of thy people shall exalt themselves to escape the vision; but they shall fall. So the king of the north shall come, and cast up a mount, and take the most fenced cities: and the arms of the south shall not withstand, neither his chosen people, neither shall there be any strength to withstand.

—Daniel 11:14–15; quoted by a black Union soldier, citing biblical reference that he felt indicated the North would win the war

* * *

17 January 1865
New York, New York

Daniel quietly made his way around the workshop attached to his home, feeling with his fingertips as he walked. He could see only shadows at best. His world was dark; Marie had been wrong. His sight still had not returned.

The panic and fear now struck with less intensity than before, and he supposed he should be grateful for that at least. Mornings were difficult, however. Now that he was home and in familiar surroundings, each day when he awakened to feel the warmth of the sun on his face through his and Marie's bedroom window, he opened his eyes expecting to see. The smell of the home was the same, the same boards creaked in the same places, but it was as though his whole world had shifted to an odd place he had no desire to experience.

Perhaps the worst of all of it was that he hated being dependent on Marie for the simplest of things. She deserved a husband who could dote on her, give her all the finer things of life she might wish for; instead, she was trapped in a marriage to an invalid. The thought tasted sour in his mouth, and more than once he wished for the courage to rid her of himself.

His hands touched the tools of his carpentry trade, his fingertips identifying each object. They were good tools, solid tools. He had been bored of them lately and had sought a vocation with more adventure, more excitement—more possibility of praise. He had been seeking the approval of the ghost of his father, and carpentry did not qualify.

How ironic, then, that the thing he wanted most was to spend some time here in this shop, working magic out of plain pieces of wood. It was laughable, really, to think that he might again be a useful carpenter. So much of what he had created had been born of pure instinct and his ability to *see* what he was doing. Now he wouldn't even be able to saw a board in half without the possibility of losing a finger.

Daniel took a deep, shuddering breath and felt his way to the corner of the room. A small cabinet housed liquor that he kept for special occasions—usually when a substantial project had come to a close and he was pleased with the results. Fumbling with the door, he eventually felt the bottle inside that still held the majority of its liquid. He unfastened the closure, put the bottle to his lips, and took a long, mind-numbing drink.

* * *

Marie sat at the small dining room table, eating her morning bread and eggs and flipping through the newspaper. So much was happening in favor of the abolition of slavery now that the focus of the war seemed to have shifted. The purpose was now no longer merely about preserving the Union; it was also about freeing the Negro, and her eyes misted in response. A constitutional convention in Missouri had just adopted a resolution abolishing slavery, and there was talk in Washington of the House passing an amendment to the Constitution that would abolish slavery everywhere in the Union.

Lincoln was entertaining the notion of talks with Confederate representatives as an attempt to bring an end to the war, but he would only countenance a total surrender and agreement to reenter the Union on the part of the rebellious Southern states. The Confederates were hardly likely to agree to such a thing. It seemed almost certain that the conflict would be settled on the battlefield and nowhere else.

Marie sighed as she looked at drawings sent in from correspondents in the field. Political cartoons told the same story: the Southern soldiers were starving, barely outfitted, and hanging on to life in some instances by the barest of threads. They had no more resources on which to draw—Sherman had effectively squelched what they might have received from their home states by way of aid.

What a sad, sad four years it had been. Marie thought of her home in New Orleans, where for years things had been so peaceful with her mother and father. Closing her eyes, she remembered the feel of the humidity and warmth against her skin, the smell of the lush vegetation, the sounds of the city, and the quieter throbs of the countryside. She wondered if things would ever be the same again, if life would ever return to normal for the people who still lived there.

Some changes are good, she mused as she looked again over the articles in the paper. Good people like the Fromeres should not have had to worry for their lives because of their skin color every time they stepped out into society. Change had been long in coming in that case, and she welcomed it despite the cost, despite the fact that holding true to principles of fairness and equality had cost her father his life and their family their home and livelihood.

Marie lifted her head as she heard the sound of something being bumped in the workshop, followed by a muffled curse. Her brow creased in worry, and she quickly made her way to the shop and entered to see Daniel rubbing his hip.

"Oh, I'm sorry, Dan—I didn't realize you were in here. Do you need some help?"

"No," he bit out, turning his back to her. "I'm fine. I can find my way around my own workshop."

Marie closed her mouth and tried to swallow the hurt that surged to the surface at his words. In all their time together, Daniel had never snapped at her in anger. He was still raw and hurting, she had to remind herself, and frustrated at the fact that his sight had yet to return. He wasn't really angry at her so much as the situation.

"I'll leave you alone then," she murmured and made to leave the room.

"Marie," he said softly.

"Yes?" She turned back at the door to look at him.

"I'm sorry. I'm very, very sorry. I find I'm rather . . . impatient with myself these days."

"I understand." She walked to his side and, placing a hand on his arm, leaned up to kiss his cheek. "Let me help you, though. Don't be so proud."

"I don't think I have much control over that," he answered.

"You most certainly do." She rubbed his arm and left him to his thoughts, her own troubled as she returned to the dining room and began to clear the remains of her cold breakfast.

* * *

5 February 1865
Savannah, Georgia
Willow Lane Plantation

Emily Birmingham Stanhope tapped her foot against the floor as she watched countless Union troops file out of her home, across the front lawns, and out into the street. They poured similarly from homes all over town and packed up their belongings from tents dotting the countryside.

There were thousands of men, and too many camp followers to count, who had stayed just over a month in Savannah and, in the process, had bled the community dry. True, Sherman was leaving some sheep behind and had shared provisions from the North with the residents of the city, but sixty-thousand-plus visitors had a way of draining one's resources.

Her neighbors just to the north stood at the edge of their property, watching the procession of men with stony expressions. The family matron glanced in Emily's direction, and Emily saw the woman say something to her husband as she looked at Willow Lane with narrowed eyes. Emily shook her head a bit. She was probably imagining things; it just seemed that of late, the neighbors had become even more vicious in their comments, more cold in their stares.

Surely the war would soon draw to a close. Now that Sherman was sweeping his way through the South and up into Virginia to meet Grant, it was impossible for the beleaguered communities to provide the Confederate troops with provisions they didn't even have for themselves. Emily was hardly sorry for that; however, she did wonder how her own little family would fare in the coming weeks and months.

She had had occasion to observe General Sherman both up close and from afar, and she could only conclude that her feelings about the man were conflicted. He was clearly not her kindred spirit; he didn't believe the black population equal in talent or capacity to that of the white, but at odds with his beliefs, he had issued Field Order Number 15, which effectively gave abandoned or captured plantations over to freedmen and former slaves.

Of one thing Emily was certain. Sherman was efficient, effective, and sought an end to the war. And although he couldn't be with every single man in his command every moment of the day, he had told them all on more than one occasion that the people of the communities through which they stormed were not to be physically harmed or threatened. Emily had heard stories—everyone had heard stories—of atrocities committed by men in blue, and she didn't doubt they were true. She was gratified to realize, however, that Sherman didn't sanction it.

So many things had changed for the better, at least in theory. The United States House of Representatives had only six days earlier passed the Thirteenth Amendment to the Constitution, abolishing slavery! It was now the responsibility of the individual states to ratify it, and Illinois, Abraham Lincoln's home state, had been the first to do so. Emily had danced and cried with Gwenyth in complete and utter giddiness when they had received word. It was a miracle Emily had thought she might never see in her lifetime, and the joy she felt in it was complete and very sweet. She missed Mama Ruth so much that she had cried even harder then, and wished for all she was worth that she could be with the woman in person to celebrate her happiness.

The realities of daily life, however, were never far behind the euphoria, and there was so very much to do now that the troops were leaving that Emily's head nearly spun with it. Willow Lane's stores were depleted, their recent harvests gone. Destitute people—refugees with nothing and former slaves—had poured into the community and were near starvation. The needs of the people were overwhelming, and Emily wanted to do more than stand by and watch.

She turned with a glance as her husband approached and laid his arm across her shoulders. Resting her head against his shoulder, she sighed a bit.

"What is it?" Austin asked, kissing the top of her head.

"I'm weary of it, and we haven't even begun."

"It will all work for the best. We can make a difference."

She smiled. "Ever the optimist. I hope you never change."

From inside the archway behind them that led into the interior of the house, a throat cleared. The couple turned, and shock from the sight nearly drove Emily to her knees.

"Joshua?" His name came from her throat on a thread of sound.

Joshua moved forward to clasp Austin's hand, and Austin pulled him forward into a warm embrace. "Joshua Birmingham, what are you doing here?" Austin asked as he slapped him on the back.

Joshua winced a bit and laughed. "I must thank you, Austin, for your generosity to me, although you were unaware." Joshua gestured behind him, and Gwenyth came forward from the shadows.

Emily reached forward and clasped Joshua to her in a gentle hug, tears stinging in her eyes. "What *are* you doing way down here, Joshua?" she asked as she pulled back and released him.

"I was not far from here—a couple days' ride—and my company was caught in an attack. I was wounded, most of my company dead or taken prisoner, so I found my way to Willow Lane. Gwenyth was good enough to care for me and not trouble you with it. You've had much on your hands," he finished, motioning to the sea of blue soldiers, both outside and still exiting the house.

"Oh, you two," Emily said and lightly slapped at Gwenyth. "We certainly would have liked to have known you were here, Joshua. It wouldn't have been any trouble at all."

"It was my idea to keep it a secret," Joshua said with a glance at Gwenyth.

"Well, not entirely," Gwenyth said in low tones and moved closer. "We couldn't be sure how the other troops would react. I didn't want to alert them to Joshua's presence until we could be sure he'd be treated well."

"And will you?" Austin asked.

"Sherman's men have told me I can accompany them north until I can be mustered out, since my men have been scattered. I'll not exactly be a part of the group, however. You know they don't mix the colored troops with the white men."

"I don't like this," Emily said, scowling. "Can you not just remain here?"

"I need to finish this, Emily. It's very near its end."

"Will you march through Charleston?"

"Yes. That's what I hear." Joshua paused. "It promises to be ugly. The men are swearing to make South Carolina howl."

Emily nodded and swallowed. She thought of Bentley, the home where she and Joshua had both been born and reared, one in the main house, one in the slave quarters. As a young teen when the war had begun, she had wanted to see all of the South burn to the ground. "It seems I'll get my wish," she murmured.

Joshua must have remembered the sentiments he'd often heard her mutter in those days of old, because he said, "Do you wish it otherwise now?"

Emily stared at a fixed point in the distance and narrowed her eyes. How *did* she feel? "I don't know. There are so many innocent lives caught up in this thing . . . I want it finished."

A shout from outside caught their attention, and Joshua straightened his shoulders. "I must be off. Austin, Emily, again, thank you for your unwitting hospitality." After another exchange of embraces, Joshua turned to Gwenyth. "I wonder if I might see you alone for a moment."

Gwenyth nodded and followed Joshua onto the wide front porch, and Emily watched them converse, her mouth agape. "I never imagined . . ." she said aloud, and then a smile slowly crept across her features. She settled back into the crook of her husband's arm and looked up at him. "I hope he doesn't die before this is all finished, because *that* is perfect." She motioned to the couple on the front porch and felt her eyes burn with tears. "He deserves someone like her. And she him."

Austin nodded. "Are you . . . That is, do you . . . Are you at peace with this?"

"This?"

"All of this." Austin motioned to the two of them, and then broadened his gesture to include the couple on the porch.

"Very much so, Austin. Very much so. I'm sorry to ever have given you cause to wonder. I did love Joshua—I *do* love him—but it's changed. It's different. You know me now the way nobody ever has, and I love you differently, more than anyone I've ever known."

"I'm grateful." Austin breathed a sigh of relief, and Emily laughed.

"Why would you worry, silly man?"

"Because I married the most beautiful girl in all the Southern states. Some things are too good to be true."

"Not this." Emily wound both arms around his waist and squeezed. "Never this."

* * *

"Gwenyth, I would have you know of my gratitude. You saved my life, and I think were I allowed a longer stay, you'd probably save my soul."

Gwenyth looked at the man who stood opposite her, handsome and proud in his blue uniform. She had polished his brass buttons herself and now dusted at his sleeve to clear away some crumbs. Her lips twitched a bit at his statement, and she sought to lighten the moment. She didn't want him to leave. "I doubt very much your soul needs saving, Joshua Birmingham."

"Not necessarily from sin, although I confess I have been known to do that from time to time. No," he said, a quick smile fading from his face. "This is different. My arm has a . . . a . . ."

She searched his eyes, and he hid them from her, ducking his head and then turning it away in embarrassment. "Joshua, are you speaking of your tremor?"

His face turned back to hers in surprise. "You knew?"

Her nod was gentle, her face sympathetic. "It has lessened of late. When we talked of your experiences on the battlefield, it seemed to cease a bit."

"Yes. I noticed it as well. I think your company has soothed me and is helping me heal . . ." He paused, uncomfortable. "Gwen, I'm not well versed in sharing my thoughts like this. Forgive me. I just, I find that I am very reluctant to leave you."

"I wish you didn't have to either," she murmured, wanting to memorize each detail of his precious face. "Would you be interested in spending time with me again, then? When this is all over?"

"I would dearly love it," he said and reached his hand toward her. She placed hers inside it and felt a thrill of intimacy and contentment. "Please, keep yourself safe and well. I will return for you."

"I will wait." The tears came then, and she wished them gone. She didn't want Joshua to feel her sorrow. "I will wait for as long as it takes."

He nodded and brought her hand to his lips, brushing the lightest of kisses across her knuckles. Her breath caught, and she wondered if her heart would break. Suppose he died and she never saw him again? The words *don't go* hovered in her throat, but she closed her mouth firmly. She would not stand between him and the things he felt he needed to accomplish. That a black man was allowed to wear a United States uniform at all was a miracle in itself, and she wasn't about to tell him she didn't want him to continue defending his newfound freedom. It was more, meant more, than either of them individually.

She bit back a sob as he released her hand and made his way down the wide front steps, turning back to look at her once again before joining the other men leaving the yard. So that she wouldn't disgrace herself in public, Gwenyth turned and walked down the porch steps herself, around the corner of the main house, and made her way to the cabin where Joshua had only recently slept.

She entered the small room and sat upon the bed that he had so carefully and neatly made before leaving. Clasping his pillow to her stomach, she cried until she had no more tears left.

CHAPTER 5

We will fight you to the death. Better to die a thousand deaths than submit to live under you . . . and your Negro allies.
—*Confederate General John Bell Hood*

* * *

7 February 1865
Chicago, Illinois

Isabelle Webb looked around herself as she walked to the post office and wondered where she'd gone wrong. Nothing felt right. Her work with Allan Pinkerton as one of his private investigators no longer held the thrill for her she thought it always would. The war and all its atrocities had made her weary, and too much time posing as a socialite had made her jaded.

There were only so many ways for a woman to make money, and that was the sad truth. Her options were fairly limited, and she had never fancied herself as much of a teacher. She had saved a fair amount of her earnings through the years and, as a result, had built herself a nice wall of security, but it wasn't enough. She didn't feel useful. She felt as though she could die the next day and nobody, really, would be the wiser or feel a loss at her absence.

She had written some of these thoughts in a letter to her longtime friend, Anne Birmingham Gundersen, but felt fairly certain it hadn't reached her in time to already expect a reply. That was why it was with some surprise as she retrieved her mail from the post office that she saw a letter postmarked from Cleveland.

Isabelle left the post office, tearing the letter open as she walked back out into the brisk February air. The date at the top of Anne's letter told her that their letters had indeed crossed. Anne spoke of the passing of her father-in-law, the hardship it had caused Ivar's little girl, and of her own impending expectancy.

Isabelle felt tears in her eyes at the news and smiled broadly, ignoring the stares of passersby as she walked. Anne was going to be a mother! *I suppose we really have become adults, Annie,* she thought and wondered if she might ever see the day that would find her with a husband and a child.

Her tears lingered, and they now fell for her own sake. She shook her head as she approached her apartment building, hating the self-pity. Feeling sorry for herself was a new experience, and the past several months she had been plagued with it. She was tired. Tired of wondering what she wanted to do with her time, tired of the war, tired of feeling so sad.

The last paragraph of Anne's letter caught her attention as she made her way into her apartment. *Camille is struggling,* it read. *She miscarried and hasn't quite recovered from her grief. I believe my mother and Cammy's friend Abby do their best to keep her mind occupied, but she battles a sadness that is hard to resolve . . .*

Isabelle pondered Anne's letter over the next several hours as she made herself busy cleaning an already clean apartment and preparing a small meal for herself. Her mind reverted to Camille's plight several times, and Isabelle finally knew what she wanted to do.

"Camille," she said aloud as she pulled a sheet of paper from her small desk in the corner of her bedroom, "perhaps we are just what the other is in need of right now."

* * *

17 February 1865
Boston, Massachusetts

Camille had read the letter from Isabelle Webb with some surprise. She didn't know Isabelle well—had only really known her through her friendship with Anne, in fact—but something in Isabelle's words tugged at her heart.

Anne tells me that life has been sad for you of late, and I'm sorry to hear this. I must admit, although my reasons are not the same as yours, that my life has felt sad as well. I wonder if you would object to the thought of our being sad together. Perhaps if you let me take care of you and you take care of me, we'll arrive at a better place . . . I don't know exactly why, but I would dearly love to spend some time with you and your good husband . . .

When Camille showed Jacob the letter at lunchtime, he seemed almost relieved, and his expression tore at her heart so, she very nearly dissolved into tears at the sight of it. He had then looked panicked, however, and quickly began dancing in a comical fashion that had become the only way of making her laugh. Laugh she did, and he had kissed her cheek. "Absolutely tell your friend to come for a visit. I will rest much easier at work knowing someone is here spending time with you during the day."

He had then gone back to work after leaving her a copy of the newspaper on the table near her elbow. She knew he hoped she'd read it instead of ignoring it as she often did anymore. It was unlike her, this feeling of despondency, and she hated it. She cried several times a day and for the silliest reasons. She didn't want to go anywhere or do anything, and sometimes it was all she could do merely to get out of bed in the mornings.

Retrieving a piece of paper and a pen, she sat at the table to answer Isabelle's correspondence. She told her sister's friend that she would welcome the company, although she couldn't promise to provide much by way of good entertainment in return.

Upon finishing the letter, she turned her attention to the newspaper, an action which would have made Jacob smile had he been there. It was with some surprise that she found herself absorbed before long in the stories printed before her. President Lincoln, earlier in the month, had apparently met with three Confederate peace delegates, but to no avail. The biggest headline of all, however, caught her attention. Columbia, South Carolina, had been almost completely destroyed by fire. Sherman was being blamed, but apparently some felt that retreating Confederate soldiers had set the fires.

Camille rested her head in her hand for a moment and thought of all the citizens who now were without homes or businesses. *What would I do?* she wondered. *Where would we go? What would we eat?*

For a brief moment, Camille forgot her own pain. She wished for all she was worth that she could somehow help, that she could find the small children who wandered without homes or even parents and feed them, clothe them, and love them. The thought of small children, though, soon brought to mind images of her own baby who was now never to be. The hated tears clogged her throat, and she shoved the newspaper aside, leaving the table and wandering aimlessly into the parlor, where she stared into the hearth until the flames died.

* * *

Across town, Robert Birmingham sat in his father's office. "They really want *my* memoirs?"

James smiled at his son. "Is that so hard to believe? You're a very good writer." He nodded and picked up a piece of paper. "I just received the letter today."

Robert took the paper from his father and read the letter from a prominent publisher in New York. He shook his head, his surprise genuine. "When you first insisted we send it in, I thought you were just being fatherly."

"I was. But it was also very, very good." James's smile still stretched across his face. "I'm proud of you, Robert. I always have been."

"Thank you, sir. I never was, that is, I never quite had . . ."

James waited patiently for him to continue.

"I never did have Luke's charisma or his huge heart. I often felt that I would never be as good . . ."

"Stop. Your mother and I never compared you to your brother, either publicly or privately. You have always had your own strengths and talents, and we wouldn't have wanted you to be another Luke." James's eyes misted. "I miss him too, son. I miss him very much. But I'm also very, very glad that you're still with us. I don't like to think of the times we came close to losing you."

"You lost part of me," Robert said, his mouth quirking into a wry half smile as he lifted up his arm, a portion of which was missing below the elbow.

"We could afford to lose that part of you. I'm grateful it wasn't worse." James cleared his throat. "Now that I've bullied you into publishing your memoirs, I feel I should ask you if you are at peace with the public reading your private thoughts."

Robert nodded slowly but said nothing.

"People need to know, son. They need to know the price that has been paid to keep this country whole. If it isn't written down, in time they will forget. Your observations of battle and daily life are some of the most stirring I've read."

Robert ducked his head, embarrassed. "Thank you. And you may feel free to put your mind at ease on my account. I have no issue with sharing my private observations. I'm still so very surprised."

"On another note, have you heard that our troops are closing in on Wilmington, North Carolina?"

Robert glanced up in surprise. "The last open Confederate port?"

"Yes, indeed. I feel this thing drawing to a close. It can only be a matter of time."

"Somebody should probably mention that to Jeff Davis and Bobby Lee."

* * *

Mary Birmingham worked her magic with the needle and thread, finishing off the last of the tiny embroidery stitches for Elizabeth Birmingham's newest table runner. "There we have it," Mary said and held it up for Elizabeth's inspection.

"Oh, Mary, you are a wonder," the older woman said. She looked at her nephew's wife with an admiring eye. "You have a gift that I've rarely seen equaled. We all learn how to do this, but your pieces are works of art."

"You're too kind," Mary said, smiling at the praise.

"Not just kind, chile. It's truth," Madeline said, and Mary looked at the Jamaican cook with gratitude. The women sat around the kitchen table, planning menus and folding linens. Mary loved the Birmingham house. Her first days of freedom were spent under this very roof, surrounded by people who wanted to help her make a better life. She was reluctant to leave Boston, although her reasons for doing so were valid enough.

The thought brought a frown to her face, and before she could erase it, Elizabeth caught the expression. "What is it?" Elizabeth asked, and Mary knew from her direct gaze that she wouldn't brook an evasive response.

"I worry about leaving. I want to see my son desperately, but this place has become so familiar to me. People in Boston are generally accepting of my marriage to Ben. At least they don't openly give us trouble. I don't know how things will be in the West. I also don't know what Ben's mother will think of our marriage. She hasn't answered Ben's letter, but his father has."

"Mary," Elizabeth said as she set her pen down, "let me tell you something of what I've heard about my sister-in-law. Sarah has been through an extremely trying emotional ordeal. It's my understanding that she has been humbled beyond words. And given Ben's past with her, she's most likely the last person whose good opinion you should seek."

Mary nodded slowly, unconvinced. "Suppose Ben wishes to mend the rift. He's spoken in warmer terms of his father lately. Mr. Jeffrey seems to be extending an olive branch. If there is a chance of reconciliation with his mother, his marriage to me will only hinder that."

Elizabeth shook a finger at Mary, her expression flat. "Do *not* lay yourself or your marriage on Sarah Birmingham's sacrificial altar. Do you understand me, Mary? You are made of sterner stuff than this, and I expect you to remember that. Do you not recall your life before? The things you have overcome? I don't care if Sarah throws you from her home and into the street. You march right back up, tell your husband it is time to be off, take your child, and live your life. Sarah has had hers to live, and what she has or hasn't done with it is her own fault. *Your* life is just beginning, and you've made a wonderful start of it with a man who adores the ground on which you walk."

Elizabeth took a deep breath and released it, her expression hardening. "Am I clear?"

Mary's lips twitched. "Yes, ma'am. No groveling."

"None!"

The women sat in silence as each resumed her activities, Mary pulling a fresh piece of linen from her basket and beginning the process of choosing the colors for her new design. A thought struck Mary, and she lifted her head. "Where is Camille? I haven't seen her here for several weeks."

Elizabeth looked up from her papers, a flash of discomfort crossing her face. "She doesn't want to leave her house."

"Oh, dear. I had hoped she was feeling better."

"Physically she's fine. Healthy as she ever was. She still hasn't recovered from the loss of her baby girl, and heaven knows that can take some time. I worry about her, but short of dragging her from the house, there's little I can do to get her out. I visit often, and so does Abigail, but . . ."

"I'm sorry to hear that." Mary was amazed that Elizabeth had been unable to draw Camille from her web of grief. As she had just witnessed herself, Elizabeth was a formidable opponent, and one not easily matched. For Camille to withstand her mother's will, she must be ill indeed. "I wish I could do something to help her. In an odd way, I understand the grief of losing a child, even one who wasn't wanted."

Mary glanced up to see if Elizabeth was shocked by her words, but she should have known better. Elizabeth merely nodded, her expression thoughtful. "Yes, Mary, you have overcome much. If you allow Sarah to get the better of you, I shall be sorely disappointed."

Mary was thoughtful as she left the Birmingham house and began walking in the direction that would take her home. Midstep, she changed her course and turned, instead walking directly to the home Camille shared with her husband. Before she really knew what she was doing, she had raised her hand to the knocker.

Camille herself answered the door and started in surprise at Mary's presence. "Why, how are you?" she asked Mary, drawing her inside and ushering her into the parlor.

"I'm well, thank you, Camille," Mary answered and sat down opposite the young woman. She studied Camille's face for a moment, noting its pale hue and the dark circles under her eyes. It was difficult to bear a child and more difficult still to lose one. To have nothing to do with one's day after the fact would be torturous.

"Can I offer you some tea or sandwiches?"

"No, thank you. I've actually just come from your mother's home, and I had commented to her on your absence. I've missed seeing you weekly."

"I suppose I haven't felt the energy . . ."

"Camille, I do understand." Mary reached forth her hands and clasped one of Camille's. "I want you to know I understand. After I birthed Elijah—for weeks after I birthed him—I was so unutterably sad. I had lost him much as you lost your baby."

"Oh, Mary." Camille dissolved into tears and with her free hand reached for a handkerchief. "And you had so few people to coddle you and love you and insist that you rest. More to the point, you were probably working away again in a matter of days. I feel so spoiled."

"No, no. Truly, that was not my intention. I just hoped to help you realize that this will pass. You will not find yourself miserable forever."

"Really? My mother has said much the same thing, but even after bearing five children, her melancholy was not so severe as mine has been. I'm beginning to worry that I am seriously flawed."

"You must believe me, you are not flawed. You're going to be well before you know it. Just be patient, and let it run its course. And if I might offer a suggestion—do your best to keep yourself busy. The less you are alone and thinking thoughts that never lead anywhere but in circles, the better things will be for you."

Camille nodded through her tears. "It's just so very hard. I don't want to leave the house."

"Perhaps just a small visit somewhere? In fact, I am walking down the street to the bookshop tomorrow around noon. If I come by, will you accompany me there? Spring is on the horizon, and it feels very nice outside."

Camille nodded, although Mary could see it was reluctant. "Perhaps just a little walk."

"Yes. Small things lead to good things."

CHAPTER 6

Though I never ordered it, and never wished it, I have never shed many tears over the event, because I believe it hastened what we all fought for, the end of the war.
—General Sherman, regarding the fires that destroyed much of South Carolina

* * *

The cruelties practiced on this campaign toward the citizens have been enough to blast a more sacred cause than ours. We hardly deserve success.
—Union corporal

* * *

15 February 1865
Charleston, South Carolina

The swath of mayhem and destruction the troops left behind them as they marched on Charleston had Joshua shaking his head in stunned wonder. By the time they were finished, barely two stones were left standing atop one another. Beautiful, tropical gardens and homes were left in utter ruin. The people who had lived in them only days before now foraged through the soldiers' camps after troops departed.

It could only be described as chaotic and unlike anything Joshua would ever have imagined. To make matters more complicated, there were bands of reckless people who followed Sherman's thousands, raiding and looting whatever they could find along the way.

It wasn't long before the countryside began to look extremely familiar, and Joshua felt his heart thumping in his chest. He had but few friends among the soldiers, none of whom marched beside him now as he realized he was approaching his former home. There was nobody to turn to and say, "I was raised here. I was a slave here," because, as he had expected, a good majority of the white soldiers were none too happy to have a colored man in their midst.

The majestic mansion soon came into view as the men swarmed over the property, walking down the tree-lined drive with driven purpose. There stood Bentley, just as he remembered it. Now that the family had gone, and Ruth along with them, he wondered if anyone occupied the main house at all.

He climbed the front steps and, with nearly detached observation, noted the condition of the cracking paint, the general wear on the house that nobody was around to fix. Joshua followed the tide of men that entered through the double front doors, the sounds of their voices and laughter fading into the recesses of his mind as he looked around himself.

So many memories. How he hated this place! And yet he could almost see Mama Ruth descending the staircase, ready to get after him for this infraction or that. He remembered Emily, bounding about with her red hair trailing behind her. He thought of Richard and his eyes involuntarily narrowed.

Most of all, perhaps, he remembered Ben—his bosom friend who had taught him to read and had risked his life trying to free Ruth, Mary, and Rose. Ben's good heart had cost him his inheritance and his relationship with his family. He was a good man, had been the very best of friends, and Joshua missed him. By rights, this home should have gone to Ben, but ironically enough, Ben disliked it as much as did Joshua.

One of the soldiers saw Joshua looking at the cobwebs and dust that had settled on what few items still remained in the front foyer. "Hey, soldier," the man said, "maybe Sherman'll take pity on you and give you this big house. He's been giving away property to Negroes left and right."

Joshua glanced at the man, hearing the sarcasm for what it was. He looked away again at the high ceilings, the grand staircase, the carpets that had once cost more than his life had been worth. "I don't want it," he answered the soldier.

"Oh, are you too good for this place, then?"

Joshua looked at the man and cocked an eyebrow. "As a matter of fact, yes." With that, he turned and left the house, shoving past the men in blue who were still entering the front doors in hopes of finding treasures. Any reply the man might have said to Joshua's retreating back was lost in the crowd, and Joshua didn't much care.

He walked down the sloping back lawn and paused at the tree where Ruth had been whipped for trying to escape and Ben had leaped upon her in defense, taking the blows on his own back for her. He continued walking, passing several rows of slave quarters until he came to the row that had been his.

Joshua pushed lightly on some of the doors, only to find each cabin empty. Bentley was completely deserted, and he admitted some surprise. He had expected that some of the people would have stayed on even after Ruth left. If nothing else, it provided folks with a roof over their heads. The earth was spent, however—the crops long since abandoned, the fields not harvested in months. What had once been splendor was now little more than weeds and ruin.

Slaves had left in droves; he had seen it throughout the country as he had moved his way south. It was hard to feel ownership in a place that had kept one in shackles, and after yearning for freedom for so long, some people seemed to want to go somewhere, *anywhere* but the plantations where they'd toiled, many had loved, and all had lost. There had to be those, Joshua knew, who stayed at their former plantations simply because there seemed nowhere else to go. The snide soldier had been correct in one of his comments—Sherman had indeed given property over to people of color who were left behind when all was said and done.

As Joshua looked at the cabin that had housed him for the majority of his life, he knew he would have been among those who left. He felt no ties, no affection for the land. The only thoughts connected to Bentley that garnered any sort of positive emotion in his heart were those of Ruth, Mary, Rose, Ben, and Emily. They were all gone as well. None of those he had loved were still there.

He heard shouts from the big house and turned to his left. The men were vacating the building, and he knew what was soon to follow. It wasn't long before smoke curled out of the windows of the upper floor, followed by flames that licked the dry wood and consumed it. The crackling of the fire echoed down the hill, and Joshua watched with little emotion as the mansion burned.

Soldiers were now approaching the slave quarters, torches in hand. Finally, they made their way down the row where Joshua stood, watching. He recognized one of the men carrying a torch. Bill was one of the kinder soldiers who often took the time to ask after Joshua's welfare and engage him in conversation.

"Hey you, Josh," Bill called to him as he approached. The man must have seen something strange in Joshua's face, because he halted when he reached him and asked, "Are you well, soldier?"

Joshua cleared his throat and gestured to the cabin before them. "I used to live here," he said.

Bill looked from Joshua to the cabin and back again. "Not a very fitting home," he said.

"No, it wasn't."

"Seems to me, then, that you should do the honors." Bill handed Joshua the torch, and Joshua looked at it, burning and fierce in his hand.

"I do believe I will," Joshua said and looked at Bill, who nodded.

Joshua moved forward a few steps and looked at the cabin that was a symbol of his life as a hostage to a corrupt system. With an angry cry, he hurled the torch through the glassless window and watched with a mixture of fury and sorrow as flames began to consume the small structure.

Bill approached him from behind and clapped a hand around his shoulders. "Well done, Josh," he said. "Let's leave this place now."

Joshua nodded and turned, tears coursing freely down his face. They left the slave quarters, Bill's arm still firmly around Joshua's shoulders. The pair elicited many stares from the other men, but nobody made a comment on their camaraderie. In fact, the air had taken on a kind of stillness as the soldiers parted to allow them passage back up the lawns toward the burning mansion.

Bill gave Joshua another reassuring squeeze as Joshua looked back over his shoulder at the destruction, and the pair quietly left Bentley. "Some good news," Bill said to Joshua as they walked down the wide, overgrown drive. "You'll never guess where Old Glory now flies."

"Where?" Joshua asked, wiping at his nose with a handkerchief.

"Fort Sumter. Right where it all started."

* * *

3 March 1865
Cleveland, Ohio

"'Lincoln rejects Lee's request for negotiation,'" Anne read aloud from the paper.

"Does it say why?" Ivar asked her as he cleaned his work boots.

"Lincoln is demanding surrender first. The Confederates appear to want some sort of negotiation 'between the two countries.'"

Ivar shook his head. "I suppose I admire them for riding it to the bitter end," he said. "They haven't given up easily."

"No. Nor did we expect them to." Anne took a sip of tea, hoping it would calm her roiling stomach. She wore a light blue dress of sturdy muslin and a white shawl tied about her shoulders, knowing that ordinarily the colors would have set off her complexion to perfection. As it was, she still lacked a decent appetite and knew that her blonde hair and blue eyes did nothing to calm Ivar's fears whenever he noticed the unusual paleness of her face. She resisted the urge to pinch her cheeks for a bit of color and continued reading the paper. "Lee's army is still holed up in Petersburg after ten months of fighting, six of which have included a siege."

"They must be near to starving by now."

Anne nodded. "This war has exacted a high price." She winced and shifted, taking a deep breath. "I wonder what would have happened differently if people had known the end from the outset."

"It wouldn't have made a difference," Ivar said, examining his boots one last time before setting them aside. "It was all inevitable." He took a close look at his wife and winced in sympathy. "Are you going to be ill again, sweet?"

"No, I don't think so. I wrote to my mother about this, you know, and she said she wasn't ill much past the first three months with each child. I should be doing much better soon then if I'm to be like her."

"I hope such is the case," Ivar said and planted a kiss on Anne's forehead. "I'll return soon. I'm going to rescue my mother from Inger."

Anne smiled as Ivar left the house. Amanda wouldn't see it as a rescue; she adored the child, and Inger kept her busy. Anne tapped her fingers against the table for a moment and wished she had something that might keep *her* busy as well. She was efficient with her work around the small home she, Ivar, and Inger shared, and she was beginning to feel a familiar sense of restlessness.

"I miss writing," she said aloud. Indeed, it had been several months since she had been in Jacob Taylor's employ as a newspaper writer, and she was beginning to feel an itch to set pen to paper. The urge to experience neck-breaking adventure along with the writing, however, was something that had passed from her life. She smiled a bit to herself, thinking that the war, near-starvation, and prison camps had satisfied her penchant for danger seeking.

There had to be something she could do with her talent, though. If nothing else, it would help keep her distracted from the near-constant nausea. She retrieved a paper and pen and began writing her thoughts down on paper; she wrote whatever came to mind, whether they be distant memories or dreams, and before long, she had filled the page completely with random thoughts.

She scowled a bit, looking over the mess with a critical eye. One theme seemed to repeat itself; a young woman, seeking adventure and learning the meaning of bravery, stepped out in bits and pieces all over the page. Anne wondered if other young girls or women had ever felt as she had, and she wondered if they would be interested in reading about the adventures of one very reckless and optimistic young woman.

Anne was preoccupied with the thought all through dinner and Inger's bedtime routine and lay awake long into the night next to her husband, wondering what to do with the musings that swirled around in her head but didn't seem to want to settle in any one spot.

* * *

4 March 1865
Boston, Massachusetts

Camille looked across the parlor at her new friend and laughed. "Isabelle, you didn't!"

"I did," Isabelle said. "Cut her hair right off and made her look like a man. Who else would she have gone to for help? A male barber?"

"Oh, I had no idea," Camille said, pulling her embroidery thread through the fabric. "I suppose I should have guessed. She didn't want to speak much of the whole of it when she returned home, and then she was off again finding Ivar. We really haven't seen her much over the past few years."

Mary sat with the women in the parlor, also working at a handcraft. "Anne is a very brave woman. She always was. I admired her as a child—you all would come down to the plantation for visits, and she was always so . . . daring and different. She played outside with the boys and didn't worry one bit about falling out of trees or messing her dresses."

"I know," Camille grumbled. "She nearly made me crazy, and I was half her size. I thought she was scandalous, you know. You should have seen me when I was told she'd been parading around town as a boy so she could write newspaper articles for Jacob. Nearly had an apoplectic fit!"

Isabelle laughed, and it was a full, rich sound. "Camille, you would have been scandalized beyond words at our antics at school, then. Oh, mercy," she said and fanned herself at the memory.

"Well," Mary said, "I happen to know of *someone else* who also dressed as a boy, and not too distantly in the past, either."

Camille tossed a pillow at Mary, who caught it with a smile. "That was for a good cause," Camille muttered.

"What's this?" Isabelle sat at attention in her chair by the fire.

"Camille dressed as a boy and snuck out here to this very house because she had heard of a threat on Jacob's life. She saved the house, if not Jacob himself, that night."

Camille muttered something unintelligible.

"Why, Camille Birmingham Taylor, if you don't beat all!" Isabelle said.

"It was nothing."

"It was love," Mary said in protest. "I find it very daring and romantic."

"It was stupid."

"Yes, dear," Isabelle said, settling back into her chair. "We all do stupid things for love."

Camille's eyebrows shot up. "You've been in love, Belle?"

"Once or twice. Maybe three times."

Camille and Mary laughed. "It's not at all fair to mention it without any details," Camille said to her.

"They're not worth mentioning. I have a habit of expending emotion on men who don't deserve it."

"Well, then, I suppose we must find you one who does," Camille said, feeling a familiar spark return—a light sensation that came from involvement in a friend's life.

"We'll do no such thing, young lady," Isabelle said, her tone firm. "I'm doing just fine on my own, thank you."

Mary and Camille looked up at her, saying nothing.

"Oh, very well. I suppose I've been a bit dour of late, but it has nothing to do with my companionship or lack thereof.

Besides, I already feel on the mend just in the short time I've been here."

Camille smiled, and this time when the tears threatened, the emotion behind them was joy. "I also feel on the mend," she said, looking first at Mary and then Camille. "The two of you are saving my mind. And I'm especially glad you're here since Jacob had to be gone this week."

"Is the inaugural today?" Mary said, looking up in surprise. "It is! I had forgotten."

Camille nodded. "I think he misses some of the elements he used to enjoy just writing for the paper instead of the headache of editing. He was looking forward to this opportunity very much."

"And Robert and Abby are with him?" Mary asked as she tied off her thread.

"They are." Camille winked at Mary and said, "I have a feeling that something is happening with those two below the surface of their casual conversation. Abby is now all a fluster in Robert's presence, and he always seems so much more lively when she's in the room."

"So Robert and your friend Abby are in Washington with naught but your *husband* as an escort?" Isabelle asked, her own embroidery long since forgotten in her lap.

"Yes."

"My, my, the scandal," Isabelle said with a shake of her head. "And here I believed Anne and I to be the only women alive who shunned convention."

"Abby has a sterling reputation," Camille said, "so most who know her wouldn't blink an eye at the thought of her vacationing with two men."

"What of those in Washington?"

Camille smiled. "I don't believe she cares overmuch."

"Good woman. I like her already."

CHAPTER 7

With malice toward none, with charity for all, with firmness in the right as God gives us to see the right, let us strive on to finish the work we are in, to bind up the nation's wounds, to care for him who shall have borne the battle and for his widow and his orphan, to do all which may achieve and cherish a just and a lasting peace among ourselves and with all nations.
—From Lincoln's 2nd Inaugural Address

* * *

4 *March 1865*
Washington, D.C.

The air around the large crowd was cold and windy, much as it had been at Lincoln's first inaugural. Jacob, his fingers gripping his pen, scribbled as quickly as he could to catch as much of the president's speech as possible. He was struck by the humble strength in which the words were offered and the sheer compassionate power of the words themselves. There were many in the Union who were not of a mind to be gentle to the vanquished. And if the word from the fields was to be believed, Sherman's army was all but demolishing the very people about which Lincoln now spoke.

"What a mess this thing is," Robert muttered to him as they stood on the front lawn of the nation's capitol. "I wonder if folks have any idea how long it will take to rebuild."

"We're not doing poorly at all up here," Jacob commented, still taking notes.

"Before long, we'll all be one country again, and from what I hear, south of the Mason-Dixon it isn't pretty."

Abigail stood with her arm through Robert's, straining to see through the crowd. "I wish I could see him up close," she murmured. "He must be very, very tired. The poor man deserves a rest." She glanced at Robert and flushed. "That is, I don't mean to imply his lot has been worse than the ordinary soldier's, I just . . ."

Robert inclined his head at her with a small smile. "I didn't think that for one moment," he said to her softly. "I, too, feel for Mr. Lincoln. But I'm afraid that as much as he deserves a rest, we'll be in a bad way if he takes one. The war isn't even over yet, and when it is, well, then the work is just beginning."

As the president's remarks drew to a close, the crowd shifted and the program continued. "We'll walk for a bit," Robert said to Jacob, who nodded.

"Meet me out in the street when this is finished," he said.

Robert drew Abigail aside. "Do you mind? I'd like to stretch my legs."

"Not at all. I was mostly interested in hearing Mr. Lincoln. A walk would be just the thing."

They strolled through the crowd in silence, each taking in the sights and sounds of people at a celebration. "Have you heard," Abigail said to him at length, "that Congress only yesterday established a bureau for refugees and freedmen?"

Robert nodded. "I did hear. I think it's a necessary thing." He shook his head. "I know I'm repeating myself, but this country is going to need such a bureau, with as many offices as we can staff, as we can possibly create."

"You know, I find it amazing that only just across the river and south a bit, people are grappling for what precious little they can find."

"Yes. The Confederate dollar is not worth the paper on which it's printed. Did you know in the South, a single stick of firewood costs five dollars?"

"I find it horrific." Abigail turned her face into the cold wind and closed her eyes, opening them momentarily to find Robert watching her. "It makes me want to do something to help."

"I agree. Perhaps in the coming weeks as the Freedmen's Bureau develops, something we can do will become apparent."

"My mother would have done something," Abigail said as they continued walking away from the capitol. "She would never have sat idle."

"I admired your mother. She was active in the Abolition Society for years." Robert chuckled. "One never wondered what she thought. She spoke her mind, and spoke it freely."

Abigail smiled. "She was an original, wasn't she? Sweet mercy, how I miss her."

Robert hugged her arm to his body. "I'm sorry you've been alone. I'm sorry Luke is gone . . ."

"Hush now, Robert. I'm sorry as well, but one thing I knew about your brother was that he cared for my happiness. He wouldn't want me to live my life out as a spinster, alone and uncared for because he was gone. He would have wanted me to continue to find happiness, I'm sure of it."

Robert let out a breath. "I know."

"Robert." Abigail stopped where they stood at the side of the street and forced him to face her. "It's good that you fancy me. It is not a bad thing at all, to my mind."

He remained quiet. Her brown hair and eyes, small figure—she was so dear and familiar to him, and he wondered if he'd finally have the courage to lay all of his feelings before her.

"I rather fancy you, too," Abigail continued. "I am a few years your senior, however. I wonder that you haven't found some pretty young thing to snatch from her parents' grasp."

"I've only ever wanted you, Abby," Robert admitted quietly. "From the beginning. Even when Luke was alive. So you can imagine how guilty I feel now that he's not."

"Then you need to absolve yourself of that guilt, because Luke would, if he could." She paused. "Robert, he's gone. But you and I are here. We can either acknowledge that we care for each other, or we can stop associating, even casually. But eventually, you will find someone to love, as will I. I would rather it be you for me and me for you, but if you feel it's something you cannot live with, then I suppose this whole conversation is pointless."

Robert considered her words, a heavy band that had been constricting his chest slowly loosening. Did he want her to find someone else? Of course not! The very thought made him sick. The wind gently blew a curl across her face, and he lifted it with his fingers. Without saying a word, he slowly lowered his face to hers and placed a soft kiss upon her lips.

When he drew back, she smiled. "Why, Mr. Birmingham, you'll have my reputation in tatters. What will the good folk of Washington say?"

"Let them say what they like. You've suddenly made things very clear to me. I love you, Abby."

"And I, you." She placed a hand alongside his face. "Now, let us enjoy each other and never again speak of guilt. It's misplaced. Are we agreed?"

"We are."

* * *

Jacob finished revising his notes and sat down to the business of writing the newspaper article detailing the events of the inaugural. This was the part of the process he liked the least; however, the day as a whole had bestowed upon him a feeling of invigoration and freedom he hadn't felt in ages. He was a newspaperman first and foremost; he loved investigating things that were just on the brink of happening. He was tired of spending time in an office, behind a desk, and he hadn't realized how restless he'd become until now.

The next day he planned to wander about town, taking in the feel of the city and her citizens at the dawn of the president's second term. He wished above anything that he could find entry across the border and into Virginia. That was where the real story lay; he wanted to see it firsthand.

His brow creased as he thought of Camille. If he thought she could bear it, he would suggest they take some time away from home and travel a bit so that he could revisit his early days of reporting. He had worked hard and saved money throughout the years, and he knew it wouldn't be a financial burden to take a leave of absence from his editorial position.

She was still so unhappy about the loss of their child. He had been shocked but had had the luxury of work to distract him from obsessing about it. It was different for women, and he knew that; it hurt him to see Camille so sad. Isabelle's presence seemed to be helping, though, and he was very grateful for her timely visit. Anne's friend was practical, humorous, and bright. She was a perfect match for his wife—he only hoped Camille would begin to show shades of her former self. The day he left for Washington, she had smiled at him with a hint of her old sparkle, and his heart had leapt at the sight.

Well, he mused as he sat back in his chair and stretched, who knew what the future held? Perhaps she would feel up to the travel, and they could observe the results of the past four years on the countryside. Provided the war soon came to the close for which Lincoln was hoping, they might be able to do just that.

* * *

4 March 1865
Salt Lake City, Utah

The celebrations had withdrawn from the main-street parades and had moved to homes that glittered and sparkled from within as the citizens toasted Lincoln's reelection. Earl Dobranski held his arm out to Charlotte Birmingham Ellis, and they strolled quietly away from the merrymaking and into the quiet night.

"I suppose William will have been asleep for some time now," Earl commented to the woman at his side.

"One can only hope," Charlotte said with a shake of her head. "Otherwise your mother might be ready to tear out her hair."

Earl chuckled. "My mother has handled boys for many years now. I'd say she and William are a fair match for each other."

Charlotte glanced at him. "I want to thank you, Earl, for bringing me here for the celebrations. The time away has been nice."

"How are things at home with your folks?"

"Well enough—my mother seems stronger each day. I suppose . . ." She paused and looked into the street, seemingly searching for words. "I suppose I'd like a home of my own now. Before, I was content at the thought of living with them forever, but now that time and distance have placed us far from Bentley, I find myself a bit restless. Isn't that odd?" she asked, looking back at him. "A widow with a child should welcome the company and protection of her parents."

Earl shrugged a bit. "I don't find it odd, Charlotte. You're an adult—why should you not want some space of your own?"

"Yes," she nodded. "As long as I'm under their roof, I'm still their child. I have my own little family now. I just never dreamed, really, that any of this would happen to me. If someone had told me what the future held, I think I would have died. But now that I'm living it, it's gratifying to know that I'm surviving." Charlotte flushed a bit and turned her head slightly. "How silly that must seem to a man who has lived his life working hard with his family."

"Not silly at all. Not at all." Earl gave her hand a small pat and rubbed her knuckles with his thumb. "I admire the woman you are, Charlotte. I admit, I probably would never have had the nerve to spend two minutes in your company back in the day when you were a young debutante on your fancy plantation."

She shook her head, her smile holding something sad. "I wasn't beautiful or captivating. I wore expensive clothing and had an impressive dowry. My parents decided who should have me, and he accommodated them. It was to my own misfortune that I loved him."

Earl knew he couldn't hide his confusion from her. "But, Charlotte, you're a very beautiful woman. You're strong and intelligent and amusing. Why do you act as though you had nothing in your favor but your parents' money?"

She looked at him with an expression that was utterly without guile. He knew she believed everything she was telling him. "Because it's true. Most suitors found me boring or stiff. Abrasive, perhaps. I just didn't know how to behave, how to relax. I was always on edge, very nervous. If my father had been a lowly farmer or someone of more humble means, I would never have found myself married."

Earl shook his head and stopped walking, halting their progress. "Who told you these things?"

"Nobody had to tell me, Earl. It was just the truth."

"I don't believe it, Charlotte. I don't believe it for a minute. And if decent men couldn't see your nerves for the shyness that it was, then I must believe that all of South Carolina is full of fools for men."

Her mouth dropped open a bit, and she looked at him with a face so innocent and like a small child's, his heart nearly broke for her. "I would have grabbed you at your first dance and never let you go," he whispered and brought her knuckles to his lips.

"Oh, Earl," she shuddered out on a light breath, "you don't know how I was. After William and I were married, I became so cold and cruel. I became jaded and heartless like my mother, and . . ."

He put his finger over her lips. "You were hurting. People preserve themselves however they can when they hurt. Now you're in a new place with a fresh start and a beautiful son. You can be the woman you were on your way to becoming when your folks interfered."

Tears formed in her eyes and spilled liberally down her cheeks. He wiped at them with his thumbs and let them continue to fall, never once telling her to hush or not to cry. When the tears seemed at an ebb, he withdrew a snowy-white handkerchief from his pocket and presented it to her with a flourish.

She laughed and accepted it with a murmur of thanks. He waited until she had tidied her face to her satisfaction and then again presented her his arm. "Now then," he said to her as they continued walking, "what sorts of things held your interest when you were young, before you met your husband?"

Charlotte blew out a short breath and considered his question. "I don't really remember—well, actually . . ."

"Yes?"

"I did enjoy dancing. I wasn't good at socializing and charming conversation, but the dancing itself I always did wish to be good at."

The strains of music floated out of a nearby house, and as they neared it, Earl stopped again and bowed deeply. "May I have this dance, Mrs. Ellis?" he asked her.

Again, her mouth dropped open in shock. "Here? In the street?"

"Of course. I much prefer moonlight to kerosene."

Charlotte glanced around them as if assessing who might see. Then, apparently throwing caution to the wind, she smiled and curtseyed. "I should be delighted, Mr. Dobranski."

Earl placed his hand at the small of her back and clasped her hand. She lifted her skirts with her other, and they began to sway together, moving in time to the music. Charlotte laughed and tipped her head to the sky, taking in the splendor of the stars and moon and the lovely scents of the calm spring evening.

Earl watched her joy, feeling a tightness in his throat, and he knew that come what may, he was going to convince the widow Ellis to become his wife.

CHAPTER 8

I doubt if history affords a parallel to the deep and bitter enmity of the women of the South. No one who sees them and hears them but must feel the intensity of their hate.
—*General William T. Sherman*

* * *

15 March 1865
Savannah, Georgia

Emily's neighbor looked at her with heated ire as they stood on the street downtown. "I hate them," she said. "I will hate the Yankees for as long as I live. They are a despicable race who aren't satisfied with their own space up north. They have to come down here and tell us how to live as well. Electing Black Lincoln a second time, and they assume that we will surrender and return to him with no hard feelings."

"Hmm." Emily tried to school her features, but she knew if she wasn't careful, she would either laugh right in the woman's face or become equally as angry and blast her with a commentary that would leave her ears ringing. In the end, she did neither.

"They call themselves gentlemen. Ha! No true gentleman, no *Southern* gentleman, would do the things those bluebellies are doing. I'm not the only one who feels this way. Why, *all* of my lady friends, practically every good woman in this town, hates the North. We're thinking of forming a society called the Daughters of the Confederacy. I know you'll want to be among our ranks."

"Actually," Emily said, switching her heavy basket from one arm to the other, "I wouldn't be interested."

"*What*? Why ever not?"

"I hate the Confederacy."

Emily left the woman gaping behind her and continued on her way to her original destination. She paused outside the door, double-checking the address she had written down on a scrap of paper and placed in her apron. Shaking her head, she thought of her neighbor's angry words and knew full well that the woman was not alone. The good women of the South were indeed outraged, and their hatred ran hard and deep. Emily's betrayal of her feelings to the woman were bound to get her into trouble, but she wasn't worried. She and Austin had a few friends, and she found she could do without the company of the rest. When she heard a light voice of warning at the back of her head, she shrugged it aside and determined to ignore those who were less than friendly.

Emily opened the door to the building and stepped inside. The Freedmen's Bureau was new and, as such, was still in its rudimentary form. They had, however, begun to do much good for the folks in town who were destitute and without food or home. "Hello," Emily said to the captain, a man named Ketchum who was given charge of this particular office. She had met with him on one other occasion and had pledged her support of their efforts.

"I've brought some books," she said, and lifted the large basket onto the man's desk. "You mentioned that the new school for colored children was in need of some. These are mostly primers that were left at Willow Lane—Mr. Stanhope's parents ran a school of their own at the plantation years ago. The books are a bit dated but should still serve some purpose."

"Absolutely, Mrs. Stanhope, and I thank you heartily," he said, shaking her hand with enthusiasm. "Your generosity is most appreciated."

"How are the children faring, sir?"

"Splendidly, absolutely marvelously. Their teachers are gratified by the rapid growth they've seen in the students. And so fastidiously combed and dressed they are! I visited myself only yesterday and was much impressed."

"I'm very happy to hear it," Emily said, genuinely impressed herself with the captain's optimism and good heart. "I do hope you will call upon us with further needs. And if you don't mind, I'd very much like to check in with you a few times a week to see where we might help elsewhere, as well."

"Mrs. Stanhope, you and your husband are very good people."

"Perhaps my motives are selfish, Captain. I seek to keep my hands busy so I don't fuss and worry at home. Times are hard."

"That they are. And we are of a like mind. Busy hands are preferable to idle ones."

As Emily exited the Bureau, she saw no sign of her neighbor and was relieved. She was hardly desirous to listen to the woman prattle on and on about the virtues of the Confederacy. To Emily's mind, it had been idiocy from the start, backed by an evil purpose. The Confederate vice president had said it himself; upon his inaugural, Alexander Stephens had told the crowd gathered outside the state capitol in Alabama that the new government was founded on the principle that the white man was superior to the Negro. What Emily had hated from the onset became an entity so reviled in her mind that she undoubtedly felt as much negative passion for the new Southern government as her neighbor did for the Yankees.

Perhaps the ultimate irony, now that the Confederacy was losing more men in battle than it could afford to replace, was that

Jefferson Davis had, only two days prior, signed a bill allowing blacks to enlist in the Confederate army. The reward was that each black man who enlisted would also be given his freedom. The insult! It soured Emily's stomach to think that the only means through which a man could legally obtain his freedom would be to defend the system that had enslaved him.

Emily was thoughtful throughout her uneventful ride home, and as she reached Willow Lane, she directed the small, horse-drawn curricle around the back of the plantation to the stables. *Please, dear Lord,* she prayed. *Please be with the president. Bless Mr. Lincoln.*

Her mental prayer continued as she entered the mansion and made her way up the stairs to her daughter's nursery. Once there, she dismissed Nina with a smile of thanks and scooped Mary Alice into her arms. She kissed the little girl's soft cheek and nuzzled her curly hair, eventually coming to rest on the floor amid the young one's toys.

"Shall we play with your dolly, Mary Alice?" Emily asked her daughter and set her down on the floor beside her. Mary Alice babbled in her infant tongue and smiled at her mother, smacking her hands up and down playfully on Emily's knee. Emily smiled at the child, her breath catching in her throat at the knowledge that this perfect little child was hers. Of all the things that occupied her life, Mary Alice and Austin were her favorites, and she spent a good amount of her time in the nursery.

* * *

Gwenyth sat alone in the cookhouse, reading over Joshua's letter a second time. He had seen Bentley burn with his own eyes, had even set fire to his own former cabin. The letter seemed to carry a tone of finality, and Gwenyth could only hope that perhaps Joshua had been able to put some demons to rest with the destruction of the place.

She glanced up from the paper and looked at her surroundings with a certain amount of fondness. She had stayed at Willow Lane of her own free will; when Austin, and his parents before him, had given her the choice to be on one of their escape trips north to Boston, she had refused. She wanted to stay behind and help.

How many faces had she seen pass through this plantation? Countless! The Stanhopes had left a legacy of freedom and dignity as they used their resources to make life better for others. She had wanted to be a part of that for as long as she could. Now, though, as she read Joshua's letter, she imagined a home of her own for the first time in her life. She wanted a place to live out her life in peace with Joshua at her side.

She missed his company. She had relished those daily visits while he was mending, had been amazed that while she had certainly known who he was before he escaped to Boston—indeed, he had lived right at Willow Lane—she hadn't felt the connection to him that she now did. Perhaps it was just as well. There were times and seasons for everything in life, and the past year had held much work for Gwenyth as she had run Willow Lane single-handedly in Austin's and Emily's absence. Emily had spent much time at home with her family in South Carolina during Austin's term of enlistment and had relied on Gwenyth heavily.

It had been a weight she was happy to bear, but now she only wished for her own place, her own life. As she knelt in prayer later that evening, she pleaded with the Lord to keep Joshua safe and to preserve them both so that they might have a chance for happiness together.

* * *

15 March 1865
Boston, Massachusetts

"This is vexing."

"What is it?" Camille approached Isabelle, who clenched a letter in her fingers.

"Pinkerton is asking me to go to Washington." Isabelle sat on the settee behind her with a drawn expression.

"Why does he want you there?" Camille sat next to her, a bit unnerved to see Isabelle looking so distressed. It was unusual.

"He wants me to spend some time in a certain boarding-house, to see if I can't learn anything about a Mrs. Mary Surratt." She paused and looked up at Camille. "There's trouble brewing."

"For the president?"

Isabelle nodded, looking pained.

"But he doesn't even travel with a large escort any longer. Now that the war is surely almost at an end, I thought it was deemed unnecessary."

"I believe that's a commonly held opinion, even amongst those closest to the president. Allan says that he's heard rumors flying about the underground . . ." Isabelle stood and began pacing the floor. "I can hardly ignore this. I just don't want to go anywhere. This visit with you all has been so pleasant."

"I can't believe anyone would have the nerve to cause outright harm to the president. An assassination? Is that the concern?" Camille shook her head a bit. "It's unheard of. I just cannot fathom such a thing." She watched Isabelle's agitated movements for a moment longer. "Why don't Jacob and I go with you? Jacob says he is looking to get out into the reporting field a bit—what better place to go than back to Washington? You saw him yourself when he returned last week. He was happier than I've seen him in ages."

Isabelle scrutinized Camille's face. "What of you, though? Do you suppose you feel up to a holiday?"

"I'm feeling stronger and better each day. I believe my walks with you and Mary have helped tremendously. The more I leave the house and move about, the better I feel. Truly, Belle, I shall be fine."

Isabelle stopped pacing and tapped her foot instead, looking at Camille for long moments, her thoughts seemingly flying in different directions. "Mention it to Jacob when he comes home. If you can come along, I would welcome your company tremendously. You can't stay in the boardinghouse with me—it will arouse suspicion. I need to do this by myself. At any rate, I'll need to leave in the morning." Isabelle moved forward impulsively and clasped Camille in an enormous hug. "I love you," she said. "And I'm very afraid."

"For me?"

"No. For the president."

"Belle, really. I'm certain that you will find the whole of it filled with nothing more than rumors or nasty speculation."

"Camille, you don't understand. There are people in this world with evil hearts."

"You're a cynic. You've spent too many years working for Pinkerton."

"I'm a cynic because I know too much. I've seen too much." Isabelle shook her head. "You don't know how I would love to believe you're right. But the president hasn't been safe since that day four years ago when he snuck into Washington in disguise."

* * *

17 March 1865
Washington, D.C.

Isabelle found herself successfully entrenched in Mary Surratt's boardinghouse. To all onlookers, she was Mrs. Watts, a plain widow who was traveling south to visit her besieged family.

The disguise was necessary; Isabelle had spent the better part of the war in Washington and surrounding cities posing as a wealthy, Confederate-supporting socialite. Therefore, she took great pains that no one remember her from before, whether on the street or in some secluded shop. Her hair was dour, her face dabbed with white powder to make her appearance pale and wan.

She now sat upstairs in her spare room, quickly drafting a missive to Allan Pinkerton. *There seem to be a few who have congregated here with regularity in the past day or so,* she wrote. *One I immediately recognized as John Wilkes Booth. You may remember we accompanied the president before he addressed the crowds at Gettysburg and attended the play in which Mr. Booth performed,* The Marble Heart.

Isabelle paused for a moment and reflected on her activities of the prior evening. When Mr. Booth had been out, she had quietly gained access to his bedroom and done a preliminary search through his belongings. Perhaps of most interest to her, and the most alarming, was an entry in the diary she had found hidden in a desk drawer. *"I have begun to deem myself a coward,"* he wrote in reference to his reluctance to fight for the Confederate cause, although he was known about town as an obsessive supporter of slavery and white supremacy, *"and to despise my own existence."*

As Isabelle had flipped through his diary, her heart had raced at the fanaticism revealed on the pages. In reference to the president's recent inaugural address, Booth had written that from his position in the crowd, he had been afforded *"an excellent chance . . . to kill the President, if I had wished."*

Isabelle frowned and continued her communication with her private-detective employer. *I do believe, Pinkerton, that this man is dangerous, unhinged. As to other particulars, he has surrounded himself by the following persons: Lewis Paine, a wounded Confederate veteran; David Herold, who is a druggist clerk and, by my observations, most probably slow-witted; George Atzerodt, a*

German whose English, I confess, is very difficult to understand; and John Surratt, a man who has spied for the Confederacy and whose mother is the owner of the boardinghouse.

They have gone out tonight, I know not where, and it is too soon as of yet for me to leave and follow them, as Mrs. Surratt believes me to be a widow of questionable health who is desirous for an extended stay here before progressing further south.

There was a chill in the air that Isabelle was certain no amount of firewood would help ease. She rubbed her arms as she placed her pen on the small table and leaned back in her chair. She felt unsettled. It wasn't because she was alone; heaven knew she had conquered that fear long ago and had conducted solitary assignments throughout the war. Pinkerton had mentioned to her in further communication when she had arrived from Boston that he was following leads on other threats from sources elsewhere in the city. Poor Mr. Lincoln—his dissenters and enemies would most likely never rest.

She was gratified, despite her confidence in her own abilities, to know that within a day or two, Camille, Jacob, Abigail, and Robert would all be arriving in the city. Although they would be staying elsewhere, she knew she would feel comfort from knowing they were in the vicinity. *I just can't seem to rid myself of this feeling of dread,* she murmured, a prayer of sorts. *I am very, very concerned.*

The slam of a door below the stairs drew her attention, and she stood smoothly, opened her own door, and crept out into the shadows of the balcony that overlooked the boardinghouse common area. Mrs. Surratt appeared from the kitchen, wiping her hands on an apron. She was a nondescript woman, dark of hair and eye, pale of complexion. She approached the five men who had entered and were now seating themselves at a large, round table.

The actor, Mr. Booth, had his head in his hands. "So goes the world," he muttered, and Isabelle crept forward to better hear him. "Might makes right."

"What happened?" Mrs. Surratt asked.

"They weren't there," one of the others answered her.

"At Soldiers' Home?"

The man nodded. "Just on the outskirts of the city. Weren't there."

"You weren't certain they would be, though."

Silence met this remark, and the men continued to brood, each in his own thoughts. A few minutes passed without comment, and then they rose to disperse. Isabelle crept back into the recesses near her door, and as she turned to enter her room, she missed Mrs. Surratt's quick glance upward at the creak of the floorboards.

She closed the door quietly behind her, her heart thudding a heavy rhythm. Soldiers' Home was just on the outskirts of the city. That was where the president and Mrs. Lincoln sometimes slept. Isabelle made her way back to the small table and added this new information to the letter for Pinkerton.

Her heart still beating quickly, she tried to settle in for the night but found herself unable to sleep. When she finally did, it was as the dawn hour approached, and her dreams were nightmares of the president, lying in state in the White House.

CHAPTER 9

I have been up to see the Congress, and they do not seem able to do anything except eat peanuts and chew tobacco, while my army is starving . . . [W]hen this war began I was opposed to it, and I told those people that unless every man should do his whole duty, they would repent it; . . . And now they will repent.
—*Confederate General Robert E. Lee, to his son*

* * *

22 March 1865
Bentonville, North Carolina

Joshua sank to the ground, exhausted. Robert E. Lee had reappointed Joseph Johnston to head the Confederate troops in the Carolinas. Johnston had thought he might try to halt Sherman's advance, and threw his force of twenty thousand men at the Union's combined forces of one hundred thousand.

To their credit, Joshua mused as he removed his boot and began massaging a sore foot, they didn't give up easily. Three days of fighting had Johnston finally abandoning the field, leaving 2,600 of his men behind, lost. Joshua shook his head and stretched, grateful for what he hoped would be a night of peace.

He opened his pack and pulled out some paper and a pen. Writing to Gwenyth seemed to help him relax, so she had become the recipient of all his correspondence. He had begun a letter to her several days earlier and now gave her a brief outline of the three-day battle.

Joshua paused in his writing, clenching his teeth against the hated tremor in his arm that had plagued him throughout the battle. If only he could be with Gwenyth for just a few minutes. The very sound of her voice seemed to soothe his spirit, and the trembling often quieted for hours, days even.

Although I am anxious to be finished with this business, I have seen the tattered, pathetic state of the enemy, he wrote, trying to divert his thoughts from his own affliction, *and one would have to be dead not to feel the stirrings of pity for these humans. Many of the Confederates are barefoot, their clothing in absolute shambles. They are thin from lack of nourishment and have a look of weariness about them that I find sad. From what I hear of Lee's army defending Petersburg, he has lost sixty thousand soldiers to desertion.*

Our numbers at Petersburg exceed one hundred twenty-five thousand, and Lee's have diminished to only thirty-five thousand. Word is that his lines of defense around Petersburg, now some fifty-three miles, show his soldiers standing a good fifteen feet apart, twenty feet in some places. How can he hope to defend with such a line? I am amazed at the tenacity of the Southern people. It should come as no surprise, however; I was raised among them.

I do wonder how much longer Lee can hope to hold his position around the city, however. Their will can only serve them until their physical abilities collapse, and I do believe that time approaches rapidly. I wish I could more fully describe the appearance of many of these men, but I'm afraid only a firsthand view would adequately tell the tale.

At any rate, Gwen, I am faring well. The soldiers are used to my presence by now, and those who gave me trouble when we departed Savannah have since found other pursuits. It isn't as though there aren't plenty of black folk among us; there are, but for the most part, they follow along behind, refugees and recently freed souls who are looking for a way to live. Were I one of them, I doubt I would have garnered a second glance from many of the men here in the ranks. Because I wear a uniform that matches theirs, however, I was a subject of derision. I have proved myself on the field of battle and have silenced their comments. There are many who speak and write the English language with less precision and correctness than do I, and I must admit to you that while I value my own hide enough to refrain from comment upon the fact, it gives me no small amount of pleasure. Here am I, an educated black amongst them! Mama Ruth would be quite proud of me, I do believe, although she would likely tell me that pride goeth before the fall.

Well, the light begins to wane, and I am weary. I intend to post this letter as soon as possible, and I hope that it finds you well and whole, and possibly missing me just a bit. I will write again soon and keep you apprised of my whereabouts. Please give my best to Emily and Austin, and keep yourself healthy.

Ever yours, Joshua

* * *

2 *April 1865*
Washington, D.C.

Jacob Taylor stood in a crowd of newspaper reporters as word spread. It had just come over the telegraph wires from a newspaperman at the scene: General Lee had withdrawn from Petersburg after Grant had driven his men from their trenches at half past four that morning, and Lee had given his suggestions to President Davis in Richmond, Virginia, that the Confederate government leave immediately and move south.

Robert Birmingham stood near Jacob's side, watching him scribble his notes and listening to the conversation buzz around them. "Lee probably hopes to join up with Johnston in North Carolina and try to stave off Sherman," Robert commented to

Jacob, "but if what we're hearing of the Rebs' condition is true, they would do well to quit now."

A man standing close by heard Robert and nodded. "Listen to this," he said. "According to this account, when Grant's men drove Lee's from the trenches around Petersburg, the dead left behind included old men and boys as young as fourteen years—without shoes."

Jacob lifted his head and stared at the man for a moment. "What is it about that doomed cause that inspires such devotion?" he wondered aloud.

Robert sighed. "They think we're invading their homeland and trying to take away their freedom. You know they refer to this as the Second American Revolution. If we thought we were literally defending our very homes, I daresay we'd all go barefoot to do it too."

Jacob clenched his teeth. "We *are* defending our very homes. This whole country is ours. It belongs to all of us. If we fail at keeping it as one, then the European kings and leaders who scoffed that a self-governed nation would never survive will have been right all along. We will have lost it all."

"Just so," Robert said as Jacob finished his notes and they walked away from the crowd, "I believe that was Lincoln's motivation from the beginning. It's evolved into something much bigger, though. Much more significant."

"I agree wholeheartedly. Not everyone will see it as such, though." Jacob took a deep breath and fished more papers out of his greatcoat pocket. Unfolding them, he made a cursory glance at a few before looking up at Robert. "Did you know that Lincoln met with Grant, Sherman, and Admiral Porter on Grant's floating headquarters on the river at City Point, Virginia? They had a two-day meeting on the best course of action to follow in order to finish this thing."

"I had heard something regarding the meeting," Robert said, "but I was unaware of the details. Do you know any more?"

"Just that Sherman came away from the meeting with a very favorable view of the president. They met once before in '61, and Sherman felt that Lincoln was weak and partisan, incapable of accomplishing his task. After City Point, though, he commented that Lincoln . . ." Jacob searched his notes. "' . . . seemed to possess more of the elements of greatness and goodness than any other.'"

"High praise, indeed," Robert said.

"Do you approve of Sherman?" Jacob asked him as they continued to walk.

Robert appeared quiet and thoughtful. "Militarily, yes. I believe he's tactically brilliant."

"Compassion isn't his strong suit."

"Not when it relates to war, no." Robert glanced over at Jacob. "Speaking of ruthless, had you heard of Nathan Forrest's defeat? I heard news of it flying around the hotel lobby before you came down this morning."

"Confederate Nathan Forrest?"

"The very one. It's one of his few defeats these last four years. Happened in Selma, Alabama. He escaped capture but lost nearly three thousand of his men along with guns and supplies."

"And what do you think of him?"

"Militarily?" Robert grinned a bit, and Jacob smiled in kind.

"Very well, militarily."

"I think he's also brilliant. As a person, I believe him to be without conscience and barbaric."

"He doesn't support Lincoln's Emancipation Proclamation."

Robert barked out laughter that lacked any real humor. "That's the least of it. The very least."

"So what do you suppose Grant will see as his next move?"

"Am I being interviewed for an article, brother-in-law?"

Jacob laughed and nodded. "I confess, some of your quotes will most likely find their way into my next piece."

Robert shook his head. "I was beginning to wonder . . . hmm. Grant's next move. Well, he'll close in on Petersburg, if he's not already there, and move into Richmond posthaste. Then I presume he'll follow Lee south and finish it."

"It feels very near the end. I hope you're correct in your predictions."

"As do I. We have all given enough."

"Do you suppose you'd like to join me in Richmond? I plan to go tomorrow."

"Yes, I would. Camille and Abby will not want to stay here, however."

Jacob shook his head. "I know they won't, but I'm afraid I will insist. I don't know exactly what we'll find in terms of resistance from the citizens, and I wouldn't put the women in harm's way, whether intentional or not."

Robert clapped his brother-in-law on the shoulder. "I'll let you tell them."

* * *

3 April 1865
Richmond, Virginia

Robert had been right—it hadn't been a pretty thing, telling the women they were not to go with them, or follow them, to Richmond. What a wise decision it had been, though. The things he had seen churned Robert's stomach, and he was glad Abigail wasn't at his side for it.

The setting the day before when he and Jacob had arrived in the city had been one of utter chaos. Departing Confederate soldiers had set fire to numerous buildings, and mobs of people ran the streets, breaking into homes and businesses, looting all they could find. Whiskey ran in the gutters ankle deep, to

Robert's amazement, and crude-looking women and even children scooped the liquid into pans and buckets.

The fires spread to the Confederate arsenal, which was filled with artillery shells and gunpowder. The ground trembled with each explosion, followed by a plume of smoke that circled into the air above the building and mixed with the smoke and ashes of existing fires. The air was thick with it, acrid and foul.

Robert and Jacob did nothing but watch and try to remain unobtrusive in their efforts to observe. When they had retired for the evening, neither spoke more than a few words as each attempted to put the day's wild images to rest.

Now Union troops entered and tried to return some semblance of order to the haggard city. Robert couldn't contain his smiles as large groups of black people cheered the Union men like conquering heroes. What an amazing day it was for them! His eyes became moist as he thought of Luke and how much his brother would have loved to have seen the expressions of joy and hope on the faces of the former slaves. They danced and shouted and embraced each other with abandon, and for one wild moment Robert thought of rushing into their midst and joining them. He shook his head, calling himself foolish, and then a small voice inside his head whispered, *Why not?*

With a shrug and a grin at Jacob, he ran into the crowd of celebrators, his arms stretched wide, not caring what anyone might think of his missing hand and forearm. He grabbed a large man whose face was turned toward the sky in unabashed glee and hugged him tight around the middle. He felt, rather than saw, the man look down at him, sensed the stiffening of surprise, and then noted the deep rumble of a chuckle that must have started in the man's toes and made its way to his head. Large, beefy arms came down around Robert's frame, and the man squeezed until Robert could hardly breathe. Robert laughed then, feeling the tears seep from his eyes and down his face, spilling liberally onto the man's faded shirtfront.

The man thumped him on the back, and Robert pulled slightly from the embrace, looking at the work-worn face and twinkling eyes. "Hallelujah!" the man said and grasped Robert's face in his big hands.

"Hallelujah!" Robert laughed and clasped the man's arm with his one hand. "Hallelujah," he said again as the man reached for one more tight embrace before releasing him and moving down the street. "God bless," Robert murmured to the man's retreating form as he watched him through eyes that still streamed with tears. "God bless you, my brother."

Jacob had caught him by then and threw his arm around Robert's shoulder with a squeeze. "Let's go down to the capitol," he shouted above the crowd, and together they ran behind Union soldiers who were on foot and horseback. As they reached the former Confederate headquarters, two men descended from their horses, one of whom retrieved a folded cloth that could only be a flag. Within moments, the two had entered the building, raced to the top, and hurried onto the roof, where they lowered the stars and bars and hoisted the stars and stripes. They stood up on the roof, uncapped a bottle, and drank to the symbol of united freedom.

Amid the cries of delight and cheers, Robert looked around and spied people who were obviously locals standing on the outskirts of the melee and crying their grief. For a brief moment, he felt morbid to be celebrating what was obviously the cause of so much pain for others. He looked down at his feet, his gaze falling upon the spot near his elbow that should have been an arm and hand. Looking up once again, he spied the man he had embraced celebrating and still shouting his praises to the host of heaven.

Robert had paid a personal price in defending the life of the Union. He had lost his brother and a part of himself. Robert glanced back at those who grieved, and while he still felt a stirring of pity, he knew that there was never a cause so foolish, so corrupt at its root, than the one supported by those who now felt that loss. Feeling Jacob's arm again around his shoulders, he turned to his brother-in-law and smiled.

"One step closer to the finish," Jacob said close to Robert's ear. "Nearly there now."

"Thank the good Lord above," Robert said and placed his hand on his heart. He looked up to where the flag snapped in the breeze and felt a sense of relief. As they made their way back down the street they had traveled, Jacob suggested they walk to Rockett's Wharf.

"I think he should be arriving any minute," Jacob said, consulting his pocket watch as they reached the water. "Yes, look!" He pointed out over the water at an approaching barge carrying with it a familiar figure, tall and lean with a stovepipe hat.

Robert watched with a smile on his face as the president was escorted from the barge with his older son, Robert Todd, and his small son, Tad. Robert leaned in as close as the crowd around Lincoln would allow and heard him say, "Thank God I have lived to see this. It seems to me that I have been dreaming a horrid nightmare for four years, and now the nightmare is over."

The president was then mobbed by the joyous black citizens of the city, who wept and sang and danced about him with happiness. One man cried, "I know I am free, for I have seen Father Abraham and felt him."

"Don't kneel to me," Lincoln said to the folks surrounding him, seemingly stunned by the response. "You must kneel to God only and thank Him for your freedom."

"He's surprised," Jacob murmured in Robert's ear. "I think he little realizes how much he has been revered by these people."

Robert nodded. So many others hated the man, it was little wonder he was shocked by such a reception.

The two men followed the president and his throng of admirers as they walked the road to General Weitzel's headquarters, the home that had been Jefferson Davis's mansion. There was no carriage to be found, and the walk was a long one. Robert was content to follow the president around all day.

As Lincoln paused a moment to rest, he stopped opposite an older black man, who removed his hat and bowed, tears flowing down his cheeks. "May de good Lord bless you, President Linkum," the man said.

The president removed his own hat and bowed to the old gentleman in silence, and the crowd all around seemed to take on a hush. Robert looked at Jacob, his jaw slackening slightly, and noted that tears had sprung into Jacob's eyes as he, too, watched the exchange.

Robert looked back at the president and the older man with a sense of awe, knowing that he was witnessing something entirely profound and meaningful, something that had never before happened in the history of the United States. A president had bowed in respect to a man of color. The image seared itself into his brain, and he welcomed it, hoping never to forget the powerful emotion that charged the air.

If I could choose one moment to remember forever, to live again and again, he later wrote in a letter to his mother and father in Boston, *that would be it. Would that I never forget even the singlest detail of the day. Never have I been so in awe of a simple act of kindness and genuine human love.*

CHAPTER 10

*The result of last week must convince you of the hopelessness of
further resistance ... I ... regard it as my duty to shift from myself
the responsibility of any further effusion of blood by asking of you
the surrender of that portion of the Confederate States Army known
as the Army of Northern Virginia.*
—*Grant to Lee*

* * *

*Though not entertaining the opinion you express on the hopeless-
ness of further resistance ... I reciprocate your desire to avoid the
useless effusion of blood, and therefore, before Considering your
proposition, ask the terms you will offer on condition of its
surrender.*
—*Lee to Grant*

* * *

*[P]eace being my great desire, there is but one condition I would
insist upon, namely: that the men and officers surrendered shall be
disqualified for taking up arms again, against the Government of
the United States.*
—*Grant to Lee*

* * *

There is nothing left me but to go and see General Grant, and I had rather die a thousand deaths.
    —General Lee, when told that the odds of breaking through the Union lines were too great

* * *

9 April 1865
Washington, D.C.

"So what exactly happened?" Isabelle entered Camille and Abigail's hotel room, removing her bonnet.

The two women stared at her in silence. Camille found her voice first. "Belle, I would never have recognized you on the street. Your disguise is perfect!"

"Thank you," Isabelle said with a wave of her hand. "I don't have long. I must return to the boardinghouse. Tell me what you know. I haven't seen a paper yet, but I figure you will have heard from Jacob and Robert by now."

They all sat together, and Camille puffed out a breath of air. "Where to start? Well, Lee left Petersburg and headed west, of course, because Grant blocked his way directly south. Grant then closed in on him from three sides as Lee followed the Appomattox River."

"Was he hoping to go *around* Grant?"

"I suppose so, yes. The reports we've seen coming in over the wires say that the whole line was besieged from the moment they left, small battles occurring at intervals, until finally yesterday at Sayler's Creek, the Union took eight thousand of Lee's men. It's a third of his army. So he communicated back and forth with General Grant, who outlined terms of surrender, and today they are to meet at Appomattox Court House."

"It's over?"

The two women nodded. "It's over," Abigail said, her eyes bright and liquid. "I suppose we'll hear all the details of the surrender soon enough."

Isabelle tapped her bonnet. "I heard rumors flying around, even at the boardinghouse, but I wanted to hear it from a reliable source." She paused, looking at her friends. "Well, then, I must be off. My work isn't finished yet."

Camille frowned. "How much longer? I can't help but worry about you. Nothing seems to have happened in the past few days. Perhaps it's a futile chase?"

"I don't think so. I wish it were. These men . . . there's something not quite right about them."

* * *

Appomattox Court House, Virginia

Jacob sent a note by messenger to the women at the hotel to alert them to his and Robert's continued absence. "I want them to know we're at Appomattox," he said to Robert. "I'd like to return, but as we're this close, it seems silly to head back to Washington now."

Robert nodded. "This is one meeting I'm glad to witness in person. The most ironic thing of all is the location."

"At Appomattox Court House?"

"No, the home in which the truce will be signed. It belongs to Wilmer McLean. Do you remember the first battle of Bull Run?"

"Of course."

"Mr. McLean's home was used as the headquarters for General Beauregard, and it was right in the line of fire. Shortly after the battle, Mr. McLean relocated his family because he wanted to be safe and untouched by the war. I find it amazing that it's in his house, of all places, where the generals will meet."

"That is amazing. How is it that you always come by the interesting information?"

Robert laughed. "Ben always asked me the same question. I keep my ear to the rails, you know."

Jacob shook his head as they approached Mr. McLean's home on a dusty, nondescript road. "I suppose you must. You're very good at it, my friend. Now what have you heard of the formation of this meeting, the preceding events?"

"The troops in the field first received word of the intended surrender," Robert said. "General Grant and his officers were resting in a field, Grant with a pounding headache. Lee's messenger rode up bearing a white towel as a surrender flag and a note from Lee himself. Grant looked at the note and handed it to his friend General Rawlins. Apparently," Robert continued, "the men were all stunned. Finally, a Colonel Duff jumped up on a log and called for three cheers. The men tried, a few wavering cheers sounded, but then they all just broke down in tears."

"I can only imagine. They must be so tired."

Robert nodded. "Then a place was selected for the meeting," he continued. "Apparently, the man Lee sent into town to find a suitable meeting place was unable to find anyone at all. The streets were completely deserted. The first man he happened to come across was Mr. Wilmer McLean, who agreed, albeit reluctantly, that his house might be used for the purpose."

"Eerie," Jacob said, his face thoughtful. "What are the odds of such a thing happening? Appomattox Court House is farther west than Lee would ever have wanted to travel in a retreat southward. It isn't as though such a thing could be planned."

"It's very strange," Robert agreed. "Oh, and I neglected to mention this detail, which I found a bit amusing. On hearing of the surrender, an aide said that Grant displayed no more emotion on his face than 'last year's bird nest.' But his headache was gone."

Jacob smiled. "I can imagine it was."

They stopped walking when they reached the front steps of the McLean home and ascended them to the front door. Jacob identified himself as an editor of the Boston paper, which must have seemed impressive enough to the Union soldier at the front door to grant them entrance.

The two men entered the parlor, where two tables had been arranged, with many chairs shoved back to the perimeter of the room. They took seats and watched as the roomful of army personnel paced and chatted in subdued tones.

General Lee arrived first at the McLean house, looking splendid in a crisp, clean uniform that was complete with accoutrements and symbols of his rank. Robert observed the man with a sense of awe. He had never met the vaunted general, and Lee's bearing matched perfectly his professional and heroic reputation. Robert couldn't help but feel sympathy for the man who had survived four hard years of brutal warfare only to lose his cause at the end along with thousands of his men. Had someone asked Robert earlier if he would ever find a reason to admire the man, he would have expressed a biased dislike, despite his own fascination with military figures. Now, however, he felt his heart reluctantly softening as he looked at the proud, tired face of the man who had advised his own leaders against the war but had served where he felt he was needed when asked to do so.

The group of men in the parlor waited thirty minutes for General Grant to arrive, and when he did, Grant was dressed in a dirty private's shirt with shoulder straps of his rank, a mud-spattered uniform, and no sword. Robert gaped at the man's appearance and forced himself to close his open mouth. Grant also looked weary, but despite his disheveled appearance, Robert was no less in awe of his presence than he had been of Lee's. Grant had become a legend, overcoming a horrid reputation and years of disrespect.

The two generals shook hands, took their seats, and spoke for a moment. Grant reminded Lee that they had met once before, during the Mexican War, and Lee remarked that he had not remembered what Grant looked like. The conversation progressed and soon became so pleasant that Grant appeared to have nearly forgotten why they were there. General Lee reminded him, and they got down to the business of the details of the surrender in McLean's parlor.

The terms of surrender were simple. The Confederate officers were allowed to keep their sidearms and personal possessions, including horses they claimed to own, and each officer and man was allowed to return safely home without trouble by the United States authorities. Grant then asked how many men Lee had and if they needed food. Lee said he was no longer sure of the number, but he was sure that they were hungry. Grant offered twenty-five thousand rations, which Lee said would go a long way toward making his men feel better and would, in his words, "do much toward conciliating our people."

Robert sat back in his chair and took a deep breath. *Just like that. Simple and kind, after trying to kill each other only yesterday.*

General Lee eventually left, and Robert moved to the window to watch him. Grant's men began to fire a celebratory gun salute. Grant moved out front and ordered it stopped immediately. As Robert watched General Lee's progression down the dusty street back to his men, he noted that the general rode sadly in the saddle, the reins held limp in his hands. Robert moved to the front door as the men in the parlor began to buy off pieces of McLean's furniture as memorabilia of the event. Robert didn't care about taking home a souvenir; he wanted to watch Lee approach his men.

Robert moved quickly down the front steps and shielded his eyes from the glare of the sun, hearing a noise rise up in the distance. Lee's men began to cheer him, and Robert noted a distinct stiffening of the general's spine. He now sat erect in the saddle, his head proud and looking straight ahead. With each group he passed, the cheers began, and then came the tears.

Robert noted people speaking to Lee, others merely passing their hands along Traveller, Lee's horse. Grown men sat on the ground and wept.

It wasn't long before Jacob was at Robert's side, quickly scribbling notes as fast as his hand would move. "You know who that is over there?" Jacob asked Robert, who glanced at the Union soldiers lined along the road.

"Which one?"

Jacob gestured with his head, still looking down at his notebook and writing. "Right there. It's Joshua Chamberlain. He was the hero at Gettysburg."

Robert's heart thumped in his chest. Luke had survived Gettysburg only to die shortly after in New York suppressing the draft riots. "I think Luke fought alongside Chamberlain," he murmured. "Mentioned it in his last letter home."

Jacob glanced up at Robert, sympathy on his face. He gestured over his shoulder to the house and said, "Grant wanted Chamberlain to be the one to accept the surrender of the troops." Looking down the street at an approaching general, he nodded. "This will be John Brown Gordon. He's a general from . . ." Jacob frowned, thinking.

"Georgia," Robert supplied, also watching the man approach. "Poor man looks miserable."

Jacob nodded, his voice dropping to a whisper as the two opposing soldiers approached each other, one to surrender, the other a clear victor. "I suppose he must be," he said. "It's not every day one loses a war."

As Robert watched, the Confederate general ordered his men to lay down their weapons. Gordon's voice was heavy with grief and defeat. Chamberlain must have sensed it and felt a stirring of sympathy, for at that moment he ordered the Union soldiers to change the position of their rifles. The men in blue shifted their weapons from a position of "support arms" to "carry arms," thus symbolizing equality and honor with the foe.

At Jacob's questioning of the maneuver, Robert explained it to him in hushed tones, feeling a sense of amazement at his presence at such an historic event. *I wish Luke were here to see this,* he thought as he watched the proceedings that were hushed with an unexpected sense of reverence.

As the men eventually began to disperse and Grant's men in the parlor began exiting the building with bits and pieces of Wilmer McLean's furniture, Robert spied Grant himself standing near the steps, speaking to an aide. Unable to resist stealing one last chance at hearing the general's thoughts, he moved unobtrusively closer and listened carefully. Grant was telling the aide that he felt no satisfaction at Lee's downfall, that he felt sad to see the defeat of one who had fought so well and so long, although he felt that the cause for which Lee fought was one of the worst for which people had ever fought, and one for which there was the least excuse.

"Well, and there is the sum of the thing," Jacob later said to Robert as they made their way away from the scene of the surrender. "Four years and thousands of ruined lives."

"And yet, I shall never forget the scene in Richmond," Robert said. "There was good to come of this mess. It only needs now to bear fruit."

"I presume the president will want to meet with Grant immediately," Jacob mused as he walked, continuing to scribble notes in his notebook.

"The president and Mrs. Lincoln have extended an invitation to General and Mrs. Grant to join them in Ford's Theater for a play in a few days," Robert answered him. "I may be mistaken, but I believe from what I overheard Grant telling his aide, they may have declined the invitation."

Jacob snorted a bit. "I shouldn't be at all surprised. Mrs. Lincoln has been jealous of Grant's popularity and has made snide and obnoxious remarks in public regarding the general and Mrs. Grant."

Jacob nodded. "If I were she, I wouldn't set foot in the same room with Mrs. Lincoln. Her behavior of late has been extremely unpredictable. Still, though, I should very much like to see the president again, even if only at a distance. Perhaps we can obtain tickets to the play. I'll see when we return to Washington if there are any more available."

* * *

Washington, D.C.

Across town, Isabelle was frustrated and fit to be tied. John Booth and his friends hadn't shown their faces at the boarding-house in days, and she had no new leads as to their whereabouts. She paced the floor of her bedroom, anxious and tired of waiting. She didn't dare leave, however, for fear of missing them or an opportunity to eavesdrop on Mrs. Surratt.

Thinking of her friends together on the other side of town, she felt a twinge of envy and wished she could be with them. By now they undoubtedly had details of the truce, and she was as desperate for news as she was for company. She could, she supposed, seek out Mrs. Surratt and ask if she had heard anything new, but Isabelle wanted to hear the story from people who would be pleased with its outcome. Somehow, she didn't feel up to pretending she was despondent at the Confederacy's downfall.

She stayed up late into the night, listening in vain for the sound of footsteps on the creaky wooden stairs and fell asleep atop her bedcovers, fully dressed.

CHAPTER 11

It is hard for the old slaveholding spirit to die. But die it must.
—Sojourner Truth

* * *

12 April 1865
Nebraska border

"I feel a million miles away from everything," Mary Birmingham told her husband, Ben, as they settled back into the stagecoach. "Chaos behind us, chaos ahead of us, but here we are right now in the middle of nothing."

"Why do you see chaos ahead?" Ben asked her, taking her hand. He moved closer, and she leaned her head against his shoulder.

"I don't know how we'll be received. I don't imagine it will be smooth or pleasant."

Ben squeezed her fingers. "We'll make our own way, find good friends. There will be those who think we're . . . strange . . ."

"Strange?" Mary laughed. "Ben, we're absolutely bizarre."

Ben sighed. "My aunt told me several weeks ago that you'd been talking about this. She said that if you mentioned your concerns, I was to tell you that she won't take kindly to you . . . hmm, how did she say it? She said that if you don't keep a stiff spine and hard resolve, she'll personally find you and give you a piece of her mind."

"She is formidable, isn't she?"

"I suggest you take her threats seriously. Formidable is a mild characterization. I would say Elizabeth is as strong as my own mother, but in a better way."

"Ben, you know your mother has changed. We've heard it from more than one source."

"I'll believe it with my own eyes when I see the changes before me."

Mary chewed on her lip for a moment in contemplation as the stagecoach rambled over the dusty road. "Would you enjoy a reconciliation with your mother, do you suppose?"

He shrugged and jostled her head lightly in the process. "She's never been a person I've admired, Mary. I can't imagine one's whole personality could undergo such a change as to make likable what was before not. Much of my reaction to her depends on *her* reaction to you."

"This is why I worry. Don't expect her to welcome me with open arms."

"Then I won't be welcoming her with open arms."

"I do not want to be the cause of conflict between—"

"Mary, if my mother can be decent to you and to us, then we might mend some bridges. I have no love lost, my anger is spent, and she means little or nothing to me. These are things that have existed since my childhood. She was less of a mother to me than an overseer. She left my rearing, my education, all of the soft tenderness of a mother, to Ruth. She didn't care much for my welfare other than as an inheritor of her empire when I was young, and now that it's gone, I see no reason for her to concern herself overmuch for my welfare now."

Mary was quiet, and Ben softened his tone. "We have overcome such tremendous odds, sweetheart, by the mere fact that we are together. I can live through anything now."

* * *

12 April 1865
Ogden, Utah

Ruth sifted the warming earth through her fingers. She would have a good vegetable garden this year. The snows were finally dissolving under the heat of the sun, and she was more anxious than she ever would have imagined to be outdoors, breathing in the fresh air and working in the soil on her own plot of land.

The snow had been such a strange thing. The children had been delighted, of course, and Ruth had taken a certain amount of pleasure in the newness of the weather, but mercy, she was tired of being cold. Spending all of one's years in a warm, humid climate did nothing to prepare one for the shock of a desert winter.

A coughing spasm had her reaching for the side of her home, bracing herself with her hand until it passed. It hadn't gone away, the wretched coughing that sometimes produced flecks of blood. She was ill and worried that her time would be over before she saw Mary, whole and happy. Sarah told her often enough that it was nothing more than a seasonal illness brought on by exposure to the cold weather, but Ruth knew in her heart it was something else.

When she recovered, she looked up at the blue sky and watched the birds dart from tree to tree. *I would like to enjoy just a little more time here, my Lord, just a bit. I haven't had enough time to accustom myself to the taste of free air . . .*

* * *

Sarah approached Ruth's fenced yard but stayed in the shadows until Ruth's coughing fit had passed. Swallowing an unfamiliar lump in her throat, she forced herself to keep walking and enter the yard. It was nothing more than a cold. It would pass, and Ruth would return to her customary good health. She would be fine—she would! Surely God wouldn't bring them all this way together only to call Ruth home before they'd been in their new dwellings a year.

Walking around the side of the house, she found Ruth studying the sky with her hand braced against the house. The look on the woman's face frightened her. Beyond the unusually pale complexion was an expression of one who was communing with her Maker.

"Don't you dare think to tell me you're ready to go, Ruth," Sarah said, trying to keep her voice light, but failing.

Ruth looked down at Sarah, a small smile crossing her face. "Actually, I was asking for more time."

"Posh. You needn't ask for more time—you're hardly sick. You're wasting God's time, as I'm sure He'd tell you were He here."

"All the same, it doesn't hurt to ask."

Sarah waved a hand in dismissal and opened the lid to a basket she held draped over her arm. "Charlotte made bread this morning, and I've brought a loaf for you."

"My goodness!" Ruth dropped her hand from the side of the house and moved slowly toward Sarah. "She's taking well to the domestic arts."

"It makes her happy," Sarah said with a shake of her head. "I had the world to give that girl. She'd never have had to lift a finger in our old life, and here she is working alongside the cook in the kitchen."

"It was all she ever really wanted. As a child in the nursery, she used to pretend she lived in a cottage with her babies."

Sarah sighed softly and looked down the street at her home. Jeffrey had worked very hard to provide a comfortable home for her, reminiscent in many details of Bentley. The home itself seemed to stand out from the few others that dotted the street, however. The town was still quite small and extremely sparsely populated, although the residents seemed to believe that the town would boom once the railroad reached it. Ogden was to become a major stopping point for the railroad, and Sarah found herself anxious for it; she was comfortable with the thought of living around many other people.

"Sometimes I just cannot believe how things have changed," she said to Ruth.

"Ben and Mary should be here soon."

Sarah glanced back at Ruth. "Why do I feel as though you're testing me?"

Ruth shrugged. "Just a passing thought."

"I know they'll be here soon. I imagine you're anxious to see them."

"And you?"

Sarah laughed. "Ruth, you know very well that they both hate me."

"Will you give them reason to hate you further?"

"You might at least try to convince me I'm wrong."

Ruth shook her head and gestured to a bench she'd cleaned off with a cloth. The women sat on it and turned their faces toward the warm sun. "What purpose would that serve now, Sarah? The history between you and your son runs deep and ugly. How you manage things from here, however, is entirely your choice."

"I cannot make him love me." Sarah hated the hurt that she heard in her own voice.

"But you can love them. In turn, they will feel it."

"Ruth," Sarah said and paused. "I don't know if I can approve of their marriage."

"Because Mary's mother was black."

Sarah winced a bit and turned her face away from Ruth. Mary's mother had been Ruth's only daughter. Her face warmed for reasons that had nothing to do with the sunshine. "Doesn't it seem wrong to you?" she finally asked and turned her face back to Ruth.

Ruth's eyes were calm and assessing, quietly judging her with their wisdom. Darn her eyes! They had always been wise. "No, Sarah, it does not seem wrong to me. They are two human souls who love each other. I don't believe God looks on it in criticism either." She paused. "You know full well that Mary appears nearly white, Sarah. If you're worried about what people think, you needn't."

Ruth's voice had taken on a flat tone, and Sarah had to wonder if she spoke with sarcasm, derision, or truth. "You make my reservations seem silly, Ruth," she said. "You make me question my entire life."

"I don't know how you can expect any different from me, Sarah. Mary is my granddaughter, and I love her. She's a person with feelings, not an animal. She's beautiful and intelligent and talented. She would make any man an excellent wife."

"I am sorry for offending you." The words were slow to come from Sarah's throat, but she did mean them. Apologizing to Ruth was something she would never have condescended to do when they lived at Bentley and Ruth had been Sarah's property. So many things had changed, however, and Sarah had nearly gone mad with it. When she had come to her senses and realized that aside from Jeffrey, Ruth was her rock, her bosom friend from youth and her emotional support, she vowed to think differently, to *be* different.

It was so difficult, though! One did not change a lifetime of opinions commonly held as truth overnight. There were issues, feelings, that lingered despite her best intentions. "I promise you, Ruth, I shall do my utmost to accept Ben and Mary and to help them feel welcome."

"I suppose that's all anyone could ask."

"Would you care to walk back with me for tea? Charlotte is preparing something that smells delicious."

"I'd enjoy that very much, Sarah, thank you. I should like to see the children also."

Sarah nodded. "They're doing well—anxious to be outside. I think all of this cold weather has been difficult for them."

The women rose and walked slowly down the street, comfortable in the familiar companionship.

* * *

Charlotte placed the tea scones on the small table in the parlor and served her mother and Ruth. She was gratified to see the expressions of delight on the women's faces as they tasted the results of her morning's work. "You like the scones, then?" she asked them.

"Very much, Charlotte," Ruth answered. "You've quite a talent."

"They're delicious," Sarah said with a nod.

"I'm glad," Charlotte said and picked up her own plate. She would have to make some for Earl the next time he came for a visit. The thought made her blush slightly, and she ducked her head, hiding her face by taking a sip of tea. She couldn't go two minutes without thinking of the man. Since their dance in the street the night of the inaugural, she had thought of little else.

"Sarah, the house looks very cozy now that all of the details are finished," Ruth said, looking around at the molding in the parlor. "Mr. Dobranski has done excellent work with all of the trim."

Sarah nodded. "Thank you. He finished the nursery only just a few days ago, and that was the last of it." The home was a much smaller version of Bentley, but still beautiful in simple charm. A gently curving staircase at the front door led to bedrooms and the nursery on the second floor. Sarah often found herself surprised that it was enough.

"I've noticed Mr. Dobranski visiting with some frequency of late," Ruth murmured to Charlotte. Her comment brought a deeper flush to Charlotte's face, and while Charlotte would have liked to have been angry, she couldn't help the small smile that turned the corners of her mouth.

"He does seem to enjoy calling on us," she said.

"Us?" Sarah's laughter was quick. "I hardly think he comes here to spend his time conversing with me or your father."

"He converses with all of us," Charlotte said.

"Yes, but he looks only at you."

Flustered, Charlotte took another drink of tea, trying to fight the thrill that her mother's words brought forth. Her cup rattled against the saucer as she set it down on the table at her elbow.

"Does he make you uncomfortable?" Ruth asked.

"Oh, no. No, not at all. I enjoy his company. He's very much a gentleman, very considerate of my feelings."

"I suspect we'll be hearing a proposal from him soon," Sarah commented with another nibble on her tea scone that dripped with clotted cream.

Charlotte swallowed and broached a subject she'd been avoiding with her mother. "How would you feel about such a thing?" she asked Sarah.

Sarah paused and looked at her oldest daughter. Something passed across her face, something Charlotte couldn't quite read. "I would be happy for it," Sarah said, "because I feel it would make you happy. I believe he would be a good husband."

It was then that Charlotte knew Sarah's expression for what it was: remorse, apology, a possible chance at absolution. Charlotte's first marriage had been an unhappy one, arranged and manipulated entirely by her parents who thought they knew what was best for Bentley. For the family. But it hadn't been for Charlotte.

Charlotte was surprised by the sting of tears in her eyes, and she averted her face, looking out the wide front windows onto the yard. When she felt in control of her emotions, she nodded a bit and said, "I would be very happy were he to offer marriage. I suspect he might, but shall try to salvage my pride if he doesn't."

Sarah snorted. "He will. Mark my words."

* * *

Salt Lake City, Utah

Earl swung the heavy ax down onto the last of the logs he was splitting for his father's new outbuilding. Eli grinned at him and said, "I knew there was a reason the good Lord gave us so many strapping boys."

"Where are the rest of them, then?" Earl grunted as he braced the ax against the fallen wood. "Why is it that I, who live the farthest away, am always the one to help with this kind of work?"

"Because your heart is the most pure," Eli said, still smiling. "And because you miss your mother's good cooking. You visit on the pretense of helping me, but I notice you always manage to stay for dinner."

Earl shrugged. "Oh, I don't know that Ogden doesn't have its share of good cooks," he said.

"Does it, now? And would one of them happen to be a pretty, young widow?"

"Perhaps."

"I've been wondering how long it will take you to gather your courage and make her your wife." Eli laughed at Earl's surprised expression. "Don't even imagine you've hidden your feelings, son. They're on your sleeve for the world to see."

"I would like to," Earl admitted. "I'm not certain . . ."

"Certain of what?"

"That I'm the sort of man she would agree to marry."

Eli scowled. "What would make you say such a fool thing?"

"She's accustomed to fancy things, manners and such. I'm not so refined. I work with my hands."

"Earl." Eli tossed a piece of wood onto a larger pile and looked at his son. "That woman has seen some hard times—maybe not so much physical hard times, but the kind that you keep inside. I don't believe she is altogether concerned with manners and social functions. She needs someone who will love her and take care of her."

Earl nodded slowly, surprised at his father's perception. "She has a hurting heart," he admitted. "I suppose I've been too worried about my own shortcomings to think I might be good enough for her."

"You'd best not let your mother hear you talk so," Eli said. "Besides, I think this place way out here has been a breath of fresh air for those folks. They left utter bedlam behind."

Earl nodded. "Lincoln gave a public address today urging the people to reconcile," he said. "I saw the papers on my way into town. It's not going to be an easy thing. The Southern folk have some mighty wounded pride, not to mention the fact that their homes have been destroyed."

"I can't imagine how it must look now," Eli said. "All that time I spent in the Southern states preaching the gospel—I never imagined that the place would be decimated in just a few short years."

"You must be grateful you and Mama brought the family this far away. It's as though we've been swept aside and protected. That's what I keep hearing Brother Brigham say anyway."

"I am grateful." Eli whistled and hefted another log onto the pile. "Those poor folks have a lot of work ahead of them."

"The country will grow. We all have a lot of work ahead of us."

CHAPTER 12

[There was] a deathlike stillness about me. Then I heard subdued sobs, as if a number of people were weeping . . . the mourners were invisible. I went from room to room. No living person was in sight . . . where were all the people who were grieving as if their hearts would break?

[I entered the east room]. Before me was a catafalque, on which rested a corpse in funeral vestments. Around it were stationed soldiers who were acting as guards; and there was a throng of people, some gazing mournfully on the corpse, whose face was covered, others weeping pitifully.

"Who is dead in the White House?" I demanded of one of the soldiers.

"The President," was his answer. "He was killed by an assassin."

—A dream of President Lincoln's, as recounted to his wife and several others on April 11, 1865

* * *

14 April 1865
Washington, D.C.

Isabelle scribbled a message to Pinkerton that was so hurried it was barely legible. Her hand shook as she penned the words, cursing in frustration as she made a mistake and scribbled it out. *Calm yourself, Belle,* she thought as she looked over her letter through eyes that blurred with tears. *There's enough time. The play doesn't begin for another ten minutes . . .*

Her plan was simple enough. Send a messenger to Pinkerton with the letter, get to Ford's Theater as quickly as she could, go inside the building, and scream the roof down. Only one hour earlier, as she had been quietly following Booth around town and had finally been able to listen as he spoke to an acquaintance in his room at the National Hotel, had she learned of their plot. She was amazed at the audacity of it; it involved not only the president of the United States but his entire cabinet as well. Unfortunately, she could be in only one place at a time, and so she chose the theater. She had to hope her message to Pinkerton would take care of the rest.

She folded the letter and sealed it, turning rapidly toward the door of her room at the boardinghouse. The appearance of Mrs. Surratt brought her up short, and she fought to recover herself. "Why, Mrs. Surratt," she said, a bit breathless. "How are you this evening?"

The woman looked at her through eyes that narrowed. "Where are you going, Mrs. Watts? I thought you said you weren't feeling well."

"Oh, I suppose I need a little bit of fresh air. I believe I'll go out for a while."

Mrs. Surratt stepped back into the hallway and slammed Isabelle's door with such force that Isabelle backed up a step, blinking. "No, you won't," the woman said from the other side, and to her horror, Isabelle heard a key scraping in the lock—the lower lock over which she had no control from her side of the door. "You've been entirely too curious for your own good. You'll stay away from my son and his associates. I'll see to that myself."

"No," Isabelle whispered, her knees feeling weak. "No!" she shouted and moved toward the door, pounding on it until her fists hurt. "No, no, no! You cannot do this! Let me out immediately—someone will hear me and you'll find yourself in trouble!"

"There's nobody here to hear you, Mrs. Watts," the boardinghouse keeper shouted back at her from the hallway, and Isabelle heard the woman's firm footsteps on the stairs. In a moment, she heard the slam of the front door.

Isabelle, think, think! her mind screamed at her as she looked wildly around the room for another escape route. The window was small and didn't open. Still, if she could break it with something, she might be able to yell to someone on the street and get help. She grasped a chair that sat beside the small desk and swung it for all she was worth at the window. It shattered, and, still using the chair as her tool, she continued to bash at the glass until the largest of the pieces had fallen through to the ground below.

Tossing the chair aside, she gingerly poked her head out and yelled for help to the empty street below.

* * *

Ford's Theater
Washington, D.C.

Jacob, Camille, Robert, and Abigail took their seats on the floor of the theater near the stage, grateful to have procured tickets at such a late date. The house was full, and in light of the recent mood in the North, it promised to host a good evening. Camille felt a surge of joy that she'd been missing for some time. Glancing at her brother, who escorted Abigail gallantly in his crisp, blue Union uniform complete with medals, she was proud that he wanted to do honor to the president by donning the uniform he once said he never again wished to see.

She smiled at Jacob as she settled back into her seat. "You do work miracles," she said to her husband. "To find last-minute tickets was amazing."

Jacob winked at her. "Anything to see you smile."

"And such a play it is! Imagine, we shall see Laura Keene in person."

The play, *Our American Cousin,* began, and Camille turned her attention to it, intent upon enjoying the evening. It hadn't been in motion long, however, before it stopped.

There was a general stir above them, followed by applause and the sudden notes of "Hail to the Chief" played by the orchestra. Upward and to Camille's right, the president of the United States entered the presidential box. Camille looked at him with a full heart and felt her eyes sting. Mrs. Lincoln, Major Henry Rathbone, and his fiancée, Clara Harris, accompanied him, and the president gave a nod, acknowledging the applause and taking his seat next to his wife.

Before long, the lights in the theater again went dim, and Camille took her eyes off the president and focused them instead on the stage before her.

* * *

Isabelle's voice was hoarse from screaming, and still nobody had heard her. It was odd; with the warmer weather, people were usually on the streets long into the night—now it was as if Isabelle was screaming into a ghost town. She looked around her room for what seemed like the thousandth time, trying to find *some* sort of solution. *Please, please! I must get out of here!*

She glanced down at her clothing, making note of the extra layer of padding she wore under her oversized dress as part of her disguise. Looking carefully at the small window, she tried to measure her chances. What were her odds of success? She thought of the president, sitting a few miles away in a theater, completely unaware of the danger awaiting him, and decided it was her only available option.

Isabelle tore her clothing off, ripping at the padding and stripping herself down to her petticoat and underclothing. With frantic movements, she thrashed about in her satchel for one of her older dresses that better suited her frame. Making quick, if not clumsy, work of the buttons, she pulled the sleeves down past her wrists and used her arms to clear the remaining shards of glass from the window frame.

After securing her letter to Pinkerton in one of her skirt pockets, she dragged the chair again to the window, this time climbing upon it instead of wielding it as a tool. The window was too small to fit her head, arms, and one leg through at one time, so instead she decided to back out feet first.

Were the situation not so dire, she might well have laughed herself silly. She knew that the spectacle she made trying to shimmy both legs backward out of the window while balancing the upper half of her body on the chair back was ridiculous. Isabelle was finally out of the window to her hips, her hands braced on the windowsill and aching with the pain of her weight shoved onto the remaining small pieces of glass.

Very slowly, she wriggled and lowered herself out of the window until she was hanging by her hands, her feet dangling from her second-story perch. *There's no hope for it,* she mused. *I hope I don't break both legs.*

The loud crunch she not only felt but heard, accompanied by the sharp, stabbing pain in her left leg, told her that she'd probably broken only the one. As she hit the ground, she rolled to her side, clutching at her leg. The haze around the edges of her vision clouded in until the street around her had virtually disappeared. As though from a far distant place, she heard the sound of footsteps sounding against the pavement, and a voice echoed in her head.

" . . . crazy, miss? Are ya tryin' ter kill yerself?"

As the young man approached, Isabelle reached with a trembling hand into her pocket and pulled forth her letter to

Pinkerton. She mumbled Pinkerton's address to the man and searched his face with tears of grief and pain running down her face. "It's a matter of life and death," she choked out and let her hand drop as he took the blood-smeared letter from her. "Go, now!" she managed to say before the darkness overtook her vision altogether and a pain inside her head crushed against her skull.

* * *

Robert smiled as the character Mrs. Montchessington stated her lines. "I am aware, Mr. Trenchard, that you are not used to the manners of good society."

Harry Hawk, the actor playing Asa Trenchard, answered her with humorous clarity. "Don't know the manners of good society, eh? Well, I guess I know enough to turn *you* inside out, you sockdoligizing old man-trap."

Robert's laughter added to that of the crowd around him. The events that followed were a blur he didn't want to remember but was certain he would never forget. Had he never been a soldier, he might not have recognized the pop of the gun for what it was. As the world seemed to slow to a standstill, he turned his head to the sound and looked up.

In a flurry of movement, a figure darted past Major Rathbone, who clutched at his arm. The mysterious figure climbed to the railing on the presidential box and leapt to the stage, his spur catching the tails of a decorative flag as he came crashing down. "Sic semper tyrannis!" the man shouted, and he wobbled to his feet and in moments had dashed awkwardly off the stage and out of sight.

"What did he say?" Robert heard Camille asking Abigail, who sat between him and his sister. *She doesn't realize what's happened,* he thought, still stunned.

"I think he said, 'The South is avenged,'" Abigail was answering her.

Robert felt bile rising in his throat as an uproar sounded in the theater, screams of "The president has been shot!" second only in sound to the sobbing of the president's wife. He rose from his seat and made his way past people who were still seated, surprised, and trying to take stock of what was happening. From the stage, members of the cast who now realized what had transpired shouted "Booth!" as they recognized the fellow actor.

Robert dashed back through the theater and around the corner, making his way up the stairs to the presidential box. He was met, once he arrived at the box, by several other soldiers who were attempting to lift the president from the floor. Lincoln's great body sagged in the middle, as there were soldiers at his feet and his head but nowhere else. Robert rushed forward and placed his one arm under the body of the man he so admired.

"Outside," someone said. "We must get him out of this place."

"You are a surgeon," a voice behind Robert sounded to another man in the vicinity. "What say you of the wound?"

"It is mortal," the man answered. "The bullet has entered the back of his head."

Mary Todd Lincoln's screams and anguished cries followed the soldiers as they bore the president's body through the theater. The soldiers carrying the president with Robert barked at the crowd to move out of the way, but people seemed paralyzed in shock. The shouts and orders continued until they finally made it outside and onto the street. There they remained for nearly five minutes until a man rushed toward them and identified himself as a Mr. Peterson. "My room is across the street," he shouted. "If he will not make it to the White House, please, use my room!"

Robert walked across the street to the boardinghouse the man mentioned, his arm still supporting the body of the president and his mind sick with worry. *Please, please don't let him die. Please, not yet! We need him so!* Entering the boardinghouse, they took Lincoln to a room on the first floor and laid him crosswise on the bed, as his frame was too large to fit on the small mattress.

Members of the president's cabinet were arriving by this time, and the soldiers were then ushered from the room. Robert lingered near the doorway, knowing the great man lay on the other side, barely clinging to life. It wasn't long before Gideon Wells, the man Robert recognized as the secretary of the navy, entered the boardinghouse in a great rush.

"He is in here?" Mr. Wells asked Robert.

Robert nodded, feeling tears form in his eyes, and Mr. Wells glanced more fully at Robert's Union uniform, and pointedly at the missing arm. Mr. Wells gestured for Robert to follow him into the room, and Robert gratefully did so, slipping unobtrusively onto a chair in a corner.

Mrs. Lincoln screamed and sobbed uncontrollably and begged for her husband to speak with her. Finally, Secretary of War Edwin Stanton demanded in angry tones that someone lead her from the room, and she was firmly escorted out. Someone murmured that the president's son, Robert, should be contacted.

All throughout the night, the vigil continued, the president's cabinet keeping watch and Robert, seated on his chair in the corner, quietly staying out of the way while his heart felt as though it were breaking. Nobody spoke to him or questioned his presence. He was still and unobtrusive; he hoped they didn't even realize he was there.

At some point in the early morning hours, word came to the men in the room by messenger that Secretary of State William Seward had been stabbed and wounded badly in his home. Further inquiry showed that Andrew Johnson, the vice president, was safe. Robert shook his head, his analytical mind going over the logistics of carrying off such a foolhardy plan.

By now, it had come to the attention of all in the room that the president's assailant had been none other than famed actor John Wilkes Booth. Booth was an avid secessionist, and Robert suddenly realized why Booth had shouted what he had when he hit the stage. *Sic semper tyrannis.* "Thus be it ever for tyrants." It was the Virginia state motto.

A parade of doctors, sixteen that Robert counted, attended the president throughout the night, and all were equally unable to do anything to help him. The wound was probed twice, but nothing else could be done.

Robert grew weary, and as dawn approached, he laid his head on his arm that rested on the back of the chair he had long since turned around. He didn't sleep but still felt a jolt when the sounds of sobbing came from the foot of the president's bed. Mr. Lincoln's older son, Robert, stood with his head resting on the comforting shoulder of Senator Sumner, his grief wrenching to behold. Again, as had happened many times through the night, Robert's eyes filled with tears.

It was nearly seven in the morning when the president's breathing ceased, only to resume its shallow course for nearly another thirty minutes. Finally, President Lincoln breathed his last. The grief in the room was palpable; Robert wondered if he would ever forget its heavy, oppressive feel.

Secretary of War Stanton symbolically raised his hat to his head, and then took it off again, placing it over his heart. He asked Lincoln's clergyman to lead those present in prayer, and when this was accomplished, those present began to quietly leave. As they did so, Stanton darkened the windows and murmured, "Now he belongs to the ages."

CHAPTER 13

I thought I did for the best.
—*John Wilkes Booth*

* * *

20 April 1865
Boston, Massachusetts

Isabelle sat propped against a mound of pillows in a bed in Jacob and Camille's guest room. She gazed out the window, barely noting that the scenery hadn't changed in the few days she'd been looking at it. She wasn't looking at anything in particular, just staring, lost in her own thoughts.

Camille had entered moments before with a tray of tea and some light sandwiches, but Isabelle hadn't the stomach for it. She needed to eat but found that food of any kind these days turned to sawdust in her mouth and became nearly impossible to swallow. The throbbing in her leg where the doctor had set and mended the broken bone was excruciating, but worse still was the pain in her mind and heart.

There must have been something she had done to tip her hand to Mrs. Surratt—asked one too many questions, perhaps. In all of her years as a Pinkerton operative, Isabelle had never bungled anything so badly. The stakes had been so very high, and she had failed. Pinkerton had told her repeatedly that she had uncovered more information on the plot to kill Lincoln, the vice president, and the other cabinet members than any of his other operatives, but it was little consolation. She doubted she would ever find a way to forgive herself.

Lincoln, dead! Just when Isabelle thought her tears were spent, she felt them well up again in eyes that were swollen and tired. She lifted her bandaged hand to her eye and rubbed at the moisture, welcoming the painful scratch of the bandage fabric against her sore skin. She had cried more tears in the past week than in her entire lifetime, making her skin raw and dry.

How she had loved and revered the president, and she was not one easily given to praise or respect, especially for politicians. Lincoln had done the impossible in holding the country together, and not only that, he had freed an entire people from bondage. Now that he was gone, she felt as though the world was a bit worse off for losing him, and she feared for those recently freed. The backlash against them would be horrific, and the one man who would have been able to keep hostile factions at bay was now taken from them all. The Radical Republicans in the Senate were already speaking of harsh, uncompromising retribution against the South, whereas Lincoln had promised peace and prosperity. Those who would suffer the most would be the former slaves.

Perhaps the worst of all of it was Isabelle's sense of responsibility; had she acted faster, followed more leads, *something*, she might have prevented the nation's future pain. She hadn't said as much to her friends, for she knew it sounded melodramatic, but in her heart she believed it as truth. The president was dead, and it was her fault. Andrew Johnson was ill prepared for the job ahead of him; indeed, the day of Lincoln's death, he had been sworn in as president in a completely inebriated state. Who could blame the man, really—the assassination had come as a shock to everyone—but to Isabelle it only served as a preamble to what lay ahead. If Johnson did see Lincoln's vision and hoped to implement his policies, he lacked the political strength to keep his senatorial opponents in check.

Isabelle sniffed and wiped at her eyes again, chewing on her lip in consternation. As for Booth himself, the cowardly actor was still on the run, hiding from the authorities who were determined to see him chased down. How she hated him! She hated him, but she didn't hold him responsible for her own mistakes in not finding him out sooner than she had.

The president's body was currently en route to his adopted home state of Illinois, and the funeral procession was taking the exact path Lincoln had followed on his way to the White House four years earlier. At Isabelle's insistence, Camille had been bringing her the paper each day, and Isabelle followed Lincoln's progress as he made his way to his final resting place. The body of his young son, Willie, had been disinterred and was making the trek with his father.

Crowds in various cities stood all day, sometimes in pouring rain, for a glimpse of the president's coffin. Black fabric was selling out faster than it could be replaced, and buildings draped in black dripped huge black tears in the rain. Miles of people, often two deep, lined the streets of cities and towns, each seeking to pay their last respects to the fallen president who had fought so hard to keep the country together.

The loss of innocence was tremendous; Isabelle realized this as she read accounts in the paper. So many citizens had held the same view as had Camille when Isabelle had been summoned to Washington. They hadn't believed someone would actually kill the president—it was simply unheard of. The shock and disbelief resounded in every Northern city and through every home.

It wasn't right! It wasn't fair! Isabelle's mind screamed and cried these thoughts throughout the long days in her bed while her leg began to heal. Her dreams were haunted by her failure, and her waking hours certainly provided her no escape from those images. Camille and Abigail interrupted her thoughts several times daily, but more often than not, Isabelle begged to be left alone.

Camille was always reluctant to leave, as she had been from the moment they first found Isabelle lying unconscious in the street in Washington. After Robert had disappeared from the theater with the president's body, the remaining threesome had come looking for her. Camille seemed to know she would be near the boardinghouse, and when Isabelle had finally awoken, her head was cradled in Camille's lap.

She was grateful for her friends; were it not for them, she undoubtedly would be drinking herself into an early grave. Perhaps it might be the better option, however; Isabelle would never be free from her wretched thoughts. No matter how far she ran, she couldn't escape herself.

* * *

26 April 1865
Savannah, Georgia

Emily kissed Austin's cheek as she reached him in the dining room, where he sat eating his breakfast. Thumping the daily newspaper down on the table next to him, she flipped it to the main headline. "They tried to burn him out of a barn, but shot him instead," she said, pointing to it.

"Booth?" Austin picked the paper up and scanned the article. "The actor asked someone to lift his hands to his face moments before he died, and he uttered the words 'useless, useless.'"

"I should say they were useless," Emily muttered as she took her seat at Austin's right. "His whole bloody brain was useless. I hope he burns for eternity." Her words were brave, but they didn't hide the tremor in her voice. She cleared her throat firmly and shoved a forkful of egg in her mouth.

"He'll be a hero forever around these parts," Austin said with a shake of his head. "And with Johnson now in office, it will not go easy for us." Austin glanced at Emily and held his hand out on the table, palm up. She placed hers in it and gave his fingers a squeeze.

"It hasn't been easy for a while, now," she answered him.

"I know. I've just been thinking a bit about this lately . . ." He trailed off and focused his gaze on the empty hearth.

Emily sensed his mood and noted the seriousness in his tone. "And where has your thinking led you?"

"I'm wondering if we should remain here."

"At Willow Lane?"

"In Savannah. In Georgia altogether."

Emily straightened a bit in her chair and took a deep breath, finally blowing it out on a sigh. "Well. I hadn't anticipated *that* train of thought."

Austin shrugged a bit. "Perhaps it's just worry. I don't believe we'll come to harm; however, it is becoming common knowledge that the Stanhopes have been part of the Underground Railroad for years. Folks around here are not looking on that kindly."

"I'm not worried about what people think. I never have been."

"It's one of the things I love most about you, Em. But we have Mary Alice to consider now."

Emily frowned. "I suppose I never imagined her being hurt in any way. Rather naive of me, really."

"Well, it's something to consider. Think on it, as will I."

"Where would we go?"

Austin brought her hand to his lips and kissed her fingers. "Anywhere. Doesn't much matter as long as you and Mary Alice are with me."

* * *

Gwenyth paced her bedroom, pondering Joshua's most recent letter. The Confederate resistance had officially ended on the eighteenth with General Johnston's surrender to General Sherman, and with the business of the war finally at an end, Joshua was mustered out of service.

He wanted to see her and planned to make his way south to Willow Lane, and it was this notion that had her worried. Even now, with things supposedly changed, Joshua would be in danger traveling by himself through the South. Her concern for his safety warred with her desire to see him again, and she couldn't keep herself still. If Emily and Austin were downstairs in the parlor, they'd surely have heard her pacing by now.

Still, she had to keep some faith in his abilities to protect himself. Large of stature and trained on a lifetime of hard work in the stables, he was now also a veteran soldier with a weapon. Perhaps her worries were for naught, and she did him a disservice to doubt him.

Gwenyth quietly made her way out of her bedroom and down the main front stairs. Exiting the mansion, she walked around to the smaller cabins in the back of the property and found the one Joshua had used during his brief stay when she had nursed his wounds. It was empty, as was her wish, and she softly closed the door behind her. It was as though he were only just gone as she looked at the bed where he'd lain, so close to death upon losing so much blood from his wounds.

She sat on the bed and placed her arms around her middle, rocking slowly back and forth. *Please, dear Lord,* she prayed. *Please help him find his way here safely . . .*

* * *

27 April 1865
Outside Memphis, Tennessee, on the Mississippi River

Joshua looked out over the water at the mayhem, his heart in his throat. Flames glowed in the river as the massive steamboat took on more water, men pouring out of her like a tide. Men atop the steamboat whose clothing was aflame leapt into the river.

Joshua had been making good time after his dismissal from Sherman's army and intended to be in Savannah within a few weeks. After being mustered out, he was given leave to keep his horse and his firearm, the latter of which came wholly unexpected. He had been making good use of nighttime travel, and now as he was making his way along the Mississippi, he had seen, to his horror, a massive explosion occur before him out on the river.

He dismounted and held his horse's reins in a tightly clenched fist. The first of the survivors who were strong enough to swim to shore was now staggering onto land. Joshua held out his hand to a man who stumbled and fell to one knee, coughing and gasping for breath.

"I don't know what happened," the man mumbled and held tight to Joshua's hand.

"I saw an explosion," Joshua commented to the man, who still continued to cough.

"Must've been a boiler," the man said. "That steamship wasn't meant to hold more than four hundred. There were a good two thousand of us on board." Joshua took a closer look at the man's clothing, which was clearly a Union uniform that had seen better days.

"You're on your way home, soldier?" Joshua asked him

At that, the man began to cry, his voice cracking. "We all are. Most of us are newly freed prisoners. Oh, life is cruel! Finally free to go home after all this time . . ."

Joshua braced the man with an arm around his shoulders and, with his other hand, released his horse's reins and reached into his saddlebags for a blanket. He shook it free of its folds and wrapped it around the shivering soldier, feeling sick to his stomach as he looked out over the river at the floating bodies and knowing that many more had probably already sunk to the bottom.

He stayed with the man and other stragglers who made it to shore long into the night, dashing out into the water himself and dragging men to the banks of the river. Locals soon gathered and began to make provisions for the survivors. It wasn't until early the next morning that he heard the estimate—seventeen hundred souls lost while on their way home at long last to be with their loved ones.

* * *

28 April 1865
Cleveland, Ohio

Anne glanced at her husband and felt her heart constrict. Ivar was taking the news of the sinking of the steamship *Sultana* especially hard, and she knew it was because he felt ill at the irony that prisoners of war were finally freed, only to die in a freakish accident. Had he not been a prisoner of war himself, he might not have felt such a kinship with the men.

As for herself, she was sick about it. She thought of how she would feel if Ivar had been on that boat. She reached over and squeezed his hand as he sat quietly next to her on the sofa. She didn't have to say anything to him, and she knew he preferred it that way. It was enough for him that she was there and holding his hand.

Finally, after many long moments of silence, he said, "I don't understand it, Anne."

"Nor do I."

He tugged on her hand and pulled her close, wrapping his arm around her shoulders. Inger was in bed for the evening, and they were enjoying a few minutes of peace and quiet before retiring themselves. Anne felt a slight flutter in her abdomen and sat up a bit.

"What is it?"

"I felt the baby." She placed a hand on her stomach and looked at Ivar in shock.

His face lifted, and a sparkle appeared in his eyes. "Are you certain?"

"Yes, I did! I felt it!"

He pulled her toward him and placed a gentle kiss on her forehead. "I love you, sweet wife."

Anne's eyes widened slightly. He was always tender with her, always kind and caring, but didn't often express his feelings in words. "I love you as well, husband." She placed an arm around his middle and snuggled close against his chest. "In the midst of death, there is life," she murmured and closed her eyes, falling into a contented sleep.

CHAPTER 14

And now, while the nation is rejoicing . . . it is suddenly plunged into the deepest sorrow by the most brutal murder of its loved chief. We are now continually passing paroled men from Lee's army on their way to their homes . . . Many have found blackened ruins, instead, and kindred and friends gone, they know not whither. Oh, how much misery treason and rebellion have brought upon our land!
—*Sergeant Lucius Barber*

* * *

3 May 1865
New York, New York

Marie tied her bonnet strings under her chin and called Daniel's name. Hearing no response, she walked through the house, room by room. Her last stop was the door leading to Daniel's workshop, and when she opened it, the smell of alcohol assailed her nostrils.

She closed her mouth and looked around a bit before speaking. When she did, she hoped she would be able to censure the schoolmarm tone that was hovering on her lips. "Daniel?" She stepped into the room and closed the door. "It's a bit early for a drink, isn't it?"

Marie eventually spied her husband seated on a stool beside his small liquor cabinet. It was becoming more and more frequent that Daniel begin his day with a drink, and she saw his behavior for the pattern that it was. She had seen good men turn to ruin because of too much alcohol, and she knew Daniel was coping with his blindness the only way he could manage.

"It's never too early for a drink," came the murmured reply. To his credit, Daniel held his spirits well. Marie had never seen him sloppy or boorish from too much drink—he became very quiet instead.

"Daniel, you needn't do this."

"What else would you have me do, Marie? It's fortunate we live on a small farm and that my wife doesn't mind weeding the garden, or we would starve. I'm useless to you, to everything."

"You're not useless, Daniel. There are many things you can do, if you'll only—"

"Marie, I cannot see!" Daniel set his glass down on a cabinet, the contents sloshing over the brim. "There is not one thing I am good for! Everything I used to do required my eyes, and now that they're gone, I may as well be dead. I can't make my furniture. I can't fight fires. I can't even operate this foolish little farm!"

Marie took a step back, bumping up against the door. She couldn't remember a time when she'd heard him raise his voice before.

"I'll leave you to your liquor then," she heard herself say quietly, and she opened the door at her back.

She was proud of herself for making her way up the hill to Daniel's mother's house without crying. Once there, she found Brenna and her own mother, Jenny, readying the wagon for their ride to the orphanage. Jenny, however, took one look at Marie's face and knew all was not well.

"What is it?"

"Nothing. It's nothing."

"Out with it, girl," Brenna said to her as she hoisted herself up on the wagon seat. "I'm Irish and stubborn. You know I'll only drag it out of you otherwise."

"Your son is also Irish and stubborn," Marie said, feeling her eyes burn with tears she was determined not to cry.

"Ah, so that's the way of it." Brenna patted Marie's knee, and when Jenny settled into place on the other side of her daughter, Brenna snapped the reins. "I might well have told ya that myself, dearie."

"This is different. He's behaving differently." Marie flushed. "I know it mustn't be easy to accept blindness, but I'm worried he'll destroy himself over it."

"Is he still refusing to do anything?"

Marie nodded. "And he's drinking now, much, much more than usual."

Jenny sighed a bit and reached for Marie's hand. "Perhaps Brenna and I have stayed away too long," she said. "We thought to allow the two of you to work through this problem together, but I'm changing my mind."

"Aye. It's time we paid the boy another visit."

"No, no," Marie said. "I don't want him thinking I went crying to the two of you. He's angry enough with everything as it is. If you go down there and take charge, he'll only resent it."

"I beg your pardon, missy," Brenna said with a glance at her daughter-in-law. "You sound as though you think your mother and I are nothing but a pair of bossy-boots."

"Well, truth be told, the both of you rather are, and in ordinary circumstances," Marie said, holding up a hand at the mothers' outraged responses, "I wouldn't mind it a bit. But these circumstances are anything but ordinary. I would love for the two of you to visit us, but if you go after Daniel the way only mothers can, I assure you he will not only resent it, but he'll withdraw further into himself."

The older women were quiet for a moment. "Does he not speak to you at all, dear?" Brenna finally asked her.

"Very little," Marie admitted and swallowed a lump that had formed in her throat. "He's told me he doesn't feel worthy of me."

"Oh, that boy! And undoubtedly he believes that if he drives you away, you'll be better for it." Brenna shook her head, exasperation clearly written on her features.

"I believe that's what he's thinking, yes."

Brenna sighed. "How patient are you willing to be, Marie?"

"What kind of question is that to ask a wife? I love him."

"I only ask because I know the boy. He'll have you crazed before this is finished."

* * *

Daniel hated himself. He knew he had sunk to a new low by taking his frustration out on his wife, and it was nothing but more proof that she deserved a better man than he. Lifting himself slowly from his stool, he felt his way down the length of his workbench, the touch of the wood familiar to his fingers.

He stopped and lifted a tool, registering its form and ridges with his fingertips. How could he have been such a fool? Thinking he needed to prove himself a hero and experience daily excitement, he had placed himself in danger and lost something precious. *I was good, though. Da, you would have been so proud of me. I was a good fireman . . .*

His father had loved everything about the United States of America. They had come from Ireland with nothing and had built a life in a new land. Gavin had loved the freedoms, the principles on which the country was founded. Even when people in the city hated him for being Irish, he looked the other way and found something to smile about. In the end, his big heart had gotten him killed, and Daniel ached with missing him.

Why is it you believe your father wasn't proud of the work you do as a carpenter and a farmer? Marie had asked him once. Her question now echoed again in his head, and he put his hands to his ears to try to block it out. Forgetting he still held the tool in his hand, he scraped the sharp edge of it against his cheek and quickly felt the warmth of blood spilling down his face.

With a curse, he dropped the tool and fumbled in his pocket for the fresh handkerchief he knew Marie would have placed there. Finding the fabric and holding it to his face, he nearly laughed at the bitter irony of it. He had been convinced Gavin would have been more proud of his work as a firefighter. Now, not only was he unable to do that, he couldn't even work in his own shop.

"I failed, Da," he said aloud and made his way back to the stool in the corner. "I'm not good for anything now."

* * *

5 May 1865
Ogden, Utah

Mary looked at the house before her with wide eyes. Elijah was inside, and she was terrified. Ben chatted with Earl Dobranski as Earl saw to the horses that had pulled the carriage carrying them from Salt Lake to Ogden, and Mary stood rooted to the spot. *I can't go in there!* she thought in a moment of panic and wondered what force it was that kept her from running like a mad woman down the street.

Earl had regaled them with tales of her son and his cousin, William, from the time they had arrived by stage late the evening before until they came to a stop in front of Jeffrey and Sarah's new home. According to Earl, Elijah stayed at this house with his grandparents, Clara, and Charlotte and her son. Ruth and Rose lived down the street only half a block away in their own home.

Mary's head was spinning with so many thoughts that she hardly knew what to absorb. Ruth had a home and income of her own! Mary never thought to see such a thing in her lifetime. And yet miracles did seem to happen—she was married to a man with whom she had been in love since young childhood, and his love and patience were giving her the strength to embrace the son she didn't know.

Ben looked at her face and smiled a bit as he approached her with Earl at his side. "Would you like to see Ruth first?"

"Yes. No. I don't know."

Earl laughed. "If I may be so bold, Mrs. Birmingham," he said to her, "I must tell you that while I can imagine your worry, it's unnecessary. The folks you knew before, well, I believe they're not the same folks who live here now. And your son will love you. Just give him time to become accustomed to you."

"Thank you, Mr. Dobranski. Thank you very much. You're kind."

"Not at all." He tipped his hat to her and she smiled. "Now then," he continued, "shall we enter?"

Taking a deep breath, Mary nodded. The door loomed bigger as they approached the front porch, and she wondered if her legs would have given way had Ben not supported her with his arm. "It's nearly noon, is it not?" Mary asked in a hushed voice. "They'll be eating their noonday meal soon—it would be impolite to interrupt."

"Mary, remember my aunt Elizabeth," Ben murmured in her ear. "Now straighten your spine. And if *that* doesn't help, for goodness' sake, think of your grandmother."

It was as though Ben had uttered magic words. Mary thought of Ruth, her proud grandmother who was now the mistress of her own home and whom she would see, presumably, within the hour, and she lifted her chin. Ruth would *never* go cowering into another person's home, regardless of who lay in wait. Even as a slave, Ruth had walked with regal bearing.

To Mary's surprise, the man of the house opened the front door himself. Jeffrey Birmingham smiled widely when he realized who stood on his front porch, and he reached for his son. Ben moved forward and grasped his father, embracing him in a quick clasp before moving back to place his arm around Mary.

Mary looked at her former master, feeling her heartbeat quicken. How very, very strange the world had become, and how very just. Jeffrey had obviously made great strides in becoming more like his son, for he took Mary's hand in his and bowed lightly over it. "Mary," he said. "Welcome to our home."

She was stunned but managed to murmur her thanks. As they were invited inside, divested of their coats, and ushered into the front parlor, Mary took in her surroundings and noted similarities between this new house and Bentley. However, there were also several differences in style that were refreshing.

Jeffrey stood before them at the parlor doorway and said, "Sarah, Charlotte, we have guests."

The two women in the parlor stood, and for a very long moment, the silence in the room was palpable. Sarah's hand fluttered to her heart as she looked at her son, and to Mary's surprise, the older woman's eyes soon flooded with tears. A quick glance at Charlotte told Mary that Ben's younger sister too was overcome at seeing him after nearly seven years of separation.

Mary felt Ben hesitate, and then he left her side and moved forward to his mother. He stood before her and said, "I'm glad to hear you're doing well."

Sarah dropped her gaze, her chin tipped downward as though she had hoped for something more. As though resigning himself completely, Ben said, "Mother."

She looked back up at his face, which now towered above hers. In his absence, her son had become a man. He reached his arms down and encircled her tiny frame with them, and Sarah's arms reached upward, trembling, to return his embrace. She then tightened her hold and sobbed quietly into his coat, and they stood thus for several minutes.

Finally she released him and dabbed at her eyes and nose with a lacy handkerchief. She was so much frailer than Mary had remembered. The illness that had afflicted Sarah must have taken its toll on the older woman's health. Ben held his hand out to Mary, and she stepped forward to take it, knowing full well that Sarah's reaction in the next few moments would determine their future with Ben's family.

"Mother," Ben said, "This is my wife, Mary."

"Yes," Sarah said and bobbed her head as she continued to wipe at her eyes. "Yes, of course. Mary, I hope . . . I hope . . . that is, I promised Ruth . . . I hope you are well, Mary," Sarah stammered, flustered.

Mary stared at the woman who had been her owner, her mistress. Could it be the same person? Who was this lady who stuttered, unsure of herself? Mary finally collected her wits and answered, "Yes, thank you. I am well."

Mary glanced up at Ben, who also stared at his mother as though her head had just come loose from her shoulders. He looked at Mary with a slight widening of his eyes and a small shrug. She smiled at him, and seeing that she was content, he nodded once.

"Ben?"

A tremulous voice behind them reminded Mary that Charlotte was also in the room. Ben turned toward her and reached for her, clasping her tightly to him when she raced into his arms. "I missed you, I did," she said. "I never wrote to you, never told you. I wasn't as brave as Emily was, but . . ."

"Shhh," Ben said and rubbed a hand over her hair. "I missed you, Charlotte. I am so glad you are happy and have a wonderful son."

"Yes." She nodded and pulled back a bit. She glanced at Mary and reached her hand out. "Mary, I . . ."

Mary moved forward and clasped Charlotte's cold fingers.
"I . . . I . . ."

Mary raised her eyebrows a bit and leaned forward.

"I owe you a lifetime of apologies," Charlotte finally
managed to say.

"I accept them all," Mary said.

"Oh. Well, yes, then. Oh," she exclaimed and glanced at
Earl. "You'll want to see Elijah. Earl, they're playing in the
back—would you mind fetching them?"

Earl touched his fingers to his hat, and Mary could have
sworn she saw him give Charlotte a light wink. She looked back
at Ben's sister to see a flush cover her cheeks, and Mary smiled.
Ruth always had said that Charlotte had been a tender child.

It wasn't long before the sounds of two young children
running through the house could be heard, and Mary felt her
knees give way. Ben caught her arm and sat her down on a
nearby divan, and Mary held her breath as two beautiful young
boys ran into the room.

The blonde one she knew to be Charlotte's. But Elijah! He
had curly, dark brown hair, a light brown complexion, and star-
tling green eyes. But perhaps the most amazing thing of all was
that in her son she saw Ben. Richard had not looked characteris-
tically like a Birmingham, and one of Mary's worst fears—a fear
she hadn't ever shared with Ben—was that when she looked at
her son she would see Richard.

She placed her hand over her mouth as her eyes filled with
tears, and she looked at a child who bore resemblances to not
only the Birminghams, but to Ruth. He was all smiles as he ran
toward his grandfather, who scooped him up in his arms and
placed him on one knee and William on the other. Mary felt the
eyes of all the adults in the room upon her, but her own gaze
was riveted on her son.

To Mary's surprise, it was Charlotte who took matters into her
hands. She rose and went to a seat next to her father and ran a

hand across Elijah's curls. "Elijah," she said in a soft voice, a child-friendly voice Mary had never heard Charlotte use. "We have some new friends for you to meet. Will you come and say hello?"

Elijah looked up at his aunt and nodded. "Oh, good boy," Charlotte said. "We always do like to meet new friends, don't we?"

She took Elijah's hand and led him over to Ben and Mary. "Elijah," Charlotte said, kneeling next to him on the floor, "this is your mother, and this is your father."

Mary's eyes flew to Charlotte's, and she felt them well up further in gratitude. Elijah looked at his aunt in some confusion, and Mary reached into the pocket of her dress. "Elijah," she said, and cleared her throat, "I have something for you. How old are you?"

Elijah looked first at Charlotte, who nodded, and then held up four chubby little fingers. "Four years old! My, you're so very big," Mary said and was rewarded with a shy smile.

She opened her hand and extended it to the boy, showing him the carved wooden whistle that Joshua had made when he worked in Boston for a carpenter. "Shall I show you how it works?" Mary asked him.

He nodded, and Mary put the whistle to her lips, blowing in it lightly. Elijah smiled and ducked his head. "It's for you," Mary said and held it to him again, "and when you feel you're ready, you can try it yourself."

Elijah took the whistle slowly and put it to his lips, blowing in a light breath of air that produced the barest of sounds. "Very good!" Charlotte rubbed the little boy's back and glanced at her son, who had come bounding over to see the new toy.

"Oh," Mary said, and reached into her other pocket. "We didn't forget William." She produced an identical whistle for Charlotte's son and smiled as he took it from her with some zeal.

"What do we say when we receive gifts?" Charlotte asked the boys.

"Thank you," both boys murmured and proceeded to blow into their whistles.

Jeffrey rubbed his forehead in consternation. "I'm not altogether certain we *should* be thanking you," he said. "By sundown we'll be ready to toss those whistles into the river. But at any rate," he continued as light, if somewhat strained, laughter floated around the room, "it's time for our noonday meal. Ben, Mary, you're just in time."

CHAPTER 15

And when ye shall receive these things, I would exhort you that ye would ask God, the Eternal Father, in the name of Christ, if these things are not true . . .
—*Moroni 10:4*

* * *

10 May 1865
Boston, Massachusetts

"Johnson declared an official end to the armed resistance against the government today," Robert commented to Abigail as the two rode along the streets in one of the Birmingham family's carriages.

"You say that with such enthusiasm," Abigail remarked to him in a dry tone.

"I'm of a mind to agree with Isabelle," Robert said and tapped his finger against his thigh. "Johnson is not prepared to handle the presidency."

"And yet Lincoln chose him as his vice president," Abigail commented.

Robert snorted in reply. "It was politically advantageous. Johnson appealed to those Lincoln couldn't reach." He waved a hand in frustration. "It's neither here nor there—what's done is done."

"Have you heard of the reward Johnson is offering for the capture of Jefferson Davis?" Abigail asked.

Robert nodded. "One hundred thousand dollars. Quite a hefty sum."

Abigail shook her head and looked out the carriage window at the evening sky. "I believe his own might just turn on him for that much money."

"I don't know about that," Robert said. "They're mighty stubborn folk. Although I do hear that more Southerners each day blame their government for their loss. Robert E. Lee will always be a hero, but Jefferson Davis is treading on thin ice."

"I wonder where he is," she murmured. "How long can a man hide?"

"I don't know. I'm tired of the whole mess of it. Tired of the war, weary of the political plots, sorry for the cost."

Abigail looked at her beau carefully for a moment and then crossed the distance between them so that she sat next to him on the rear-facing bench of the carriage. The steady clop of the horses' hooves and gentle commands from the driver faded into the distance as she took his face in her hands.

"What is it?" she asked. "You're on edge in a way I haven't seen for a while. Since you came home from the war, in fact."

He closed his eyes briefly and reached up for her hand, entwining her fingers with his. "I have been able to think of little else since returning from Washington," he admitted quietly. "Watching the president die . . . I've seen so many men die . . ."

Robert paused, and Abigail let him sort through thoughts without interference. "When he took those last few shuddering breaths and I knew his soul would soon leave, as Luke's left, as did so many soldiers I knew, Ben knew . . . Lincoln was a soldier as much as any of us. To lose him now at the end . . ."

Abigail nodded but remained silent.

"I suppose I don't want to think of it anymore, but I can't seem to help myself."

"What would you do right now if you could do anything in the world? What would you enjoy spending your time doing?"

Robert was quiet for a moment as he considered her question. "I don't know," he finally said. "I wish I could change everything from the beginning somehow."

"Well, since that's an impossibility, how would you feel about trying to make a difference for people who have lost everything?"

"How do you mean?"

Abigail patted his hand. "I've been doing some thinking of late. My life is a solitary one, and I have resources at my disposal. I've considered going to Virginia for a time to see what can be done to help."

He looked at her carefully. "There are many who wouldn't welcome your help."

"True enough. But there are many who would. Think of the Negroes who are now free but who will receive little in terms of aid from the locals, their former masters. I would like to try anyhow."

Robert nodded. "I'm sure the Freedmen's Bureau would welcome all the help folks are willing to offer."

Abigail settled back into the seat. "At any rate, should you find yourself looking for a cause to embrace, I can assure you I would welcome the company."

"You can't mean to suggest that I would simply let you go without me."

"I was rather hoping you might say such a thing." Abigail looked at him sideways from under her bonnet, and Robert's mood suddenly felt a bit lighter.

"Were you, now?"

"I was."

"And I suppose you know that we cannot very well travel together unchaperoned."

She smiled. "Were you thinking of inviting your parents along, then?"

"Hardly."

"Hmm." The carriage continued to roll along gently down the street, and they swayed with the rhythm.

Robert lifted Abigail's hand to his lips and kissed it. "Abigail, this is hardly a romantic setting, but I must ask you now or lose my nerve. Will you marry me?"

Her eyes misted, and she looked at him with a poignant smile. "Absolutely. I was beginning to wonder if I would have to do the asking myself."

"Will you marry me soon?"

"Tomorrow, if you'd like. I have no other plans."

"Tomorrow it is, then. And then on to Virginia?"

"On to Virginia."

* * *

14 May 1865
Ogden, Utah

Ruth sat alone in her parlor after Ben and Mary left to spend some time with Elijah down the street. The past nine days since their arrival and acceptance of her offer to live with her temporarily had brought her nothing but joy, and to see her two "children" so happy together filled her heart with contentment.

The day of their arrival had been one of such happiness for all of them that Ruth's eyes misted slightly at the memory. They had stayed up late into the night sharing stories of the past several years that had seen them apart, and each day when she saw their faces at her breakfast table, Ruth was surprised and thrilled anew at their presence.

The couple had decided to leave Elijah in his current home with Charlotte and William, Jeffrey and Sarah, rather than abruptly pull him from that which was familiar. In truth, Ruth suspected it was a relief to Mary, who had confided to her that she was at a loss as to how to behave like a mother. "I don't know what to do," she had said that first night with a hint of tears.

"It will come now, child. Don't you fuss about it," Ruth had told her. "You just need some time to get used to each other."

It was indeed getting easier for Mary, who told her just that morning that Elijah laughed and embraced her each time she appeared. "He's a very loving child," Ruth had told her, and it was true. Elijah was special, despite his unfortunate paternity.

Ruth rocked slowly in her rocking chair by the hearth that contained a small fire to ward off the spring morning chill. In her hands she held a book of scripture that Ben had given her the night before. She ran a finger along the spine of the book, wondering what it was going to mean for her personally.

She had begun reading the night before, and to her surprise, it had held her attention rapt until early in the morning. Ruth knew her scriptures. She knew the Old and New Testaments and the words of Christ as well as she knew anything. Her surprise had come, she supposed, by the haunting feeling that she was reading something familiar about the Savior in the Book of Mormon. It claimed to be another testament of Him, and she was beginning to suspect that it was.

In her time spent in Utah, Ruth had learned something of the people who had begun settling it nearly twenty years earlier. They were industrious, clever, hardworking, and had given their all for that which they believed. They had been driven from their homes in the United States, their violent departures often occurring with the blessings of state governments, until the only place they could find refuge was beyond the borders of the country.

Ruth had reserved judgment, however, because of a few things that had bothered her. First of all, polygamy was practiced by some of the Church members, including their prophet, and it seemed a very odd thing indeed to her. Second was an issue that Ben himself had discussed with her—that of the priesthood. Ben had described the priesthood to her as the power to act in the name of God, a power that was currently unavailable to black men.

"How are you, of all people, at peace with this?" Ruth had asked Ben.

"When I first arrived here in Utah, I wasn't at peace with it when I realized what the policy meant. I thought I would have to leave the Church altogether because I was so unsettled about it. I thought I'd made a huge mistake."

Ben paused for a moment, reflecting. "I heard of a man named Elijah Abel. He was a black man who had received the priesthood from Joseph Smith. His further temple blessings were denied him by Brigham Young, yet this man still stayed true and firm in the faith. I knew I had to speak with him.

"He was gracious and patient with me—he must have seen my anger and frustration, although I thought I hid it rather well. He told me of his convictions and his faith that the Lord would make things right in the end. He told me to pray sincerely about it, to open my mind and heart and see where I was led.

"I took it to the Lord and told Him that if He wanted me to accept it, He would have to put my mind at ease about it Himself. And He has." He paused. "I don't believe it will be forever," he said quietly. "And I don't understand it at all, except that there are some things God must care for in His own time. Perhaps the purpose is His, perhaps the issue is man's. At any rate, I plan to ask Him about it when I die."

"What of the blessings that will be denied you and Mary, as well as your children? Do you not worry over this?" Ruth asked him without rancor.

"I think of it often. It's as though I know in my heart that someday all will be rectified. I don't know why things are this way, but perhaps it's my test in this life. It must be my leap of faith and trust in God. I know He loves me, and I know He loves Mary. I also know He was pleased at our union—I felt it in my heart. The rest I must leave in His hands."

Ruth had smiled at him then and placed a hand alongside his cheek the way she had so many times in his youth. Now as she thought back on the conversation, she wondered if she would be able to find faith for herself the way he had, for while the book she held in her hands certainly rang true to her heart, the practices of the people who believed in it did not.

* * *

Ben watched Mary with her son and smiled when Elijah threw his arms around Mary's neck with abandon and laughter. Mary's eyes lit up, and she placed her hand at the back of Elijah's head, embracing him and rocking from side to side. Elijah was quickly becoming used to this woman who came over every day to play with him and William, and Ben was glad to see some of Mary's earlier reservations melt away in the face of her own unacknowledged competence.

Ben had worried that seeing Elijah might bring to Mary's mind sad or painful memories of Richard, but she seemed happy and at peace, and so he was grateful. For his own part, it had been a bit of a challenge. Every reminder that Mary was a mother was only a reminder to him that his own brother had brutally raped her. He didn't fault Elijah, but he wondered if he would ever be able to fully forget why the young boy even existed.

Mary must have sensed his mood, because as Elijah ran from her to grab a toy, she looked at him with a questioning expression.

He shrugged. "Just thinking."

"Of what?"

"Many different things, I suppose."

"You have that angry look on your face." Mary scooted closer to Ben and placed a hand on his knee. In a low voice, she said, "You're thinking about Richard again."

He put his hand atop hers and shook his head. "Am I so easily read, then?"

"Ben, I remember Richard as a spoiled, willful, and cruel boy who met his just end. I take satisfaction in knowing that he is not living a life of luxury somewhere—I feel justice has been served. You and I both know that such is not always the case."

Ben nodded.

"He had to meet his Maker knowing full well what he'd done with his life, things he did both to me and to others. And in spite of all that, something beautiful came from something awful." She motioned to Elijah, who was making his way back to her side.

"Mama," he was saying. "Look!"

Mary glanced back up at Ben. "The memories are fading," she murmured, "and my life now is all I could have hoped for."

Ben looked at her with a sense of wonder. *Please*, he prayed in his heart, *help me also find a sense of peace with this. Help me forget about Richard. I doubt I'll ever be able to forgive him, but help me to at least forget.*

* * *

Earl and Charlotte watched the scene quietly from the doorway to the nursery. "They're good together," Earl whispered in her ear. "They'll be fine parents for that boy."

Charlotte nodded, her expression unreadable. "You know he lost his inheritance, his home, his family trying to help her escape. I often wonder what it would be like to inspire that kind of compassion in someone."

"Do you fault him still for having attempted it?"

Charlotte looked at him in some surprise and stepped a bit away from the door and quietly closed it. "What prompts you to think I ever did?"

Earl merely looked at her with one eyebrow raised.

"Oh, very well. I'd like to be able to pretend I was the paragon Ben was, but I wasn't. I thought he was insane."

"And yet now you are accepting of their union. I wonder why the change of heart."

Charlotte flushed. "Must you be so direct?"

"I'm a coarse farm boy. I know little else."

"Ha. Well, if you must know," she said, walking down the hallway away from the nursery, "I nearly died in childbirth. Ruth stayed with me and cared for me. I admitted to myself then that she was truly my mother, more than my own had been." A tear escaped her eye and rolled down her cheek. "It was then I began to see her as a person, not as our property."

"I believe that sooner or later, all people come to a realization of the truth," Earl said, "if not in this life, then in the next."

"And you," Charlotte said, wiping her cheek, "are your family abolitionists?"

Earl smiled. "My mother is the daughter of a Cherokee."

"Ah. Of course."

"Charlotte," Earl said as they began descending the front staircase, "I wonder if you would do me the honor of another visit to Salt Lake next weekend."

"Certainly, I would be delighted. May I ask for what occasion?"

"A special one. But I believe for the time being, I shall keep it to myself."

"Oh. Well, then."

At the base of the stairs, Earl took her hand in his and kissed her fingers. He smiled at her and removed his hat from the hat tree in the corner. "I've taken the liberty of asking your parents if William might remain here, if that suits you."

Her eyes widened slightly in surprise. "Was he a nuisance for your mother the last time we visited? I wish she had said something to me about it—"

"No, no. I merely wished for you to have some time to yourself. And with me."

"Oh. Oh, well, yes. Yes, certainly." Charlotte felt extremely unsettled, caught off guard, and she was under the impression that Earl was enjoying her discomfort immensely.

"Until then," he said with a slight bow and placed his hat on his head. As he left the house quietly, Charlotte closed the door behind him with a small snort.

"Coarse farm boy. He's no more coarse than am I." With that, she went off to quiz her mother.

CHAPTER 16

I hereby repeat . . . my unmitigated hatred . . . to the perfidious,
malignant, and vile Yankee race.
—Secessionist Edmund Ruffin

* * *

14 May 1865
Savannah, Georgia

Emily's flame-red hair stood in stark contrast to the curly
black hair of the student to whom she bent close. Running a
finger along the sentence in the book before them on the child's
desk, she spoke the words aloud. "The boy ran," she said. "Now
you say it."

"The boy ran," the little boy answered.

"Good. Now point to the word that reads 'ran,'" Emily said.

The young one pointed to the appropriate word with his
thin finger.

"And which letters are in the word 'ran'?"

"R . . . a . . . n . . ." the boy told her.

"Excellent." Emily put an arm around the boy and gave his
shoulders a squeeze. "You're learning so quickly. You'll be
reading this whole book before long." Emily glanced up at her
surroundings and saw scenarios similar to hers. Gwenyth sat

next to a young child, as did several other women, most former slaves. They were volunteering their time to the school for colored children, and Emily found she looked forward to each session with eagerness. At least twice a week, sometimes thrice, she and Gwenyth attended to the needs of the children in whatever capacity their teacher directed. If they weren't also consumed with keeping Willow Lane afloat, Emily would have spent every day at the school.

When classes came to a close for the day, Emily stood near the teacher, Miss Weston, an escaped slave who had been living in the North for several years. She had recently returned to her former home to assist in the education of the children, and Emily respected her enormously.

"Thank you again, Mrs. Stanhope. I do so appreciate your time. You as well, Miss Stanhope," Miss Weston said to Gwenyth, who approached the pair after dusting the apron of a little girl's dress.

"Thank you for allowing us to share in your class, Miss Weston," Emily said to the woman. "It cheers me every day we come. These children are wonderful. And I understand you have received visits from Captain Ketchum?"

"Yes. He is most solicitous of our needs."

Emily nodded in satisfaction. "I do believe he has a good heart. He has mentioned to me on more than one occasion how very impressed he is with the condition of the children—their neat appearances, their good behavior, and the results on their exams. He says it gives him much pleasure to report those things back to the Bureau's headquarters."

Miss Weston smiled. "I'm very glad to hear this," she said. "We are rather a case for scrutiny, being some of the first to educate former slave children."

"Your efforts are well worth your time," Emily told her. "I am very much in awe of your talents."

Gwenyth and Emily left the small building and made their way around to the back. Emily stopped speaking to her companion midsentence when she noticed that their carriage was most obviously missing its pulling power. "Where's the horse?"

Gwenyth frowned and walked around the outhouse. "As if he could be hiding back here," she muttered and looked up at Emily in confusion. "I don't know."

Emily stood with her hands on her hips and looked off into the distance in all directions. "Gwen," she finally said, stating the obvious, "I do believe someone has made off with our horse."

"Well," Gwenyth answered and stood next to Emily, "someone obviously was tremendously desperate to make off with it in broad daylight."

"That could be anyone south of the Mason-Dixon." Emily sighed. "I suppose there's nothing for us to do but to start walking." Emily's brow furrowed in a deep frown, and she chewed on her lip as they left the schoolhouse. The worry that had been tugging at the back of her mind over the last few weeks was quickly moving to the fore.

It wasn't as though the two miles to Willow Lane was a taxing walk, but neither woman said much along the way. As they neared their destination, Emily finally said, "Everybody is poor and in need. It's probably nothing more than that."

Gwenyth nodded but remained silent. What neither woman mentioned was that this would be the second horse to disappear in less than a week. Austin had been at a town meeting earlier and had exited the building to the same fate. Willow Lane had only one horse remaining, which really was more than most of their neighbors had. Because Austin and Emily had so readily hosted Sherman's troops, when the Union soldiers had left town, they had allowed the Stanhopes certain "privileges." Emily was left to wonder if those privileges, along with her own uncensored mouth, were now landing them in trouble. If they were to lose their last horse, Emily was at a loss to think of how they would manage. It set her heart to tripping a bit as she considered that fate, and she was suddenly very angry that people had stolen not just one but two of their most valued possessions.

"I'm sure you have the right of it," Gwenyth finally said. "It's probably nothing."

Later that night as she readied for bed after reading Mary Alice a bedtime story and seeing her safely tucked into her bedroom down the hall, Emily voiced her concerns to her husband. "It isn't as though it might not just be a coincidence. After all, people are hungry and destitute and need horses for plowing their fields, as all the other animals are gone . . ."

"However?"

"However, I can't help but feel a bit unsettled about this. Tell me I'm wrong."

"You're wrong."

"I don't believe you."

He smiled. "Good. You shouldn't."

She sat down on the bed and watched him disrobe. "Do you think we're being deliberately targeted?"

He hung his shirt over the wardrobe door and shrugged. "I wouldn't be at all surprised."

"Austin, it's all my fault. I've made it no secret that I hated the Confederacy—now I've jeopardized all of us."

"Emily." He leveled her with a stare that she had come to recognize as his you're-being-unreasonable expression. "My family has been involved in politically dangerous activity for over one hundred years. You're hardly the cause of this. In fact, I'd say you're a rather appropriate addition to the family legacy."

She leaned her head against one of the large posts at the foot of the bed and closed her eyes. "I'm afraid."

Austin had removed his prosthetic leg, so he now hopped over to her side. It was a feat he usually did with some flair to make her laugh, but as her eyes were closed, he figured the extra effort would be for naught. "Em," he said, holding the same bedpost for balance and placing the back of his fingers alongside her cheek. "We're going to be fine. I won't let anything happen to our family."

"Oh, Austin." She opened her eyes. "You're so noble. And I respect that you would give your life to keep us safe. But I'm not willing to risk it. Have I ever told you about my Uncle James's brother-in-law? He operated a newspaper in New Orleans. When he printed one too many articles that painted the South in an unfavorable light, his Confederacy-loving neighbors beat him to death."

"Em, I don't think that—"

"To *death*, Austin. Beat him to death. We don't have the luxury of believing folks here would be any different."

"Sweetheart." Austin leaned his shoulder against the bedpost and gripped both of her shoulders in her hands. "If the situation here becomes so dire, we will leave. Do you understand? We'll leave. In fact, it's something I give considerable thought to each day. I believe the time is drawing near."

Emily took a deep breath. "Very well. Do you give your word?"

"As a true blue Confederate veteran soldier."

Her lips twitched. "Do you not mean true gray?"

"Indeed. Now get yourself changed for bed. Mary Alice will be up with the bluebirds."

"That's true enough," Emily grumbled as she rose from the bed and wrapped her arms around Austin's waist. "Just once I wish the child would sleep a bit longer."

Austin kissed the top of her head and held her tightly against him. He closed his eyes and hoped he had been successful at keeping his own worry out of his voice. Judging by Emily's relaxed demeanor, he decided he'd achieved his goal. Austin knew that sentiment about the Stanhopes was anything but positive these days. Once word had leaked out about his family's activities throughout the years before and during the war, the reception he'd received around town had been decidedly chilly at best.

He would have to watch closely. If politics in the South stabilized, the fervor might die down. Hatred against the North was rampant, though, and if their vanquished pride wasn't enough to keep people angry, their hunger and poverty would.

* * *

15 May 1865
Richmond, Virginia

Isabelle moved alongside Camille slowly, using her crutches to help her walk. "Are you certain you're not tiring?" Camille asked her with a frown.

"I'll speak up if I am," Isabelle answered her. "Anything is better than lying in bed."

"I'm still not altogether sure this was a good idea for you," Camille said. "The doctor was very vocal about not moving you any great distance again. He told me privately that we should never have moved you from Washington to Boston in the first place."

Isabelle snorted. "I don't trust doctors. Besides, I believe I know what's best for my own health, thank you."

Camille eyed her askance with a half smile, which she hid. It was good to see Isabelle show signs of her former spunk. Camille and Jacob had begun to worry about her welfare in the month since Lincoln's passing. Isabelle had largely taken the blame for his death on her own shoulders and couldn't seem to listen to reason concerning the matter. Even a visit from Pinkerton hadn't done much to assuage her troubled state of mind. He had told her repeatedly that she wasn't to blame, that she had moved on the intelligence she had uncovered as quickly as possible, but she was not to be convinced. She had remained certain that she hadn't done everything in her power to discover Booth's details quickly enough.

When Robert and Abigail had surprised the family with an extremely quick wedding, followed by an equally surprising announcement that they wanted to venture south and work with the Freedmen's Bureau, Camille had felt a pang of envy at their new venture. When they had suggested that she and Jacob come along, Camille had also invited Isabelle but had been unsure of her friend's wishes.

The change seemed to have done Isabelle some good, however, for she acted more like her former self each passing day. She, Camille, Robert, and Abigail spent the daylight hours in the service of the Freedmen's Bureau, and Jacob explored the city as a reporter in the field, transmitting his reports back to the paper in Boston via newly repaired telegraph lines.

Camille hefted the basket she carried onto her other hip, redistributing the weight of the food and supply rations inside. She shielded her eyes from the sun for a moment and looked down the street. Blackened chimneys were visible as far as the eye could see, the buildings mere shells. "They might have thought of the people they were leaving behind before they burned the place to the ground," Camille muttered.

"I don't think they much cared," Isabelle said with a wince as her injured leg was jarred by a rock in her path. "Retreating armies aren't known for their willingness to leave resources available to the enemy."

"Yes, but what of their own?"

"A good majority of their own had already fled. Most of them are living with relatives in remote areas well outside the cities."

"Well," Camille said, "it still doesn't seem right to me. Not everybody left—here we are on our way to deliver food, after all."

The women walked along in relative silence for several minutes, turning this way and that according to a map given them at the Bureau. When they finally approached their destination, they stood outside the front door of a charred but largely intact home that had obviously once been very beautiful.

Camille's knock upon the front door produced a young woman of roughly fifteen years who opened it a crack and peered out at them with mistrust clearly stamped on her features. "Yes?" she said.

Camille introduced herself and Isabelle and asked if the young woman's mother might be at home.

"Y'all are Yankees," the young woman said in a flat tone.

Camille stared at her for a moment before responding. "We are. But we're good Yankees."

"A Yankee's a Yankee."

Isabelle impatiently tapped at the wall of the house with her crutch and said to the girl, "Are you hungry? When was your last decent meal?"

The girl thrust her chin a notch higher. "I don't know what business that is of yours."

"It's our business in that we have food, good food, for several people here in this basket. Now if you don't think you'd like it, we'll just be on our way." Isabelle nudged Camille, who again shifted the heavy weight of the basket and looked at her, wide-eyed. She began to follow Isabelle down the front porch stairs when the girl called out behind them.

"What do we have to do for your food there? Sign an oath of loyalty?" The young woman's brave words couldn't disguise the tremor in her voice.

Isabelle turned back around and eyed the girl carefully. "What is your name?" she asked.

"Sally." The chin went up another notch.

"Sally, your mother was in the Bureau offices yesterday and signed the oath herself. That's why we came to be here with this food."

Sally's mouth dropped open a fraction. "The *Freedmen's* Bureau? She would never!"

Camille stepped forward and set the basket down, breathing a sigh and stretching her back. "Sally, your mother has mouths to feed. Things often change when a woman is looking into the faces of her hungry children."

"Well, she won't have to worry about that any longer."

"What do you mean?" Isabelle asked her with narrowed eyes.

"She died late last night. She's had consumption for weeks." Sally's eyes welled up, but she kept the tears at bay.

"And your father? Has he yet to return home?" Camille asked her softly.

"Papa died at Shiloh. We've lived all this time without him—I figure we'll do just fine now without Mama. We don't need your *Freedmen's* food."

"Where is your mother now?" Isabelle asked the girl, inching closer to the door.

"I told you, she's dead."

"I know that. Where is she though? Here?" Isabelle gestured toward the house with a crutch.

"In the parlor," Sally replied, and a tear slipped from her eye. She brushed at it with a hasty motion, scowling as though ashamed the hated Yankees were witness to her grief.

"We need to get her out of the house. The rest of you will be sick. Where are your younger brothers and sisters?"

Sally motioned to the right with her head. "Upstairs in the nursery."

"And you have," Camille paused as she retrieved a paper from her apron pocket, "two sisters, ages eight and six, and a ten-year-old brother?"

Sally nodded wordlessly. "But we aren't going anywhere. I won't let anyone take us to an orphanage or give our house to someone the likes of y'all."

Isabelle rolled her eyes. "We don't want your house."

Camille glanced at Isabelle and tried not to choke on horrified laughter. Her companion in compassion was taking an impatient approach, but she didn't know why she was surprised. Isabelle was nothing if not practical, and the girl's stubborn reluctance to accept help would be beyond Isabelle's comprehension.

"Sally," Camille said, interrupting before Isabelle could throw out another caustic remark, "most likely we can find a friend or relative who would be in a position to come and care for you and your family. We have no desire to take you from your home and place you in an orphanage. And as much as I'm sure you're perfectly capable, wouldn't it be nice to have a bit of help?"

Sally stared at the pair on her porch, refusing to agree or disagree with Camille's question. She finally said, "When the Yanks stormed in after Davis left, all our colored help ran off. Just left. Mama was outraged that they were out singing and dancing in the streets. She would *never* have gone to the Freedmen's Bureau begging for help from people who are here to help colored folk."

"You're surprised your 'help' up and left?" Isabelle asked her with one eyebrow raised.

"This was their home. They had obligations to us, to my mama."

"This wasn't their home. This was their prison." Isabelle's tone was flat. "And for your information, missy, the Freedmen's Bureau lends aid not only to freed slaves but also to whites who are willing to sign the loyalty oath to the Union. Eat the food or don't eat it, I don't much care. We'll send someone around to make arrangements for your mother's burial." Isabelle turned once again, this time thumping carefully down the steps, leaving Camille little choice but to follow her or be left behind with the sullen child who would have liked nothing more than to carve out her Yankee heart.

Sally stared at them as they left her property; Camille glanced back once at the girl's thin frame and her defiant, frightened expression. "She's afraid," Camille said.

"She's a fool. She's old enough to know better."

"She's also starving. She may not be thinking clearly."

"When a starving person is handed a basket of food," Isabelle bit off, "she should take it first and ask questions later. I know what it's like to be starving to death."

"You do?" Camille glanced sideways at her in surprise and tried to keep up with her angry strides. The woman had suddenly become quite proficient on her crutches.

"I was caught on the wrong side of the Vicksburg siege. I've been so hungry that roasted rat was a delectable meal." Isabelle shook her head. "Of all the causes worthy of death, theirs must be the most ridiculous." Isabelle gestured at the ruined landscape with her crutch. "Look at what you've done to yourselves," she shouted to the charred rooftops. "And for what? A hypocritical notion of freedom?"

Camille stopped with Isabelle and bit her lower lip to stop its trembling. Tears had formed in Isabelle's eyes, and the anger Camille heard in her voice broke her heart. "Look at this mess." Isabelle turned back to Camille with huge eyes. "What an awful, interminable mess! And the one man who might have been able to help clean it up is gone."

"Well, then, I suppose we'll just have to pick up where he left off," Camille said through a voice clogged tight with emotion. "He's gone, but we're still here. And we can make a difference, one life at a time."

"Oh, Camille. I don't know if you realize just how bad it is." Isabelle's head sunk a bit in despair, and Camille wished for a sign of her earlier anger. "It was in the papers just this morning— the farther south one goes, the worse it gets. Columbia, Charleston—utter ruin. Blackened, burned, no crops or livestock, gardens nothing but weeds. People have *nothing*. And when we try to help, they refuse it on pride." Isabelle glanced back at Sally's house in frustration. "If they were so bent on winning or dying, they ought to just have stepped in front of a cannon and been done with it."

"I don't believe the entire Southern population is bent on denying Northern help. Sally's mother was evidence enough of that. A mother will want to feed her children. It will take time, but things will be fixed to right. Jacob said he's heard that men are already hard at work repairing the damage Sherman did to the railroads all throughout the South. Many of the soldiers are nearly home now, just in time to get some good crops in the ground." Camille paused and eyed her friend in sympathy. "Folks are resilient. The hatred may hang on for some time, but it will heal."

"One life at a time," Isabelle murmured, repeating Camille's phrase as she wiped at her eyes. "Yes. One life at a time." Isabelle turned around and headed back in the direction of Sally's house.

"Where are you going?" Camille called after her and trotted to catch up to her.

"I'm going to make that girl eat. And if she refuses, I'll roast her a rat."

CHAPTER 17

The surgeons and matrons ate rats and said they were as good as squirrels, but, having seen the rats in the morgue running over the bodies of the dead soldiers, I had no relish for them.
—*Confederate soldier in a Virginia hospital.*

* * *

25 May 1865
New York, New York

"Just plain old darn foolishness, really. Nothin' more than a waste of life."

Daniel listened to his friend Michael with half an ear as he listened for the sounds of the chickens and tossed them some grain. He appreciated Michael's visits; Michael was a firefighter and meant well. Daniel suspected Michael felt responsible for the blindness—the two had been partners at the fire that night.

"Texas, you say?" Daniel asked, more to be polite than out of any real sense of curiosity. His head was pounding, and he wanted a drink.

"Palmetto Ranch. Union cavalry attacked the Confederate outpost. Fought for two whole days. The Rebs lost but maybe five men. We lost thirty and over one hundred were taken captive."

Daniel grunted. "Someone should have told them the war is over."

"I reckon so. Sounds like we have returning troops headed our way some. A couple of days ago in Washington, Grant's men marched through, then just yesterday Sherman's men. I hear it was a grand parade—over a hundred fifty thousand men marched by in right smart uniforms while the crowds cheered like madmen."

Daniel nodded, still listening for the sounds of chicken scratching. He imagined Michael was probably propped up with his elbows resting on the fence that surrounded the chicken yard. Daniel felt so far removed from the rest of the country—the rest of the world, really—that he struggled to immerse himself in the conversation. He wanted to care about the fact that thousands of soldiers were returning safely to their homes and that they had been privy to wonderful parades of adoration along their way, but he couldn't summon the emotion. *I can't see . . .* was all he could think, every minute of every day. It consumed his every waking hour until he went to bed at night, and when he awoke, he wished he could sleep the day away. The only thing that took away part of the sting was a good, stiff drink. He knew he was fast becoming dependent upon it, though, and if he cared about his life a bit more, it might have concerned him.

"I'm sure people were happy to see the men returning," he commented to Michael in an effort to bear at least part of the conversation.

"Tens of thousands lined the streets. It was a real hero's welcome. Oh, and had you heard? Jefferson Davis was captured in Georgia!"

Daniel nodded. "Wearing a dress, or some such nonsense?"

"That's what they say—apparently Mrs. Davis wanted to help him escape, and so she ushered him out the door in his night wrapper, and as he left, a servant threw a shawl about his head. I hear the whole way to Virginia he was taunted something fierce by Union soldiers."

"Where is he now?"

"Fort Monroe, Virginia. Word is they won't even let him leave his cell."

Daniel moved a bit to his left and found the walking stick he'd propped against the side of the house. Replacing the feed bucket on the nail in the wall, he grasped the stick and felt his way to the fence. Michael cleared his throat a bit as Daniel neared and exited the chicken yard, fastening the gate closed behind him.

"Daniel, if you ever need anything, that is, if I can ever help with anything, you know I would do it."

"I do, Michael, and I thank you for that. I wish you'd stop blaming yourself for this, though. It's not your fault, you know."

"Oh, I, well . . . I didn't say that . . ."

"I know. You didn't have to—I can hear it in your voice each time you visit. I'm grateful for your visits, but you don't need to come here because you feel guilty."

"I don't feel guilty," Michael said, sounding a bit embarrassed and stunned that Daniel would speak so bluntly.

Daniel waved a hand at him. "Forget I said that. How about a drink? Would you like to join me inside?"

"It's a bit early for a drink, I believe. I need to be on my way back into the city, besides."

Daniel shrugged. "As you wish. Perhaps next time."

"Yes." Michael paused, and Daniel listened for the sound of retreating footsteps. When they didn't occur, he waited for Michael to say something else. "You take care of yourself, Dan."

"I will."

Finally, the footsteps sounded, and Daniel heard Michael mount his horse and trot away. He turned his back on the sound and felt his way toward the house, fighting the surge of panic that often overtook him as he wondered if the wrong step would take him from his property and have him lost somewhere in the streets. If only it weren't so dark. He had become terrified of the dark, and it was now his constant companion.

* * *

Marie stood next to her mother and smiled at the trio of people who currently toured the school. Brenna had told her and Jenny on the ride into town that three men with close ties to a prominent bank were looking for charities to support. With any luck, they might choose the school as one of those beneficiaries. "I don't care one fig what their reasons are," Brenna had said, "just so long as they open their wallets."

Now, Brenna walked the men around the facility and explained the functions and purposes of each major item or area. She also skillfully maneuvered the conversation to include those things wherein the school was lacking, and Marie smiled at her abilities. She was indeed a formidable woman. Would that Daniel could now adopt some of that tenacity.

The thought of her husband brought a worried, frustrated skip to her heart, and she fought back a frown. Daniel hardly seemed to be improving in his spirits. He said all he wanted to do each day was maintain the farm while she volunteered her time at the school, but money was becoming scarce, and she was unsure of what she should do. She could hardly hold him responsible for work he couldn't possibly do now that his sight was gone, but there must be something he could do to contribute in such a way that he would feel useful. Were she to suggest that it was time for her to find paid employment, he might never pull himself from his wretched, self-pitying stupor.

I don't know what it's like to be blind, though, she couldn't help thinking, as she always did whenever she was tempted to become too frustrated with him. She could only imagine the fear and anger he must feel each day when he opened his eyes to the darkness. It hurt her, though, that he seemed so easily able to close his mind to her; even when they were in the same room together it was as though she were alone. All of her questions to him were rewarded with monosyllabic answers that told her little or nothing, and he never sought her out to ask for her help or opinion, as he would have in earlier times.

Brenna drew closer with the three businessmen, and Marie snapped her mind back to the present. Her mother-in-law was introducing her and Jenny to the men, all of whom regarded them with smiles and tips of their hats. The last of the three, whom Brenna introduced as Mr. Holmes, took Jenny's hand in his and bowed over her fingertips, kissing the air just above them, and then proceeded to do the same to Marie.

"Ladies," Mr. Holmes said with a certain amount of flair, "it is absolutely a pleasure to make your acquaintance."

Marie quirked a brow at Brenna, who scowled at her, and turned her attention to the fawning gentleman. "Likewise, kind sir," she said.

"Oh, you are a Southern belle," he said. "Such a delightful accent you speak with."

"Louisiana," Marie admitted. "New Orleans, to be specific."

One of the other two gentlemen spoke up at her comment. "Perhaps you've heard of the mess that happened down in that neck of the woods just today?"

Marie shook her head and glanced at her mother. "I don't believe I have. Have you?"

Jenny shook her head, and Brenna shrugged.

"Well," the man said, "not exactly your home, but fairly close by—a warehouse full of munitions in Mobile, Alabama, exploded, destroying nearly eight city blocks and killing over three hundred people."

"Oh, dear," Jenny replied. "How awful for their families. Is there a suspected cause?"

"No," the man replied. "Odd, too, really—the papers say that otherwise that area has been relatively unscathed through the whole war."

"It's a shame," Marie murmured. "Even still there are effects of the war."

"Yes," Mr. Holmes said. "I imagine you and Mrs. Brissot are grateful to be far away."

Marie's mother nodded. "We're safer here." Marie glanced at her mother. The men would never imagine exactly how much danger she and Jenny had been in at home in New Orleans. Even if memories among their former associates were short and it were safe for them to return, Marie wasn't sure she'd ever be able to face the memories of her father and his last days there.

Marie's brows drew together in a slight frown. The folks there had never made it easy for her—she had been branded undesirable long before her father had ever begun printing controversial newspaper articles.

"Ah, but we've spoken of unpleasant things," Mr. Holmes said with regret in his voice. "During our next visit we must be certain to bring naught but smiles to these lovely faces."

The other two men with Mr. Holmes were a bit older than he, and they looked at him with unreadable expressions. Marie wondered if they were forced to endure the younger man's declarations of charm with each visit they made. She smiled a bit at the thought, and Mr. Holmes caught her expression, smiling warmly at her in return. "Until then," he said with another tip of his hat.

When the men left the building and Brenna returned after seeing them out, she burst into laughter. "Well, Marie," she said, "you may be single-handedly responsible for our good fortune."

"They're going to fund the school?" Marie asked.

"They are indeed, thanks in no small part to the smitten Mr. Holmes."

"Posh," Marie said with a wave of her hand and began to straighten books on a shelf that were already perfectly straight.

"It's true, dear," Jenny said with a smile on her face. "I do believe the man was quite taken with you."

Marie felt herself blush. Her own beauty was something she'd been uncomfortable with for years. As an adolescent it had only invited trouble, and she had long since learned to ignore it. Daniel had often remarked upon it in the most gentle of terms, at least until his accident. Now he seldom seemed to notice anything but his whiskey bottle.

"I'm a married woman," Marie said in protest, and to her frustration, the mothers only laughed.

"You *are* a married woman," Brenna agreed in her lilting Irish voice, "but you are also beautiful beyond words. When you grow to be one hundred years old, you will still be beautiful beyond words."

"That she will," Jenny said with no small amount of pride. "She looks like her father. Mercy, but he was a handsome man."

"Ah, Mama." Marie moved to her mother's side and placed her arms around her for a quick embrace. "Wasn't he? The handsomest man in all of Louisiana."

"I should like to have met him," Brenna said. "I believe he and my Gavin would have gotten on quite well."

"They would have." Jenny nodded. "They were of a like mind on many, many things."

"Perhaps they are together even now," Marie said. "Perhaps they watch us from heaven and laugh."

"Yes, yes," Brenna said, her eyes crinkled and smiling at the corners. "Gavin was a laugher, bless him. Loved to laugh, that man."

The mothers' good humor carried Marie throughout the remainder of the day with a lightness in her heart. It wasn't until she reached her home that an increasingly familiar heaviness returned.

The house was dark; of course it would be, because whether or not the lamps were lit made no difference to Daniel. She entered quietly and lit the lamps herself, noting that he had been in the kitchen and tried to clean up after himself. A few telltale crumbs remained on the counter along with some spilled droplets of the stew she had made the day before and kept.

"Dan?" she called, and made her way through the house to their bedroom, where she found him sitting in the corner in a chair he had once made in his shop. "Here you are. How are you, sweetheart?" she asked, trying to force an ease into her voice that she didn't feel.

"Well enough," he answered and turned his cheek upward slightly when she kissed it. The faint smell of alcohol clung to him; it was becoming an all-too-familiar scent when she was near him.

She told him of her day, of the men who had agreed to offer generous funds to the school. He answered politely enough, but without any real interest or conviction. When the pause in conversation became uncomfortable, she finally said, "The mothers have invited us to their house for dessert. I thought I would have some stew and bread and then we could walk up the hill for a visit."

"You go ahead. I don't much feel up to a visit right now."

Her patience finally snapped. He always found reasons to never leave the house, despite numerous pleadings and urging on her part. "Why, Daniel?"

"I just don't feel well."

"Could it be that you've imbibed a bit too much? It seems to be a common problem with you these days." There. She'd finally said it.

His pause was lengthy, and in the dim light she could see the muscles in his handsome jaw working as though he were clenching his teeth tightly. "How I choose to spend my time during the course of my miserable day is none of your concern," he said.

"Your day is miserable, Daniel, because you choose it to be thus. And as your wife, I daresay your drinking habits are most definitely my concern."

"Who do you think you are to tell me I choose to be miserable? Did I choose to be blind, Marie?" He leaned forward in his chair, his grip on the arms white-knuckled. "You think I *chose* this?"

"No, I don't think you choose to be blind. You *do* choose, however, to hole yourself up here day after day, and no matter how much I beg and plead, you refuse to leave this house. The world is still revolving, Daniel, and I would very much like you to experience it with me!"

"I can't very well experience that which I can't see! You go on and live your life, Marie. 'Experience' life, and do not concern yourself with what I do or do not *choose* to do!" By this time, Daniel had risen from his chair with such agitation that it fell over behind him, crashing into the wall.

Marie turned and fled the room, her vision blurred by tears as she left the house and walked down the dusty street in the direction opposite of the mothers' house. It wouldn't do at all for them to see her upset. She would walk for a bit, compose herself, and then simply go to their house for dessert and tell them that Daniel wasn't feeling well. For the time being, however, she allowed her tears free rein, and they fell down her cheeks in a steady pattern.

How was she ever to make things right? How could she possibly help heal a man who refused to be healed? He was effectively driving her away—she couldn't very well beg him to continue loving her the way he once had if he no longer felt himself capable of doing so. Her thoughts swirled in different directions until her breathing finally calmed and she was able to clean her face with a handkerchief. With a deep breath and a resolution to spare the mothers her own anguish, she turned back and headed up the hill to their house.

* * *

Daniel sat on the floor in the bedroom wishing he could take back every selfish thing he'd said to Marie. Heaven help him, but she was the one person on earth who meant more to him than anything, and he was making her run from him. In his mind's eye he could see her lovely face, her dark hair and violet eyes. He should be grateful, he told himself, that he couldn't see the pain he was causing her.

He didn't deserve her; he probably never had. It was fate's cruel way of showing him that someone far worthier than he should have her by his side. He wished there were a simple way of ending their marriage without causing disgrace upon her head; then she would be free to remarry and live the life she deserved to have with a man who was whole and courageous.

Perhaps she would grow weary of him and finally leave on her own—surely society wouldn't condemn a woman who fled a husband so deep into his cups that he was near death. It would be his gift to her. Other men had drunk themselves into an early grave; so would he. If she were a widow, she would be free of him.

He drew his knees to his chest and laid his forehead on them. *Da,* he moaned quietly in his heart, *I'm a failure. I'm a failure . . . I'm so sorry.*

CHAPTER 18

And also, ye yourselves will succor those that stand in need of your succor; ye will administer of your substance unto him that standeth in need; and ye will not suffer that the beggar putteth up his petition to you in vain, and turn him out to perish.
—Mosiah 4:16

* * *

29 May 1865
Cleveland, Ohio

Anne looked over the stack of papers on the table with a sense of satisfaction. She'd always written fairly short pieces for newspapers, never an entire book. Her decision to write down her experiences as a Union soldier had provided her with a creative outlet she hadn't realized she would enjoy so much.

The book was an adventure story, of sorts, detailing her activities before, during, and after the war, and she knew people would believe it all to be the fanciful workings of a woman's imagination. They would never believe it to be the truth that it was.

The evening light had long since vanished, and she sat near the flickering light of a lantern at the dining table. Ivar approached her from behind and placed his hands upon her shoulders and massaged gently. With a small moan, she rolled her head first to one side, then the other. "I'm stiff from sitting here so long," she said.

"Are you finished?" he asked her.

"I believe so. Will you look over it for me one last time? I know you've read it before, but I'd like one final nod of approval."

"I would be honored."

She looked up over her shoulder at his face, searching for signs of sarcasm. When she found none, she knew she shouldn't have been surprised. "You're very good to me, Ivar Gundersen," she said.

"As are you to me, Anne Gundersen."

"Most men would dismiss a project of this sort as utter foolishness." She was still for a moment. "Of course, most men would have been horrified at discovering a woman posed as a man for *whatever* the reason."

"You will recall I *did* disapprove."

"But you didn't turn me in. Not until I was at death's door. You let me march right along beside you into battle. Saved my life, too." She leaned her cheek against his hand and closed her eyes. "Sweet mercy, I loved you even then."

He bent down behind her and embraced her, placing his arms around her growing abdomen. "And I loved you. Despite the fact that you were reckless and stubborn."

"Well, and aren't you glad I was? We would never have met, otherwise."

"We are fortunate, then." He nuzzled her ear with his nose. "*I* am fortunate. You could have chosen any man in that regiment."

She smiled. "I wanted only one."

* * *

The following morning, after helping Ivar see to the animals, Anne and Inger walked hand in hand into town to mail Anne's manuscript. She was satisfied with it; Ivar had given it his stamp of approval and also agreed with her that it wouldn't hurt to submit it with her initials instead of her full name.

Inger skipped along, taking two steps to Anne's one, chattering as though her mouth contained an endless stream that would never run dry. Anne smiled, knowing why the child slept so well each night. The amount of energy it took each day to be Inger was staggering.

Upon leaving the post office after seeing the manuscript safely tucked away, Anne turned to her young stepdaughter. "Would you like a treat, Inger?"

"Yes, please! A peppermint stick?"

"A peppermint stick it is, then. Let's cross the street, and we'll go into the store."

Anne allowed Inger free rein in the store and watched the child wander from barrel to basket, staring in delight at all the items within each. The store itself was a delight—Anne surmised that she probably enjoyed it as much as Inger did. The various barrels were filled with nails, tools of all kinds, and everyday items that a woman wouldn't want to find missing in her house. The shelves held bolts of fabrics of all kinds and patterns, spools of thread, and various foodstuffs. The place fairly shimmered with silks, satins, taffeta, and brocade as well as the more serviceable materials—cotton and calico. The store always smelled fresh to Anne, full of surprises and items with which one could make a vast array of things. The possibilities were endless.

It wasn't long before the front door opened again and Anne recognized the young mother who entered. "Hello, Madeline," Anne said to the woman who carried a newborn in her arms and tugged along two young girls behind her.

"Well, hello, Anne," Madeline answered her, smiling though her eyes had a weary look about them. "What brings you into town today?"

"A few errands and a treat for Inger. And you?"

"The same. I need a few yards of fabric—I'm making summer dresses for the girls." Madeline motioned to her daughters, twins, who had found Inger and were examining the barrels with her.

"Oh? You know, I've a fair hand with needlepoint and embroidery, but I've never made much by way of clothing. I'd love to learn to make some things for Inger—do you suppose you might show me how sometime?"

Madeline's eyes lit up a bit. The difference was so subtle that Anne wondered if she had imagined it. "I would be happy to teach you how," the woman said. "It would be a welcome change to enjoy some adult company."

"Wonderful! I shall look forward to it."

Madeline motioned to Anne's midsection. "I understand you're expecting—this is your first baby?"

"Yes," Anne said. "I'm a bit nervous, having never done it before. I'm nothing but a puddle of tears some days, too, which doesn't help."

Madeline laughed a bit. "It does pass, although it takes time. I'm still a puddle of tears after this one," she said, lifting the baby in her arms. "With the twins, though, after a few weeks I was feeling fine again."

Anne nodded, momentarily placing on her reporter's cap and assessing the woman's appearance. Fatigue definitely lined Madeline's eyes and face, and a certain sadness seemed to lurk there as well. Deciding the woman needed a friend, Anne set a time and date for her and Inger to visit and asked if she might also bring Ivar's mother along.

Deep in thought about Madeline but not entirely certain why, Anne finally left the woman in the store after paying for Inger's peppermint stick. A man Anne recognized as Madeline's husband passed them as they left, brushing against her shoulder and jostling her into the side of the building. Anne's involuntary grunt didn't elicit so much as an apology or acknowledgement from the man as he continued his way into the store and called out to his wife.

Anne rubbed her shoulder a bit and looked at the now-closing door in some irritation. "Did he hurt you, Mama Anne?" Inger asked, reaching for Anne's hand.

"No, sweet. I'm fine, just a bit surprised."

"Yes indeed," the astute child answered. "He was quite rude."

"Perhaps he was just in very much of a hurry. It must be milking time soon. I imagine he needs to get home to his cattle." Anne clasped Inger's fingers and led her across the street. As they passed the post office, she was hailed by an employee who came running out with a bundle of letters for her. "You just missed these when you were here before, Mrs. Gundersen," he said breathlessly.

"Thank you." She took the bundle with a sense of anticipation. Letters from friends and loved ones—how she looked forward to hearing from them. Atop the stack was a letter from Emily. She smiled at it, missing her cousin and wishing they lived closer. Emily had become a woman that Anne would gladly have counted as a friend even if there had been no relation between them. In addition to that was the fact that Emily and Austin had helped her save Ivar's life, and she would be forever grateful. Anne balanced the heavy stack of envelopes in her hand and was glad there were so many. She would savor these treats for after dinner this evening during her quiet time with Ivar.

Anne waved at Madeline, who by now was leaving the store across the street. Her delight with the mail was momentarily shadowed by worry over this woman she hardly knew as she saw Madeline's husband brusquely exit the store behind his wife and soon take over the lead, walking several paces ahead of the woman and the three children. Anne let Inger ramble incessantly as they walked home and unfortunately registered perhaps half of what the child said. She couldn't shake the memory of Madeline's sad eyes and decided she would make it her new mission to see some happiness sparkle there instead.

Later that evening, as she sat with Ivar over their lovely stack of mail, Anne frowned at Emily's letter. "They're not doing well," she murmured.

"Who's not doing well?" Ivar was absorbed in a letter from a fellow soldier he'd known at Andersonville.

"Emily and Austin."

Ivar looked up, instantly alert. "What is it?"

"Their neighbors are becoming hostile now that the Stanhope family activities are common knowledge."

"How hostile?"

"So far a couple of stolen horses and cold stares. Emily's worried, though." Anne paused. "Emily doesn't worry about much."

Ivar was silent, and Anne glanced up from the letter. "It could get much uglier," he finally said. "Already there's talk of open hostility toward former slaves and their friends."

Anne nodded. "I've heard."

"I will write to Austin," Ivar said. "Tell him they're welcome to move this way—they'll have a home if they need one."

"I'll include your letter with the one I write to Emily." Anne frowned and looked back down at the paper in her lap.

* * *

1 June 1865
Savannah, Georgia

Gwenyth held tight to Joshua and felt tears seep out of her closed eyes. He had made it to her safely! She had hardly been able to believe her ears only moments before when he had quietly crept up behind her in the cookhouse and said, "I wonder if a man might find a meal around here."

"Joshua, I feared for your life," she said to him as he slowly rubbed his hand across her back. "I worried you would be killed before you ever made it this far."

"I'm here, safe and sound," he said and gave her a squeeze before releasing her. He took both of her hands in his and smiled. "My, are you a sight for sore eyes."

"Oh, stop. I look wretched. I've been working in the garden all morning, and I'm filthy."

"You're beautiful. You could be covered in mud and still you'd be beautiful."

"You are a charming devil, aren't you? My mama warned me about men of your kind."

He grinned at her and leaned forward to snatch a kiss from her startled lips. He sobered a bit and looked at her for a moment before closing his eyes and kissing her more slowly, and with more purpose. My, but he had never kissed her before! She decided it was probably a good thing, else she would never have let him go. Just when she was sure she was set to melt into a puddle of mush on the floor, he released her and took a steadying breath.

"I've put you in a compromising position, Miss Gwenyth," he said on a shaky laugh.

"Oh, I don't so much mind," she said, but it came out as more of a whisper than anything.

When he grinned at her again, she felt behind her for a chair at the rough butcher-block table and sat down hard. "I can't believe you're standing here in front of me," she murmured.

He pulled out another chair and sat near her at the table. "I would have walked the whole country to return to you," he said, his eyes serious. "You've been my hope."

Gwenyth put her hand on her heart, emotion thick in her throat. "You know, I worried that you thought you had feelings for me because I nursed you back to health after you'd been shot."

He shook his head with a crooked smile. "Mama Ruth nursed me back to health on more than one occasion. I never felt the same things for her that I do for you."

Gwenyth turned her head away for a moment, awkward with what she wanted to say. "Joshua, I know . . . that is . . . I realize that in the past you were sweet on Emily. I . . ."

He put up a hand to forestall anything further she might say. "I was younger then. She was all I knew, and we were close friends because of our ties to her brother Ben. I thought I loved her more passionately than I really did, but there was something vital missing."

"What was that?"

"I hadn't met you."

"Oh." She nodded a bit, trying to hide her embarrassment.

"I met you after Emily and Austin married, but I was here for a short time, and I was confused and anxious about going north . . . I didn't have time for anything in my head but myself. I wish I hadn't wasted that time—things might have been different. I might have convinced you to come north with me, or I'd have stayed behind with you."

She shook her head. "I was needed here still, and I would never have allowed you to stay behind for my sake. The past is the past, and it's all well and good." Again she averted her gaze from his scrutiny. "I hate to sound so girlish about it. I'm sorry to have mentioned you and Emily—it really is none of my business. I suppose," she shrugged, "I don't know. I would hate to be second in someone's heart."

He smiled and shook his head, reaching for her hand. "Never. You are not second in my heart. I've been waiting for you my whole life."

"Oh, you must stop saying such things," she said, wiping at her eyes, "or I'll never stop crying."

"Let's talk of other things, then," he said, still smiling and looking oddly pleased with himself. "What do you hear out of Washington these days?"

Gwenyth paused and took a breath, trying to collect herself. "Hmm," she said. "Well, on the twenty-ninth, President Johnson proposed his plan for 'Restoration.'"

"And is that the same plan as his Congressional plan for 'Reconstruction'?"

"No, it differs. And this plan offers a general pardon to all persons involved directly or indirectly with the 'existing rebellion.' Except for a few key Confederate figures."

"Jefferson Davis being one, I would think."

Her face brightened a bit. "Oh, and this will be of interest to you! Congress has just equalized pay for its black troops."

Joshua's expression was one of stunned amazement. "I never would have dreamed . . ."

"Isn't it incredible? I believe we have the Radical Republicans in Congress to thank for these kinds of changes. Emily and I have discussed them at some length."

Joshua nodded. "On my way here I saw the beginnings of several new state and local governments that even have black members officiating. I suppose my fear is that as more Southern states are readmitted to the Union, the Republicans will lose their power and be voted out of office by the Southern elite."

"We'll see a backlash, then. A nasty one. There are already rumblings—rumors out of Mississippi that the locals are prepared to punish the former slaves for the South's misfortune."

"Officially or unofficially?"

Gwenyth winced. "Both, most likely. But what we've heard so far is talk of legislation . . . I'm afraid that for us and people like us, times are going to be as uncertain as they have been for the last four years. Lincoln is gone, and we do not have ourselves an ally in Johnson."

Joshua squeezed Gwenyth's hand. "We'll survive. Not only that, we will flourish. And we are going to find joy if it kills us."

Gwenyth smiled at that.

"How are Austin and Emily? And Mary Alice? All healthy and well, I hope."

Gwenyth sniffled and nodded, but she felt herself stiffen a bit with an anxiety that had become a constant companion to her and the rest of the household. "Healthy, yes, but trouble's brewing."

"What sort of trouble?"

"The neighbors and 'better folk' of the city have not taken kindly to the fact that the Stanhopes have been in the slave-freeing business all these years. When they realized that Austin himself was involved, well, they're none too pleased about it."

"I see. Have they been threatened?"

"Not yet. Not directly, anyway. I worry that it's only a matter of time, however."

* * *

The silence of the night was shattered by the sound of crashing glass. Emily and Austin were roused from their sleep by the noise and rushed downstairs to find that a large stone had been thrown through their front window. Upon it was scrawled a message that made Emily's blood boil, then turned it to ice. She looked into her husband's pale face and said, "It's begun."

CHAPTER 19

I would that ye should impart of your substance to the poor,
every man according to that which he hath, such as feeding the
hungry, clothing the naked, visiting the sick and administering to
their relief, both spiritually and temporally, according to their
wants.
—*Mosiah 4:26*

* * *

8 June 1865
Ogden, Utah

Mary watched her sister-in-law with a sense of amazement.
Charlotte was speaking to Ruth as though Ruth were her
mother or grandmother. It had been years since Mary had seen
Charlotte behave with such guileless charm and enthusiasm, and
she supposed the things Ruth had been telling her must be true;
the Birmingham women had undergone some incredible trans-
formations. "I don't know that I'd trust it," Mary had said to
Ruth, who had promptly answered her, "Saul became Paul,
young lady. If he could change, anyone can change."

Charlotte was officially engaged to Earl Dobranski, and she
was in a state of subdued euphoria. She wasn't one given to
histrionics or demonstrations of great emotion, but it shone in

her eyes—the woman was extremely happy. While part of Mary was irrationally jealous that Charlotte suddenly had a favorable relationship with Ruth, she couldn't help but be happy for her. Earl treated her with affection and respect; Mary had never seen that in Charlotte's first husband, William.

"Earl originally had hoped to run for sheriff here in Ogden," Charlotte was explaining to Ruth, "but he was too late in entering the elections. He has a good offer with a building company in Salt Lake City, and he's asked if I will mind living there."

"And will you?"

"Oh, no! I don't mind at all. It will sound harsh of me, I suppose, but I believe I would enjoy living my life away from under my parents' roof. I never imagined such a thing was possible."

The conversation continued, and Mary excused herself from the two women on the pretense of checking on the welfare of the boys, who were playing in Ruth's backyard. She wandered slowly through the charming house and stood for a moment at the kitchen window, where she could observe her son and his cousin undisturbed.

Her mind swirled with thoughts—good ones, mostly. The changes she had seen in Ben's family were positive: Sarah and Jeffrey treated her kindly; it was wonderful to be with Ruth again; Ben was everything she had ever hoped he would be; and her son was growing more attached to her daily. She thought often of religion, however; it was impossible not to living in such a place. The few neighbors they had in the area were kind, for the most part, and Mary had to wonder if they even realized she was black. Her features were classically white, her skin tone light, and she had often been mistaken for a white girl of some exotic descent. She couldn't decide how she felt about that when she looked at her grandmother with such love and pride, knowing full well that Ruth would never be mistaken for a white woman. She even felt a sense of guilt that she might be tempted to pass herself off as white when she and Ruth had personally overcome so many obstacles.

Ruth had begun attending church with Ben in a tiny building down the river; the congregation numbered perhaps fifty on a full day, and Ruth had told Mary that the women, while perhaps not altogether warm, had yet to throw her out of the building. She had even read the book of scripture Ben had given her. She said she believed the Book of Mormon to be a true testament of the Savior, but she was a bit at odds with some of the Saints' philosophies.

Those were also Mary's concerns. Ruth had gone a step further, however, by actually reading the book. Mary had yet to do even that. She was afraid that she would believe it to be true also, and then she would have to finally choose whether or not to embrace her husband's religion. If she ultimately decided against becoming a member, would it not drive a wedge between her and Ben? She couldn't imagine that it wouldn't, despite his reassurances to the contrary.

They often spoke of where they wanted ultimately to live, and Mary was content to remain in Ogden. The railroad was on the horizon, and Ogden was to become a major stopping point for it, bringing new growth and industry to the city. Ben had mentioned that some people at church were concerned that the railroad would bring in scores of non-Mormons certain to change the face of the tiny community, but truth be told, it gave Mary a glimmer of hope that she wouldn't then be one of the few in the area who wasn't Mormon.

William and Elijah played well together, and Mary smiled as she watched them interact. Very rarely did they quarrel, and when they did it was usually over, all forgiven, very quickly. It was amazing, really. They played together and not because William's parents owned Elijah. What a difference had come about for one generation.

Mary shook her head at herself and smiled a bit. She had assumed that when she had her freedom and her Ben, all of her problems would be solved. She had never imagined the complications of religious beliefs factoring into the whole of it. Wasn't it enough to believe in God and be done with it? Why was it so important to commit to one faith over another? They were questions she was going to have to answer for herself—she knew that nobody else could do it for her. She thanked her lucky stars that she had a husband who wasn't pressuring her to see his point of view.

Elijah spied her at the window, and his beautiful green eyes danced. "Mama!" he shouted, followed by something entirely incomprehensible but which she interpreted as an invitation, or perhaps a demand, to go outside and play. With a smile in return, she did.

* * *

8 June 1865
Richmond, Virginia

Jacob had been watching with interest as the city of Richmond and her outlying areas slowly began to be rebuilt. Residents and soldiers who had survived the war had come home to a place they barely recognized, but they did not wallow long in self-pity. With an energy born partly of self-righteous fury at the ignominy of their defeat, they attacked their problems with a vengeance. Crops were planted, buildings were assessed for damage and possibility of reconstruction, and the Freedmen's Bureau and other aid societies from the North did their best to feed the starving, which included most of the South.

Camille was busy from sunup to sundown, and Jacob was glad to see her becoming her former self, following the sad miscarriage. It had taken time, but that time did seem to be healing her wounds. She and Isabelle were working diligently with the Bureau to see people's needs met, and more specifically, seeing to it that "Stubborn Sally" was eating the food they continually supplied to her and her younger siblings.

Politically, Congress continually warred with the new president, and with the South in such a state of chaos, many people were left feeling extremely unsettled. Typically, however, the North flourished. It was the condition of change and confusion that most fascinated Jacob, however, and he was grateful for the change of pace.

He approached the warehouse where Robert was currently working with a team of men assessing damage. The warehouse was one of many buildings that had been demolished by departing Confederate soldiers. Jacob smiled when he saw his younger brother-in-law. Robert was putting his good, analytical brain to positive use for the men with whom he worked.

Jacob waited for a moment until Robert was free before approaching him. "Everything seems to be going along smoothly," he said.

Robert nodded. "I think this one can be repaired relatively quickly. Not like the last one we saw. It'll have to be torn down the rest of the way and completely rebuilt." He lowered his voice and glanced behind him. "They assume I'll be of no use when it comes to the physical labor because of this." He lifted his arm that reached only to the elbow.

Jacob snorted in support of his friend. "They've obviously never seen you work, have they?"

"That's what I told them. I'll just have to prove it to them, I suppose. You know, I'll probably spend the rest of my life proving myself."

"Not to those who matter. We already know."

"Speaking of those who matter," Robert said with a grin and a slight flush, "any chance you've seen my wife this morning?"

Jacob smiled back at him and clapped him on the shoulder. "Working hard, as always. She said she was going with Isabelle and Camille to visit Stubborn Sally. After that, I believe they had a few more visits to make this afternoon."

Robert nodded. "As much as I'm glad we're all doing this, I confess I'd like to kidnap my wife for another honeymoon. I hardly ever see her."

Jacob laughed. "Sad but true. Life intrudes on the best-laid plans."

* * *

When Jacob left him a few minutes later, Robert watched him depart with a fond thought or two. Camille's husband had been nothing but good to him, and he had come to value him as a cherished friend. Camille was becoming more and more herself with each passing day, and Isabelle was slowly starting to heal from her ordeal over the president's death.

There were times when the death weighed heavily on Robert's mind too, and sometimes he allowed himself a moment or two of genuine grief before turning his thoughts elsewhere and losing himself in other activities. Abigail helped him immensely; he couldn't imagine his life without her in it.

Shortly after his marriage to Abigail, Robert had taken some time alone in Luke's old bedroom in his parents' house. He had closed the door and locked it behind him and wandered the length of the room, looking at all the things that used to belong to his brother. Finally, he had sat down on Luke's bed and spoken to him for some time, in hushed tones, about his marriage to Abigail and their hopes for the future. He hadn't really expected a response at all, and indeed he hadn't received one except for a very reassuring feeling of peace. A calmness settled over his mind and heart, and he had felt that Luke had heard him and was also content with events.

Abigail, too, had made her peace with Luke. Shortly after Luke's death, the family had had him disinterred and buried in a family plot in Boston. Abigail told Robert she had visited the grave and placed flowers upon it, shed a few tears, and told Luke good-bye. She, also, felt a sense of tranquility that all was well, and Robert was grateful for whatever forces were at work on the other side. It allowed him and Abigail the peace of mind they needed to move ahead with joy and hope.

* * *

"Sally," Isabelle said to the young woman, "we would like you to know that we're very grateful you've been eating the food we've been bringing to you." There. She'd said something nice. She glanced at Camille, whose lips were twitching in an effort not to smile. Camille had made Isabelle promise that she'd be nice to the young woman for a change.

Sally eyed Isabelle with something akin to intense dislike before finally replying through a tightly held jaw. "Thank you for bringing the food, Miss Webb."

"I trust you and your brother and sisters are healthy?"

Sally nodded once.

"You know, Sally," Camille said, "Abigail—Mrs. Birmingham, that is—recently lost her own mother to an accident."

Isabelle, Abigail, and Sally all looked at Camille for a moment, most eyebrows raised, as Camille flushed. "I just thought you might be interested to know that you're not alone in your feelings of loss."

Abigail came to Camille's rescue with a smile at Sally. "It's true. It hurts for a while, sometimes a long while, and you'll never not miss her, but it will get easier."

The girl's chin raised its customary notch. The women had become accustomed to the defiant movement that really was more a cover for impending tears than anything. The young girl apparently arose each morning and dressed herself in clean but worn clothing and pulled her hair back into a respectable braided coiffure that her mother must have taught her to do. Each time the women visited, usually unannounced beforehand, Sally looked ready to receive guests for tea. Something in Isabelle's heart twisted, now, at the pride evidenced in the younger woman's raised-chin gesture. She had been Sally's age when both of her parents had died, and that sad, familiar show of strength was a trait she saw in herself. Truly, Sally was not much different than the girl Isabelle had been.

The women had come to realize the dire straits the young family must have been in once they got a good look at the parlor. The furnishings were shabby at best and few in number. Sally had gone to great pains to explain to them that the Union soldiers had divested them of their best things. The home itself must have once been a grand affair, but the years of war coupled with a lack of appropriate maintenance had taken their toll. It was but a shell of its former self.

After a few more moments of stiff conversation, the women took their leave. As they walked away from the house and down the street, Camille exclaimed in a huff, "You might not have looked at me as though I had just sprouted horns. I was merely trying to help the poor girl feel better."

Isabelle and Abigail both laughed. "Yes, but you just shot it right out of the blue," Isabelle told her. "There was no prelude, no introduction to the topic."

"Well, she makes me uncomfortable," Camille grumbled. "There's no pleasing her."

"She's hurting," Isabelle said, her smile fading.

"Oh, a fine one you are! Here I must practically *beg* you to be kind to the girl and now you admit she's hurting? Every single time we visit her, I'm forced to listen to you go on and on about how ungrateful she is and how you'd like to just leave her alone for a couple of weeks to see how she fares on her own." Camille glared at Isabelle. "Isabelle Webb, you are making me insane!"

"You're not the first, and I'm sure you won't be the last." Isabelle grinned at her before nodding a couple of times and adding, "Yes, I admit she is hurting. She reminds me of someone I once knew."

"You are an interesting piece of work, you are," Camille said.

"I'm so glad I came along, today," Abigail said. "You two are much more interesting than the army officers at the Bureau. All they do is exchange war stories."

Camille made a face. "Ugh. I have a war story of my own, and I don't care to relive it by talking about it again and again."

"Ironically, though, Robert tells me that your shared experience at Bull Run brought the two of you closer together—forged a bond, if you will. He felt much kindlier toward you after that."

"He did?" Camille smiled. "Well, yes, he's right, and we both noticed it. Things were different after that."

"Which Bull Run? The first or second?" Isabelle asked.

"First. The only one I needed to see. The whole of Washington had turned out for the event. I ponder on it now and wonder at our idiocy. What makes folks think they can show up to a battle site and imagine it will be a day's worth of fun entertainment?" She shuddered. "Almost like people were expecting an evening at the theater or something."

"And even that's not safe anymore," Isabelle murmured. "There are no guarantees. I don't suppose there ever were."

Later that afternoon and toward the evening hours, Isabelle found herself restlessly thinking of Sally. When she finally could stand it no longer, she borrowed Camille and Jacob's horse and carriage and rode out to visit the young woman by herself. It was no longer than five minutes from the boardinghouse where Isabelle and the others were staying to Sally's home, and in that short time, Isabelle began to question her sanity.

With a shrug as though she had nothing to lose, she secured the horse and slowly made her way to the front door, heavily leaning on her cane. Her leg pained her badly at night when she had been moving around on it all day. Worse, however, was her pounding heart. Shaking her head at her own foolishness, she rapped on the door.

A few brief moments later, it was opened a crack by Sally herself. When she saw Isabelle, she opened it a bit wider to reveal a face that was slightly swollen and eyes that were red-rimmed and watery. "What do you want?" the young woman asked her, hostility edging her words.

"I came to have a visit with you, if you don't object."

"I do object. Good night."

"Sally, wait. Please." Isabelle's hand stayed the door that would have otherwise slammed shut in her face. "Please, just for a moment."

"I've eaten all the food you brought. Now leave me in peace."

"No, no, I'm not here to make sure you've eaten. I just want to speak with you."

After an interminable pause, the door opened wide enough to grant Isabelle entry, and Sally led the way to the parlor, where one lone lantern was lit.

"Where are the children?" Isabelle asked her as they sat down.

"Upstairs in the nursery. They're already down for the night."

"Is it usual for them to go to bed so early?"

"Lately it is. They've been a bit ill."

"Why didn't you say something?" Isabelle asked. "We can have a doctor look at them."

"I can't pay for a doctor."

"You don't need to pay for one. The Bureau will provide one."

"The Bureau, the Bureau." Sally turned her face away and stared into the empty hearth. "I've had enough charity from the Bureau."

"It's not charity."

"What is it, then, if not charity?"

"Love."

Sally looked at her through heavily lidded eyes. "Love? Do you call what the Union has done to this land love?"

Isabelle shook her head. "It's so much more complicated than that, Sally. And besides, I didn't come over here tonight to have a political debate with you."

"Then why are you here?"

"I'm here because I understand you. When I was your age, I lost both of my parents. It was me and my younger sister and nobody else. No aunts or uncles, grandparents—nobody. We survived on our own, and it hurt like the very devil."

Sally looked at her wordlessly but with a slightly stunned expression.

"If someone, especially a recent enemy, had come to my door offering help, I would have behaved exactly as you have. But there were so many times—too many times—that my sister and I went to bed hungry. I wish someone had been there to insist that I eat food they provided."

"You say such things easily enough now that the time has passed."

"Yet it's true." Isabelle winced a bit. "I hardly see my sister anymore. She works in Chicago, and we don't keep much in contact. It was a hard life for us, and we eventually grew apart. I accepted work with Pinkerton, and she did other things."

"You worked for Allan Pinkerton?" Sally sat up a bit in her chair and sniffled, wiping her nose with her handkerchief.

"I did. Still do, occasionally."

Sally's interest was clearly piqued, but she was obvious in her attempts to hide it.

"Not everyone has heard of him. How is it that you know who he is?" Isabelle asked her.

"I've read all about him and how he is the first private investigator ever to hire women to work as his operatives."

Isabelle nodded. "That's true."

Sally looked down and traced a pattern on her skirt with her forefinger. Without looking up, she said, "I imagine it was exciting."

"At times it was. Many other times it was mundane. Waiting, watching, listening in on people's conversations, following them around . . . I often found myself wishing I were somewhere else."

Sally cleared her throat and finally looked up at Isabelle. "How did you hurt your leg?"

"I fell out of a window trying to prevent President Lincoln's assassination." Isabelle took a deep breath after her declaration. She had not yet had to explain to anyone other than the Birminghams what had happened to her on that fateful night. The tightness in her chest eased a bit and wasn't as severe as usual when she thought of it.

Sally's eyes were large and round, her mouth forming a soundless O.

"I obviously failed."

"I'm . . . sorry," Sally said.

Isabelle smiled at her. "Are you really? You needn't say so for my sake."

"I find it cowardly to shoot a man in the back of the head," Sally said. "I saw him pass by on the streets when he was here after President Davis left town. I thought Mr. Lincoln looked very tired. He didn't look villainous at all."

"He wasn't a villain. And he cared very much about making things good again for everybody."

"This war, this awful, awful war," Sally began, and bit her lower lip. "My daddy is gone, my mama is gone," she said, and Isabelle heard the tears in her voice. "I was only eleven years old when my daddy left. I was Jenna's age. There are times when I can't even remember his face."

Isabelle nodded her sympathy and let the girl cry. "It will get easier," Isabelle finally said when Sally had wiped her eyes and nose.

"Are you happy?" Sally asked.

Isabelle sat for a moment, too stunned to answer. Was she happy? When was the last time she'd really been happy? "I have happy moments," she said at last. "I am lonesome much of the time, so I find that my happy times come when I am with my friends."

"Why have you never married?"

"I haven't found a man yet who would like to be married to a Pinkerton operative."

Sally smiled. Isabelle was surprised by the girl's expression because she realized she'd never seen it before.

"Sally, some of the other workers and I were looking into your family records," Isabelle said, careful to avoid use of the word *Bureau,* "and we've discovered that you have an aunt who lives in West Virginia. Do you know her well?"

"That would be my mother's sister, Ingrid." Sally's brows drew together in thought. "I don't remember her much—I believe the last time we saw her was before the war, but Mama did often talk of going to stay with her."

"You know, when the dust finally settles and some sort of local order returns here, there will be those who insist you and your brother and sisters are looked after by an adult."

"I can care for us."

"I know you can, but you're only fifteen. You must believe me, folks will intervene. This is why I mention your aunt. I would think it would be far preferable for you to live with a relative who has your best interests at heart rather than someone you don't know."

"It would be preferable for us to be left alone."

"That is not going to happen, Sally. I don't want to upset you, but I do want you to consider your options. Let me help you contact this aunt and see what we can discover about her situation."

"You and your sister were left alone."

"My sister and I ran. We ran until we had no more options, and then we were placed in a home for orphaned girls. I wish we would have had an aunt at our disposal."

Sally's mouth clamped shut.

"Just consider it, and when I see you again, we can discuss it some more. Is that fair?"

Sally nodded. When Isabelle stood and leaned on her crutch with a wince, Sally stood as well and walked her to the door.

"Thank you for allowing me this visit, Sally. I know you didn't want to allow me entrance, let alone speak to me."

"Think nothing of it," the girl mumbled.

"I'll see you again soon." As Isabelle left the house and made her way to the carriage, she wondered if she'd done any good or just wasted her time. One thing was certain, however; *she* definitely felt better.

CHAPTER 20

My son, peace be unto thy soul; thine adversity and thine afflictions shall be but a small moment . . .
—*Doctrine & Covenants 121:7*

* * *

16 June 1865
New York, New York

When Daniel's friend Michael had invited him into town for a before-dinner drink, he had taken him up on the offer for lack of anything better to do with his time. The smells and sounds of the bar, so similar to the one in which he had fought pugilist matches before the war, turned his stomach and yet felt like home simultaneously.

Marie and the mothers were working late at the school, busy with new supplies and equipment bestowed upon them by some wealthy benefactors. Not that she would have cared if Daniel were home—Marie had studiously avoided any contact with him beyond cool conversation since the night he had exploded at her for calling him to task over his drinking. It had been weeks, and he couldn't blame her. He had become someone he didn't recognize, and he was utterly useless to her.

All of the old feelings he used to associate with the bars in his former days came crashing back upon his shoulders. He hadn't realized how much Marie had become a balm for his soul in the time he'd known her. He had come to the bars to fight, not because he needed the money, but because he'd been fighting his anger over his brother's death years before, as well as his own sense of inadequacy.

One night when the fighting had nearly killed him, he had made the decision to enlist in the navy and get far away from the things that haunted him. In that time, he had met Marie and had begun to feel a new sense of life, of joy. Now he was blind—a carpenter by trade who couldn't see. He couldn't care for a wife, much less make her happy. All of the old feelings of doubt were back with a vengeance. He wanted to laugh at himself. Whom had he been fooling to think that he could live a life of happiness with a beautiful woman?

You had a life of happiness with a beautiful woman. You're throwing it away. Daniel stiffened a bit in his chair and wonder if someone had spoken in his ear—someone who sounded suspiciously like his dead father. Michael must have sensed his discomfort, because he asked, "Is something wrong, Dan?"

"No. Nothing." Daniel relaxed a bit and tried to ignore the truth he knew he'd heard in his mind. He ran his finger along the edge of the drinking glass in front of him and imagined what it looked like, judging by the feel. His ears picked up every sound in the room—laughter, discussions, people who were finishing their workdays and stopping for a quick drink before heading home.

Daniel's father had never indulged in drink. First of all, his life had been the farm, but even when he had spare time, he had wanted to spend it with Brenna and the boys. He had seen his family near starvation and ruin in Ireland, so the blessings they enjoyed and worked so hard for in this new land were ones he wanted to share with his family.

Daniel thought of Marie, and his heart tripped. He wanted to be with her, too. So much that it hurt. He had behaved abominably to her, even before his blindness, with his insistence on pursuing a career as a firefighter. It was a noble profession, of that he had no doubt. But he had tossed aside Marie's feelings in the matter and had turned his back on the business he had so lovingly nurtured through the years. Suddenly his carpentry hadn't been exciting enough—he couldn't prove his worth to anyone through it, or so he had thought. Now what he wouldn't give to be able to see his tools and workshop again.

A conversation at the next table caught his attention, and after a moment he wished it hadn't. ". . . nothing like the draft riots last year, though," one man was saying. "There was blood in the streets. Negroes lynched and hanging from trees or beaten to death, and it didn't stop until troops from Gettysburg rode into town."

Michael must have noticed that Daniel heard the conversation, because he said, "You weren't here then, were you, Dan?"

Daniel cleared his throat. "No, I was still away with the navy."

"It wasn't a pretty sight. Wasn't a darn thing we could do to stop it, either. All the firefighters in New York weren't enough, and most of them were rioting as well, anyway."

"I know. The orphanage and school where Marie works was burned to the ground, and many firemen stood by and watched it happen."

Michael was silent for a moment. "I'm sure they had their reasons. It was a hard time for everyone."

"They did have their reasons. It was a colored orphanage."

"Listen, I'm sorry about your wife's orphanage, but you weren't here. You don't understand how frustrating it was for people who didn't think the draft was fair. It wasn't fair, either— what sense did it make to free the black man so he could come north and take our jobs?"

"And we've just been overrun, haven't we, by people who have stormed up from the South to take our jobs?"

"I suppose you can be high and mighty because you enlisted." Michael paused, and Daniel heard him taking a swig of his drink. "Isn't it just too bad that we weren't all so noble."

"My father was shot during the draft riots while trying to save the life of a black man," Daniel said, staring with his sightless eyes down into his drink. "My feelings about the draft riots are a bit raw."

"I'm . . ." Michael appeared to be fumbling for words. "I'm sorry, Dan."

Dan waved a hand in his direction.

"Listen, I need to be getting home. I'll drop you at your place."

Daniel nodded and stood, waiting for Michael to take his elbow and lead him outside to the waiting carriage. As he left the bar, the air around him felt heavy and laden with old pain and old memories—and he wished to never go there again. If he were going to drink himself to death, he could do it from the comfort of his own home.

* * *

"Mr. Holmes, truly, it isn't necessary that you stay. I should think you would want to be on your way home by now," Marie said as she placed freshly folded sheets into the linen closet at the orphanage.

"Nonsense. I wouldn't dream of leaving you ladies unattended this late in the evening." Mr. Holmes looked oddly out of place holding an armful of clean bedding.

Marie's lips twitched. "We're often here quite late, and besides, the ladies who stay here overnight with the children are here as well. We're perfectly safe, you see."

"At any rate, there are still books to be unpacked in the schoolroom, and you will be needing my help with those."

"Very well. If you insist, I don't suppose I can convince you otherwise." Marie finished stocking the linen closet and closed the doors. She then made her way into the schoolroom, calling good night to several of the children who were already snuggled into their beds for the evening. She blew them all one large, collective kiss, and they all laughed and caught it.

"The children do seem enamored of you, Mrs. O'Shea," Mr. Holmes said to her as they reached the adjoining schoolroom and closed the door.

"They're sweet, and I love them," Marie replied. "I was a teacher in New Orleans."

"You don't say. Well, that would certainly explain your easy way with them."

"Marie!" Jenny called to her from across the room where she was unpacking a stack of primers. "There's another box here, if you have a moment."

Marie nodded and crossed the room, amused and irritated that Mr. Holmes was on her heels.

"I see you've brought help," Brenna said from the next shelf over.

"The help insists on staying with us," Marie answered. "Mr. Holmes has very solicitously offered to stay and offer his protection."

Brenna laughed. "Protection from whom, Mr. Holmes? The children?"

"It's very late, Mrs. O'Shea," Mr. Holmes said a bit stiffly. "I only thought to help."

"Of course, of course," Brenna said. After all, her expression seemed to say to Marie, the man *had* given the school a substantial amount of money. "It's very thoughtful of you. We're unaccustomed to the attention, I suppose."

"This surprises me, I admit," Mr. Holmes said. "I should think your husband would make it a point to accompany you home on these late nights." The last was directed at Marie.

She straightened her spine and looked at the man. "My husband is ill," she said.

"I'm sorry to hear that."

"Yes."

The four worked in slightly strained silence for the next several minutes until the majority of the unpacking was accomplished. When Marie stood back and examined the new supplies, some of her agitation melted away.

"These are beautiful, Mr. Holmes," she said and motioned to the new books. "We can't thank you enough for your generous contribution."

"Time spent in your company is thanks enough," Mr. Holmes said, bowing low to the three women. "If you're certain you're well enough to make it home, I'll leave you to it."

"Quite certain, thank you," Jenny said with a smile. With her dismissal, the man took his leave. When he exited the room, Marie sank into one of the students' benches. Brenna looked her squarely in the face.

"Marie," she said, "I've heard your wishes to let Dan heal in his own way, but my patience is running thin. Not only does he look wretched when I *do* see him outside, you also do not look good. You've lost weight, and you look as though you never get a decent night's sleep. I've had enough of this standing aside."

Marie turned her hands palm up. "Do what you will," she said, hearing the weariness in her own voice. "I am running dry of solutions."

"Does he speak to you?"

Marie shook her head. At this, Jenny interrupted. "Do you speak to him?"

"Not much," Marie admitted.

"Girl, whyever not?" her mother demanded.

"He tells me to mind my own business," Marie exploded. "I've tried to help him, to take care of him, but all he does is snap at me."

"That boy may be too big to turn over my knee," Brenna said, "but now that he's blind, perhaps I can catch him unawares."

"Mother!" Marie was shocked that Brenna would be so cavalier about her son's disability.

"Well, it's true enough. I did not raise that boy to behave so abominably."

"But he's lost his eyesight. He feels frightened and useless."

"Pooh! People lose their eyesight every day in this world. Do they snap at their families and turn to drink?"

Marie fumbled for a response. "I'm certain some do—I know I would be terribly afraid if I were suddenly blind."

"If you feel that way," Jenny said, "then why on earth do you not speak to your husband?"

"Mama, I tried. I tried in every way I knew how. It's as though he wants me to leave. And sometimes in his sleep, I hear him crying out to his father that he's failed."

Brenna shook her head and sat next to Marie. "Oh, that boy. He was always trying to please Gavin. What he never understood was that Gavin was already pleased."

"Did Gavin ever tell him?"

"Marie!" Jenny was shocked at Marie's impertinence.

"No, Jenny, 'tis all right. It's a question that deserves asking, and now that you have, Marie, I'm not sure Gavin ever did tell Dan he was proud of him."

The room was quiet as the women sat absorbed in their own various thoughts.

"Did he tell Collin he was proud of him?" Marie asked in muted tones as her mind whirled and she began to fit information together as pieces of a puzzle.

Brenna thought for a moment and then nodded. "Collin was our reckless one, much like Gavin. He took life by the throat and embraced what Gavin saw as the real American dream. Gavin was quite vocal about his admiration for that." She let out a sigh and drummed her fingers on the desktop. "Dan was much more pessimistic about the things that went on here in New York. People were leery, if not downright nasty, to Irish immigrants, and it chafed at Daniel something fierce. Gavin didn't want to see it, or chose not too. Dan had a hard time overlooking it."

The ride home was a quiet one for the three women who were each pondering how to go about helping the same person. When they reached Brenna's farmhouse, she turned to Marie. "Dear, I wonder if you would do something for me."

Marie nodded, and Brenna continued. "Would you wait here with your mama for a bit? I'd like to go speak with my boy."

"Certainly." Marie climbed down from the wagon with Jenny, and the two of them wordlessly entered the home as Brenna continued on down the hill to Daniel and Marie's house.

* * *

When Brenna stepped inside Daniel's home, it was dark. She lit a lantern that hung just inside the doorway and called out to her son.

"I'm here," he answered from her immediate right. Startled to realize he was so close, she nearly dropped the lantern.

"Boy-o, you gave me a fright," she said and made her way to the dining room table where he sat alone.

"Why are you here, Ma? Have you come to tell me Marie's gone back to New Orleans?"

"And why on earth would she go back there, I wonder? So the locals can torch her like they did her home?"

Daniel had the grace to look chagrined.

"And what would make you think she had reason to go anywhere?"

"Where is she, then?"

"She's up at my house with her mother for a visit. I see you've not let Marie cut your hair for a while."

"I wouldn't know."

Brenna scoffed at that. "Can you not feel it? Or did your fingers fall off in that fire too?"

"Mama, why are you here?"

"I suppose I'm feeling a bit sorry for myself that my one son who always took care of me, who always took the time to check in on me, hasn't come by to see me for weeks."

"Well, seeing is the problem, I suppose."

"Your feet don't know the way up the hill? The house hasn't moved. Everything's still in its proper place."

"I haven't much felt up to visiting."

"Well, you're lucky you are, that your da isn't around. If he were, he'd have pounded your door off your hinges by now. To see his son that he was so proud of sitting here doin' nothing? Mercy, he'd have your ears ringing."

"You have me confused with the wrong son, Ma. Collin was the one Da was proud of."

"Posh. Collin nearly drove your da mad. The boy was reckless and foolish, and no matter how much we loved him, we couldn't save him from himself. Now *you,* on the other hand— your da didn't worry about you, except that you were too serious by half. He wanted your happiness above all else, and he was worried you'd never let yourself have it."

Daniel was silent, and it broke Brenna's heart. To see him sitting there defeated, unhealthy, and unkempt raised every motherly instinct she possessed to make it all better. What frustrated her more, however, was the knowledge that she couldn't do it for him.

"I never saw your da more proud than the day he came home after seeing your workshop for the first time," Brenna continued as though merely making casual conversation. "He was so amazed at your talent, and he spread the word far and wide that his son was the best carpenter in the business. After he saw some of the pieces of furniture you made, he told me, 'Brenna, that boy is so good, he could do it with his eyes closed.'"

"He didn't say that."

"Yes, he most certainly did. Proud he was, so very proud . . ." Brenna's voice trailed off as though she were contemplating the past, but in truth she was swallowing her tears. *Gavin, how did we not see that he needed this from you?* she asked her husband. When she had composed herself, she added, "He once told me that no man on earth would ever make a better husband than you would. And speaking of which, I need to get back home and send your wife on her way. Say something kind to her, will you? She's quite concerned for you."

Daniel nodded once but remained silent. Brenna approached him and put her arms around him. She kissed his cheek and again felt the tears swell. Before he would notice, she moved away from him, called her good-byes, and left the house.

CHAPTER 21

And little children also have eternal life.
—Mosiah 15:25

* * *

25 June 1865
Cleveland, Ohio

Ivar was returning from milking the cows when he spied his daughter sitting alone under a tree near the house. Upon closer inspection, he realized she was softly crying, and the sight chilled his blood. Inger was a happy child; she rarely cried. He hurried to her side and sat next to her in the grass.

"What is it, sweet?"

Inger sniffed and wiped at her eyes. "I miss Bestefar."

Ivar smiled at her gently and pulled her onto his lap. He cradled her head against his chest and slowly rocked back and forth. "I miss him too, Inger." He held her close until her tears finally began to subside and she sat up a bit.

"Do you suppose he watches us?" she asked, her eyes moist.

"I'm sure of it. Does that make you happy?"

"A bit. I'd rather he were here watching us."

Ivar laughed and stroked her cheek with the back of his fingers. "So do I. But we must be patient—someday we'll see him again."

"Papa, sometimes you're sad too."

Ivar looked at her in surprise. "What makes you say such a thing?"

"Sometimes you look like you're ready to cry. Is it because you miss Bestefar too?"

It was true, he often felt bouts of sadness, but it was not all owing to his father's death. His memories of the war and his experiences in the prison camp hung heavy at times, and as much as he wished he could forget, he knew he never would. Inger was too young to understand, and so he merely told her that, yes, it was because he missed her bestefar.

After her tears had dried completely, she said she wanted to go and play in the house for a while. He nodded and watched her scamper inside, wishing that grief over her grandfather's death would be the worst thing she would experience in her life. His mood had shifted with her observant comment, and his mind was flooded with images of pain and anguish from the last four years.

He closed his eyes and turned his face upward toward the sky, feeling the warmth of the sun as it shot through the leaves of the tree. Sometimes his time away from this tranquil little farm seemed like a distant dream or something from another life. Other times it was as though his mind was still there. Were he given the choice, however, he would do it all again because it had led him to Anne.

* * *

When Anne left the house with Inger in tow, Ivar was sitting against a tree trunk, apparently contemplating the meaning of life. She blew him a kiss and made her way to her mother-in-law's home across the field. Amanda was waiting for them on the front steps, and so the three began the half-mile walk to Madeline's house.

"You're sure you don't mind coming along again?" Anne asked Amanda.

"Not a bit. She's a sweet girl—she could use a mother in her life."

Anne nodded. "There's something happening in that house. I can't put my finger on it. I just hoped that an extra pair of eyes might be able to spot it."

Amanda tipped her head toward Inger and raised her eyebrows at Anne. Anne smiled with a bit of a wince and whispered, "She's having a sad-missing-Bestefar day."

Amanda made a sympathetic face and murmured a few compassionate words in Norwegian. She ruffled Inger's hair, and when the little one looked up, Amanda took her hand and smiled at her. "Are you all right?" she asked the child.

"I'm just having a sad day," Inger said. "Mama said sometimes she has sad days about her brother. He died during the war."

Amanda nodded sagely. "Yes, yes he did. Mama does have sad days sometimes. Even Bestemor does. Do you know what helps me feel better?"

Inger shook her head.

"I say a prayer."

Inger looked thoughtful, and Anne made a mental note to be more diligent in her prayers with the girl. They said grace over meals and recited a little prayer at bedtime, but Amanda said she often just talked to God as though He were a Father sitting right next to her. It couldn't hurt, Anne had thought, and it would probably be good for Inger.

They reached Madeline's house in short order and entered at her beckoning. Inger ran off to play with Madeline's twins, and Amanda took the baby from Madeline's arms so she could show them her most recent sewing projects. "This is a dress I'm making for the baby," she said. "It's nearly finished, but see here, it needs more lace."

Anne nodded and admired the small dress, making note of a slight tremor in Madeline's hands as she handled the fabric. "Would you like to see what I'm working on for the older girls?" Madeline asked Anne.

"I would love to, although I'm not certain you should see what *I'm* doing," Anne laughed and settled next to the young woman on her sofa. "You gave me the simplest of projects, and I'm afraid it looks rather fearsome."

"Oh, surely not," Madeline said and smiled until Anne pulled the dress from her satchel. "Oh, dear."

Anne laughed long and hard. "You see? I need your help, desperately."

"Oh, I see what you've done," Madeline said and joined in Anne's laughter. "It's simple enough to fix."

Anne glanced around the sparsely decorated parlor and dared give voice to a comment she'd held in reserve on their last visit together. "Madeline, with your talent I would expect to see all manner of decorations in your home. Now, are you a woman like my mother who gives everything away as soon as she makes it?"

Madeline shrugged a bit, her face unreadable. "My husband didn't much care for the way things looked when we married. I had . . . many things about." She sighed and glanced over her shoulder. "My first husband died at Gettysburg. My current husband is actually his brother."

Anne fought to keep her mouth closed. It had wanted to drop open in surprise. "Madeline, I had no idea. It must have been such a challenge for you."

She nodded. "I loved my Bill very much. We were sweethearts from childhood. The twins are his children. My husband, Edmund, is Bill's older brother. He had always expressed an interest in me . . . After Bill died, it seemed only natural . . ." Her voice trailed off, and she left the thought unfinished.

Anne stole a glance at Amanda, who was looking at Madeline with a firmly set jaw. Anne knew that look all too well—if Amanda and Madeline were closer friends, Madeline would have received a tongue-lashing like no other for hitching herself to a man she obviously didn't love. Anne had to pity Madeline, though. Not all women had been raised to believe they could survive without a man.

"I see," Anne said. "So the baby is Edmund's daughter then."

"Yes. He wanted a son."

"Don't they always?" Anne said, trying to lighten the conversation. It was a stretch for her, however; Ivar had never begrudged Inger for being a girl, and Anne's own father had always treated his daughters with the same love and attention as he had his boys.

"Bill didn't," Madeline murmured.

Anne nodded slowly, searching for a reply. Really, though, there wasn't one, and so she remained silent. Conversation eventually turned back to the children's clothing, and Madeline helped Anne fix the mess she'd made of Inger's prospective dress. The hour passed quickly, and at its close, Madeline said, "I must be about dinner now."

No sooner had the words left the young woman's mouth than the sound of a slamming door at the back of the house gave them all a start. "Please, I must get busy. Edmund is early," Madeline said. Her face was pale, and a visible vein thudding in her neck belied her agitation.

Anne nodded, and Amanda passed the sleeping infant back to her mother. They found Inger and bade their good-byes to Madeline and the children, planning another visit together in a week's time.

As they walked back home, Anne was silent for some time. Finally, she asked Amanda, "So what is it?"

"She's still in love with her first husband."

"And you think she never should have married Edmund."

"I wouldn't have."

Anne smiled. "You're also a woman of strong stuff, Mama. I doubt Madeline believed she could have survived on her own once Bill died."

"She reminds me of a frightened little bird."

"Exactly." Anne nodded. "And Bill was probably very tender with her."

"What do you know of Edmund?"

"Very little. I'd be better off asking you, as you've lived here for so many years. Did you know those boys as children?"

Amanda shook her head. "Not much. Only ever saw them in passing. Bill was a friendly boy, always smiling. Edmund was more sullen, if I remember."

"And you didn't know Madeline well?"

"No. She lived farther out. She and Bill must have met in school."

"Hmm." Anne tried to decide if anything at all could be done for Madeline. She couldn't very well try to convince her to forget her first husband—and why should she? If Edmund were a jealous man, however, and begrudged Madeline her memories of his brother . . . after all, he had made her throw aside things from her former life—simple things like decorations for a parlor.

"The house they live in now," Anne said, "it was Bill's?"

"Yes."

"And where did Edmund live before Bill went off to war?"

"With their parents, I believe."

Anne rolled her eyes. The scenario she was piecing together did not paint Edmund in a favorable light. The noble younger brother went off to war, so the sullen older brother stayed behind to claim the house, the wife, and the children.

Amanda glanced at Anne. "You'll be treading on thin ice to go interfering in a marriage, you know."

"I'm sure I don't know," Anne said, trying to look innocent. "I would never interfere in a couple's marriage."

"Anne, there's *nothing* you wouldn't do if you felt the reasons were the right ones."

"Well," Anne sniffed. "Suppose he's not nice to her. He certainly doesn't seem to be."

"That's a different thing altogether. But we have no reason to believe he isn't. Just because she mourns her first husband doesn't mean the second one is hurting her."

"I'm sure you're right."

"No, you're not. You say that to keep me quiet."

Anne laughed and put an arm around Amanda's shoulders. "I would never want to keep you quiet, and that is the honest truth," she said, placing a kiss on her cheek.

"Ah, Anne," Amanda said, putting an arm around Anne's waist. "Such a good daughter you are. Your mother must miss you terribly."

"Oh, my poor mother—I gave her fits."

"No! I can't imagine."

* * *

25 June 1865
Savannah, Georgia

"Out with 'em, Stanhope! We know you're hiding them freed Negroes of yours!"

Austin looked at his wife, who crouched next to him behind the front window. Next to her were Gwenyth and Joshua. A few angry men with torches had gathered on Willow Lane's front slopes, and from the sounds of their voices, they'd had too much to drink. There would be no reasoning with them, so the most Austin could hope for was to keep them at bay until they grew tired and went home.

The shouting and taunting continued until one foolish man grew brave enough to throw his torch through the window next to the front door. With a shout for the others to get back, Austin picked up the torch and hurled it back outside, not really aiming at anyone specifically but still catching the man who had thrown it square on the shoulder. The man cried out in pain and roared his outrage.

Just as Austin was prepared to face an onslaught of torches, he heard a shout from beyond the front borders of Willow Lane. It was with an intense sense of relief that he spied the local authorities on horseback who had come to look into the cause of the commotion.

Austin glanced at the other three with him and felt weak with the pounding of his heart. Emily must have felt much the same, because she sank to the floor. "Perfect timing," she murmured. "Much longer and the house would have been in flames."

Austin stood and looked out the window that was now broken shards of glass. As the crowd dispersed, a couple of men on horseback approached the house and dismounted. Austin unlocked the front door and allowed them entry. They were Union soldiers, career men who had decided to make a life of the military and were now serving as enforcement for the interim governments currently establishing themselves in the Southern states.

"You folks all right?" one of the men asked them.

"Well enough," Austin answered. "Mighty grateful for you fellows."

The man touched his fingers to the brim of his cap. "You send word if trouble returns."

"I'm sure it will," Emily said. "This isn't going to go away."

"I understand it has something to do with your helping colored folk," the second man said. "If that's the case, I doubt there are too many places this far south these days where you'll find any kind of refuge."

"We'll manage," Austin said and glanced at Joshua and Gwenyth.

The first man also looked at the other couple in the foyer. "I wish you all luck," he said and took his leave.

Austin closed the door and locked it, laughing a bit nervously at the folly of it, considering that the window beside it was now smashed. Emily was looking at it and shaking her head. "And we only just had the other one repaired," she said with a sigh.

Austin motioned for the trio to join him, and he made his way into the parlor. The clock in the foyer struck one in the morning, and he suddenly felt very tired. As they sat, he joined Emily on a small sofa. "We can't stay here," he said without preamble. "We're going to have to find another place to live. I've received a letter from Ivar Gundersen that I've given considerable thought. They live in Ohio, and while I appreciate his offer, I've been thinking more along the lines of moving out west. To Utah, where Emily's family is."

Austin may have imagined the spark of interest that lit Emily's eyes at his comment, but they would discuss it later. He was glad to see it, though; he had hoped she would agree with his thoughts on the matter. "Our time here is done." He motioned with his hand to the front of the house. "We're obviously not safe."

"I worry it's because I'm here," Joshua said.

Austin shook his head. "Joshua, this predates you by decades. The locals were furious with us long before now. That's a burden you needn't carry."

Joshua glanced at Gwenyth. "This is a good time to tell you, I suppose, that Gwen and I are to be married."

Emily smiled. "Finally, you say something. I knew it. Congratulations to the both of you. When is this to be?"

"As soon as possible, I suppose," Gwenyth answered.

Joshua nodded. "The sooner the better. We need to decide where we're going, as well."

Gwenyth sighed. "This place is all I've ever known."

"You'll bloom wherever you're planted, you know," Emily told her. "You're a brilliant person—of that I have no doubt. Do the two of you have any preferences for where you'd like to live?"

"Well," Joshua said, "I enjoyed my time in Boston very much and found that I enjoyed working with my hands. I had a

promising position before I enlisted, and I've since been in
contact with my employer. He's said there is a job waiting for
me if I wish it."

Austin looked at Gwenyth. "How do you feel about
Boston?"

"I think I would enjoy it. I suppose I won't know until I'm
there, but what I really would like is for our life together to
start." She motioned toward Joshua.

"Mary loved Boston," Emily said. "She absolutely loved it. I
think it might be a place that will treat you both well." She grew
misty-eyed. "More partings, more changes. How many must we
all endure in one lifetime?"

CHAPTER 22

Oh, may my soul commune with thee
And find thy holy peace;
From worldly care and pain of fear,
Please bring me sweet release.
  —Lorin F. Wheelwright, "Oh, May My Soul Commune
with Thee"

* * *

1 July 1865
Ogden, Utah

Ruth dreamed she was walking along a path that was lined with trees and all kinds of beautiful things. She longed to stray from the path every now and again, but she knew that to do so would halter her progress and keep her from her destination. She wanted to see her husband again, and she knew he was waiting for her at the end of the path.

He had been dead for so many years. He hadn't even seen their daughter, Mary's mother, raised. She missed him so much, even after all this time. What she wouldn't give just to see his face again. Well, she would! She knew he would be there if she could just keep moving and placing one foot in front of the other.

Others jostled her on the path, many not even stopping to apologize for nearly bumping her into the bushes. They were also in a rush to reach the end, and they had little concern for those they might bump along the way. Every now and again, a person would give her a bit of a shove that she was sure was intentional.

More than the rude ones, however, were the kind ones who helped to catch her and break her fall when she stumbled. They embraced her and smiled and wished her well. She took heart from these kind ones and kept her pace.

Finally! She saw him standing at the end of the road—her sweet, sweet husband who waited for her with tears shining in his eyes. Next to him stood their daughter, Lily. They, in turn, stood near someone who exuded warmth and love, which energy gave her the strength to reach them at the end. It was her Savior who stood near her husband—she would know Him anywhere.

As she approached her husband, she noticed that he held a small, black book in his hand. It was the very book of scripture she had received from Ben. She glanced up at her husband's face in surprise and saw him smile and nod a bit. *But,* she wanted to say, *what of all the strangeness? What of their view of us?* She glanced at her Savior. *How can they claim to be Thy people?*

The answer resounded in her head as clear as day. *All things explained in due time . . .*

When Ruth awoke, she felt tears on her face, and her arms ached to embrace her husband. She heard a knocking on her bedroom door and couldn't collect her thoughts enough to bid the person either wait or enter.

The door cracked open a bit, and Mary peered inside. "Mama Ruth!" She rushed to Ruth's bedside and placed an arm around her shoulders as Ruth sat up. "I heard you crying—are you ill? Do you hurt?"

Ruth placed her arms around Mary and cried. "I was with your granddaddy and your mama and my Lord," she said. "I want to go back there again."

"Oh, Mama." Mary stroked her hair and rocked slowly back and forth, much as Ruth had done for her as a child.

"It's true. He told me the book is true," Ruth cried. "I knew, of course, but he held it there in his hand."

"What book, Mama?"

"The Book of Mormon. You must read it, Mary, and we will discuss it. Promise me you will."

"I will. I'll read it. Perhaps you should rest now."

"Just stay with me for a moment longer."

Mary nodded and settled back against the pillows, her arms still firmly around her grandmother. Her own tears silently fell on Ruth's graying head as she considered the dream. Ruth was not a person given to strange whims or flights of fancy. The dream must have been very real to her. Ruth herself had taught Mary from the Bible, and knowing the importance of dreams, Mary could hardly dismiss this one.

Finally, Ruth settled back into an easy sleep, and Mary lay awake, thinking.

* * *

Salt Lake City

Ellen Dobranski glanced at her new daughter-in-law while she kneaded the bread that lay in a lump before her on the countertop in her kitchen. Charlotte sat at the table looking content, feeding William his breakfast. "Thank you for inviting us over again," Charlotte said. "I worry we'll overstay our welcome."

"Nonsense," Ellen said. "I enjoy the company, and with Earl leaving the house so early, there's no reason for you and little Will to breakfast alone. Are you enjoying your new house?"

"It's wonderful," Charlotte said. "I've never had a home of my own."

"It's not as big as what you're used to."

"It doesn't matter. I do believe I'd be happy these days in a shack," Charlotte laughed. "And Will so adores Earl. What a wonderful father he's become."

Ellen's heart melted a bit more each time Charlotte spoke so highly of her Earl. She had worried a bit that Earl was taking on a spoiled Southern belle whom he would never be able to satisfy, but Charlotte was proving herself to be a woman of whom Ellen approved.

"He does take well to children. Always has, that boy."

Charlotte nodded. "I believe it. He knew just how to handle Will from the very beginning." She shook her head. "That long wagon trek, I hardly knew what to do with myself. I felt as though I'd stepped off the face of the earth."

Ellen smiled. "It must have been strange for you."

"It was. And with my mother nearly beside herself, it was difficult."

"How is your mother? It's been several weeks since my last visit to her."

"She's well. I believe she's worried about Ruth, though."

Ellen looked up from her bread dough. "I wasn't aware Ruth is ill."

Charlotte nodded. "She seems to be worsening. She coughs up blood more and more frequently these days, and her energy is severely limited."

"Has anyone seen to her?"

"We've had doctors visit, but they all say the same thing— she has consumption, and there's little to be done." Charlotte winced. "I don't like to think about it. None of us are ready to let go of her yet."

"Perhaps I'll pay her a visit soon."

Charlotte looked up with such hope in her eyes that it saddened Ellen. "Do you have something that can help her? Medicine or a special herb, perhaps?"

Ellen hated to disappoint the young woman. "I'm afraid I don't have a cure," she said with regret. "But I can help ease her pain and discomfort."

Charlotte's face fell, and she turned her attention to her son with a nod. "I'm sure she would appreciate any help at all," she said.

"What of this new project Earl's company has been commissioned to do?" Ellen said, seeking to distract Charlotte from her melancholy.

"It's rather odd, really. From what Earl says, Brigham Young has an idea for a meeting hall, and construction is to begin in September."

"Why is that odd?"

"Well, the design itself seems strange to me. From Earl's description, it seems rather like an overturned washbasin. Its design will accommodate many people, and the sound will travel well throughout the entire room. That in itself is admirable, really, but I can't say as I've ever seen a building that looks like this one will."

"It won't be the first time we've done something strange around these parts," Ellen said. "And speaking of which, what do you think of the Mormons?"

"Generally friendly, hardworking. Of course, I married one, so that should say I speak highly of them—of you." Charlotte flushed.

"Do you know much about the religion itself?"

"Not much. Earl and I have had a few discussions, but nothing beyond that."

"It's really very simple, Charlotte," Ellen said as she wiped her hands on a dishtowel. "This is Christ's restored church. Just as it was in days of old."

Charlotte nodded. "Earl has suggested I read the Book of Mormon."

"That would be a mighty good place to start. Now then," she said to William, who had finished his breakfast and was straining to be let down from the table, "shall we weed the garden? I need some helpers, you know."

William trotted along behind Ellen, who led the way out into the vegetable garden at the rear of the house. Pointing to each weed and bending over to show the boy how to pull them, she oversaw his amateur attempts at weeding.

"Mrs. Dobranski," Charlotte said, and Ellen looked up at her daughter-in-law.

"Yes?"

"Will you think less of me if I decide I don't care to be a Mormon?"

"Certainly not. You're good for my son, and that's my first concern. For your own peace, however, I do hope you look into it and find it to your liking."

Charlotte nodded. "I will try."

* * *

Ogden, Utah

Ben shook hands with the man who was to be his new employer. "Thank you, sir," he said. "I'll give you my best."

"I have no doubt," Mr. McPhee replied. "Mr. Brian from the Salt Lake Telegraph office recommends you highly. Said you were one of the most dedicated workers he ever had."

"Thank you, sir."

"Listen, it's late in the day now. Go home and come back in the morning. Fair enough?"

"Fair enough." Ben said his good-byes and left the downtown telegraph office. The streets were dusty and sparsely populated, both in businesses and residences. The view of the mountains, however, was incredible. He had forgotten how much he loved the landscape, and the valley that now housed his small family was beginning to feel very much like home. The city was nestled in an area just at the foot of the mighty mountains, which were green in the spring, brown in the summer, and white with deep snow in the winter. The mountains were like giant arms that encircled their residents, and some of Ben's favorite moments lay in watching the morning sun climb over them and bathe them in a beautiful glow. The early morning air was exhilarating, and he loved watching the sunrise from his comfortable vantage point in Ruth's backyard.

Talk of the coming railroad was big in Ogden; rumor had it that Brigham Young was disappointed that Salt Lake City wasn't to be the hub that Ogden was to become. Ben was relieved, however, that the railroad was certain to bring in new blood, and he and Mary had discussed it numerous times. His conversations with Ruth over his religion and Mary's race had caused him much thought and not a little anguish. He was often blessed, however, with reassurance in his heart that all would be well concerning it. And with the promise that the community would most likely evolve in a diversified manner, he was becoming of a mind with Mary—that Ogden just might prove to be a good home for them.

Ben began walking up the hill that led to Ruth's home, his brow furrowed in thought. He was glad to have employment secured; he had nearly exhausted his savings over the last few years, and at any rate he felt restless without some kind of work to keep him occupied during the day.

He was worried about Ruth, though. Mary had tearfully returned to their bedroom early that morning to tell him of Ruth's dream. "She's near the end, I can feel it," Mary said. "If anyone deserves a rest, she does. I'm just not ready to let go of her yet."

"None of us are, sweetheart," Ben had told her, and it was true. Ruth was a rock, a solid foundation for the family, and they all depended on her, including his own mother. Sarah still denied that there was anything seriously wrong with Ruth, despite evidence from the doctors and facts they could all see with their own eyes.

It was all a part of life, really, Ben told himself. People died. Luke had died right in his arms, and Ben had still survived. The sting hurt less over time, although the emptiness still remained. He knew it would hurt when Ruth died, but life would continue. Tears burned in his eyes, and he felt foolish to be crying as he walked up the street.

By the time he reached Ruth's home, he had pulled himself together. He entered and found Ruth seated in the parlor, wrapped in a blanket despite the warmth of the summer after-noon. "How are you feeling?" he asked her and sat next to her on the sofa.

"Well enough," she said before breaking into a coughing spasm.

"And where is Mary?" he asked.

"She was hovering too much," Ruth said with a weak smile. "I sent her off to play with Elijah and Rose."

Ben nodded. Elijah was now staying with them as Charlotte and William had moved to Salt Lake City. The boy seemed to be adjusting well enough and had bonded beautifully with Mary. Rose, Mary's younger sister, also had moved her things into Ruth's home, but the bulk of her day she still spent with Clara. The two had been companions from birth and were inseparable. She seemed to be enjoying Mary's company after being apart for so long, so for the most part, the days were filled with happiness for all concerned.

Ben took stock of Ruth's appearance—her face was entirely too pale for his liking. "Have you eaten anything today?" he asked her.

"A bit. Mary forced some broth down me."

"Are you hungry now?"

"No. Ben, listen." Ruth paused for a moment, thinking. "I want you to baptize me."

"Are you certain? You had so many reservations . . ."

"There are things I am now willing to leave in God's hands and accept on faith. I knew that book of scripture was truth from the moment I first read it."

"I'll be happy to baptize you, Ruth. When would you like me to?"

"As soon as possible, but if I can, I'd like to wait for Mary."

Ben looked at her for a moment. "Ruth, you may be waiting for a long time then, I'm afraid. I don't know that Mary has any interest at all in the Church."

"She promised me she would read the Book of Mormon."

"Very well. We'll give her some time."

"Did she tell you of my dream?"

Ben nodded. "I understand it must have been wonderful."

"It was! There he was, just waiting for me . . . and my sweet Lily . . . I can't begin to tell you how beautiful it was. I didn't want to wake up. I wanted to stay there with them forever."

Ben clenched his teeth, determined not to let Ruth see his emotion. "You'll have your chance soon enough," he managed.

"Sweet Ben, I will miss you. I will begin work on a new home, though, all right? Just as I came here and prepared this house for all of us, I'll do the same there."

Ben settled next to Ruth on the sofa and placed an arm around her frail shoulders. He pulled her close and held her for a long time, neither one saying a word.

* * *

7 July 1865
Washington, D.C.

Isabelle had been closely following the prosecution proceedings of the conspirators who had been rounded up, tried, and found guilty for the assassination of the president. President Andrew Johnson and Secretary of War Stanton were convinced that Booth and his conspirators had somehow acted on orders from the Confederate government, even going so far as to suggest that Davis himself was behind the plot. But for now, there were four who were sentenced to hang.

She stood in the arsenal grounds of the Old Penitentiary Building with a large crowd as the four people were brought forth and climbed the thirteen steps to the hanging platform. Isabelle wasn't sure what she expected to feel—a sense of vindication, perhaps? All she knew for certain, as Booth's associates were led up onto the scaffold, was a deep stab of anger. Lewis Powell, George Atzerodt, David Herold, and Mary Surratt each took seats upon the platform as the charges against them were presented.

Isabelle shifted a bit in the hot sun and adjusted her bonnet. She wore a day dress of bright red calico, perhaps her own morbid way of celebrating the event, and winced at the tightness of her corset. She should have had Abigail loosen it a bit for her that morning before leaving for the capital. The confines of her clothing somehow seemed worse than usual in the oppressive heat of the day.

General Winfield Scott Hancock oversaw the proceedings, and General Hartranft read the charges against the four conspirators while someone held an umbrella to shield Mrs. Surratt from the sun. Isabelle knew a momentary flash of compassion for the woman; she deserved to spend time in prison, perhaps, but her own son, John—one of Booth's main accomplices—was not even present. He had fled the country, probably for Canada, but had yet to be captured. It didn't seem fair that, although Mrs. Surratt had provided a place for the insane group to meet, her son was free while she died in his stead.

Isabelle knew from speaking with Pinkerton that it was rumored General Hancock did not want to see Mrs. Surratt hang; she wondered if he would delay the proceedings while hoping for word of a stay on the older woman's account. Finally, after some time, it became clear that no word would be forthcoming, and the prisoners were ordered to stand.

Isabelle's heart increased its rhythm as cloth sacks were placed over the heads of the accused and ropes put around their necks. Sweat trickled down the back of her neck and was absorbed into the material of her dress, and she knew that her underclothing beneath her corset was drenched both from the heat and from the anxiety of the moment. Lewis Powell, from beneath his hood, shouted, "Mrs. Surratt is innocent and doesn't deserve to die with us!"

Isabelle's heart was in her throat as Atzerodt yelled out, "Good-bye, gentlemen. May we all meet in the other world!" She clenched her teeth as her breathing increased, wanting the thing to be done. Finally, General Hancock clapped his hands, and the board was knocked out from beneath the four, leaving them to sway morbidly in the summer sun.

As Isabelle left the stockyard to return to her friends in Richmond, she found herself shedding tears, and the only thing holding gulping sobs inside was her corset. She relived the moments of terror and feelings of utter helplessness she had experienced in Mrs. Surratt's boardinghouse when she had realized the president was about to be murdered and she was helpless to prevent it. Her mending leg throbbed as though in punctuation to her feelings, and she suddenly couldn't wait to leave the city.

Voices trailed around her as though coming from a great distance, murmurs that the country had just seen its first execution of a woman. The press was present in full force, and Isabelle knew she would be reading all about the day by the morning edition of any one of a number of newspapers. She had even seen a large box camera set up on the threshold of the stockyard to immortalize the event on photographic plates.

Was the execution just? Isabelle didn't know. The only one thing she knew for certain was that she didn't want to think about it anymore. With a shuddering sigh, she mopped her tears on her handkerchief and wiped her nose, shielding her face from others by pulling her bonnet closer about her face. She couldn't remember a time when she'd ever cried in public. Regardless of the justice or injustice of Mrs. Surratt's punishment, Isabelle determined to put it behind her. She straightened her shoulders and made her way into the city streets with the crowd around her.

CHAPTER 23

And ye will not suffer your children that they go hungry, or naked . . .
—Mosiah 4:14

* * *

11 July 1865
Richmond, Virginia

Camille sat on the orphanage floor with one child on her lap and one on either side. She read to them from a storybook that she had enjoyed as a child and was content to see their fascination with it. The children were refugees, really, a mixture of children varying in skin hues and heedless of their differences or similarities. They were all children without parents, and they didn't notice much beyond that.

Those who Camille might have guessed would object to the desegregated nature of the orphanage were high enough in status that they could afford to be apathetic; the place was full of neglected, poor children. What did it matter, black or white? Beneath them was beneath them, and that was the end of it. Surprisingly enough, Camille and the others were learning, it was the middle to lower classes of white citizens who objected to a mixing of the races. They were stubborn in clinging to old tradition and refused to allow "coloreds" to be on equal footing with them.

The children were beginning to thrive on the attention they had received in just the few weeks since the orphanage had opened. Their little stomachs were filling with good food, they were bathed daily, and their clothes were repaired and regularly washed, and in some cases they were outfitted in entirely new clothing altogether. They were given shoes and a few personal belongings; they had kind, gentle hands to see to their welfare each day. It was more than many of them had ever had.

Each day, well-meaning citizens rounded up more children who had been living on the streets and the outskirts of town, and Camille worried that eventually they would have to start turning them away. There were only so many beds, and unless the Bureau could fund another orphanage, there were young ones who would still be without homes.

The child Camille held in her lap was a two-year-old girl of mixed parentage. Her hair was curly and unruly, the texture like that of the little black child who sat at Camille's right, but this girl's hair was blonde. Each morning when Camille arrived to help the orphanage workers get the children up and going for the day, this little girl, Iris, ran to Camille with her hair ribbons and demanded that she make her "look pretty."

Iris was slowly worming her way into Camille's heart, and it worried her because she knew the day would eventually come when she would have to say good-bye. How she wished she could take *all* of the children home with her to Boston when she and Jacob decided it was time to leave. It wasn't a realistic dream, though, and fanciful as she was, Camille knew better than to indulge in such thoughts for very long.

Across the room, Abigail sat with a young boy in her lap. He was roughly six years of age, as near as the adults could tell, anyway, and he walked with a severe limp. Something had happened at birth, or perhaps in the womb, to impair his development, and one leg was twisted and hadn't grown correctly. Camille suspected that Abigail was having the same trouble with young Jeremy that Camille was having with little Iris. The children were so trusting and loving, and it was hard to be angry with them for long, even when they were naughty.

As for Isabelle, she hadn't so much as cast a shadow on the threshold of the orphanage. Sally had taken ill with a severe fever—they could only assume the same one that had taken her mother—and Isabelle spent every free moment with the girl that she could. Camille worried about the contagious nature of the fever for Isabelle's sake, but Isabelle wouldn't hear of anyone else caring for Sally. The younger brother and sisters had gone to live with their aunt in West Virginia, but the aunt had requested that Sally not join them until she was well. Isabelle had muttered something vile under her breath about the woman when she had heard that news, but willingly—insistently— stated that she could care for Sally herself.

"Again, again," the children chanted to Camille, who had reached the end of the story.

She laughed. "Very well. But I'm afraid you'll tire of the story before long."

In response to her comment, Iris tapped the book with her little forefinger. "Again," she said.

"Again it is, then," Camille said and turned back to the first page.

* * *

Across town, Isabelle sat with Sally as the girl's fever continued to soar. Isabelle was exhausted. She had sat up with Sally through the long night, bathing her forehead in cool water and listening to her delirious ravings as the fever seized her brain. The things she heard broke her heart. Sally cried out for her mama and papa continually and occasionally mentioned her brother and sisters who were now safely in West Virginia.

Isabelle tried in vain to help the girl eat. What she did manage to get into her stomach came back up mere moments later. She drizzled water into her mouth on a regular basis, but Sally's lips were becoming cracked and dry with her body's lack of fluid. The doctor had come and gone three times already, offering Isabelle no more advice than to do what she was already doing.

Isabelle prayed, sang songs, and told Sally stories until she had nearly exhausted her repertoire, which was quite extensive if she did say so herself. Her sudden attachment to the young woman caught her by surprise, but she was unwilling to leave her side until the bitter end, if need be.

The hour was approaching late afternoon, and Isabelle sat next to Sally's bedside in the front parlor, which was cooler than the bedrooms on the second level. The day was sultry and uncomfortable; Isabelle had stripped down to her petticoats and chemise and dared someone to come to the door. She fanned Sally's face with an elegant Indian fan she had found in Sally's mother's bedroom and dripped beads of water over the girl's face and into her parched mouth.

Sally moaned and turned on her side, opening her eyes. This time, her gaze was lucid and focused on Isabelle's face. Isabelle immediately dropped the fan and reached for a cup of water she had nearby. With a gesture for Sally to rise up a bit, she helped the girl drink some sips of water before laying her gently back down on the makeshift bed.

"My eyes are burning," Sally said.

"I know, sweet girl. You have a dreadful fever. Here, let me rinse out this cloth, and we'll put it on your eyes."

She dipped the cloth into the basin of water on the side table and placed it, fairly dripping, onto Sally's burning eyes and forehead.

"Am I going to die?" Sally asked her in a voice that was reed thin.

"Not if I can help it," Isabelle answered her.

"My mama died."

"I wasn't here."

"How long have I been sick?"

Isabelle dipped the cloth in the basin again and wrung it out loosely. "Nearly a week."

"So today is the . . ."

"Eleventh."

"Well, how do you like that," Sally said and coughed. Isabelle helped her down a few more sips of water, after which the younger woman replied, "Today is my birthday."

"The eleventh of July is your birthday?"

"Yes, ma'am. I'm sixteen years old today. When I was a young girl I rather imagined myself betrothed by now. That cursed war got in the way."

"Didn't it though? That cursed war got in the way of a lot of things. You just have to get yourself better so that we can find you someone to be betrothed to, now that the war is over."

"Mmm," Sally said and shook her head slightly from side to side, then winced with the movement. "I don't know that I'd like to be betrothed just yet. Perhaps I'll become a Pinkerton operative."

"You may do whatever you'd like," Isabelle said with a slight smile.

"Did the town step out to celebrate the Fourth of July last week?" Sally asked with as much of a smirk as she appeared to be able to muster.

Isabelle laughed out loud. "What a sense of humor you have, Sally. The troops here celebrated, and many of the freed slaves did as well, but no, I'd say that not many locals were happy to celebrate."

"I'm not surprised."

"It's your country too, you know," Isabelle said softly and without rancor. "It always was."

"I suppose it was," Sally said, her tone matching Isabelle's. "My lips hurt."

"I'm sure they do—they look like the Sahara." Isabelle helped Sally sit upright again for another drink.

"Have you been there? To the Sahara?"

"Not yet." She laid Sally back down.

"I think I'd like to go there sometime. And you know, ever since my mama received that fan," she said, gesturing to the sideboard where she must have seen the fan resting, "I've wanted to go to India."

"I'll make a proposition to you, Sally," Isabelle said, resting her elbows wearily on her knees. "If you get yourself better, I'll take you to India."

"You will?" Sally rolled to her side and lifted the cloth off her eyes, squinting at Isabelle in pain despite the low light. "You won't make me go and live with my aunt?"

"I won't make you do anything you don't want to do. You're practically a woman now. I have but ten years on you."

"You're twenty-six years old?"

"Or so."

Sally smiled a bit through her cracked lips. "My mama didn't like to admit her age either. Funny—my papa didn't have a problem admitting his."

"Men usually don't. That's because they become distinguished as they age. Women merely age."

"My mama was beautiful."

Isabelle winced in pity for the young girl, glad she couldn't see her reaction because of the cloth covering her eyes. "I'm certain she was," Isabelle said. "In fact, I've spent some time looking at your photographs. You have a beautiful family."

Sally was silent for a moment. "There's not much left of my beautiful family."

"They live on in your heart. Your mama and papa are in you."

"Just as yours are in you?"

Isabelle smiled and closed her eyes. She'd never considered it. "Yes, now that you mention it. Mine live on in me."

* * *

Jacob knew he was in trouble the moment little Iris looked up at him with her big brown eyes and lifted her arms up to be held. "Oh dear," he said as he hoisted her into his arms and smelled her sweet, freshly scrubbed skin and hair, "Cammy was right."

Robert, who stood to Jacob's side, laughed. "We should never have come here, you know."

"Well, hello," Abigail said as she approached Robert and kissed his cheek. "Have you men come to see us safely home?"

"Actually, yes. It's much later than usual," Robert said.

"I know." Abigail motioned with her head to an adjoining room whose door was closed. "Cammy's in there. A young mother came in today, and she's been laboring for hours now."

"How young?"

"Fourteen, fifteen, maybe."

"You're not serious," Robert said.

"Very. She worked on a plantation and was all but turned out into the street. She doesn't know where her family is, or even what's become of them. The father of the baby is dead."

Jacob frowned as he gently bounced Iris in his arms. "I don't mean to sound callous, but I don't know that Cammy should be in there. If she should have a relapse into her own bad memories . . ."

Abigail shrugged. "She insisted, Jacob. Wild horses couldn't have held her back."

Iris laid her little head on Jacob's shoulder and yawned. In her arm she held a small doll that she cradled next to her body. Jacob rubbed her back and looked around for a place to sit.

Abigail pointed to a nearby rocking chair and smiled as he settled himself into it, looking more than a little unnerved.

"I'll see how long Camille plans to stay," Abigail told him. "But first, Robert, there's someone I'd like you to meet." She led her husband by the hand across the room to a far corner where the boys' beds were situated in a row. Some of them held children who were already sleeping, exhausted from having played hard all day. On one, however, sat a boy who looked at a book.

"This is Jeremy," Abigail said, and Jeremy looked up from his book. "Jeremy, I'd like for you to meet my husband, Mr. Birmingham."

Jeremy slid to the edge of his bed and awkwardly stood, offering Robert his hand. He balanced most of his weight on his one strong leg. Robert swallowed the sudden lump that had formed in his throat at the grand gesture and show of respect coming from such a thin little frame. He extended his hand to Jeremy and said, "How do you do? It's a pleasure to meet you, Mr. Jeremy."

Jeremy nodded. "Fine, thank you. How d'you do, sir?"

"I am well, thank you." He gestured for Jeremy to return to his seat on the bed and he pulled a chair over to the bedside for himself. "I see you're reading a book?"

Jeremy nodded. "I's only jus' learnin'. Miz Abby's teachin' me."

"It's a fine thing, to know how to read."

"I'll be the firs' ever in my family."

"And where is your family, Jeremy?"

"Gone. Mama died of the fever, and Daddy done got sold las' year. Las' we heard, he died of the fever too."

"I'm very sorry to hear that. My brother died not long ago. It's very hard, isn't it?"

Jeremy nodded, his expression solemn. "I miss 'em somethin' fierce. Mama more, though. Daddy never did like me much."

Because of his infirmity? Robert didn't ask, and Jeremy let the subject drop. "Tell me about your book," Robert said and barely noticed when Abigail slipped away to check in with Camille.

* * *

"She's so small," Camille whispered to Abigail after pulling her aside and out of the young mother's earshot. "The midwife is worried."

Abigail glanced at the young woman who lay writhing in pain on the small bed. A couple of other women from the orphanage stood close to her head, murmuring words of encouragement to her.

Camille knotted her hands together and appeared not to notice it. She was so worried for the girl, Angelina, that her stomach hurt. Abigail must have noticed her discomfort, because she said, "Jacob and Robert are here to take us home. Are you ready to leave or shall I tell them you're staying?"

"I'd like to stay."

"Are you certain? I don't know that you should, Cammy."

"I want to be here for Angelina. If she loses the baby—even if she doesn't—she's going to be so sad and confused . . . I don't want to leave her."

"Well enough. I'll tell the men. Would you like Jacob to wait?"

"No, no. There are enough beds here. I'll just stay the night." Camille turned back to Angelina as the young girl cried out again in pain. She hurried back to the bedside and barely registered Abigail's departure.

The hours continued, and still Camille stayed close to Angelina's head, speaking to her, trying to keep her distracted and clenching hands with her when the pain became unbearable. It was well into the wee hours of the morning before the baby finally emerged into the world, and Angelina's cries split the night with a sound unlike anything Camille had ever heard.

Tears stung her eyes as she ached for the girl who was but a child herself.

The baby was apparently healthy, if not a bit small, and the midwife motioned for Camille's help as some of the other orphanage workers came running into the room. She hurriedly wrapped the baby in a clean cloth and thrust the quiet little girl into Camille's arms. "I must hurry," the midwife said. "She's horribly torn and losing a tremendous amount of blood."

Camille glanced at Angelina's worn body and felt the blood begin to drain from her head. "Stay with me," the midwife snapped at her and finished the business of cutting the baby's cord. "Now, take the baby to her mother."

Camille did as she was told, rubbing some of the blood and fluid from the child's head and face as she made her way to Angelina's head.

"Angelina, sweet," one of the other women was saying. "Come dear, open your eyes. Angelina . . ."

By the time the sun rose, Angelina was dead. Camille held tight to the infant, relinquishing her only long enough that she could be fed by a wet nurse. "Please, just let me hold her for a bit longer," she asked the other women who would have taken the child to give Camille some rest.

"Sweet girl," she said in a tired voice as she rocked the baby. "Let me tell you about a very brave young woman. Her name was Angelina, and she was your mother." Tears fell from Camille's eyes and onto the baby's head.

CHAPTER 24

The errand of angels is given to women, and this is a gift that as sisters we share.
—Emily H. Woodmansee, "As Sisters In Zion"

* * *

15 July 1865
Salt Lake City, Utah

Mary stood for a few uncertain moments on Charlotte's doorstep before finally finding the courage to knock on the door. It wasn't long before she heard footsteps sounding from inside the house, and then Charlotte opened the door, the look of surprise on her face unmistakable.

"Mary! What on earth are you doing here? Come in, come in." She opened the door wider and ushered Mary into the front parlor, which was situated to the left of the entryway. Mary looked around herself in curiosity; she had yet to see Earl and Charlotte's home. The woodwork adorning the ceilings and the railing on the front staircase leading to the second floor was simple but beautiful, and it shone as though it had been recently polished.

"Oh, Charlotte, your home is just beautiful," Mary breathed as she placed her bonnet and gloves into Charlotte's waiting hands.

Charlotte beamed. "Earl did all of it. Isn't it lovely? I'm so very proud of him."

Mary nodded and took a seat at Charlotte's gesture. "You have every right to be. It's a work of art. His craftsmanship is every bit as impressive as anything I ever saw back east."

"I know. He's wonderful." Charlotte's eyes danced, and a becoming flush adorned her cheeks.

"You seem so happy, Charlotte, and I'm happy for you. I've never seen you so beautiful."

"Oh, Mary." Charlotte's eyes misted a bit, and she blinked. "What a wonderful thing for you to say, and I'm grateful for such a compliment because you have seen me at my very worst behavior. I feel like a completely changed person." She paused for a moment and then asked, "Now, what brings you so far from home?"

Mary hesitated before answering. How was she possibly to tell this woman with whom she had very little in common other than an unpleasant past that she'd experienced a nagging feeling over the past several days that she needed to come for a visit? "You know, Charlotte, I've been pondering many things for a few weeks, and I've just felt that maybe I've needed to talk to you about them." She spread her hands wide. "I'm quite confused myself, but here I am."

"Well, isn't that interesting? What sorts of things have you been pondering?"

"I've been reading Ben's book of scripture lately and wondering about many things . . . this culture we now live in . . ."

Charlotte nodded with a smile. "Earl's mother gave me her copy of the Book of Mormon, and I'm nearly finished reading it."

"What do you think of it?"

"Amazingly enough, and especially after talking with Earl about it, I find I'm believing it."

"Do you think you might ever be baptized?" Mary asked her.

"I don't know. I suppose if I believe the book, then baptism would be the logical next step."

"But . . . do you not wonder about some of the practices of this church? What of the polygamy?"

Charlotte let out a breath and pursed her lips in contemplation. Her blue eyes studied the fireplace for a moment before she nodded. "I wondered about it, and from what I understand, it was necessary as a way to stabilize and expand the population when the pioneers first arrived here."

"Then why is it still practiced?"

Charlotte shrugged. "I'm not certain—perhaps habit? I do know that the Lord doesn't intend for it to last permanently."

Mary's eyes widened a bit. "How do you know this?"

"It's in the Book of Mormon itself. The Lord specifically states that such a thing is to be practiced only during certain times of necessity and only under His express direction."

Mary frowned. "I don't remember that."

"I'll be happy to show you—it's in the first portion."

Mary nodded absently. "There is another thing . . ."

"What other thing is that?"

Mary glanced at Charlotte with her blonde hair and blue eyes and wondered if she'd made a huge mistake in considering confiding in a woman who used to view her as property. Taking a deep breath, she plunged ahead. "I'm black. Half, anyway."

Charlotte's brows drew together in confusion. "And?"

"And I will not be allowed to receive any temple blessings because of it."

Charlotte laughed a bit. "I'm sure you're mistaken," she said, a smile still hovering around her mouth.

Mary shook her head, feeling tears threaten. She considered it a very commendable feat that she held them at bay. "It's true. People of African descent are not allowed to participate in the priesthood or priesthood ordinances."

The smile fell from Charlotte's lips. "But . . . why? Mormons are opposed to slavery—I hear it often from my neighbors when we discuss the war."

"I don't know."

"Surely Ben doesn't support this. I can't believe he'd willingly be a party to such a thing."

Mary shrugged. "He's spoken to other black members of the Church—even considered leaving at one point because it bothered him so much. He tells me he eventually took it to the Lord, and that he felt at peace, that the policy won't always be so."

"Have you also taken it to the Lord?"

Mary shook her head. "I don't want to."

"Why?" Charlotte moved from her chair to sit next to Mary on the small sofa.

"I'm afraid I won't receive the same answer Ben did. That I won't receive an answer at all. Then what shall I do?"

Charlotte smiled. "So it's a matter of bravery. What does your grandmother have to say about that?"

"Ruth? I haven't spoken to her about it. She has found her own peace, her own belief in the Church. It's caused me to think on it, but it hasn't answered my own questions."

"Is Elijah here with you in town?" Charlotte asked her suddenly.

"No, I left him home with Rose and Ben. Ben has started working at the telegraph office, but Rose takes good care of him."

"And how long did you arrange to be gone?"

Mary shrugged. "A few days."

"Perfect. You can stay here with Earl and me and have plenty of time to do all the soul-searching you need without the distraction of a home and a son."

"Oh, no, Charlotte—I didn't intend to impose. I plan to make arrangements at the hotel down the street."

"Nonsense. We have a guest room right here, and I shall be offended if you don't use it."

Mary cocked her head to one side and studied her sister-in-law. "How is it, Charlotte, that you can be so good to me?"

Charlotte seemed a bit taken aback at the bluntness of the question, and then blushed. "Oh, Mary, you mustn't ask me. I am repenting of a lifetime of ill thought, taught to me by my mother, and I am ashamed sometimes at the memories."

"We'll say no more of it, then," Mary said. "I appreciate and gladly accept your gracious offer."

* * *

Mary had done everything Ben had told her to do when searching for an answer. She read the scriptures and faithfully, fervently said her prayers that night as she knelt on the floor in a soft cotton gown. She wasn't sure if she should expect angels or heavenly voices sounding from the sky, but a general feeling of contentment wasn't at all what she had been hoping for.

She climbed into bed, feeling strangely calm and yet disappointed. Sleep was long in coming, but when it finally did, she floated on enormous clouds of white, her mind light and carefree. The images then began to appear, scenes of herself and all of her family, dressed in white and together within the halls of an enormous palace. As the image came into sharper focus, she saw herself and Ben and several children led by Elijah standing together in harmony and love.

They were an eternal unit, a family, bestowed with all the blessings the Father offers His children, and she knew it with all of her heart as she viewed the scene. *This shall be yours, if you choose it . . .* A voice, gentle and yet piercing, sounded in her mind, and her heart was so filled with love that she was certain she would burst with it. *In due time, this shall be yours . . . You must trust me and stay strong in your faith . . .*

* * *

Charlotte flew down the hall in alarm, Earl dogging her footsteps. "Charlotte, perhaps she wants to be left alone," Earl whispered after her as she reached Mary's door. He rubbed his eyes in sleepiness and caught Charlotte's shoulder as she prepared to knock down Mary's door.

"Can you not hear her in there?" Charlotte demanded. "She may be ill!"

"She's not ill, she's weeping."

"Earl, I am going into this room!" Charlotte knocked twice and then opened the door when Mary didn't respond. She saw Mary, lying on her side like a small child and crying as though her heart would break.

"Mary," Charlotte whispered and then quickly approached the bedside, gathering Mary's shoulders into her arms. "Mary, you're dreaming. It's all right, you're just dreaming."

Eventually Mary opened her eyes and looked at Charlotte, who hovered close to her face. She ceased crying for a moment and took stock of her surroundings. She then slowly sat up and slid to one side as Charlotte sat on the edge of the bed.

"Are you well now?" Charlotte asked.

"Oh, Charlotte," Mary whispered, her lip trembling. She felt a surge of love for her sister-in-law and an overwhelming sense of awe at the beauty of her dream. She put her arms around Charlotte's shoulders, and when Charlotte returned her embrace, Mary turned her head and cried on the other woman's shoulder for several long moments. "I'm so very glad you made me ask," she murmured.

* * *

21 July 1865
Ogden, Utah

The water in the river was cold, but thankfully the air outside was blazing hot. Ruth barely noticed the temperature as she stepped into the water and to Ben's waiting arms, where he baptized her a member of Christ's church. Her experience was made all the sweeter when Mary followed soon on her heels, then Rose, and then, wonder of all wonders, Earl baptized Charlotte.

Four baptisms in one day—Ruth couldn't have been happier. Jeffrey and Sarah had come along to show their support, along with most of the local congregation, and the air around them all was filled with a sense of calm. The family had been extremely worried about Ruth's health and the water temperature, but their concern was for naught as soon as they made it back to Ruth's house and she was warmed by clean, dry clothing.

After the newfound friends and neighbors had departed, and as Ruth sat with her family, she looked at each of them and found something good. She had worked hard her entire life and had fought for the things in which she believed. She had raised two beautiful granddaughters and had seen them taken from lives of unhappiness and captivity and into the light of freedom.

She found pride in the way she had raised Sarah and Jeffrey's children, for truly the task had been hers and they all knew it. Ben was a good, good man. Charlotte had been given a good foundation to which she had found the strength to return. Emily, sweet Emily, far away in Savannah—she had a heart of gold and the courage of ten men. Perhaps Ruth's biggest regret was that she might not again see Emily while in this life.

Clara and Rose—the inseparables. Rose had happily accepted Mary's suggestion that she be baptized; Ruth wasn't certain that Rose understood it all, but she was fifteen years old and possessed a bright mind. Mary would see to it that Rose read the scriptures and said her prayers.

The day turned into evening, and eventually the guests rose to leave. Sarah embraced Ruth, and Ruth felt the woman's love. It had been a hard, complicated life between the two of them, but in the end they understood each other. Jeffrey hugged her too, and she felt warmed by his support. Here was a man who had finally come into his own and taken charge of his life and the elements in it that he could control.

Ben, Mary, Rose, and Elijah eventually settled in for the night with smiles and kisses all around. It had been a good, good day. As Ruth changed her clothes and then knelt down beside her bed, she thanked her Maker for a good and productive life.

Then she closed her eyes and went to sleep.

The following morning when Mary looked in on her grandmother, she found her still and with a gentle smile about her mouth. Mary knew in that moment that Ruth was gone, and she quietly set down her laundry basket and walked to Ruth's side. She knelt by the bedside and clasped Ruth's cold fingers.

Oh, sweet Father, she thought as the tears began to fall, *keep her until we shall meet again.*

* * *

24 July 1865

Sarah was inconsolable. All of Utah celebrated the coming of the pioneers to the valley, but she was locked in her bedroom where she'd been for the two days since Ruth's death. *I should never have let her get into that ice-cold river—she was fine before that! She joins that fool church and look at where it gets her!*

Jeffrey tried to tell her that Ruth's health had been failing, but she would never believe it was so bad that she had been at death's door. Ruth had been with Sarah as long as she could remember. When Sarah had crumbled and nearly died herself, Ruth had picked up the pieces and run the plantation all alone, even during the midst of a war that drained all of its resources.

Now, here they were in this new place, and one of the reasons Sarah had made peace with it was because Ruth had been with her. Ruth was gone! The bitter tears fell afresh from eyes so sore they were nearly swollen shut. Sarah didn't think she had any tears left in her to shed, but apparently she'd been wrong.

Oh, God, please! I need her, I need her! Please, you mustn't take her from me. I love her! She is my sister, and I need her! Sarah didn't know when she'd moved from her bed to a chair, and from the chair to the floor, but she lay in a heap next to the hearth, unable to move other than to sob as though her heart were broken.

The bedroom door opened, but she didn't respond or turn to see who it was. She heard light footsteps crossing the room and then felt hands and arms around her shoulders, pulling her from her prostrate position on the floor. She opened her eyes enough to see who held her tight—it was Ellen Dobranski. The little woman wiped Sarah's nose with a handkerchief and dabbed at her sore eyes.

"You will be all right," Earl's mother told her. "You will heal."

"I don't think so, Ellen," Sarah sobbed into the other woman's shoulder. "She was everything to me. Most of our lives I didn't even tell her—I treated her in the most horrible way one person can treat another, and then when I told her I was sorry and that I loved her, she only lived a short time . . ."

Ellen laid her cheek against Sarah's head. "It will pass. You just let it all out."

"I will never be happy without her here. I need her so much."

"She is still close by. Just give it some time, and you'll see she is still right here."

Sarah pulled back and looked at Ellen. "It's that *church!* If she hadn't gone into that freezing water she'd still be alive. Why would God take her when she believed she was doing the right thing?"

Ellen shook her head with a smile. "You know it's not the Church. Ruth's time was marked long before she ever decided to be baptized. She's been ill, Sarah. You haven't wanted to see it."

"But why would He take her from me?"

"You need to think of Ruth for a moment, not yourself. Think of her life. It was long, and she was tired. She did what she came here to do. She proved herself worthy to her Maker, and He let her come home. Now your test will be to live worthy so you can see her again."

Sarah's tears slowed a bit as she considered Ellen's words and the flood of calm that engulfed her heart. She no longer felt so desperate or frantic. "Do you believe that?" she asked Ellen in a whisper.

Ellen nodded. "I do. I live my life by that." She paused. "You must know that there is another life after this one."

Still, Sarah whispered through her tears. "I had hoped."

"Well, now is your time to start believing. Would you like me to teach you?"

"Yes." Sarah nodded, although the movement hurt her congested head. "Yes, I would like to learn."

"Very good. The first thing we need to do is get you bathed. Is your bathing room through here?" Ellen asked, pointing.

Sarah nodded.

"Fine, then. I'll have Jeffrey bring up some water."

As Ellen set about the business of caring for her, Sarah watched her with a sense of awe and wondered what it was the woman had said or done to lighten her spirits. Not really knowing what it was, but also not in a position to argue with her, Sarah followed her instructions, and as her bath water was brought up by a very stunned Jeffrey, she bathed away two days' worth of sorrow. When she finished, Ellen was there and said she would stay for as long as Sarah needed her.

Sarah thought of a quote Ruth had always said—something about the Lord opening a window when He closed a door—and she wondered if perhaps Ruth herself hadn't told the Lord that Sarah would need another strong woman to help her along.

* * *

25 July 1865

Ben dedicated the gravesite, and the family waited silently as the coffin was lowered gently into the ground. Ben's heart constricted, and he forced himself to remember that Ruth wasn't actually in that box, that for her this was just another beginning. It was hard, though, so very hard. Their time together here at the end had been so short, but he was grateful for a lifetime of good memories spent with her. She had raised him with virtue and with principles that he would live by forever.

Mary was coping well—better than he had expected, in fact. She was grieving, but not so much that she was incapacitated. She seemed to step in where Ruth had left off, and it was as though some of her grandmother's strength had seeped into her frame. The younger girls were having a harder time of it, but Mary kept them busy and laughing as much as she could.

Life would be different for all of them without Ruth. The entire family had been stunned at the depths to which her death had affected Sarah. Had it not been for Ellen Dobranski's timely arrival, she might well still be grieving in her bedroom. Ben felt a sense of satisfaction in it, not in a vindictive sense, but perhaps more in a feeling of justice. To know that his mother had loved Ruth so very much and depended on her strength and friendship—he was very content to know this.

Jeffrey had been unusually quiet the past few days. When Ben had spent some time with him after informing him of her death, Jeffrey had admitted his admiration and attachment for Ruth. Ben wondered if there might be more depth to his feelings for her than he let on, but he didn't ask, and Jeffrey didn't offer. "She was such a good woman," Jeffrey said, raising a glass in salute to her. "A bright and wise woman. I wish . . . ah, but what are wishes anyhow? I have many regrets."

"You gave her freedom," Ben reminded his father quietly and wondered why he was offering comfort to the one who had been a part of keeping her enslaved for years. When had he found it in his heart to begin to forgive? Perhaps he had learned it from Ruth herself.

Jeffrey shook his head. "What a sham that life was. Who did we all think we were? It wasn't soon enough. She had but a taste of freedom. I'll live with it for the rest of my life."

"Perhaps it's enough that you realize it. Many will leave this life without even a notion that the system was wrong."

"You knew. How was it that you knew? You were so young . . ." Jeffrey shuddered and leaned forward in his seat, resting his elbows on his knees. "Ah, so many regrets."

"Father," Ben said and waited until Jeffrey looked up into his face. "I forgive you. It's now time for you to forgive yourself."

Jeffrey had stared at his son, his eyes bright with brimming tears. Now as the dirt was shoveled onto the coffin, Ben figured that those tears summed up the emotions of everyone present. So many, many tears had been shed over the passing of this noble woman. It was only sad for those who were left behind to live for a time without her, though; Ben could only be happy for Ruth, herself. She was where she had wanted to be.

CHAPTER 25

Wherefore, a commandment I give unto you, which is the word of God, that ye revile no more against them because of the darkness of their skins . . . but ye shall remember your own filthiness . . .
—*Jacob 3:9*

* * *

27 July 1865
Savannah, Georgia

Emily thanked the shopkeeper and left the store, giving her list another cursory glance. She had finished her tasks and was ready to go home for dinner. She met Gwenyth, who was crossing the street, and together they made their way back to Willow Lane.

"Is Austin finished?" Gwenyth asked her.

Emily shook her head. "He probably won't be for another few hours. He said there were details that were taking some time to arrange."

"But the sale is complete?"

Emily nodded. "It will be by the time he comes home. He said he would negotiate another week into the contract so that we'll have some time to finish shipping or selling whatever is left."

"Who is buying the plantation?"

Emily shrugged. "A scalawag from Atlanta. Seems to have grand ideas for the place."

"I should think the locals will appreciate a scalawag over a carpetbagger."

Emily scowled. "I should think they would appreciate the fact that they've driven us out of our home. I don't believe they'll much care one way or the other who lives in it after we're gone."

Gwenyth nodded, and the women continued in silence. They reached the plantation, and Gwenyth headed for the cook-house while Emily went to check on Mary Alice "I'll join you in just a moment," she called to Gwenyth.

The house was staffed with a mere skeleton of a crew who had stayed on because Austin still managed to pay them fairly well. Emily and Austin had moved them all into the mansion from their smaller homes in the back out of concern for their safety. The young woman who cared for Mary Alice while Emily conducted other business was a sweet girl whom Emily trusted implicitly. As was always the case, when Emily arrived in the nursery, Mary Alice was all smiles.

Emily indulged herself in a moment of play with her daughter before preparing to pick her up and take her out to the cookhouse so that she might help Gwenyth see to dinner. Before she could go through the motions of leaving the nursery, however, Gwenyth arrived on the threshold, out of breath and panic-stricken.

"Joshua has gone out to the school," she breathed in gasps. "Miss Weston sent a messenger saying someone has set fire to it."

Emily looked over to Nina, the young nanny. "Will you stay here for a bit longer with Mary Alice?"

The girl nodded, her eyes huge. Almost as though to comfort herself from the fear, she picked up Mary Alice and held her close. "I'll be here for as long as you need me," she said.

"Let's go," Emily said to Gwenyth. She winced a bit as Mary Alice let out a cry behind her, but she resolutely closed the nursery door. *I'll make it up to you, sweet,* Emily thought as she rushed back down the main front stairs. She was about to head out the front door when a thought struck her and she ran for Austin's study. Grabbing a chair, she dragged it over to a tall bureau and stood on the upholstered seat. Feeling around the top behind the lip of decorative molding, she curled her fingers around one large rifle and a brace of pistols. Next to the weapons was a haversack full of ammunition.

She handed one of the pistols to Gwenyth, who had followed her into the room, and said, "Courtesy of the Confederate Government." The other pistol she placed inside the sack along with the shells. She jumped down from the chair holding the rifle in one hand and slinging the haversack over one shoulder.

"You cannot possibly go walking through town with that thing in your hand," Gwenyth told her.

"You're right." Glancing about for a possible solution, Emily snapped her fingers and reached for the inner folds of her skirt. Moving quickly to Austin's desk, she grasped his letter opener and thrust it into the skirt pocket, cutting a sizeable hole in the fabric. She then rather awkwardly shoved the rifle down through the hole and against her leg. The very butt of the rifle protruded from the pocket, so she hurried to the front hall and grabbed a shawl that lay draped over a hat tree next to the door.

With the rifle securely hidden, if not a bit bulky, and her arm wrapped firmly around it, she nodded once at Gwenyth. "Are you ready?"

Gwenyth nodded, her eyes luminous and fearful. As they quickly made their way out of the house and across the front lawn, she said, "I'm worried about the school, but I must admit I'm more worried about Joshua. If whoever set that fire is still in the area, he won't be safe. They say that in Alabama and

Mississippi, there are lynch mobs out and about nearly every night now."

"We'll be there soon, Gwen." Emily patted the other woman's arm with a gentle touch that belied her general feelings of anxiety and urgency. "Besides, what on earth would cause you to think that I expect any kind of trouble?"

Gwenyth looked at her askance and, seemingly in spite of herself, laughed. As the women continued to walk at their brisk pace the two miles to the schoolhouse, dusk eventually began to fall. Emily glanced up at the sky as they neared their destination and said, "It's later than I thought. We must have spent more time downtown than I'd realized."

Gwenyth nodded, her breathing becoming a bit labored. "The staff had already prepared and eaten dinner by the time I made it to the cookhouse."

"Well, Austin should be home soon, then. That's good—did you happen to leave word with anyone as to where we were headed?"

"Yes, I told Evan."

"Good."

The women smelled the burning building before they saw it, but before long the smoke that rose above the trees became apparent. Emily gritted her teeth. "Why? A children's school-house, for heaven's sake."

"A *colored* children's schoolhouse," Gwenyth murmured beside her, her gaze on the smoke that lifted high into the evening sky.

* * *

Austin left his meeting with the esteemed Mr. Smith, satis-fied that he'd protected his family's interests as best he could. The bank was holding for him the hefty sack of gold Mr. Smith had paid for Willow Lane—not nearly its full worth, but enough to get the Stanhopes out of Georgia and settled somewhere new. He had some money deposited in various accounts in the North, thanks to his parents' insight years ago, and felt some sense of security in knowing he could access those funds when necessary.

He whistled a bit as he stepped out onto the street, feeling strangely optimistic despite the fact that he'd lost well over half of his family's wealth in the past few years. The thought of being virtually forced from his boyhood home and inheritance didn't even dampen his spirits as he thought of Emily and Mary Alice and the fact that they were all he wanted in the world. *Money be hanged,* he thought to himself. *I have a family.*

The first blow came out of nowhere and hit him on the back of his head, sending him sprawling into the street. His training as a soldier was of no use to him, for by the time he managed to clear his aching head, he was beset by a large circle of men, all of whom proceeded to do their best work on a defenseless man with one leg who lay prostrate in the street.

* * *

As the pair of women approached the burning building, the heat overwhelming even at a distance, they saw Miss Weston and several others gathered around the blaze. Crews of men were doing their best to keep the fire contained, but it was clear that the building itself was lost.

Miss Weston wrung her hands and paced the ground in agitated strides. As Emily and Gwenyth approached her, she saw them and ran to meet them halfway. "Oh, Miss Stanhope," she said to Gwenyth. "Your fiancé was here, and then some men came—they'd been drinking or they mightn't have been so brave . . ."

"Where did they take him?" Gwenyth asked her, clutching at the woman's arm.

"Off in that direction," she said, pointing. "They had torches. I wouldn't be at all surprised if they set this fire."

"Have you sent for anyone from the Freedmen's Bureau?" Emily asked the distraught teacher.

She nodded and swallowed. "Captain Ketchum will hopefully arrive soon, and I hope he brings troops. We may need them for further protection if not for help in putting out this fire."

"When they arrive, please tell them we've gone looking for Mr. Birmingham. This way, you said?" Emily asked, pointing.

"Yes."

"How long ago?"

"Fifteen, maybe twenty minutes."

Emily dropped her shawl to the ground and pulled the rifle from her skirts. When Gwenyth moved to open her reticule and withdraw her pistol, Emily put a hand on her arm with a silent nod to the men who fought the fire, all of them white. Miss Weston's eyes had grown huge at the sight of the rifle, but she refrained from comment as the women headed off into the trees.

"Be careful how you use that pistol, Gwen. If anyone has to shoot a white man tonight, it should be me, not you. I don't care what the defense—it would not go well for you in a courtroom. I want you to have it, but if there are any witnesses, I'd rather them remember the hotheaded white woman with the red hair who carried a gun, not her black friend."

Gwenyth nodded grimly; she opened her reticule so that she would have access to the weapon if need be, but for the time being it remained hidden. "They could be anywhere by now," she whispered, hearing the desperation in her own voice.

"We have an advantage."

"What is that?"

"They've been drinking. Have you ever noticed how stupid men get when they drink?"

Gwenyth smiled in spite of herself. "My granddaddy was the worst. Used to sing saloon tunes at the top of his lungs."

* * *

Joshua closed his eyes as his face was slapped for what felt like the hundredth time. The men roared with laughter and taunted him, calling him vile names and insulting his parentage. *The Lord is my Shepherd, I shall not want,* he thought as he sought desperately to go to another place in his mind.

How was it that he could survive horrific battles during two years of warfare and then find himself at such a crossroads? It was as though the men knew the Stanhopes were involved with the small school, and they lay in wait after lighting the fire, not really caring whom they would capture as that person unwittingly fell into their trap. That it turned out to be a colored man was a surprise that had the men giddy in drunken delight.

The men led him deeper into the forest, hitting him repeatedly with the butts of their guns, their taunts and abuse dogging his every step. They had tied his hands behind his back and encircled him so completely that any chance of escape was temporarily blocked. He knew if he tried to run, he'd be shot down in the dirt before he made it ten feet.

He fought a desperate sense of panic as he thought of Gwenyth and how she would react when she heard the news of his death. His heart ached for himself and for her, and he was forced to calm his mind a bit so that he might think of a productive solution to his dilemma. *I don't really know that there is much of a productive solution,* he mused as the men led him to a clearing in the trees. *Pray for a miracle, I suppose. Yet who even knows I'm missing?*

* * *

The two women progressed further into the woods, and Emily prayed for some kind of direction. She kept her eyes strained for light and her ears for any hint of sound. They walked on for several more minutes before her prayers were finally answered and Gwenyth spotted a faint light off in the trees.

They crept closer as quietly as possible, and as they neared the torches, which numbered six, Emily was grateful for the men's loud conversation that was occasionally "hushed" by one or the other of them. In the midst of the men stood Joshua, his back straight and tall despite the blood that oozed from his temple and down his cheek.

Emily put her lips close to Gwenyth's ear and whispered, "How should we do this?"

Gwenyth shrugged a bit and answered back, "Hide in the trees and start shooting?"

Emily looked back at her and eventually nodded. It was as good a plan as any—it wasn't likely that the men would simply turn Joshua over to them at their insistence. In fact, they were probably some of the same men who had been terrorizing the Stanhope house.

Separating from Gwenyth and taking cover in heavy undergrowth, Emily took a deep breath and checked the rifle. It was a good thing she hadn't accidentally pulled the trigger while it had been hidden next to her leg or she'd have blown off her own foot. The thing was already loaded. With hands that shook slightly, she raised the rifle to her shoulder and prepared to try to save the very man who had taught her how to use one.

She fired a shot over the heads of the men and leaned behind a thick tree for protection. The men were startled and disoriented, calling out in confusion until one started toward her direction. Gwenyth must have noted his intent because she fired a shot from her position many feet away.

Emily used this new distraction to leave her hiding place and skirt around the outside of the circle, again taking cover behind thick trees and bushes. She reloaded and fired again, this time allowing her shot to come dangerously close to several men's feet. By now, Gwenyth was on the move, as was evidenced by her next shot, which came from an entirely different direction.

"Come on out and show yourselves," one of the men shouted.

Emily and Gwenyth were saved from reply by the sound of hooves in the distance that grew closer with each moment. The men in the circle looked at each other for a moment in consternation. "Did you tell anyone to meet us here?" one asked another.

"No, fool! *We* didn't even know we'd be here!"

It was enough to have the men scattering in all different directions, but some of them apparently chose the wrong path because she heard them apprehended by the soldiers, who had obviously been sent by Miss Weston.

"Oh, sweet mercy," Emily breathed and staggered into the clearing to see Gwenyth, who was already throwing herself into Joshua's arms. With a cry of dismay, Gwenyth reached up and removed a rope that had been placed around Joshua's neck and flung it far into the trees.

Emily's eyes filled with tears, and she stepped toward the couple, laughing a bit when they both turned to her. She stood with them for some time in a three-way embrace until they heard the sound of hooves entering the clearing. "Did you catch some of them, then?" she asked over her shoulder to the man in a blue uniform who approached on horseback.

"We did. Are you all well?" he asked them.

"Well enough," Emily answered. The man on the horse held his torch a bit closer for a better view, and his face registered his surprise.

"Mrs. Stanhope?"

"Yes," Emily replied, suddenly feeling a bit cold.

"We've been out looking for you."

"Why?" Her legs felt weak, and she leaned on the rifle butt, shoving the end of the gun into the dirt.

"Your husband, ma'am," the soldier replied, removing his cap. "He's been taken to the hospital."

* * *

"He'll end up dead for certain if I don't get him out of that hospital," Emily muttered under her breath as she, Gwenyth, and Joshua were delivered to Willow Lane in a carriage provided by the soldiers. "He's now nothing more than a sitting target. Why don't we just invite the locals to go on in and finish the job they started?" With a comment of thanks to the driver of the carriage, the three made their way into the house, Joshua with a cloth tied to his head to stop the flow of blood from where he'd been hit with the butt of a gun.

Emily placed her fingertips on her temples and tried to organize her thoughts. According to the messenger, Austin had been attacked on his way home and left bloodied and beaten in the street. The city hospital was nearby, so that was where he'd been taken when found. As she looked at Joshua and Gwenyth, however, she realized an immediate concern with an immediate solution.

"There are many things out of my control," she said to them and motioned for them to follow her to Austin's study, "but there are some within it."

Gwenyth sat next to Joshua on a sofa and fussed over his head wound and places on his wrists where he'd been tied with rough rope. "Emily, we need to go to the hospital," Joshua told her as she whirled the numbers on Austin's safe. Once she had it opened, she reached inside and pulled forth a bag of gold coins. She turned to face her friends after slamming the safe shut with energy born of pure adrenaline.

"This will get you to Boston and then some," she said. She handed the money to Gwenyth. "You remember the dresses we used to put the women in—the ones with the hidden pockets?

Of course you do, you were doing this long before I was. Put on one of those and hide these coins in it."

Joshua and Gwenyth stared at her, openmouthed. "Emily, we're not leaving," Joshua said.

"Oh, but you are. Joshua, your life is forfeit if you stay here one more day. The fever against this whole family is too high. You both wanted to head to Boston—you're doing it now rather than later. Austin and I will be out of here in a week and on our way to Utah. I've been corresponding with Mary. I'll send her a letter in the morning telling her we'll be there a bit sooner than we expected. Austin has our travel plans ready, bless his heart. We'll take the railroad as far as the lines run and then the stage the rest of the way."

"We are *not* leaving you here to do all of this on your own," Gwenyth said. "Especially as we don't even know the extent of Austin's injuries yet."

Emily's eyes filled with tears. "Please, for me, leave. If you stay, you may die, and I can't bear it. If you want to help me, you'll keep yourselves safe and notify me as soon as you make it to Boston. I'll write to my aunt that you're on your way, and you'll have a place to stay for as long as you need until you get yourselves settled."

"I don't like it," Joshua said.

"If you stay here, I won't be able to do one blessed thing. I'll be worried sick about the both of you all the time. If you love me, I beg of you, leave. Take a stage north and west until you reach the Mississippi, then book passage on a steamer. The major Atlantic ports still aren't open, or I'd suggest you just hop on a ship that would take you right into Boston harbor."

"How can we do this, in good conscience?" Gwenyth asked Emily, tears beginning to fill her eyes.

"We have got to get out of this place," Emily said, standing. "The two of you need to go first. Joshua—all of this, all of our struggles, our misery growing up together—now you have your freedom, and how will you enjoy it if you're swinging from a tree by your neck?"

The couple stood and embraced her. "Now, I'm going to the hospital," Emily said. "You stay here and pack, and for heaven's sake, do not leave the house until morning. The stage will be running by then."

"You can't go to the hospital by yourself," Joshua told her.

"Joshua," Emily said and lifted the haversack she'd carried over her shoulder through the night, "I'm tired and angry. I swear by my own grave, if someone so much as looks at me wrong, I'll shoot him."

* * *

It was much later in the evening, as she sat at the bedside of her bruised and battered husband, that Emily released the tears that had been building through the night. She sobbed quietly into his side, his shirtfront absorbing the moisture and the noise. She finally gave way to her exhaustion and sat on the floor, her head resting on the bed. When Austin awoke well after midnight, he smiled through cracked lips to see flame-red hair next to his arm.

CHAPTER 26

*I was soon at my old boyhood home. My folks were expecting me
. . . There was no "scene" when we met . . . but we all had a feeling
of profound contentment and satisfaction . . . I found that the farm
work my father was then engaged in was cutting and shucking corn.
So, the morning after my arrival, I doffed my uniform of first lieu-
tenant, put on some of my father's old clothes and proceeded to wage
war on the standing corn.*
—Leander Stilwell, 100th Indiana

* * *

*28 July 1865
Richmond, Virginia*

Camille held baby Angelina over one shoulder and bounced
Iris on her knee. The wait to hear from the interim state government regarding her and Jacob's pending adoption of the two
little girls had seemed interminable. She hoped to hear something when the mail was delivered today and figured she would
probably scream the roof down if she didn't.

It hadn't been long after Angelina's delivery that Camille had
approached Jacob regarding her desire to have the little girls as
her own, and to her immense relief, he had agreed. "We'll need
to act on the adoption as soon as possible. We probably won't be

here in Virginia much longer," he had told her. "They need me back at the main office."

"Are you ready to go back?" she'd asked him.

"Yes, I believe I am. I've grown a bit homesick for Boston."

She had nodded. "I have too," she confessed. "I'm ready to go home."

Now as she looked around the orphanage, she realized how much she would miss it—not just the children, but also the other women who were so generous in volunteering their time and energy to these little orphans. She spied her brother Robert in the corner reading with young Jeremy. He and Abigail too were waiting on adoption papers and had plans to take Jeremy home with them when they left Virginia. Robert had spent every available moment with Jeremy since the moment he'd first met the boy and had become very attached to the child. When Camille and Jacob told the others of their plans to adopt the little girls, it was as though a light had come on in Robert's eyes, and he realized such a thing could be possible for him, Abigail, and Jeremy.

When the mail finally arrived and the orphanage director carried it back to the orphanage, the long-awaited news was finally delivered; the adoptions were finalized and the Taylors and Birminghams were now proud parents. Camille was so happy when she heard the news that she hugged the little girls to her and cried.

* * *

Robert sat in a small chair in a remote corner of the room with Jeremy on his lap. "Jeremy," he said very softly to the young boy, "we've just received some very important news in the mail. This news says that, if you'd like, you can live with Miss Abigail and me and we can be a family together. Do you think that is something you might like?"

Jeremy looked very thoughtful for a moment. "Does that mean you'd be my pa and Miss Abigail would be my ma?"

"Yes, that's what it means."

"Yes," he said slowly. "I believe I'd like that. D'you suppose you might be patient with my leg n' all?"

Robert wanted to cry. "Of course I will, Jeremy. Your leg is no problem at all to me. I admire the strength of your character. I would very much like to be your pa."

"Well, sir, I think that would be right nice, then."

* * *

Isabelle laid down her cards and said, "Gin."

"You're cheating," Sally said to her. "You have been from the start."

"I most certainly have not. And besides, you've won the last three hands."

"Well," Sally sniffed, "there's something awful shifty about your expression when you win."

"My dear, that is simply the expression of success—I suspect the very same one I see on your face when you win."

Sally sat back against the cushions of the sofa and smiled. "Fair enough, I suppose."

"How are you feeling?"

"Better today than yesterday, even. I'm tired of looking at this old parlor, though. I'd very much like to go outside."

Isabelle considered this. "I suppose we can do that for just a bit." She helped Sally to her feet and, with the younger girl leaning on her arm for support, walked her to the front door. They stepped outside into the sunshine, and Sally turned her face toward the sky.

"Mmm," she said. "That feels divine."

"It's hot," Isabelle complained.

"It's hot inside."

"That's true enough, I suppose," Isabelle said and stepped with Sally out onto the front porch. She used a cane now to aid her walking instead of her cumbersome crutches. "If I fall, I'll be taking you down to the ground with me," she warned Sally.

"Won't we be a sight, then. A Yankee and a Rebel facedown in the dirt."

"It's happened before."

"True. And sad."

Isabelle glanced at the girl in some surprise at her perception. "You're right. It is sad. Was sad. But it's done now."

"Perhaps the shooting part. But folks aren't going to let it die for many years to come. That's what I think, anyway. People are very proud and determined in their hatred."

"How do you come to know so much?"

"My mama was full of hatred. That's why I didn't believe it when y'all came to my door and said she'd gone to the Bureau for help. She was so angry. Hated, *hated* the Yanks."

Isabelle nodded. There wasn't anything to add to such a statement. Truth was truth, and there wasn't much arguing with raw emotion. "How do *you* feel? Here you are, walking down your drive with me."

"You're tolerable, after a bit," Sally said with a glance at Isabelle and a smile. "I don't hate the Yanks. I do wish they hadn't killed my pa, though."

"There are children in the North who are saying the same thing about the Rebs."

"Y'all took nearly all that we had."

"We would have given all that we had, too. We just had more to spare." Isabelle looked at Sally with a small shrug, meaning no harm. "It was important that we all stay together."

Sally pulled her gaze away from Isabelle's and looked out over the street. "We could have been friendly neighbors."

Isabelle shook her head and said softly, "It wouldn't have worked. Some of the Southern states had started to consider seceding from the Confederacy near the end. Before long, the Confederacy itself would have dissolved."

"I still think it would have worked," Sally mumbled under her breath as she looked down at the dirt. Isabelle smiled and allowed Sally's pride one final protest and refrained from commenting. It was a difficult thing to be on the losing side of a game, let alone a war.

"I am sorry about your pa," Isabelle said to her. "I know how much it hurts."

"I know you do." Sally gave Isabelle's arm a little squeeze, and it surprised the older woman. "And I'm sorry that you couldn't protect your president. I'm sure it must have made you feel plumb awful."

Isabelle noted Sally's labored breathing and suggested they retire to the swing on the front porch. "My leg is getting a bit sore," she said. They climbed the steps at a slow pace and gingerly sat on the front porch swing together.

"It did make me feel plumb awful," Isabelle said. "I figured it was all my fault. If I had done my job better, it could have been avoided."

"That's plain silly. You didn't pull the trigger now, did you?"

"Well no, but . . ."

"You didn't want Lincoln shot, did you?"

"No."

"You can't be responsible for the actions of a crazy coward."

"Why, Sally! And here I thought you'd probably hold a special place in your heart for the man."

Sally scowled. "That he was a coward was poor enough. The more I think on it, the more I figure he was probably as mad as a March hare. That's no hero."

"No. No, it isn't." Isabelle paused for a moment. "Have you given any more thought to your immediate future?"

"I know you told me to consider being with my brother and sisters, but I really had hoped you would take me to India."

Isabelle closed her eyes. "I was afraid you would remember that conversation."

"Well, of course. I'd likely be dead to forget that one."

"What it will probably require is that I obtain temporary guardianship over you—either until we return and you go live with your aunt or until your eighteenth birthday."

Sally nodded. "I would be fine with such an arrangement."

Isabelle shook her head. Would *she* be fine with it? She was hardly mother material. "I would expect your compliance in everything. Is that clear?"

"Absolutely."

Isabelle took a deep breath. "I've never been one to go back on my word, and I am truly so very glad to see you recovered. If all of the legal arrangements can be made regarding guardianship, I'll gladly take you there."

"Were you really so worried I would die?"

Isabelle hesitated, then nodded. "I really was. Sally, you were very, very ill. The doctors suspected that you were stricken with the same fever that took your mother."

"There was a time I thought you hated me. I wouldn't have been surprised if you had let me go."

"I never hated you. I was frustrated with you because I wanted you to survive and take that survival from whichever source offered it," Isabelle said.

"Have you never heard of pride?"

"Pride has no place in the face of survival."

"Sometimes pride is all one has left."

Isabelle paused and smiled. "I believe, Sally, that we'll have to agree to disagree about pride."

"Fair enough."

CHAPTER 27

I have fought against the people of the North because I believed they were seeking to wrest from the South its dearest rights. But I have never cherished toward them bitter or vindictive feelings, and I have never seen the day when I did not pray for them.
—General Robert E. Lee

* * *

1 August 1865
New York, New York

Marie surveyed Daniel's workshop with an eye for dirt. It had lain dormant for so long that dust was beginning to gather on the tools and benches. It was a bright morning, the sun radiant in the sky, and she had chosen to stay home and pay some special attention to the extra housework that had fallen behind.

As she began to run a clean cloth over the items, she contemplated the recent weeks in her small household. Things were good between her and Daniel, and she was grateful to both God and the mothers for helping it to be so. Something amazing seemed to have happened that night weeks ago when Brenna had spoken with Daniel alone. It was as though she had ignited a spark of his former self that had been hiding inside.

Daniel spent much time now outside with the animals and the garden. While he had done so before, his attentions to the small farm were sporadic and lackluster. Now he greeted each new day with a sense of optimism and seemed to enjoy the time he spent working. He had thrown out all of his bottles of alcohol and had suffered the side effects of withdrawal from the liquor with a stoicism and strength that reminded Marie very much of the man she had first met and fallen in love with.

His attention to her and her needs had increased tenfold, and rather than seeing himself as a hindrance in her life, he instead sought to make things a bit easier for her. He began by cooking simple dinners while she worked at the orphanage and school. At first they were often burned and tasted horrendous, but they both laughed about it—something he had not been able to do since his accident. As time progressed, his culinary skills improved and then became exceptional—to the point where she often requested his help even when she was home in the evenings.

He was tender again and thoughtful, and he never raised his voice in consternation or anger at her. It provided a relief to her that seemed immeasurable. Her home was tranquil and loving, and as an added happiness, she had a suspicion that she might be expecting a baby.

She dusted thoroughly and carefully, wiping the rag over each surface and item. The workshop saddened her, in a way; it was as though the person who had worked in it had died and those left behind never had had the heart to disrupt the tools from the way the carpenter had left them. She picked up a lathe and looked at it carefully, wondering what it would feel like to run the tool over a piece of wood.

Marie found a scrap of wood on the floor and placed it on the workbench. She began working the lathe against the wood, struggling to make the movement smooth and effortless. She was so caught up in her efforts that she was startled to see a pair of arms creep around her from behind.

Daniel's hands ran down the length of her arms to where her hands held the tool and his voice was light in her ear. "Not quite so rough," he said. "Here, more like this." He guided her movements against the piece of wood, slowing and lengthening her repetitions. "Do you feel the difference?"

She nodded, breathless. "How do you know . . ."

"I can feel it and hear it. I heard when I came in that you were doing it all wrong." He smiled against her ear and placed a kiss on it to lessen the sting of his criticism.

"Well, I should say that for a beginner I was making a fine attempt."

"Yes. But before long you'd have been slicing into your own hand."

"Daniel, the difference in this old piece of wood is amazing. Sweetheart, you must miss this so much."

He nodded and pulled his arms to rest around her waist, leaning his chin on her shoulder. "I do miss it."

"You know by the sound and the feel how things are supposed to work in here—why don't you try something?"

"Oh, Marie—it's not the same as seeing it. There are things I wouldn't know unless I took a good look, and we both know by now that it's not going to happen."

"I can be your eyes. Explain it to me, and I'll tell you how things look. What I don't know right away I can learn."

He must have heard the earnest pleading in her voice because he eventually capitulated. "Very well. We'll make something simple."

"How about a box?"

He laughed. "A box, eh? I think even I can manage a box."

"Could we make a box that had legs on it?"

"Rather like a trough?" he asked.

"Well, I was thinking rather like a simple baby bed."

"Why would we make a baby's . . ." His voice trailed off and his arms tightened around her waist. "Are you? Marie, are you telling me . . ."

"Yes." She twisted in his arms and placed hers around his neck. "I believe we're going to have one of our own. I'm fairly certain, in fact. It's early yet, but . . ."

He kissed her neck, and she heard the gruffness in his throat before he managed to clear it. "I'm very happy, Marie. I only wish I could see it."

"You will, with your ears and your hands. And mercy, but newborn babies smell so good. You'll be a wonderful papa."

"Have you told the mothers?"

"Not yet. I wanted to tell you first. I'm very, very happy, Daniel, and I love you very much."

"I love you, sweet Marie. I'm so grateful you didn't leave me. I gave you plenty of reason."

"Nonsense. I knew things would right themselves."

"You did?"

"Well, I hoped, anyway."

Daniel rubbed his hands across her back and then down her arms. "We have much to do, then, don't we? I suppose we'd best get busy making that box."

* * *

1 August 1865
Cleveland, Ohio

Anne sipped her tea and shook her head at her mother-in-law, who sat across the table from her. "I'm telling you, it wasn't a shadow. I saw bruises on her arm."

Amanda set down her own tea and folded her hands on the tabletop. "Supposing you're right, Anne, I'm not sure how we can help her."

"I don't know, I don't know." Anne put her head in her hands. "Is that poor woman supposed to live her whole life with a man she doesn't love who beats her?"

"No, she isn't, and if he's truly beating her, then even the authorities will step in."

Anne snorted. "We hope they will. Some folks just think that what goes on between husband and wife is nobody else's business."

Amanda shook her head. "The sheriff here is a bit different. He's already locked up one man for that very thing. It seems that the sheriff's mother was beaten to death by his stepfather. He didn't take kindly to that."

Anne let out a small sigh. "Then perhaps we stand a chance."

"I'm in favor of seeing Madeline safe, but a couple of bruises on her arms doesn't mean he's necessarily beating her."

"If her arms are bruised, he can't be treating her kindly."

"How do you propose to examine the rest of her? Demand that she show you her ribs?"

"I just might! That husband of hers . . . the more I think of him swooping down like that after his dead brother's wife and property . . . And you yourself said he's always been sullen and disagreeable."

"I don't believe I said 'disagreeable.'"

"Well, it certainly fits well with 'sullen.'"

"Anne." Amanda smiled and refilled her daughter-in-law's teacup. "Take it slowly. We'll watch Madeline closely, and if he's hurting her, we'll eventually know."

"I hope we won't be too late."

"What have you heard about your manuscript?" As far as subject changes, it was rather abrupt, but Anne had come to expect it of Amanda, and she smiled. The older woman's mind jumped from one subject to the next with amazing speed.

"I believe they're going to publish it. The publisher has sent word that they want to buy it, but they mentioned that it sounds too much like the fanciful dreams of a young woman— going off to war as a young man and all that. They suggest that the public will never believe it actually happened."

"Fools, all of them." Amanda turned up her nose a bit. "They've obviously never met you."

"You defend me because you know me, Mama."

"Of course not! I defend you because it's true. You saved my boy's life. I don't suppose they believe that's true, either."

"Probably not. It doesn't matter. I enjoyed writing it all down, and in a way I felt better after I did. I think Ivar still struggles a bit with some of the memories." Anne shifted in her seat, her growing midsection becoming more cumbersome with each passing day.

"My sweet boy," Amanda murmured. "He was always such a gentle child. He felt very strongly about going, you know. When his friends enlisted in the war, and they with their wives and children, he didn't feel right about staying behind."

Anne nodded, remembering. "He showed me pictures Inger had drawn for him—things you sent in the mail. He loved receiving those. Ah, Mama," she sighed. "He was so good to me. He took such good care of me, and I fought it every step. He kept me close to his side both in camp and in battle. He was the only one who knew just from looking at me that I was a woman. And even when he told me he knew, he promised not to turn me in. I don't know many other men who would have done that." Anne didn't realize her eyes had misted over until one tear spilled down her cheek.

"He was with me when Mark and Jed were shot, you know."

Amanda nodded. She remembered the young men well.

"I nearly collapsed right on the field of battle and would have been shot myself if Ivar hadn't stepped in and dragged me off. We were all tent mates. I was devastated when they died, absolutely sick about it. I lost much of my enthusiasm after that. I believe that was when I began wishing I was back in Boston."

"Why didn't you leave?"

"I told myself that I needed to finish what I'd started. But you know, when I think back on it, I believe I just couldn't bear to leave Ivar. I loved him so much, and even when I was almost dead in that first prison camp and Ivar finally turned me in, I wanted to stay with him."

The tears fell more freely now, and Amanda let her keep talking as she wiped away a few tears of her own. "When I heard he was in Andersonville—well, the reputation of that horrid place had already begun to precede itself. I wasn't sure if we'd even find him alive." Anne shuddered. "Oh, you should have seen him, standing there all tattered and starved, but so straight and proud. He didn't bow to anyone but God."

Amanda reached across the table and clasped Anne's fingers and held them tightly. "You've never told me this," she whispered to Anne.

"I suppose I didn't want to think about it. Even now it hurts, but not so much that I want to vomit."

Amanda winced at Anne's crudity but laughed in spite of herself. She rose slightly out of her chair and kissed Anne's fingers. "How fortunate we all are that you enlisted, my sukkerklump."

Anne smiled. "Sugar lump" was a phrase usually reserved for Inger, and Anne felt oddly pleased to have it bestowed upon her.

* * *

3 August 1865
Boston, Massachusetts

Gwenyth looked around herself at the small, cozy attic room in the Birmingham mansion and smiled. She set down her travel valise and removed her dusty gloves and hat. The trip had been amazingly fast and amazingly conflict-free. She and Joshua had done exactly as Emily had suggested, using the stage, a steamer, and the rails to reach Boston, and once there, they both breathed a huge sigh of relief.

Mrs. Birmingham had received a telegram from Emily alerting her to Gwenyth and Joshua's pending arrival, and she was ready for them when they appeared at her doorstep. Gwenyth was given Mary's old bedroom, and Joshua now slept out in one of the finished groomsmen's rooms over the carriage house. "Until you two are married," Mrs. Birmingham had said, "these quarters will work well for you."

Gwenyth had ducked her head in slight embarrassment and didn't feel comfortable explaining that Joshua had never been anything but a gentleman with her, that he had slept on the floors of whatever lodging they had found, and that he had made every effort to adhere to strict propriety. She had glanced at him and then away again quickly when he winked at her.

Now, as Gwenyth washed up in the washbasin against the wall and changed into her nightdress, she thought fondly of Mary and wondered what the girl's first thoughts had been as she had finally slept in a cozy room of her own. *It must have been wonderful, Mary . . .* How nice it was to finally see one of the places where the Stanhope family resources and energy had gone. All those years that Gwenyth herself had stayed behind in Georgia helping to keep the machine of escape rolling forward—it was gratifying that now she was finally able to see a slice of that herself.

Holy Father, she said as she knelt down beside her bed, *I thank Thee with all that I am for a good life, a good man, and a good start at a new life. I thank Thee for this sweet little room and all the young women who have enjoyed it. Please bless us and be with us all forever . . .*

CHAPTER 28

Though deepening trials wend your way,
Press on, press on, ye Saints of God!
Ere long, the resurrection day
Will spread its life and truth abroad,
Will spread its life and truth abroad.
    —*Eliza R. Snow, "Though Deepening Trials"*

* * *

5 August 1865
Wyoming Territory

"We should have waited, we should have waited . . ." Emily chanted it under her breath until Austin looked as though he wanted to wrap his fingers around her throat and squeeze.

"Stop, Emily. Please, stop. I'm fine. I'll be fine."

"Austin, you're white as a sheet under those bruises. I know your ribs are hurting you—you're just too brave to admit it."

"Emily, you can absolve yourself of any responsibility in this. I was the one who insisted we leave on schedule."

"Absolve myself? You are a funny man, Austin Stanhope. I had complete control of the situation—one well-placed kick to your midsection would have sent you crying to your bed." She shook her head. "I knew better, I knew it!"

Mary Alice awoke from her restless nap and began to cry. The dust from the stagecoach wheels was thick and intruded into the hot interior, and Emily imagined they were all riding into the pits of hell. They bounced over what must have been a large boulder, and Austin groaned in spite of what Emily knew were his best efforts to be stoic.

The nausea that had been plaguing Emily for nearly a week now rose up again in her throat, and she reached blindly for the pan she'd been using at various points in the journey. Mary Alice, still crying, staggered across the stagecoach interior and climbed onto Emily's lap while Emily retched into the pan.

When she finished, Austin handed her a canteen full of water and patted his leg for Mary Alice to climb upon it instead of her mother. "We're almost there," he said to Emily who was ready to sob like her daughter.

"Oh, just admit you're miserable too," she said to Austin. "It'll make me feel better if you complain just a bit."

"Very well, I admit it. I ache from the crown of my head to my one remaining foot. In fact, I almost hurt where the other one used to be too."

Emily shifted in her seat, trying to find a comfortable position that kept her as motion-free as possible. "Thank you," she said to Austin.

"Emily?"

"Yes."

"Are you expecting?"

Emily looked at him, her expression blank. "I assumed I had some sort of illness."

"Hmm. That may well be."

"Oh, no. Another baby?"

"Do you not care to have another?"

"Well, yes, I assumed we would have more, it's just that," Emily gulped, "it hurt so very much the last time . . ."

"I wasn't there the last time," he reminded her. "I'll help you."

"Yes, yes, that's true. And Ruth. Ruth will help me too." The carriage jounced again and Emily hit her head on the window. Austin's jaw was clenched tight against the pain, and Mary Alice started another round of wailing. "If we ever make it, that is . . . We should have waited. I knew we should have waited . . ."

* * *

5 August 1865
Boston, Massachusetts

Joshua opened the letter from his sister, Mary, with anticipation. It had been some time since he'd heard from her and Ben.

Dear Joshua,

I hope this letter finds you well. I understand that this is probably the case, as Emily tells me in a letter I received just a couple of days ago that you and Gwenyth are to be married and are even now on your way to Boston. I am so very happy for you, and wish you and Gwenyth all the best. Please tell her for me.

Now, I must share some news with you that is hard to write and I suspect will be even harder to read. Joshua, Mama Ruth has passed away. She was ill. I don't know if you remember my other letters mentioning this, but she finally was taken by the consumption. I would have you know that she was happy here in her last days. She built a beautiful home and kept a wonderful garden—she finally had a patch of earth that was all hers, and she bloomed in it.

Her death has been a harsh thing for all of us. We are all still grieving and trying to fill the void she has left behind, but we know it cannot be filled. It will only be so when we see her again on the other side, and I would have you know that I have great faith in this. I know she is waiting for us, Joshua. She wants us to live full lives here so that we can see our Savior again with no regrets.

Sweet brother, how I wish I could be with you in person to share this hard news. I would embrace you and shed a tear or two, and then I hope we would smile over our memories of her. I worry that Emily will miss the letter I'm sending off to her—she will most likely arrive here expecting to see Ruth, and I feel her pain already.

Please, should the opportunity for extensive travel ever present itself, visit us and know you always have a place to rest your head here in our home. We live in the home that Mama Ruth built; she left it to us upon her death. It is full of memories of her, and I smile when I think ot them.

I love you dearly,

Mary

Joshua stared at the paper in his hand and read it through again with a racing heart. Grief overtook him then, and he sobbed over his loss. It was some time later that Gwenyth found him and, upon hearing the news, placed her arms around him and held him close.

* * *

8 August 1865
Boston, Massachusetts

Robert and Abigail walked behind Jeremy as he explored his new home. "You lived here with *your* mama?" he asked Abigail.

"I did. She was a good lady too. You would have liked her, Jeremy."

"Did she get the fever?"

"No. She was hurt in an accident. A carriage accident."

"I'm very sorry."

Abigail placed a hand on the boy's head. "Thank you, Jeremy. I'm very sorry too, because I miss her. But she would have been so happy to know that you're going to be living in this house now. My, she would have smothered you with kisses and given you all kinds of treats."

Jeremy smiled at that.

"I suppose we'll have to do it for her," Abigail continued. "And also, Papa Robert's family lives just down the street. And they'll be very happy to meet you as well."

"And likely as not, they'll smother you with kisses and treats too," Robert said, his tone dry. "Your grandmother Elizabeth has a soft spot in her heart for little boys. Especially those who like to read." He winked at Jeremy and motioned for him to make his way up the stairs to the second floor.

Jeremy's progress was slow, but his new parents weren't in any hurry, and they let him navigate the stairs on his own. When they reached the landing, Robert gestured off to the left and led Jeremy to his new bedroom. It was a former guest room and, as such, was rather formal in its appointments.

"I know it feels rather like an adult bedroom just now," Robert said, "but I'm bringing some of my favorite toys and playthings from my parents' home for you to have. Then it won't seem quite so . . ."

"Tedious," Abigail supplied.

"Yes, tedious, in here."

Jeremy nodded, his expression solemn. "I like the room jus' fine, Papa Robert. Thank you."

Abigail reached down and wrapped her arms around the boy's frail frame. She kissed his cheek, laughing a bit when he ducked in embarrassment.

Robert winked at the boy. "Always made me a bit crazy when my mother did that to me too," he said. "They just can't seem to help themselves."

* * *

A few blocks away, Jacob and Camille were settling Iris and Angelina into their new bedroom across the hallway from their new parents. Camille had pulled from storage many of her dolls and playthings and placed them on chairs and bureaus in the bedroom. Iris's eyes were occupied for some time as they took in all of the new things and her new surroundings.

"Do you suppose she'll be homesick?" Jacob asked Camille under his breath as they watched the little one gently touch the dolls.

Camille shrugged. "She was fine all the way here," she said. "I suppose this will seem strange to her at first, but perhaps if I lie down with her until she falls asleep, she'll feel more comfortable."

"I wonder if we shouldn't put Angelina in our bedroom for a bit," Jacob said, looking at the small baby's bed they had purchased from a woman in Richmond. "She'll awaken Iris with her cries in the middle of the night."

Camille nodded. "We can move the bed." She smiled as Jacob went about the business of seeing the small crib settled into their bedroom. He was so very serious about his new role as a father, and she was constantly hiding her smiles from him for fear he would think she was mocking him. On the contrary, really; his concern for their new children warmed her heart and made her feel all the more affectionate toward him.

* * *

8 August 1865
Richmond, Virginia

"Well, it is official, Sally Rhodes. You are now my legal ward." Isabelle snapped the letter in her hand with a flourish and smiled at the girl seated across from her at the dining room table.

Sally clapped her hands together. "Wonderful. I told you my aunt would have no qualms about any such thing. More likely than not she's worried that I'd infect her with something awful were I to move in with her."

"Oh, no, certainly not," Isabelle said, although she secretly agreed with Sally. "Perhaps she sees this as a good educational opportunity for you."

"A good educational opportunity for a good Southern girl does not include a visit to India. Why, there are heathens and wild animals in such far-off places," Sally said in exaggerated tones, blinking her eyelids rapidly and wielding an imaginary fan.

"Now, then," Isabelle said, smiling at her antics, "I know you're anxious to go, but we must prepare first. I need to form an itinerary that will be beneficial to us and our needs, and we need to create a list of things to pack. Is there any chance at all that you have a steamer trunk or two somewhere in this house?"

"I don't believe so." Sally's face fell.

"It's of no concern," Isabelle told her. "I shall simply send for a few of my things." Isabelle took a sheet of paper and a pen and began to write a list.

"Who will send them to you?"

"My sister, if I pay her enough."

If Sally noticed the edge to Isabelle's voice at the mention of her sister, she didn't comment on it. She merely nodded.

"I shall do some research to see what kind of clothing we'll need to bring along," Isabelle said, writing on her paper and talking more to herself than Sally, "and any other things of import." She glanced up. "I do expect you to bring along a journal."

"Oh, must I sketch? I'm absolutely horrid at sketching."

"I don't mind so much if you don't sketch, but I do expect you to keep a daily journal of our activities. You'll forget so many things if you don't write them down."

Sally nodded. "I'll do that. I'll write down everything." She paused. "Isabelle?"

"Yes?"

"I'm not going to want to come home."

Isabelle smiled. "You will. It's always good to come home at the end of a trip."

"Do you feel that way about Chicago?"

"I used to," Isabelle said, considering. "It hasn't felt so much like home lately, though, so I suppose that's why I haven't been in a hurry to return."

"So where is your home, then?"

"I'm not entirely certain. I don't suppose I've found it yet."

"I suppose this place will always be my home," Sally said, glancing around the dining room. "It doesn't feel so much like it without my papa and mama, though."

"Well, at least the house is securely in your name," Isabelle said. "It was proven paid for and legally yours when you come of age."

"What will become of it in the meantime?"

"I suppose we'll cover the furniture and lock it up tight." Isabelle paused. "Do you have any other wishes for it?"

Sally shrugged. "I suppose not. I had rather hoped my aunt would return with my brother and sisters. Most of their things are still here."

"Your aunt indicated that she does not wish to leave West Virginia. We can send your brother and sisters' things to them, however. Would you feel better about that?"

Sally nodded. "They must miss some of them. I don't think they fully realized they weren't coming back here."

"We'll pack their things in a trunk tomorrow and send it to them."

"Thank you."

Isabelle waved a hand. "Think nothing of it. Now, the last item of concern is your health. We must be certain you're well enough to travel before we leave."

"I'm fine."

"I know you think you are, but we do not want to find ourselves in a far-off land and you with a relapse. I'd rather deal with that from the familiarity of this country."

Sally scowled. "My wretched illness is going to ruin everything."

"Your wretched illness precipitated everything. If you hadn't become sick, I would never have promised you this vacation."

Sally appeared to consider this. "That's true enough, I suppose. Thank you, wretched illness."

"Thank you, indeed," Isabelle muttered. "Wretched illness turned my life on its ear."

"Oh, posh," Sally said with a smile. "I do believe you're looking forward to this vacation with as much anticipation as am I."

Isabelle was loath to admit it, but she was. She glanced up at Sally and smiled in return.

* * *

9 August 1865
Boston, Massachusetts

The evening was warm, but not uncomfortably so. The sun had finally sunk low enough in the sky to cast the Birmingham backyard into shadows that were scattered across the lawn and the beautiful flower gardens. Gwenyth held a bouquet of those very flowers in her hands as she approached Joshua down an aisle that had been made by close family and friends who were seated on comfortable chairs.

Joshua felt his heart swell with pride that the woman approaching him was to be his bride. The only bittersweet thought he had was that he wished Ruth could have seen such a marvelous day in his life. No sooner had the notion materialized in his mind than he felt Ruth near his side as though she were alive. He was so startled by the sensation that he turned slightly to glance over his shoulder, only to spy the arbor that had been erected for the occasion.

I'm so proud of you, my boy . . . As clear as day, he heard her voice in his mind, and his eyes smarted with tears. When Gwenyth arrived at his side, she frowned a bit in concern. He smiled at her through his watery eyes and reached for her hand, squeezing it in reassurance.

The ceremony was simple and to the point, conducted by a pastor at their local church, a friend of James Birmingham's. After the vows were spoken and Joshua kissed his bride, hoping forever to remember how beautiful she looked in the gown of white taffeta Mrs. Birmingham had procured for her, he glanced about at the family in gratitude as they came forward to offer their congratulations. Who were these people who were so kind and generous with their time and resources? Ah, but he knew them well, as if they were family members of his own.

The Northern Birminghams had been regular visitors to Bentley through the years, and Joshua had spent many a summer playing with Luke. What a shame that Luke's life had been cut short in its prime—he would have liked to have seen him again. He accepted James's offered hand and shook it warmly, thanking him repeatedly for his generosity. "I would love nothing more than to see you succeed with your carpentry," James said to him as they stood near the arbor, "but know that should you need it, I'll always have a job for you with my company."

"Sir, I cannot thank you enough for all you've done. I'm overwhelmed."

James shook his head. "It's been my pleasure, Joshua. My wife and I have always thought highly of you, and you've exceeded our expectations."

As James moved away, he accepted a warm embrace from Elizabeth Birmingham and thanked her for caring so well for Gwenyth's needs on such a special day. Elizabeth beamed at him. "She looks like a queen, does she not? I especially love the spray of flowers Camille placed in her hair. It's a day a woman should remember fondly forever."

"I believe she will," Joshua murmured as he glanced at his new wife. She was so beautiful to him that his heart ached.

"And don't you look splendid in your dashing uniform," Elizabeth said to him, drawing his attention again. "Your grandmother would have been so very proud."

To Joshua's surprise, Mrs. Birmingham's eyes misted. He hadn't remembered how much the Boston Birminghams had respected Ruth, and to see her emotion was comforting. "You know," he confided, feeling a bit sheepish, "I believe she was here today. I felt her with me."

"I'm certain she wouldn't have missed it for anything," Elizabeth said to him and dabbed at the corner of her eye with a lacy handkerchief. Her sage-colored silk gown rustled with the movement, and it made him aware of all the sights and sounds of the evening. He never wanted to forget the way all of the women were dressed in gowns as beautiful in color and variety as the flower gardens that surrounded them. The men were handsome in tailored suit coats and hats. The people in his and Gwenyth's life had dressed especially well for this occasion—for *their* wedding—and he was touched by it.

He folded his hands together in front of him and took a moment to enjoy the scene, noting as he had before that he no longer clasped his hands to still the tremor that had once plagued him. When the tremor had first come upon him, he had often sought to hide it either by stuffing his hand into his pocket or firmly grasping it with the other. It had taken some time, but the involuntary shaking had eventually subsided and then ceased altogether as his relationship with Gwenyth had progressed. He could only see her as his healing angel, although she modestly denied it.

Gwenyth disentangled herself from her well-wishers and approached him, lifting her voluminous skirts in her hands so as not to trip. She tipped her face to his, her eyes dancing and her smile beautiful. "This is the most lovely evening of my life," she said to him.

He placed an arm around her waist and pulled her close. "Mine as well," he whispered in her ear.

CHAPTER 29

We cannot change the hearts of these people of the South, but we can make war so terrible . . . and make them so sick of war that generations [will] pass away before they again appeal to it.
—William T. Sherman

* * *

9 August 1865
Cleveland, Ohio

Anne and Ivar sat under the tree in their front yard on a blanket with their dinner spread out before them. Inger chatted happily, and Anne took a few moments from the busy day to turn her face with appreciation to the sky that had covered with clouds and might threaten rain later in the evening.

"I do love rain," she said. "Can you smell it in the air?"

Ivar nodded. Sometimes the rain reminded him of the storms that soaked the prisoners of Andersonville in a deluge that left them shivering and damp, but when those memories surfaced, he forced himself to reach back further to times in his childhood when he had sat inside the barn with his father as the rain poured outside. He told Anne of this memory now, and she smiled.

"What a cozy picture," she said. "Were you very young?"

"Yes. At least Inger's age, and then as I grew older."

"Can we sit in the barn when the rain comes tonight, Papa?" Inger asked, tying a blade of grass into a knot with her small fingers.

"I think that's a good idea, Inger. I would like that very much."

"And Mama can come too. With the big baby and everything."

Anne's mouth quirked into a smile. "Yes, it's rather hard for me to go anywhere these days without the big baby."

"Was I so very big in your belly too?"

Anne glanced at Ivar, a bit stunned. She hadn't anticipated the day when Inger would begin to ask such things. Judging by the look on his face, he clearly hadn't either.

Ivar cleared his throat. "Mama didn't have you in her belly, Inger. Do you remember when Bestemor and I told you that your other mama died?"

Her face scrunched up in confusion, and she shook her head. Truthfully, Ivar had to admit he was grateful that Inger had no memories of her mother. Berit had been a self-absorbed woman who had no interest in having a child. She had left him and Inger before Inger was old enough to remember her face and then had died in New York.

"Did my other mama love me?"

"Of course she did," Anne said. "And now she's in heaven, very happy that I love you too."

Inger nodded, satisfied, and her parents both breathed sighs of relief. The air had turned heavier in the past moments, and Ivar looked to the sky. "We may be able to sit in the barn sooner than we thought," he said. "Why don't we finish our dinner and take these things inside so they don't get all wet."

Inger agreed, very seriously, that this was a good idea. The quilt was one that Bestemor had made, after all, and it wouldn't do to have it sopping wet with food all over it. They finished their dinner quickly and took the supplies inside just as the first drops of rain began to fall.

Inger squealed as they left the house by the backdoor and ran out to the small barn. The rain fell faster, the drops large and delightful. Anne smiled as they reached the barn and hustled inside, leaving the doors wide open to enjoy the view. They sat on overturned barrels and watched the sheets of moisture soaking into the ground. The drops were loud on the roof, and Inger picked up one of the many kittens that frequented the area, holding the little thing tight and explaining to Anne and Ivar that the raindrops were frightening it.

Ivar gathered Inger onto his lap, kitten and all, and pulled Anne close with his other arm. They stayed thus, content, for a very long time.

* * *

The rain continued long into the night and fell well past midnight. Anne wouldn't have realized it had it not been for a loud knock upon the front door. Ivar rose from their bed, and she followed him, rather alarmed. When they opened the door, they were shocked to see Ivar's mother standing on the threshold in a hat and coat.

"Mama!" Ivar pulled her inside and shut the door firmly behind her. "What are you doing?"

Amanda removed her sodden hat and shook it, turning to Anne with a strained expression. "I've had a horrible dream," she said. "About Madeline."

Anne was confused, still trying to shake the cobwebs of sleep from her brain. "What do you mean?"

"She's hurt, and she needs help."

"Mama, it was likely just a dream. We've been talking so much about her lately that . . ." Anne stopped speaking when she took a good look at the expression on Ivar's face. He was watching his mother very intently, anything but exasperated or amused.

"Mama has had dreams before," he said slowly. "Do you suppose this was like the others?"

"Exactly like the others," Amanda said. "I saw her as clear as day, lying on the floor in her kitchen, bleeding and not moving." She turned to Anne. "I should have listened to you sooner," she said, her tone worried. "Now I fear it may be too late."

Anne shook her head, taking one of Amanda's hands in hers. "You were right, though. We couldn't just go barging into their home and accuse Edmund of beating her. Now that we know, we can help her."

Amanda nodded. "We must go to her right away. By morning it may be too late."

"I'll get dressed," Ivar said. "The two of you stay here."

"I'll go with you," Amanda said.

"Mama, it's pouring rain outside."

"As though I haven't been outside in the pouring rain before." Amanda shook her hat again and put it back on her head.

Quite frankly, Anne wanted to argue that they should all go and see to Madeline, but Inger was asleep and someone needed to stay with her. "Where will you take her?" Anne asked Ivar as he walked quickly toward their bedroom to change his clothes.

"My house," Amanda answered for him. "I have plenty of room for her and the children."

"Will you come and get me when you reach your house, then?"

Amanda nodded. "I'll send Ivar back and you can come."

Anne leaned forward and kissed Amanda's cheek. "Be careful," she said.

* * *

Ivar chose a wagon that had been inside the barn, a small one with hay on the bottom. He threw two heavy blankets atop the hay and hitched the wagon to a pair of horses, to whom he apologized profusely for dragging them from their sleep and out into the rain.

As he directed the wagon to the front of the house, Amanda emerged, and he shook his head. He should have known his mother would brook no argument when it came to having her way. He helped her into the wagon and signaled the horses.

The ride to Madeline's house would ordinarily have taken but a few minutes, but with the rain coming down so fiercely, the journey was slowed considerably. By the time they reached the home, Ivar had devised a plan as to his course of action should Edmund give them trouble.

As it was, Edmund appeared to be nowhere in sight. They pounded on the front door to no avail, and Amanda eventually took it into her own hands to try the door handle. It opened, and they entered. Amanda walked directly to the kitchen and nodded when she saw Madeline, prostrate on the floor. "Just as I saw her," she said to Ivar as she knelt by the young woman's head.

Madeline's face was bruised, and she was bleeding from a cut just below her temple. "Madeline," Amanda said and tapped her cheek. "Can you hear me?" Amanda turned to Ivar. "I'm going to find the children," she said. "When I bring them here, you carry Madeline to the wagon. I'll lie with them back there and keep them covered."

Ivar nodded, and Amanda left the kitchen on legs that trembled. She worried that Edmund might have harmed the children too. It was with extreme relief that she found the three of them sleeping soundly in a small bedroom at the back of the house. She roused the twins first and told them that their mother was very sick. She gave them a moment to recognize her, and then told them that she would take them to a place with their mother where they could play with Inger all day.

They rose sleepily from their bed, and she helped them quickly dress with stockings and dresses she found in a small chest of drawers. Once this was accomplished, she went to the baby's bed and scooped the infant into her arms, wrapping her securely in her blanket.

By the time she ushered the children into the front hall, Ivar had scooped Madeline into his arms and was ready to leave. He had found a coat and draped it over her listless form and nodded to his mother to open the front door. They made their way to the wagon and situated Madeline and the children atop one blanket. Amanda climbed into the wagon with them, still holding the infant, who by now had awoken.

Amanda explained to the older girls that they were going to cover themselves with the blanket and try to keep the rain off of their mother. They were looking at her, fearful, but nodded and followed Amanda's instructions. The baby cried, and Amanda began singing an old Norwegian lullaby, holding the child close with one arm and the blanket over them all with the other. The twins also had their little arms in the air, lifting the blanket over their mother and protecting them all from the rain as though they were in a tent.

The baby stopped fussing, and still Amanda sang, looking at the twins and offering them small smiles. Their eyes were huge and confused. She stopped singing for a moment, long enough to ask them, "Would you like to see Inger soon, even though it's so late at night?"

They both nodded wordlessly. Amanda nodded back at them and resumed her soft song.

* * *

By the time Ivar entered the house, Anne was ready to climb the walls. "Is she alive?" she asked him.

He nodded. "Alive but not awake. The twins are very confused and afraid—my mother suggested we take Inger over to them."

Anne nodded and turned toward Inger's bedroom, rousing the little girl from a very sound sleep. They dressed and finally made their way over to Amanda's house, and by now Inger was chatting with the enthusiasm of a young child going on an unusual adventure. Her mama and papa had never awoken her in the middle of the night before to play with friends.

When they entered Amanda's house, Inger ran to the twins and embraced them. They seemed relieved to see her, and Inger said immediately that they should see the toys she played with when she visited her bestemor. Anne followed the little girls into the guest bedroom where Inger's playthings were and lit a few lanterns.

By the time she found Amanda and Madeline, Amanda had already made a soft bed for her on a sofa in the front parlor and covered the woman with clean blankets. She was washing the blood from Madeline's face and doing her best to assess the damage when Anne entered the room and knelt beside her mother-in-law.

Ivar stood near Madeline's head, his face grim. "I think I should get Dr. Child," he said. Anne looked up at him and nodded.

He left the house, and Anne turned to Amanda. "Does she have bruises along her body? Any areas of discoloration?"

Amanda nodded and lifted the blankets to show Anne. She unbuttoned Madeline's nightdress and pulled it aside to reveal several large cuts and bruises splashed liberally across the woman's midsection. Anne shook her head slightly. "I don't have a practiced enough eye to know if she's bleeding from the inside," she said. "Her organs, I mean."

Amanda shrugged and covered the woman up again. "I don't either. Hopefully the doctor will know."

Anne gingerly ran her fingers along Madeline's head and felt a large bump at the back. "She must have hit her head on something," she murmured, "or else something hit her head."

Amanda paused for a moment, thinking. "She was lying on the floor near the kitchen table. I wonder if he hit her, and she fell against it."

"Was he home when you got there?"

"No. Nowhere to be seen."

"He's probably hiding out at his parents' house. We need to send the sheriff over," Anne said, derision heavy in her tone.

The women passed the next thirty minutes in relative silence, taking turns checking on Madeline's breathing and feeling for her heartbeat to be certain she still lived. Eventually, Ivar returned with the doctor, who began an examination of the young woman immediately.

Anne left the room with Ivar to check on the children, and Amanda stayed with the doctor. The girls were playing as though they hadn't a care in the world. Inger looked up at her parents, who stood in the doorway and smiled from ear to ear. "This is such fun," she said.

"Well," Ivar said with a yawn, "I'm glad you're having such a good time."

"Can we do this every night, Papa?"

"No."

The three little girls looked at him, crushed.

"But," Anne interjected, "the twins will probably be staying here at Bestemor's house for a little while. Won't that be fun? Then you can just cross the field whenever you'd like to see them."

Inger looked at the twins. "That will be good," she said to them with a nod.

Anne smiled and followed Ivar into the kitchen. She lit a lantern on the table, and they sat, looking at one another. "An eventful evening," she finally said to him, reaching for his hand.

He nodded. "It's a good thing Edmund wasn't home."

"Were you expecting trouble from him?"

"No. I was afraid I might kill him."

"Ah. Speaking of retribution, we do need to notify the sheriff. Do you suppose it can wait until morning?"

Ivar rose. "I didn't think of that. It probably shouldn't wait—that would give him time to flee." He placed a kiss on her cheek and left the house through the backdoor.

The doctor eventually emerged from the parlor, and Anne met him in the hallway.

"I believe she'll live," he said. "I didn't see evidence of internal bleeding, but I can't be certain. Her pulse is steady and strong, and she is still breathing regularly. My supposition is that she probably has several cracked ribs, from what I could feel, but we'll know better when she awakens."

Anne nodded. "Is there anything we should do for her in the meantime? Anything for which we should watch?"

"I've left some laudanum with your mother-in-law to give her when she awakens. I suspect she'll be in an intense amount of pain." He paused. "You suspect the husband of this?"

"Yes. I've suspected him of causing her unhappiness for some time, but she's never said anything."

"We need to notify the police."

"Ivar has already gone to the sheriff. I hope he wasn't your means of transportation here."

Dr. Child chuckled. "No. I brought my own horse. Now you notify me if her condition seems to worsen."

"Doctor, will you testify to her condition in court, if need be?"

"I will. I'm usually one for staying out of a marriage, but he has no right to lay her at death's door."

CHAPTER 30

Were these things real? Did I see those brave and noble countrymen of mine laid low in death and weltering in their blood? Did I see our country laid waste and in ruins? Did I see soldiers marching the earth trembling and jarring beneath their measured tread? Did I see the ruins of smoldering cities and deserted homes? Did I see the flag of my country that I had followed so long, furled to be no more unfurled forever? Surely they are but the vagaries of mine own imagination . . . But hush! I now hear the approach of battle. That low, rumbling sound in the West is the roar of cannon in the distance.
—Private Sam Watkins

* * *

9 August 1865
Salt Lake City

Emily emerged from the stagecoach in Salt Lake City dusty, sick, and ready to collapse. When she saw Mary and Ben standing near the office, she ran and clasped Mary to her, sobbing.

Mary hugged her tightly, alarm sounding in her voice. "Emily, what is it? What's wrong?"

"I'm sick! I'm expecting a baby, and I've been retching for two weeks. Austin was beaten to a pulp before we left Georgia, and he's barely moving, and Mary Alice has been crying almost nonstop."

"Shhh," Mary said, rubbing Emily's filthy back. "You're here now. Everything will be fine."

Ben touched Emily's shoulder. "Does Austin need help?" he asked her even as he was moving toward the stage. "Yes," Emily cried. "He'll tell you he doesn't, but he does."

"Are you tired?" Mary asked, still clutched tight in Emily's grasp.

"Yes. We're all exhausted. We haven't slept hardly at all since Nebraska."

Mary chuckled. "Come now," she said, holding Emily back a bit and wiping at her cheeks. The tears had left streaks and splotches that were comical to behold. "Ben and I have booked two rooms at a very nice hotel here in the city. We'll get you cleaned up and have a good dinner and a decent night's sleep before we head out to Ogden in the morning. Would you like that?"

Emily nodded miserably.

"Now, then. Where's your little girl whom I have yet to meet?"

"I don't know. In the stage, I suppose."

Mary laughed out loud and hooked her arm through Emily's. "Let's go see if we can't find her, shall we? Besides, you haven't even hugged your brother yet."

* * *

After baths and a much-needed nap, the little Stanhope family was refreshed and ready for dinner. They met Ben and Mary down in the hotel restaurant and settled down to a cozy meal.

"We cannot thank you enough for arranging all of this for us," Austin said. "We obviously were not in good condition upon our arrival."

At his comment, Mary began to laugh again, and Ben's lips twitched. Emily smiled and ruefully admitted, "True, we'd seen better days."

"Oh, Em," Mary said and clasped Emily's hand. "I shouldn't laugh at your expense. I'm just glad you all made it in one piece. Especially given your condition," she said, nodding toward Austin.

"Yes, what exactly happened?" Ben asked him.

Austin shook his head and began explaining between careful bites of his food. "The local populace wasn't too happy when they learned what we'd been doing all through the war and before. They began harassing us harmlessly enough, I suppose, but by the time I'd finalized the sale of the plantation, they were spoiling for a real fight. I had finished the business of the sale, and as I left to go home, I was jumped from behind and smacked around a bit. That was that, really. They had their fun and left me."

Emily explained what had happened, meanwhile, to Joshua. Mary's jaw dropped. "I haven't heard that from him yet." She paused as though remembering something and placed her fork carefully beside her plate. "Emily, speaking of which, I believe you may have missed my last letter."

"What is it?"

"You know Ruth had been sick for some time, yes?"

Emily swallowed and placed her own fork aside her plate. "Yes."

"She's . . . gone."

"Gone? She's dead?" Emily's voice was barely above a whisper.

"Em, I'm so sorry. I know this is fresh news to you—the rest of us have had some time to grieve. You don't know how much I wish I could tell you otherwise."

Emily just stared at Mary and Ben, her mouth slack. The tears began to fall, and soon she sobbed so that her shoulders shook. "Will you excuse me for a moment," she managed and left the table.

Mary glanced at Ben and Austin. "There was no easy way to tell her," she said as though trying to convince herself. "I'll go with her." Mary rose and followed Emily up to her room. Once there, she sat on the bed and rubbed Emily's back as Emily sobbed her grief into her pillow.

* * *

Late that evening, Ben held Mary close to his side as they lay in bed, both of them trying to sleep but failing miserably. "She'll be fine," Mary told Ben for the third time. "She needs to let it out, as we all did, you remember? I cried buckets."

"I know. I just wish she could have known before her arrival so she wouldn't have been expecting to see her."

"Oh, I think things probably worked out for the best. Can you imagine her state of mind on that miserable coach ride if she had known Ruth wouldn't be here when she arrived?"

"That's true enough," Ben admitted. He kissed Mary's head and said, "So, all things considered, are you generally happy?"

"I'm very happy."

"And my mother treats you well, even when I'm not around?"

Mary laughed. "Yes, Ben. She treats me well. Much better than I'd ever expected."

"Do you suppose the girls are all right back at home with Elijah?"

Mary raised herself on one elbow and looked at her husband with the aid of the moonlight that streamed through the window. "Why are you so full of nervous questions tonight, Ben?"

He let out a sigh. "Things are going well. I'm almost afraid to open my eyes and find it all a dream."

"Some dreams do come true, you know," Mary said, settling back down into the crook of his arm. "I know mine did."

* * *

The morning dawned fresh and bright, and Emily awoke feeling refreshed. She roused herself from bed and looked to see that Austin and Mary Alice were still fast asleep. Careful not to disturb their rest, she quietly washed and dressed, pulling her hair back into a simple bun. She left the hotel room and quietly made her way downstairs to the dining room, requesting some tea and crackers and hoping that she'd be able to keep them down.

She hadn't been sitting long at a small table overlooking the street when Ben joined her. "You're up awfully early," he said to her with a smile.

"I couldn't sleep anymore."

He must have noticed the telltale puffiness around her eyes from her copious tears the night before, because he said, "Em, I'm so sorry about Ruth. We've all been devastated, but as Mary said, we've also had some time to accustom ourselves to it."

Emily nodded and felt fresh tears form in her eyes. "I can't believe I missed her."

"She's not so very far away, you know."

"That's what Mary said."

"It's true." Ben reached for her hand, and she held it, glancing at him with a little smile.

"It's so good to see you again," she said. "Not hiding this time, not in uniform, but healthy and happy. And I'm so happy for you and Mary."

"Thank you, Em. And I'm happy that you found yourself a good man."

Emily nodded and wiped at her tears with her napkin. "As am I. He is a good man—I've been so worried about him."

"He seems awfully resilient to me," Ben said. "Any man who can survive a beating and then cross the open plain with a sick wife and screaming two-year-old seems darn near capable of anything."

She smiled. "I hope he'll continue to heal well. The doctor told us we need to keep his ribs tightly bound, but he can't draw a decent breath."

Ben shook his head. "Do you remember the time I was kicked by the horse at Bentley and Ruth cared for me? We wrapped my ribs at first, but then when she saw how hard it was for me to breathe, she took the wrapping off and left it off. After that, she always insisted that it was the better option."

Emily nodded a bit and took a sip of her tea. "If it was good enough for Ruth, it's good enough for me. Today the wrap comes off."

"Now, tell me more of Joshua."

She filled her brother in on Joshua's doings during the last part of the war and of his pending marriage to Gwenyth. "In fact," she said as she finished talking about him, "I imagine they're probably married by now. I wish I could have been there to see it."

"He saw Bentley burn to the ground, hmm?" Ben mused, looking out the window at the street. "I wonder if it brought him any satisfaction."

"It would have brought *me* satisfaction. Wouldn't it have for you too?"

Ben nodded. "Not many happy memories were associated with that home. And yet it's where we spent our time with Ruth and each other . . ."

Emily nodded and looked down into her tea, stirring it slowly with her spoon. "But could you have lived in it had it been spared? Could you have actually gone back and claimed it and then made a good home in it?"

"I suppose there might have been some satisfaction in seeing Mary as mistress of the mansion, but ultimately you're right. There were so many ghosts in that house."

Emily glanced up at him. "Do you ever think of Richard?"

"Occasionally. I only wish I could conjure some pleasant memories of him."

"As do I." She paused. "Ben, how are our parents?"

Ben took a deep breath. "Emily, our mother has become the greatest enigma I've ever known."

"How do you mean?"

"She's . . . she's not the same. You saw her at her worst, when she was out of her head?"

"Yes."

"Well, she's come to her senses again, but it's as though she's been granted a new lease on life—almost as though she's beginning from . . . well . . . the beginning."

"How does she treat Mary?"

"Well." The surprise in his voice was evident. "I was convinced that when we arrived, Mother would be horrible, and Mary and I would stay here only long enough for Elijah to become accustomed to us before we packed up and moved far, far away. Instead, she's been apologetic and almost unsure of herself—it's as though she's intimidated by the lot of us."

Emily stared at her brother. "I believe you must surely be exaggerating much of this."

"I swear by all things holy that I speak the truth. She is not the same woman who raised us."

"That's true enough. Ruth raised us."

"You know my meaning. Sarah has definitely changed."

Emily raised her eyebrows, her eyes open wide, and tipped her head to one side, considering. "I suppose stranger things have happened."

"Yes." Ben smiled. "Ruth told us more than once that if Saul could become Paul, then Sarah's heart could soften."

Emily cupped her chin in her hand and continued stirring her tea. "Ah, Ruth. She was so wise. Ben, I will miss her so very much. When we lived so far apart, I knew it was still well because I could get to her if I needed to. Now I can't."

"I know." Ben smoothed a hand over her hair.

"Did she suffer much?"

"No. She had been ill, but she didn't seem to suffer unduly. It was her time, Emily, and she was ready. She wanted to go, wanted to be with her husband and daughter again."

"And Clara and Rose? They are doing well without her?"

"Well, they have moments of sadness, but Mary keeps them with her, and they help her with Elijah."

"Do the girls have other friends in the neighborhood their age?"

Ben shook his head. "The area where we live to the north is very sparse, and the girls are actually the only ones their age in the valley. It's good they have each other."

Emily smiled. "I'll wager I won't even recognize little Elijah, not to mention the older girls."

"They're anxious to see you."

"I'll have to do my best to remember how to sign. Clara will be disgusted at how much I've forgotten."

"It will return quickly. Your hands will know what to do. Even mine did after so many years away from her."

Emily slowly chewed one of her crackers. "Does Clara stay with you and Mary?"

"She does, and Mother and Father don't seem to mind, although they have tried to communicate more effectively with her. She was used to only Ruth and Rose once you left Bentley. I think if we tried to separate those girls, they'd put up a fight. It's just easier this way."

Emily nodded and rubbed her forehead. "Let me think— who am I forgetting. Oh, Charlotte! Now, whom did she marry?"

"Earl Dobranski. They're doing quite well. They live here in Salt Lake. We'll stop by their house and see them before we leave."

"I'm glad. *She* had changed when William was born, I remember that quite well. I didn't recognize her at all. She became quite pleasant."

Ben laughed. "She's still quite pleasant, even more so now. Earl is very good to her, and she seems extremely happy."

"Ben, I'm not quite certain how to proceed now."

"What do you mean?"

"I was almost more comfortable with the routine—I had become accustomed to Mother being awful, and I'm not sure how to behave around her now. And with Ruth gone, everything is just all . . . wrong." Her eyes misted over again, and she rubbed at them.

"Be patient with yourself and with her," Ben said. "You don't have to become the best of friends in the blink of an eye. This much I can tell you, she's very nervous about seeing you again. She's convinced you hate her."

"I did."

"Well, I suppose the way I've come to see it is that life is only half over to this point. How we choose to live the other half is our decision alone."

* * *

Emily embraced Charlotte with genuine warmth when the group stopped by her house later in the morning. "I'm so happy to see you doing well," she told her older sister, and Charlotte returned the sentiment.

"Emily, I'm sorry about Ruth. Sorry for all of us, really, but for you especially. I know you would have liked to have seen her again."

Emily nodded. "Thank you, Charlotte." She would have said more, but a little face peeking around a corner distracted her gaze. "William?" she asked, disbelieving.

"Oh, yes!" Charlotte beckoned for the little boy to come to her, and he did with a few self-conscious skips. "Will, this is your Aunt Emily."

Emily bent down to his eye level and gently touched his chubby little cheek. "My goodness, little Will," she said. "What a handsome boy you've become. I'm sure you don't remember me, but it's very nice to see you again."

William hid his face in his mother's skirts, and Charlotte let out an exasperated huff. "Oh, for heaven's sake," she said. "He chooses to be shy at times."

Emily stood up and laughed. "It's no more different than Mary Alice," she said. "You see where her face is." She pointed to her daughter, who had her face buried in Austin's neck.

The families sat in Charlotte's parlor and chatted for a while, bringing each other current on their lives and what was happening in the South. "So Bentley is gone," Charlotte said. "I used to imagine that someday it would be mine." She paused and continued, almost as though to herself. "I never imagined I would prefer a home like this one so much more."

It might have been an arrogant comment had it been delivered differently, but Emily recognized it for the guileless remark that it was. Charlotte had indeed changed, and it was good.

CHAPTER 31

America has no north, no south, no east, no west. The sun rises over the hills and sets over the mountains, the compass just points up and down, and we can laugh now at the absurd notion of there being a north and a south . . . We are one and undivided.
—Private Sam Watkins, at the end of the war

* * *

15 August 1865
Boston, Massachusetts

The Birmingham family sat in the family yard, the adults in the gazebo and the children playing on the lawn. Elizabeth held her husband's hand and smiled as she watched Jeremy try to entertain Iris. Their youngest son, Jimmy, now fifteen, held Camille's baby and produced amusing noises to make the little one laugh. So far he was short on luck, but he seemed determined to make it happen.

It was a good life, after all. Elizabeth still missed Luke, but she had faith in her God that He would keep her son until she could see him again. Anne had written a letter that had arrived just that afternoon, saying that all was well and she was keeping busy trying to maintain pace with Inger despite her growing pregnancy and lack of energy.

Robert and Abigail were happy together; it pleased Elizabeth enormously to see them prospering and moving past their own personal grief at Luke's death. Robert, as a father to Jeremy, made her eyes fill with tears. He was so tender with the young boy and treated him with such respect. Jeremy's bright mind was like a little sponge, and Robert was delighted to fill it with as much as each day would hold. Robert's war memoirs had recently been published in book form, and he was becoming increasingly popular as a lecturer at schools and universities.

Camille and Jacob were a bright, vivacious couple, and their banter made Elizabeth laugh. The spark that had gone out of Camille's eyes with her miscarriage earlier in the year had returned, and she was a wonderful mother to the two little girls now in her care. Jacob was content in his position as editor again, his masculine heart completely tied in knots by the attentions of his new two-year-old daughter. If Iris so much as fell down, he was on his feet and scooping her into his arms to be certain she wasn't hurt. His father-in-law watched him with a shake of his head. "Just wait until that little girl starts receiving suitors," he said to Camille.

With the family was the other set of Birminghams—the Southern set. Joshua and Gwenyth, now married and moved into a small home of their own, joined the family gathering. They were content, and it pleased Elizabeth to see it. They had both walked a long, hard road, and they deserved whatever happiness life had to offer them. Joshua was working as a carpenter's apprentice—for the same crusty old gentleman who had employed him before his enlistment. Gwenyth volunteered her time at a school in town, and the couple seemed happy to just be in one another's company.

All in all, Elizabeth had much for which to be grateful, and she was. She and her husband both had their health, their children were flourishing and happy, and the war was finally at an end.

* * *

New York, New York

Marie was cleaning the schoolroom when she heard the door open and close behind her. She smiled. It had been a long day, and she was bone weary. She knew now for certain that she was expecting a child and was grateful to have a cause for her sudden exhaustion. Daniel had taken to riding into town and picking her up at the end of the day. He had employed the services of a young boy from town to act as his second pair of eyes both in his workshop and as he drove about the city.

Daniel had become his former self, right down to his temporarily lost sense of humor. She was so grateful to have him back and even more grateful that he had rediscovered his talent in his workshop. He had begun filling simple orders again, taking his time with each project and working with his hands and ears rather than his eyes.

She turned now, expecting to see her husband standing in the doorway. Instead, to her surprise and disappointment, she saw Mr. Holmes. "It's late, sir," she said, trying to keep the smile fixed to her face. "Is this something that can wait until tomorrow perhaps?"

"Mrs. O'Shea, Marie," he said, and Marie stiffened.

"I do not believe I have given you leave to use my given name."

"We must stop fooling ourselves, Marie. I know you must find me as attractive as I do you."

Marie moved back and placed a bench between them as he continued his approach. "I do not find you attractive, Mr. Holmes, and I must insist that you leave. Now."

"Come now," the man said, doffing his hat. "I know your husband has undergone some recent hardships—you must be craving better companionship."

"Sir! I love my husband very much, and I insist that you leave right now." Marie put her hands behind her to the shelf at her back and felt for a heavy book with her fingers.

He continued his advance, and she pulled the book from the shelf. When he was close enough that she was sure she wouldn't miss, she hurled the book at him, hitting him squarely in the chest. He yelled out in startled surprise, and as Marie was groping for another book, she heard a familiar voice at the doorway.

"Marie, is there something you need help with perhaps?"

"Daniel!" Marie skirted the bench and ran to the door, grasping her husband around the waist. "I'm so glad you're here, because I'm ready to go home. This man is Mr. Holmes, and he was just leaving."

Mr. Holmes crushed his hat down upon his head, his face red with fury and embarrassment. Daniel stood stock-still as the man moved toward the door, but suddenly at the last moment, his foot moved. Mr. Holmes fell to the floor on his face, and Marie buried her own face in Daniel's shirtfront to stifle her laughter.

"Oh, dear," Daniel said. "I'm blind, you know. I didn't see you."

With a muttered curse, the man left the building. Marie's laughter turned to tears, and she cried as she put her arms around her husband's neck. "I was so worried, but the thing that frightened me the most was that you would hear of this and believe I welcomed his attentions."

"Sweet, I heard the whole thing from the doorway. And even if I hadn't, I would have known you wouldn't play me false. Come now. Let's go home. I've been working on a project all day that I'd very much like for you to see. It was one I had begun before my accident."

When they arrived at home, Daniel led Marie into the workshop with his hand over her eyes, jesting with her that if she had his condition, such measures wouldn't be at all necessary. She laughed and then stopped when he removed his hand. Before her sat a rocking chair, beautiful in its simplicity. "Oh," she breathed, her hand on her heart.

She moved forward and slowly ran her fingers along the smooth wood planes. Finally, she turned and sat in it. "Oh, Daniel, can we keep it, or is this for a client?"

"It's for you. It always was."

"Oh, sweet man," she said and left the chair to embrace him. "I love you so very much."

"And I love you, Marie. Thank you for helping me find my eyes again."

From the living room, the mothers watched the tender exchange with teary eyes. "Oh, enough," Brenna finally said to Jenny. "Let's make them some dinner, shall we?"

"Yes. Dinner indeed."

* * *

Cleveland, Ohio

The swelling in Madeline's face had receded, but the bruises remained as stark reminders of her ordeal. She sat in the parlor, which was an improvement from her long convalescence in Amanda's guest room. Anne sat with her, as did Amanda, while the little girls played outside.

"I am embarrassed to be such a burden," Madeline said. It was a sentiment she'd voiced several times before. She winced as she shifted on the sofa.

"Are you certain we shouldn't be wrapping those ribs?" Amanda asked Anne.

Anne shook her head. "I'm exchanging mail with Emily, who says that Austin now also has broken ribs, and Ruth's advice was always to leave them unwrapped."

"Ruth must have been quite a woman."

"That she was." Anne smiled a bit and turned to Madeline. "You're not a burden. We gladly took you in."

"Indeed. The only thing you need be embarrassed about was marrying that man in the first place," Amanda said, wagging a finger in Madeline's direction.

Anne closed her eyes and shook her head before saying to Madeline, "Although we realize you were probably very worried about your future and that of your girls." She glared at her mother-in-law, who shrugged and continued her knitting. "And aside from that," Anne said to the young woman, "Mama has decided she'd like to do something like this on a permanent basis."

Madeline's brow wrinkled in confusion, so Amanda explained. "I would like to provide a home, of sorts, for women and their children who may need a temporary place to stay, for whatever the reason. It's something Per would have liked very much, and you are my first arrival, Madeline."

"Well . . . that's wonderful, Mrs. Gundersen. Thank you so very much. I appreciate your hospitality—I don't know what the children and I would do otherwise."

"Well, we do have some other good news for you," Anne said, reaching into her satchel. "These are your official papers of divorcement, signed by the judge this very morning. You are no longer bound to Edmund."

"You haven't told me much about that night," Madeline said, accepting the papers from Anne. "Where did the sheriff find him?"

"At his parents' house," Anne scoffed, "just as I thought. He was hiding in their woodshed. As it happens, the doctor testified yesterday to the judge of your condition when he arrived here that night. Edmund is in jail awaiting trial, and the judge told Ivar that he believes Edmund will be behind bars for a very long time."

Madeline bit her lip, her eyes welling. "I can't thank you enough. I will never be able to repay your kindness and help."

"You just get yourself better," Amanda said. "It's all you need to think about. And Anne and I are planning a weekly quilting gathering here at my house to help give us all some needed company. There are many women in town who have heard about a new book written by an A. B. Gundersen, and they're begging to know more." Amanda winked at Anne, who grinned.

"Their husbands won't believe it's true, but I'll wager the wives will."

"What's true? Did you write a book?" Madeline asked Anne.

Anne took a deep breath. "Would you like to hear a story?"

Madeline nodded, and Amanda smiled when Anne glanced over at her. "Go ahead, sukkerklump. It's a story I could hear a million times."

* * *

Richmond, Virginia

The ports were finally open again, and Isabelle and Sally stood on the shore with their trunks, ready to board. "Do we have everything?" Isabelle wondered aloud and pulled a worn list from her pocket.

"You've looked over that list four times in the last hour," Sally told her, "and everything is done and ready."

"How are you feeling? Are you well? Shortness of breath? Do you feel feverish?"

"Oh, mercy," the girl muttered. "Isabelle, I am *fine*. What on earth has you so blessed nervous?"

"I've never been responsible for someone else before," Isabelle admitted, tapping her foot against the docks. "I've only ever traveled alone."

324 N. C. ALLEN

"You must relax, or you're going to make yourself sick. I'm fine and healthy, we have had our trunks packed and ready to go for two days now, the house is boarded and locked, and we shipped the toys off to my aunt's house. Everything is done, and I promise you, I will not be a burden."

"I know you won't," Isabelle said, taking a deep breath. "Very well. I'm relaxed."

"Mmm hmm," Sally said, glancing at her askance while looking toward the ship with great excitement. "Isabelle?"

"Yes?"

"Thank you. For everything. I absolutely cannot wait to see India."

* * *

Ogden, Utah

It had been nearly a week since their arrival in Ogden, and Emily still had not gone down the street to see her mother and father. Her parents had visited, but each time they had come, she had told Mary to make her excuses and had retired to her and Austin's bedroom at Mary's house.

Mary and Ben had given her and Austin Ruth's former bedroom and had told them that they were welcome to stay for as long as they needed. Austin was even now making plans to build a home in the adjacent lot with the money he had garnered from the sale of Willow Lane. It was a fraction of the plantation's true worth, but it was enough to build them a nice home on a small lot, and he and Emily were both content.

Perhaps it was because she was sleeping in Ruth's bedroom, or perhaps it was because so much time had been spent in recent days reminiscing about her, but Emily had had a dream the night before that had left her shaken and ashamed.

Ruth had come to her, right in that very bedroom, and had taken her to task for making Sarah suffer without a word from her own flesh and blood. "People have *told* you of the strides your mother has made and still you deny her even a polite greeting," Ruth had said to her.

"But Ruth," Emily had cried, "I miss you so much, the only person I truly want to see is you."

"Well, now you've seen me, young lady. Now you get yourself on over to your mother's house and tell her you're sorry for being rude."

Emily had cried and cried, unable to believe that Ruth would come down from heaven just to chastise her. "Emily," Ruth had said then, her tone a touch gentler, "I love you, sweet girl. You'll see me again. Now go and be the person you were raised to be."

Emily played for a long time in the backyard with Mary Alice and Elijah before screwing up her courage enough to visit her mother. She took strength from the children and hugged her daughter to her tightly, rubbing her cheek against the little girl's face. Ever since the moment her baby had drawn that first breath, Emily had vowed that things would be different between her and Mary Alice than they had been with her and Sarah. "I will be a good mother to you," Emily had whispered to her newborn, and she still remembered the burn of tears that had fallen when she'd thought of her relationship with her own mother.

"Well, Mary Alice," she finally said, lifting the little girl under the arms to look her in the face, "wish me the best of luck."

Mary Alice laughed. Emily wasn't sure whether or not to take her daughter's reaction as a good omen. She left the children under Mary's watchful eye after Mary's kiss and hug of encouragement. And so it was that Emily now stood on Sarah and Jeffrey's front porch, unable to lift the knocker but equally unable to turn away. She should have waited until Austin returned, if only for the moral support, but it was too late now. With a hand that trembled, she lifted the knocker and let it sound loudly.

Sarah herself eventually opened the door, and Emily blinked in surprise. She didn't know why she'd assumed her parents would have an abundance of servants—she knew they had a cook, at least—but here was Sarah, deigning to open her own front door.

"Oh, Emily," Sarah said, her hand fluttering at her throat. "Why, you're so beautiful."

Emily's brows shot skyward. Her mother had never said those words to her in the entire duration of her life. "Th . . . thank you."

"Please," Sarah said, remembering herself, "come in, come in."

Emily entered and made an awkward attempt to embrace her mother. Sarah made a small noise of surprise and willingly closed her arms around Emily's middle. "I'm so glad you've come to see us," Sarah said, and Emily, unable to speak, nodded.

"This way," Sarah said, releasing her and leading her into the front parlor. "Come and have a seat. I know you've not been feeling well . . ."

"It's true," Emily admitted, finally finding her voice, "but more than that, I've been avoiding you."

Sarah sat in a chair opposite Emily's and nodded slightly but remained silent.

"I've . . . not known what to say." Emily looked around the parlor for a moment and noted several things from Bentley. It was as though bits of the past were thrown into an unreal present. "I've been grossly impolite, and I would ask your forgiveness for that."

"Have you been speaking with Ruth?" Sarah asked her suddenly, and Emily's head shot back to meet her mother's direct gaze.

"I'm sorry?"

"She's been with you, hasn't she?"

"I . . . yes. She . . . I had a dream."

Sarah smiled. "Ruth always made you apologize to me for your rude behavior as a child, do you remember?"

Emily nodded slowly.

"Your tone just now was as though we were hurled back a good fifteen years."

Emily couldn't help but smile.

"Ruth was the mother to you that I wasn't, Emily, and I know this. She was also my very best friend, although I never did treat her as such. When she died just now, I . . ." Sarah glanced away for a moment, her eyes shiny, "I didn't want to live anymore either. I was very angry at her for leaving and not taking me with her. A good woman told me that I must stop thinking of myself and think of Ruth for once.

"I also know that I gave birth to children who could see truth and right for what it was, even when I was blind to it. I thank God that He has given me one more chance to make something better of myself. All I cared about was Bentley, but then you probably already knew that."

Emily didn't want to nod, but she did anyway. "You were raised to believe it was the most important thing in life," she said.

Sarah smiled a bit. "You're a kind young woman to give my behavior such allowances."

Emily shrugged, uncomfortable. It was an unusual thing for Sarah to take such frank responsibility for herself and her actions.

"Emily, please look me in the eye." There was a shade of the former, strong Sarah. Emily did as she was asked. "I am sorry, my daughter, for not being a better mother to you. I am sorry for having caused you pain and for being cold."

Emily's eyes burned with tears that quickly spilled down her cheeks. "Have *you* been talking to Ruth?" she asked her mother.

Sarah laughed. "Yes, actually, I have. She has told me in no uncertain terms exactly what I have done wrong in this life and what I need to do to mend it. I am not a perfect woman, and I never will be. I fight old prejudices daily that may never completely leave my mind, but I am trying. And your father, God bless him, is taking very special care of me."

Emily had to suppose that God did, indeed, work latter-day miracles, because she never in her wildest dreams would have imagined her mother apologizing to her for a lifetime of hurts. "You know, Mother," she said through her quiet tears, "I must apologize, too. I said many hurtful things to you intentionally, and I am sorry."

"Gladly accepted," Sarah said with a nod as a shadow crossed the threshold of the room.

"Father." Emily stood with a smile and walked into his open arms.

"How I've missed you, my little redhead," Jeffrey said as he held her tightly.

"And I've missed you."

"It's good to have you here, sweet girl. Welcome home."

AUTHOR'S NOTES

Chapter 6—As Joshua leaves the burning Bentley with the soldier named Bill, Bill tells him that the U.S. flag was then flying over Fort Sumter. In reality, this didn't happen for a few more days, the day, in fact, when Columbia, South Carolina, fell. I played with the dates a bit as a fitting end to that segment, for Joshua's sake.

Chapter 9—Jacob Taylor quotes Sherman's praise of President Lincoln at the meeting at City Point, Virginia, and while the quote is accurate, Sherman didn't say it until many years later, reflecting back on that particular meeting. Sherman mentions in that same quote that he never saw the president again, and, of course, he wouldn't have. Sherman returned to his soldiers, and days later, Lincoln was shot.

The men discuss a defeat of Confederate General Nathan Forrest, and it may interest the reader to note that in December 1865, on Christmas Eve, Nathan Forrest and a handful of other former Confederate officers met in a home in Tennessee and formed the Ku Klux Klan, with Forrest as its first Grand Wizard. On his deathbed, Forrest repented of his activities and apparently had a change of heart regarding his past.

Also in Chapter 9, Lincoln pays respect to an elderly African American by doffing his hat and bowing to him. This is a true account and one that has moved me to tears on more than one occasion. I find it beautiful and stirring.

Chapter 10—In this chapter, where Grant "speaks to his aides" regarding his feelings toward Lee, those are his actual sentiments. They were, however, taken from his writings, penned years later and based on his reflections on those events. They weren't comments he actually made at that time.

Also interesting to note is that Mrs. Lincoln had actually made snide comments about Mrs. Grant and the general. She was, according to what I've read, quite emotionally unstable and jealous of the general's popularity. People are often surprised to learn this of Lincoln's wife.

Chapter 12—The account of six soldiers carrying the president's body from Ford's Theater is a true one, but they were all told to leave once they arrived at the boardinghouse. Because I have a soft spot in my heart for Robert, and also because I wanted an eyewitness to the scene, I had Gideon Wells fictitiously invite Robert into the room with him. In truth, Mr. Wells didn't take a soldier into Lincoln's death room, although the room itself was filled with many people.

Modern analysts suggest that President Lincoln might have survived his gunshot wound had the surgeons not probed the wound with their bare fingers and then with a metal probe. There were soldiers in the Civil War who suffered worse head wounds and actually lived. According to sources I've read, it was a questionable practice even at the time, but three times his wound was examined in a way that makes modern physicians shudder.

Chapter 13—The sinking of the steamship *Sultana* really happened, and to me it is such a cruel irony. Seventeen hundred Union soldiers who had survived life in Southern prison camps lost their lives while they were on their way home. It's one of those things that is just simply hard to understand.

Chapter 31—I struggled a bit with the issue of Anne and Amanda helping Madeline to escape an abusive husband because of the modern feel of such a thing. It wasn't so very long ago that women were subject to their husbands' whims with few or no rights of their own. However, as I thought back on my own legacy of family women, I knew that I had subconsciously patterned Amanda Gundersen after a very real woman. My great grandmother, Ragna Amanda Oien, was every inch the strong woman that my Amanda in this story is, and I knew when reading back over her dialogue that my flesh-and-blood great-grandmother would have uttered every one of those words had she been faced with the same situation. She would also have opened her home to women and children who needed it, as many women of that day actually did. They were a sisterhood, and they loved and cared for each other. Perhaps the concept of a protective "shelter" isn't such a modern one after all.

BIBLIOGRAPHY

Axelrod, Alan. *The Complete Idiot's Guide to the Civil War.* New York: Alpha Books, 1998.
*Author's note: Regardless of how the title of this book, included in this list, reflects upon my intellect, I have found it to be an excellent source offering a clear, concise reference detailing a broad overview of the Civil War.

Bowman, John S. *The Civil War Day by Day—An Illustrated Almanac of America's Bloodiest War.* Greenwich: Dorset Press, 1989.

Catton, Bruce. *A Stillness at Appomattox.* New York: Doubleday, 1953.

Davis, Burke. *The Civil War, Strange and Fascinating Facts.* New York: Wings Books, 1980.

Davis, Kenneth C. *Don't Know Much about the Civil War.* New York: Avon Books, 1997.
*Author's note: See above comments on the Axelrod book. The same apply here.

Long, E. B. *The Saints and the Union—Utah Territory during the Civil War.* Champaign: University of Illinois Press, 1981.

McPherson, James, and Mort Küntsler. *Images of the Civil War.* New Jersey: Gramercy Books, 1992.

Miller, William J., and Brian C. Pohanka. *An Illustrated History of the Civil War.* Alexandria, Virginia: Time-Life, 2000.

Sadler, Richard W., and Richard C. Roberts. *Weber County's History.* Ogden, Utah: Weber County Commission, 2000.

Varhola, Michael J. *Everyday Life During the Civil War: A Guide for Writers, Students and Historians.* Cincinnati, Ohio: Writer's Digest Books, 1999.

Ward, Geoffrey C., Ken Burns, and Rick Burns. *The Civil War.* New York: Knopf, 1990.

Wheeler, Richard. *Voices of the Civil War.* New York: Penguin, 1976.

GLIMPSES OF
THE CIVIL WAR

PHOTOS FROM CIVIL WAR REENACTMENTS
BY AL THELIN